HOT ZONE

BOOK ONE IN THE ZULU VIRUS CHRONICLES

A Novel by

Steven Konkoly

Copyright Information

Copyright 2017 by Stribling Media. All rights reserved. Except as permitted under the U.S. Copyright Act of 1976, no part of this publication may be reproduced, distributed or transmitted in any form or by any means, or stored in a database or retrieval system, without the prior written permission of the author, except where permitted by law, or in the case of brief quotations embodied in critical articles or reviews. For information, contact:

stevekonkoly@striblingmedia.com

Work by Steven Konkoly

Fractured State Series—Near-future black ops thriller
"2035. A sinister conspiracy unravels. A state on the verge of secession. A man on the run with his family."

Fractured State (Book 1)
Rogue State (Book 2)

The Perseid Collapse Series
Post-apocalyptic/dystopian thrillers
"2019. Six years after the Jakarta Pandemic, life is back to normal for Alex Fletcher and most Americans. Not for long."

The Jakarta Pandemic (Prequel)
The Perseid Collapse (Book 1)
Event Horizon (Book 2)
Point of Crisis (Book 3)
Dispatches (Book 4)

The Black Flagged Series—Black Ops/Political thrillers
"Daniel Petrovich, the most lethal operative created by the Department of Defense's Black Flag Program, protects a secret buried in the deepest vaults of the Pentagon. A secret that is about to unravel his life."

Black Flagged Alpha (Book 1)
Black Flagged Redux (Book 2)
Black Flagged Apex (Book 3)
Black Flagged Vektor (Book 4)
Black Flagged Omega (Book 5)

JET BLACK (Novella)
Wayward Pines Kindle World:
GENESIS
(Compilation of novellas set in Blake Crouch's Wayward Pines story)

To my family, the heart and soul of my writing.
I couldn't do this without their tireless support and love.

About Hot Zone

First. A huge THANK YOU for your continued readership and warm friendship over the past seven years. Before publishing my first novel, *THE JAKARTA PANDEMIC*, in 2010, if you had suggested I might be writing books for a living—I wouldn't have believed it. That dream came true in 2013, and I have you, *the reader*, to thank for it. You created a monster, and that monster has no shortage of stories to tell.

When I started batting around ideas for a new series last year, I kept thinking about *THE JAKARTA PANDEMIC*, and how it had become immediately popular, much to my delight—and surprise. As a new author, I had no reason to expect any success with this book, but the story resonated with readers right out of the gate and emboldened me to continue writing books. I knew fairly quickly that I wanted to return to those roots for the series I would launch in 2017.

HOT ZONE represents a full-circle return to the type of thriller that launched my writing career. A close up and personal look at a rapidly unfolding catastrophe, from the "average" citizen's perspective.

—A new doctor struggles against the odds to save patients, until she is forced to take action to save her own life.

—A divorced police officer balances the demands of his department with the needs of his son, as the madness spreads.

—A young couple embarks on a perilous trek to escape the inexplicable tide of violence pushing against them.

—A reluctant scientist is pulled into the middle of an unthinkable scenario.

—A government agent is sent on a dubious mission in the outbreak zone.

You'll quickly get to know this diverse cast of characters, spread across a rapidly dying city—**as their individual stories of survival and loss merge into one.**

Welcome to the *HOT ZONE*
and the *ZULU VIRUS CHRONICLES!*

Book two, **KILL BOX**, will be available in fall 2017.

Chapter One

Dr. Lauren Hale leaned against the cool tile wall and took a moment to regroup. She closed her eyes and rubbed her face, taking several deep breaths. Just the thought of walking back through the emergency room doors made her nauseous. At this point, she'd been on her feet for close to fifteen hours, seven hours longer than her scheduled shift. Staying a few hours past the end of a residency shift wasn't unusual, especially a day shift, when she could rely on a full night of sleep to recuperate—but this was something entirely different.

The emergency room had been slammed with a steady flow of patients all day, the number of check-ins increasing hourly. So far, none of the attending physicians had hinted at releasing her from the ER. The arrival of the second shift in the late afternoon had barely made a dent in the overcrowded waiting room, which left her less than optimistic about her chances of leaving when the overnight shift arrived. They were slammed. The line to check into the ER now snaked as far as she could see along the sidewalk leading to the parking lot.

She slowly exhaled through her mouth and opened her eyes. Back to work. Before she pushed herself off the wall, the doors swung inward, revealing Dr. Larry Cabrera, her supervising physician. He stepped inside the small hallway and removed his blue face mask. Lauren straightened, momentarily blanking on where she should go next.

1

"I'm heading back in, Dr. Cabrera. Just needed a few seconds," she said.

"That's fine, Dr. Hale," he said. "We could all use a few. I'm hoping to get you out of here for a few hours when the third shift arrives. I'll start rotating people out a little at a time once I get a handle on who actually shows up."

"Is the third shift light?"

"A little. Same crap that's apparently making its way around the city."

"Any idea what we're dealing with?" she said.

"At first I thought it might be a late season flu wave. Fever. Headaches. Drowsiness. Fatigue. Now I'm not so sure. The headaches seem too severe. Migraine level. And I haven't seen a single patient with a cough or runny nose."

"The volume of patients arriving within such a compact period of time strikes me as odd. Have you ever seen this with the seasonal flu?" she said.

"We occasionally get swamped with flu cases during the fall and winter months, but when I say swamped, I mean a full waiting area that we clear over the course of the day. Not a growing mob outside the entrance."

"At what point do we shut down the ER?" she said.

Dr. Cabrera gave her a quizzical look. "Shut down?"

"I mean stop accepting patients," she clarified. "Shut the doors. At least temporarily."

"I hadn't given that any thought. Nothing like this has happened before," said Dr. Cabrera, his voice trailing off.

"I better get moving," she said. "I need to work my way through the general examination unit."

"How long has it been since a patient has moved out of there?" said Dr. Cabrera.

"At least three hours," she said.

At the start of her shift, the general examination area still served its original purpose. Patients were escorted from the waiting room, thoroughly assessed, and often subjected to a battery of tests intended to determine the underlying cause of their symptoms. By midmorning, they had filled most of the Emergency Department's one hundred and fifteen beds, mostly with patients reporting similar symptoms. They'd reserved a few critical care beds, along with an intensive diagnostic and treatment unit bed for acute emergency cases like heart attacks and car injuries that could not be diverted to other hospitals.

"We've filled every bed in the hospital, and all of the area hospitals are reporting the same thing," he said. "I don't see this getting any better."

Shouting erupted beyond the swinging doors, from the waiting room. Moments later, a nurse dressed in dark blue scrubs burst into the hallway.

"We have a problem!" she yelled. "One of the patients is getting violent!"

"Shit," said Dr. Cabrera, already barreling past the nurse. "Where are the cops?"

"There's another disturbance outside," said the nurse, following him. "They just left."

Lauren took off with them, entering the ER waiting room in time to see a massive black man shove a young black woman into a group of patients scrambling to escape the mayhem. The woman stumbled backward, losing her balance and toppling a mother trying to get her toddler out of the way.

The three of them hit the tile floor, the young woman landing on the kid, who let out a pitiful scream. A man dressed in a tracksuit yelled a few obscenities at the attacker after getting out of his seat to intervene.

Before the Good Samaritan took more than two steps, a thick fist jackhammered his face, exploding his nose. The man dropped to his knees, blood covering his mouth and chin. To Lauren's horror, the giant aggressor gripped the bloodied man's head with both hands and pulled it into his rising knee. The violent impact made a sickening crunch, snapping his head backward at an unnatural angle and exposing the front of his neck.

3

When the crazed attacker pulled back his jackhammer fist, with the obvious intention to strike the man in the neck, Dr. Cabrera lowered his head and rammed straight into the lower right side of the guy's back. The doctor knocked him far enough away to disrupt the lethal blow, but the man didn't go down. Not even close. Roaring, the enraged attacker grabbed Dr. Cabrera by the lapel of his white lab coat and swung him into a very recently vacated row of metal chairs. The doctor bounced off the chairs and fell to the ground, instantly scrambling backward on his hands and feet to get away from the man bearing down on him.

Without thinking, Lauren charged through the panicked crowd of patients, arriving in time to deliver a downward kick to the back of one of the man's knees. The sudden strike buckled the joint, dropping him to the floor momentarily. He lashed out at her closest leg, knocking the Dansko clog off her right foot.

She staggered backward in fear, tripping over a patient that had curled up in the fetal position on the floor. Landing hard on her back, she lay there unable to draw a breath while the grunting madman lumbered slowly in her direction, his murderous eyes locked onto hers. Lauren pushed against the floor with her arms, rising into a seated position—the wind still knocked out of her.

The man stepped over the curled-up patient a few feet away and snarled.

"Kill you, bitch."

"Stop. Please. Just stop," she begged, scooting desperately along the floor. "We can help you."

"Kill youuuuuu," he howled before lunging at her.

Before the full weight of his two-hundred-and-fifty-pound body pinned her to the hard floor, she curled into a ball, wrapping her arms around her head. Her brain instantly switched into raw survival mode, transmitting one message—protect your head. There was nothing she could do to fight this guy. She was at the mercy of others now.

The first blow cracked one of the fake ribs on the right side of her rib cage, blasting her with a sharp, excruciating pain. She resisted the instinctive reflex to lower her arm to protect her ribs. A second, more powerful punch followed almost immediately; agony overrode instinct. The moment her arm moved to her side, the man hammered the side of her head with a single blow, bouncing it off the arm she had tucked underneath.

She lay pinned beneath the monster, too stunned by the attack to react. When the assault did not immediately continue, she opened her eyes and flicked them upward. The man had a police baton under his neck, both hands clawing at the officer behind him. She felt some of the weight lift and didn't waste a second analyzing the situation. She grabbed the nearest chair and pulled herself free of his legs. As she scrambled free, a pair of strong hands lifted her to her feet, a familiar, muffled voice barely breaking through her terror.

"I'm getting you out of here," he said, wrapping her arm around his shoulder.

He guided her to the swinging doors that led to the ER examination and treatment areas. Glancing over her shoulder, the short journey unfolded like a surreal, slow-motion scene from a horror movie.

Three police officers wrestled the attacker to the floor, one of them pressing a stun gun into the side of his neck. The man's legs twitched in synch with the rhythmic crackle of the electricity as they pressed him against the tile. The waiting room had vacated around the pile of officers, leaving two catatonic patients upright in their chairs. As Dr. Cabrera pulled her through the doors, she could have sworn that one of them was moving her lips without making a sound. The Good Samaritan in the blue tracksuit sat propped against the chairs along the far wall, eyes rolled back in his head—face smashed. *What the hell just happened here?*

Chapter Two

David Olson poked the thick bed of gray ashes in the lakeside fire pit, hoping to unearth a few dying embers. Starting a fresh campfire was easy enough, but there was something profoundly satisfying about reviving the previous night's fire. He dug his walking stick deep into the sunken pile, immediately rewarded with a wisp of smoke and a faint orange glow. Perfect. David cleared the area around the ember and gently topped it with a small bundle of twigs and bark shavings he'd dried next to the fire last night.

Within moments, the single tendril of smoke that had risen from the ashes of the rock-lined pit morphed into a steady smolder. The first flame of the morning crackled through the twigs soon after that. By the time the kindling fully caught fire, David had arranged three modest logs over the blaze in a teepee shape, filling the gaps underneath with sticks and a few thin strips of wood chopped with his hatchet from the logs. He had the makings of a solid campfire.

His only real challenge at this point was waking his teenage son for "breaking-camp pancakes." The three logs would go quick. After that, they'd have to resort to some of the sketchy stuff they had found near the lake. Soggy, dead wood likely passed over by the rest of the campers that had passed through during the early summer. He'd set it next to the fire to dry, but there was only so much you could expect from deadwood. The cast-iron griddle he'd lugged for miles needed to go over the fire immediately. The first pancakes would be ready within twenty minutes.

David gently blew on the fire, encouraging it to rise, before walking over to their low-profile, two-person tent. He unzipped the front screen and stuck his head inside, wrinkling his nose at the dirty-sock smell.

"Josh, time to wake up," he said, in a far too civil tone for a teenager accustomed to sleeping in until noon. "We need to eat and pack up. It's a long hike out."

Predictably, his son didn't stir inside the thick mummy bag. He grabbed the bottom of the bag and shook it.

"Rise and shine, Josh. Time to get moving."

Josh groaned, his voice muffled inside the down cocoon.

"You up?" said David. "I have to start cooking the pancakes in a few minutes."

His son mumbled something a little closer to modern English.

"Give me a sign of life. At least get your head out of the sleeping bag."

"I'm up," said Josh. "Sort of."

"I'll get some coffee brewing, too," said David. "We'll need to filter enough water for the hike back. If you could get that going, I'll have the pancakes ready by the time you fill the CamelBaks."

Josh unzipped the bag partway, lifting his head out of the sack. He brushed the unruly mop of hair from his face, squinting at David.

"I'm up. Sort of. What time is it?"

"A little before seven," said David. "If we start out of here by eight or so, that should put us back in the parking lot by noon. Grab some lunch on the way through Bloomington. Maybe check out the campus. Then home."

"I'm still joining the Marines, Dad," said Josh, lowering his head.

"Then I suggest you report for water-filtering duty ASAP, or I'll wake you up drill-instructor style. Trust me. You don't want that."

"I'm up. Seriously."

"See you in a few," said David, backing out of the tent.

David knew better than to directly engage in the Marines versus college battle. Having enlisted in the Marines right out of high school, he didn't occupy the high ground—and he saw nothing wrong with Josh enlisting. He just wanted to be certain that his son had adequately researched all of his options before making a decision—especially since the kid had the grades for college.

Actually, he had the kind of grades that made a kid competitive for an ROTC scholarship and other options that gave him a college degree first. Then again, Josh could enlist and go to school on the G.I. Bill later, if he decided to get out of the Marines.

That was how David had done it. Got out as a corporal after four years at Camp Pendleton, then got his associate's degree in criminal justice. After a few years with the Westfield PD, he'd started night school to get a bachelor's degree in the same major. Presto. It wasn't the traditional route to getting a college degree, but the end result was the same—plus he'd dodged student loans.

On top of that, he'd seen a bit of the world and earned a steady paycheck since graduating from high school. Not a bad deal at all. Still, David wanted his son to give each opportunity serious consideration. His own mediocre high school academic performance had left him with far fewer prospects.

If Josh followed in his father's footsteps and enlisted in the Marines, it would be based on a well-explored decision. At the very least, it needed to look like one. His ex-wife would kill him otherwise. She was already convinced that their son's stubborn interest in the Marines was David's idea. It wouldn't hurt to have Josh mention a university visit or two when he returned to his mother after this trip.

David walked back to the fire pit to tend the small blaze he had created. It would be short lived, but hopefully enough to ignite the larger pieces of deadwood—or at least start them smoldering. If they didn't catch right away, he'd use them to prop the frying pan he'd lugged into the wilderness. There wouldn't be a lot of time to fuss around if that was the case.

He had the dry and wet components for the pancakes in separate containers, requiring little more than a transfer of contents from one to the other. A quick shake of the bag, and he'd have the batter they'd need to cook the pancakes—a breaking-camp ceremony they'd shared every summer since the divorce. Eight years, and they'd only run into trouble twice getting the fire right.

He really wanted this morning to be perfect. If Josh enlisted, this could be their last summer camping trip in the Hoosier National Forest. He'd start his senior year this fall, and the Marine Corps liked to ship high school graduates away right after graduation. Especially graduates with high SAT scores, who might have second thoughts about spending the next four years in a barracks instead of a college dorm.

With that somber thought, he rearranged the rapidly burning logs so he'd have a flat enough surface for the pan—just in case the dark logs arranged along the fire's boundary failed him. He didn't want the end of the trip to be a disappointing memory for his son.

Chapter Three

Emma Harper sat across from her husband, skimming the restaurant's menu—not finding what she wanted. They had a two-and-a-half-hour layover in San Juan's international airport, and she'd hoped to grab some authentic Puerto Rican food.

"You want to try another place?" said Jack. "Looks more like traditional Spanish fare than local stuff."

He'd read her mind, or the look on her face. One and the same much of the time. She wore her heart on her sleeve, so to speak, making it easy for him.

"This is the only place that didn't look or sound like some kind of chain restaurant," she said. "Paella might be nice. Are you good with the menu?"

"As long as you're good with it," he said. "I don't see chips and salsa."

"I never thought I'd say this, but I don't think I could eat chips and salsa again for a month," said Emma.

"You did put a considerable dent in the cruise ship's tortilla chip inventory," said Jack.

"Are you saying I ate too much?" she joked.

"I'm not saying another word," said her husband, closing his menu. "This looks good."

Emma turned the menu toward him and pointed at the first page. "We can order the grown-up version of chips and salsa. Tapas."

"Are you saying I'm not a grown-up?" said Jack.

"I'm pleading the Fifth, too," she said, putting her menu down. "I can't believe this vacation is over."

"It's not over until I say it's over. Last mojito in paradise?" he said, squeezing her hand.

"Why not?" said Emma, checking her watch. "We still have another ten and a half hours until one of us has to drive."

"It's going to be a long day," said Jack. "I might have two."

"Or three," she added.

Their waitress appeared, taking their drink and tapas order.

"Do you think your territory survived without you?" said Emma.

"Sales probably improved," he said. "It certainly has little to do with my effort. More like luck of the draw."

It was an old joke between them. Jack worked a local sales territory for NevoTech, a top international pharmaceutical and biotechnology company based in Indianapolis. Three years ago, a territory on the south side of Indianapolis ranked number three out of sixty for sales in the region, a feat that would have earned the territory manager an all-expense-paid trip to Mexico or the Caribbean—if it had one. In this case, the territory had gone without a sales representative for more than half of the year and had become the tongue-in-cheek rally cry for more vacation days. The longer the reps stayed away from their territories, the better the sales!

"Maybe Nevo will pay for next year's trip?" she said.

"And maybe they'll select you to represent headquarters at one of the trips," said Jack.

She worked as a financial analyst for NevoTech's Benefit Plan Investment team, a promotion she'd landed after spending five years in various finance positions within the company. Occasionally, they selected high-performing employees from the various departments to attend division sales awards trips. Kind of a spread-the-goodwill program designed to keep the corporate drones from complaining too loudly about the lavish rewards and bonuses heaped on the sales force.

"That would definitely fall under the luck-of-the-draw category."

"Then unless we both get lucky, looks like we need to start saving again. Or settle for an inside cabin next year," said Jack.

"Once you go balcony, you can't go back," said Emma.

"We could always do one of those third-rate all inclusives," said Jack. "Might need to get a series of shots before we go."

"As long as they have chips and salsa."

"You and your chips and salsa," he said, taking her hand again. "I'll go anywhere—as long as it's with you."

She stared into his bluish-gray eyes, seeing that he'd shifted gears from jokester to devoted husband in the blink of an eye.

"I love you, Jack."

"I love you more," he said, suddenly breaking the serious gaze. "You heading up with me to grab Rudy?"

"I hadn't planned on it," she said hesitantly. "Thought I'd grocery shop and get the house back in order. I'd go Saturday, if your mom doesn't mind holding on to him for another day."

"I'm sure she wouldn't mind, though I hate to make him wait."

"He has no concept of time. We could have driven around the block or gone on a nine-day cruise," she said. "Why don't you take off early, have breakfast with your mom and get back by the early afternoon. We can grab dinner somewhere outside in Broad Ripple, with our boy."

"Sounds like a capital plan, my love," he said before moving his menu off the table to accommodate their inbound drinks.

Once the waitress departed with their entrée orders, Jack raised his mojito.

"To another amazing vacation, with the most amazing woman in the world."

"Back at you," she said, clinking her glass against his.

"Did you just call me a woman?" said Jack.

"Probably," she said before taking a long sip.

Even inside a bustling airport, her mojito tasted like vacation. Emma considered the sweet rum concoction to be the queen of tropical drinks. Perfect for any warm weather occasion, or non-occasion. She made a mental note to buy the ingredients needed to extend their vacation over the weekend. The weather prediction called for mostly sunny in the high seventies. Perfect for an evening on their backyard patio. Suddenly, the prospect of leaving paradise didn't sound so bad. Another paradise awaited, until Monday—when they both returned to the real world of jobs, bosses and corporate responsibilities. Until then, she'd take it one mojito at a time.

Chapter Four

Eugene Chang eased the Cessna 206H Stationair into a wide left turn, dropping his altitude from two thousand feet to eight hundred feet during the course adjustment to his upwind leg. With the Indianapolis Executive Airport clearly visible through the pilot's door window, he passed his approach information over the airfield's designated common traffic advisory frequency (CTAF) and scanned the sky around him. The airport was a non-towered facility, so he was on his own to determine if it was safe to proceed with the landing.

Clear skies and a late afternoon sun simplified the task. He didn't see any nearby aircraft. With the upwind run nearly finished, and the airport roughly at his eight o'clock position, Chang banked the Cessna left and crossed in front of the airfield. He was effectively circling the airport, part of a traffic-pattern ritual determined by wind direction.

He dropped to four hundred feet on the downwind leg before turning to the base leg and his final approach. Despite the continued lack of competing traffic in the sky or on the runway, he dutifully relayed his actions over CTAF—just in case. The big sky around him could get very crowded, very fast, a bad scenario on final approach.

With the aircraft's nose lined up with the runway, he slowly dropped altitude and bled power until he reached the sweet spot where everything got quieter, and the Cessna felt like it was slipping through the air with little resistance. His approach was rewarded with a textbook, minimal-bounce landing at the northern end of the runway. He throttled back after a few seconds on the runway, slowing the aircraft to a safe taxi speed.

Chang turned the plane onto the nearest taxiway connector and made his way to the main tarmac, where Montgomery Aviation, the field's sole fixed base operator, would take over. They'd inspect the aircraft and refuel it before moving it into covered storage at the field, where he could access it at any time.

One of Montgomery Aviation's service staff guided him into one of the spaces reserved for their signature clients, and chocked the Cessna's wheels once the aircraft was stationary. When the technician gave him a thumbs-up, he left the engine running and squeezed betweenthe two front seats to get into the rear passenger compartment. A few seconds later, he was on the tarmac with his briefcase and a small carry-on bag.

"Welcome back, Dr. Chang," said the technician, offering a hand. "Can I run those to your car?"

"I got it, Jeff. Thank you," said Chang. "Hey, whatever you guys did to the engine made a big difference. She didn't feel sluggish at all."

"I figured you might notice, Dr. Chang. We replaced the oldest cylinder with a brand spankin' new one. No more gunking up after a month or so. On top of that, we cleaned the shit out of the engine. Every nook and cranny we could reach without taking apart the case. The way you run this bird, you might consider a thorough cleaning like that every few months."

"Put it on the calendar, and we'll work around my flying schedule, when it gets closer," said Chang.

"Sounds good, Dr. Chang. I'll have the head shed send you an email with the tentative date."

"Thanks, Jeff."

He nodded goodbye and started to walk away, not meaning to be rude, but not exactly in the mood for a conversation after the five-hour flight.

"Dr. Chang?"

Maintaining what he hoped was a neutral face, Chang spun slowly around to face Jeff.

"Do you have any flight plans this weekend?" said Jeff.

"Nothing solid," said Chang. "I need to catch up on things at the lab after my trip."

"If you don't mind, I'd like to lower the left wing's rear spar. Just a small adjustment. Looked like you're still flying a little left-wing heavy. Might take a few adjustments and a little trial and error to get the roll tendency out of her, but it'll be worth it in the long run."

"Was it that obvious?"

Chang's arm was a little stiff from applying constant pressure to the controls. In fact, he'd engaged the autopilot two hours into the flight to give his arm a rest. It was more an annoyance than a real problem. One he'd put up with since he'd sold his Cessna 172 Skyhawk and upgraded to the Stationair last fall.

"Been doing this for close to thirty-two years. I've been meaning to bring it up, but didn't want to hit you with too much at once after you bought her—and it's not a critical fix. I've run out of fingers and toes counting the number of pilots I've known that flew a crooked plane for years out of habit. It's an easy fix on a Cessna. I can tackle it in a few hours, honestly. I just can't guarantee I'll get it all done at once. Weekends are getting busier."

Chang walked back to the aircraft, well aware that he might not get out of here for a while. Jeff could easily tack another hour onto his already long day, if no other aircraft arrived to interrupt. Given the few private flights he'd seen in the air north of Indianapolis on the way in this afternoon, today had the potential to turn into one of those marathon conversations. Still, he couldn't shrug off the man's sincere offer to help, and he suspected Jeff could use the opportunity to rack up some paid moonlighting hours.

"I can stay put for the weekend," said Chang. "I appreciate you taking care of me, and I'd be happy to pay the shop's regular hourly rate."

"I'll give you a discounted rate since this is on the side," said Jeff, producing a business card from one of his pockets. "Give me a call Saturday if you change your mind about taking her up. Sunday is supposed to be a clear, sunny day."

He took the card and stuffed it in his wallet, removing one of his own.

"Thanks again, Jeff. You guys have my personal number, but I'm not the best at keeping track of that phone. There's a business mobile number on this card that I monitor all the time."

"Great. I'll buzz you when I finish. If you don't hear from me by close of business Saturday or I don't hear from you, it'll be Sunday. Definitely won't go longer than the weekend," said Jeff. "Hey, I'll let you go. You must be bushed."

"Sorry I'm not a little chattier, Jeff," said Chang. "I feel like I packed three weeks into three days on this trip."

"No problem, Dr. Chang. I tend to run my gums a little long from time to time, or every time," he said, followed by a deep laugh. "You take care."

"You too," said Chang, shaking Jeff's hand.

He always felt this way after returning from Edgewood Chemical Biological Center (ECBC), the U.S. Army's primary chemical and biological weapons defense research facility. Twice a year, a dozen of the top virology researchers in the United States descended on the center to receive classified briefings on current and projected biological threats against the United States. Edgewood shared current intelligence and research insights, hoping to glean direction from the scientists, many of whom worked for or consulted on behalf of massively wealthy companies or universities with far bigger research budgets.

It was an informal outreach program, with the hope of streamlining some of the desperately needed research and development work in the realm of defending against and preventing the deployment of biological weapons against U.S. and allied populations. Nearly three years ago, a barely thwarted biological attack against multiple targets on the East Coast had turned this mostly ignored threat into a potentially lucrative business, spurring a new era of interest in the field.

Nearly every major pharmaceutical company devoted significant resources to the development of vaccines, "fixed-spectrum" antibiotics and next-generation biologics to keep Americans safe from the next attack, and university research laboratories across the nation started programs to seize the seemingly unlimited supply of grant money shaken loose from the federal budget by politicians.

It had taken on the air of a reckless frenzy, but in the end, when the fervor died, like it always did with these things, his field would have benefited—and the core group of virologists that expended vacation days to attend these secretive, off-the-books meetings would be better positioned to make sustainable advances in the fight against weaponized microorganisms.

The meetings were kept secret because the attending scientists represented a wide range of corporate and academic entities, all racing against each other to make the next big breakthrough in the field. Any perceived form of collaboration between them would very likely put their jobs in jeopardy, even though the group took careful measures to ensure no proprietary information was disseminated. Outside of the classified Edgewood briefings, the scientists spent most of their time alone with the Army's researchers, who kept their confidence.

This was why he kept returning to the unofficial conference. The Army researchers stood on the front line of a silent war that threatened millions. Any help Chang could provide them to keep them ahead of the next bioweapons attack served the greater good. Not to mention the fact that his friends at Edgewood had pointed him in the right direction a few times regarding his own research.

He patted the aircraft's wing before he left, giving the red and white Cessna a long look. The six-seater was a significant upgrade from the Skyhawk, giving him a little more range and a lot more piece of mind. He'd flown several single-propeller aircraft over two decades as a licensed pilot and had never felt this comfortable. The Stationair was a pleasure to fly on long trips, and fun enough when all he wanted to do was get into the air. Put the lab well behind him, and below, in this case.

It also provided an additional layer of anonymity to his

"unofficial" travels. NevoTech would have to conduct some serious surveillance and private investigative work to figure out where he had vacationed this week. Landing field records were spotty at best, especially at the fields he utilized. He paid in cash for everything, not that he had incurred many expenses. Mainly fuel. Piecing together this puzzle would be an expensive effort, not that he put it past his employer. They had a lot riding on his research.

NevoTech's stock price had been in a steady decline prior to the announcement that the company would take the lead in developing several prophylactic, boosterable treatments and vaccines for the most pressing bioweapons threats. Once the new vaccine direction was announced, profit projections skyrocketed, floating in the high tens of billions of dollars and bringing the stock price with it. The bioweapons-related field represented a new era of blockbuster drugs, with guaranteed government contracts and an unlimited public demand. All the more reason to take measures like a private aircraft to ensure the secrecy of his travels—and job security.

Chapter Five

David Olson turned his pickup truck onto the main road that cut through Highland Ridge, eager to sink into his well-worn recliner later tonight and watch the Cubs game. As much as he mourned packing up their gear and saying goodbye to the idyllic lakeside campsite, by the time he'd hiked three-quarters of the way back to the parking lot, his mind became focused on one thing: heaving that monstrosity of a backpack into the pickup bed and getting back to the comforts of home. His son had felt the same way.

The mind had a funny way of shifting gears. One minute you couldn't get enough of nature. The next you couldn't stand another minute of it. Same thing had happened on their Florida trips back when he was married. Nobody wanted the last night to end. They always enjoyed a few happy hour cocktails beachside, followed by a leisurely sunset dinner. A late night walk in the sand to dip their feet in the ocean one last time. They'd practically have to drag Josh back to the hotel room. The next morning, it was back to reality—everybody looking forward to getting home.

Unfortunately, with both of them tired after the long hike out of the forest, initial enthusiasm for the campus visit idea pretty much died on the short drive to Bloomington. Stuffing themselves at the Steak 'n Shake near the College Mall killed it completely. Neither of them felt like exploring the university on shaky legs and full stomachs, so they bypassed the university and beat most of Indianapolis's rush-hour traffic. They hit a few backups northwest of the city on Interstate 465, but managed to get to their turnoff before the masses escaped from work.

"What do you feel like for dinner?" said David.

"Pizza," said Josh. "Definitely pizza."

"Pizza it is. I'll order us a loaded with cheesy bread for the Cubs game."

"Two orders of the cheesy bread?" said Josh. "With blue cheese dressing."

"Sounds like a plan," said David. "I need to run out to Kroger after we offload the gear and clean up. Grab some groceries for the rest of the weekend. You want omelets for breakfast?"

"That'd be great, Dad. Maybe some hash browns?"

"Patties or the shredded kind? Or home fries?" said David.

"Uhhhh…"

"I'll get both, and some cheddar cheese to melt over them."

"Awesome!"

"Just don't tell your mother," said David.

His ex-wife had been on a bit of a healthy-eating kick for the past year, declaring war on carbohydrates, cheese and sugar. Rather than push back against her requests to honor their son's forced diet changes, he politely agreed to do his best at the house. When they were out at a restaurant, all bets were off. He wasn't about to play menu police with his boy. Pizza and cheese-smothered hash browns hardly qualified as "doing his best," but he'd been informed by Josh that, "Mom occasionally falls off the cheese wagon." As far as David was concerned, his son had more than earned the right to eat whatever he wanted after spending more than a week in the woods.

"What about some nachos? They'd go great with the game," said Josh.

"Now you're pushing it," said David. "Plus you can get those tomorrow night at the movies."

"Sweet," said Josh as David turned the pickup onto their cul-de-sac.

Their two-story, red brick and vinyl siding home became visible as soon as he completed the turn. Two houses from the end of the long cul-de-sac, he was tucked away nicely in a quiet, friendly neighborhood, with protected forestland behind his house. Protected by town zoning laws that required a strict percentage of "green space" in all of the neighborhood developments. Unless a tornado knocked the trees down, a possibility in central Indiana, the forest wasn't going anywhere. A good thing, because he valued the privacy it gave him, as most cops did.

"Looks like the grass took a hit," said Josh.

"Yeah. I kind of expected as much," said David. "Great weather for camping. Not so great for the lawn."

He'd set the sprinklers up and soak the ground off and on over the next week, hoping for the best. Worst-case scenario—his lawn got a three-week jump start on browning. The rest of the lawns in the neighborhood would join his shortly. Late June and July were hot and dry around here.

David drove just past his house and stopped, backing his truck into the driveway, as close as possible to the garage without hitting it.

"Another successful camping trip, buddy," he said, patting him on the shoulder.

"It was a good one, Dad," said Josh. "Maybe we could get the kayaks up next year. We can skirt the edge of the lake and pull in at designated camping areas. Day hike from the sites."

"Not a bad idea. Never thought of that," said David. "We could probably haul more supplies that way. Set up a base, and then move on. I like it. If you want, we can take the kayaks out to Eagle Creek Reservoir tomorrow. Spend a few hours paddling around."

"I'd be up for that," said Josh.

"Great. We can head out after breakfast," said David, pressing the garage door opener.

While his son offloaded their packs, David made his rounds through the house. His brief yet thorough exploration served two purposes. First, to make sure the house hadn't sustained any obvious damage during their absence. Overflowed toilets. Broken washing machine hoses. Animal infestations. Dead sump pump. Whatever the home-owner fates might have decided to randomly throw at him while he wasn't here. Second, to ensure that nobody had broken into the house—and decided to wait for him.

As a veteran Westfield police officer, he'd sent enough criminals to prison over the years to keep him constantly looking over his shoulder. His professional life had only caught up with him once, when the brother of a recently incarcerated meth-cooker took a few swings at him with an aluminum baseball bat outside Starbucks.

Fortunately for everyone involved, the kid was blind drunk, his home-run swings missing wildly from start to finish. On top of that, half of David's shift had been inside the coffee shop at the time, easily overpowering the guy without much of a fight. How the dude had missed the three squad cars parked in a row behind him baffled everyone. Maybe he didn't care, which was why David checked every door and ground-floor window for signs of forced entry, and looked in every closet before fully relaxing at the end of a shift.

Finishing his quick tour of the ground and second floors, he turned his attention to the basement. He'd taken special precautions with the basement, since the space offered a lot of hiding places, especially the unfinished areas he used for storage. The door leading to the basement had a deadbolt that could be locked and unlocked from both sides, but only with a key. It sounded a bit Hannibal Lecterish to have a lock on the outside, but it gave him peace of mind that nobody could break in through one of the full-sized, sunken window wells in the basement and get upstairs. Likewise, nobody could break in up here and slink into the basement to hide.

David inspected the deadbolt, finding it locked. Fishing a key ring out of his pants, he opened the lock and turned on the stairwell lights. A quick inspection of the basement windows showed no problems. The only way to get in would be to smash a window. Satisfied that some small-time junkie wasn't hiding in his house, he headed back upstairs.

The house felt a little stuffy, so he adjusted the thermostat, hearing the air-conditioning unit kick in outside. Always a good sign, too. So far everything still appeared to work! Aside from moving some sprinklers around, he could kick back with his son and enjoy the rest of the weekend. Walking into the kitchen, his hopes for a low key last few days of vacation faltered. The LED message box on his answering machine blinked FULL. Shit. He'd never come home to a full message box before.

He pulled his cell phone from his pocket and powered it. The device had been powered down since he left the house with his son over a week ago, one of his nonnegotiable vacation procedures. The department and his ex-wife had pressed the panic button one too many times over the past several years, cutting a planned vacation or long weekend short. He'd solved that problem by turning off his phone. It was amazing how nobody had a crisis when they knew his personal LoJack system had been disabled.

When his cell phone grabbed the nearest cell tower signal, it buzzed for several seconds as text message and voicemail notifications filled the screen. Shit. Every number was a Westfield PD extension or a personal cell number from an officer on the force. The calls and messages had started yesterday morning. Something big must be up.

With his son still cleaning the tent and rinsing their camping tools, he decided to break protocol and give the station a call. If there were a true emergency, he'd feel terrible not pitching in. David pressed speed dial for the duty sergeant.

"This is Sergeant Jackson. David?"

"I just got back with my son from camping, Sergeant. Saw a ton of messages."

"Shoot. I hate to ask while you're still on vacation, David, but we're down a few officers in each shift. Some kind of flu virus or something going around. Pretty bad from what we've heard."

"Food poisoning?" said David. "A bad batch of meat at Del Rayo on any given day could take out half the department."

Jackson laughed. "No kidding. Take my ass out for sure. No. It's definitely not your garden-variety bug. The hospitals in Indy are slammed, and their PD is struggling with absences. Way worse than us. The hospitals in the northern suburbs are starting to fill up, too. I could really use your help to fill at least one of the shifts."

"How soon?"

"As soon as you can get in," said Jackson.

"How many officers are out?"

"Twelve," said Jackson. "I really wouldn't ask if I didn't think it was necessary."

"That's more than a few. Let me call my ex. She mentioned heading out of town with her boyfriend at some point this week. If she's around and doesn't have a problem with me cutting my time with Josh short, I'll get over to the station ASAP."

"Thanks, David. Let me know as soon as you hear so I can start working on a duty roster that keeps people off double shifts."

"I'll be in touch soon," said David, ending the call.

Damn. He wished he hadn't turned on his phone. The thought of giving up two days with his son didn't sit well. The thought of calling his ex and asking her to take Joshua back early, knowing that she wouldn't give him time back in the future, made him feel resentful.

"Stop it," he mumbled to himself.

He couldn't let this ruin what had been an exceptional week with his son. Two days wasn't the end of the world, nor would it make a dent in his relationship with Joshua. If anything, he could still order pizza and cheesy bread…even make nachos, and enjoy the Cubs game with his son before bringing him to his mother. Jackson would have to settle for him showing up later tonight.

David leaned against the refrigerator and dialed Joshua's mom, secretly hoping that she was out of town. In that case, there was no way he could take a shift. He wasn't going to leave his son alone at home overnight and risk losing visitation privileges to fill a shift he was under no contract obligation to fill. Only a declared state of emergency was grounds for recalling officers from vacation. A little flu bug hardly qualified.

When the call went to voicemail, he left a quick message explaining the situation. After that, he searched through his contacts list for alternate numbers and repeated the message on her home phone and work line. That was it. He'd done his part. The ball was in her court now. He'd take a shower and knock out the grocery run so he could maximize the time with his son, if forces conspired to put him in a patrol car later tonight.

Chapter Six

Dr. Hale paused outside the ER conference room door long enough to catch the gist of the conversation. She wondered how her bruised face might alter the discussion. Additional police officers had been permanently stationed in the emergency room after the attack that nearly killed her, but with an increasing number of patients exhibiting aggressive behavior, it was only a matter of time before someone was seriously injured again. The guy wearing the tracksuit lay in the hospital's critical care unit, still unresponsive after twenty-four hours. Lauren had been moments away from joining him. She felt lucky to walk away from the same rampage with a mild concussion, splitting headache and two severely bruised ribs.

The room calmed when she entered, before breaking into a round of clapping and applause. The noise aggravated her pounding head, but she smiled through it, not wanting to dampen the one light moment her colleagues had probably experienced all day.

"The karate kid is back," said Dr. Cabrera, patting her on the shoulder.

"What did I miss?" she said.

"What didn't you miss?" he said. "Things are getting worse out there—and in here."

Dr. Zachary Wu, head of the ER department, quieted the group of doctors and nurses that had been packed into the small room.

"Dr. Hale, welcome back," he said, barely pausing long enough to sound sincere. "We have five minutes. Let's make them count."

"I don't want to rain on anyone's parade here," said Dr. Jeff Owens, one of the ER's most experienced doctors. "But the current situation is unsustainable. Frankly, what we're doing here no longer falls under our mission. And now they want to pull back some of the police?"

Dr. Hale interrupted. "I thought they added police."

"They did, but the police department has its own staffing issues. Half of them are sick," said Dr. Wu. "They don't have enough officers to patrol the streets let alone guard the hospitals."

"Babysitting these patients is not our job," said Dr. Owens. "We wouldn't need this kind of police protection if we moved infected patients out of our beds. With the ER slammed like this, we're barely mission capable."

"That's the hospital's call," said Wu.

"Then we need to have a heart-to-heart with hospital administration," said Owens. "Because we're caught in a perpetually worsening cycle here. Most of our beds are occupied by these mystery virus patients, who require constant observation by our security staff and the police. What are we looking at now? One out of ten patients getting aggressive?"

"At least," said Dr. Cabrera. "It seems to be getting worse."

"On top of that, we have patients exhibiting symptoms of advanced neurological damage!" said Dr. Owens.

"What?" said Lauren. "What do you mean?"

She vividly recalled the two patients sitting upright in the ER waiting room, seemingly oblivious to the raging lunatic that had cleared the rest of the patients from their seats. Something hadn't been right with them, but they'd gone unnoticed until the room emptied. Then there had been the guy curled up into a fetal ball on the floor, nowhere close to the rampage. Strange behavior for sure.

"While you were out of the ER, we started to see some unusual symptoms in an increasing number of patients. Seizures in particular. A lot of speech pattern disruptions, too. Some memory loss," said Dr. Wu.

"Sounds like encephalitis," she mumbled.

"What was that?" said Dr. Cabrera.

"Or meningitis," she said.

"Son of a bitch," muttered Cabrera. "Leave it to the resident to put two and two together."

"Can't be encephalitis," protested Dr. Owen. "Not in these numbers."

"I agree," said Dr. Wu. "This is something entirely different. Something nobody's seen."

"Have we sent any of the patients to radiology? An MRI would show swelling," said Dr. Cabrera.

"A polymerase chain reaction test of cerebrospinal fluid would be conclusive," said Hale.

"I thought you were studying emergency medicine?" said Cabrera.

"I'm interested in a pediatric emergency medicine fellowship," she said, suddenly very aware that the entire room was focused on her.

"We're not doing spinal taps," said Dr. Wu.

"Damn right we're not," said Dr. Owen. "We can send some patients on to radiology. Bring an anesthesiologist down for the spinal taps."

"All of the attending physicians can do a spinal tap," said Cabrera.

"Not anymore. This group is shot," said Dr. Owen. "How much sleep have you logged in the past forty-eight hours?"

Dr. Cabrera started to calculate the number.

"The answer to that question is *not even fucking close to enough to mess with the spine*," stated Dr. Owens. "And I don't anticipate any of us getting any sleep soon. We've lost three doctors and six nurses from the overall rotation already."

"Lost?" said Dr. Hale.

Dr. Wu grimaced and shook his head. "Some just disappeared. Slipped away when nobody was looking. The others are sick. Same symptoms. Dr. Edwards is strapped to a bed in the psych wing. We didn't want to keep him here."

"That's where half of these patients should be right now," stated Dr. Owens.

"Jesus," said Dr. Hale. "Is anyone else…sick?"

"Good question," said Dr. Owens. "Dr. Edwards didn't give us much warning."

"Let's get back to the question of police protection," said a young-looking doctor toward the back of the conference room. "If the patients are getting worse and the police are disappearing, where does that leave us? I have to be honest. I'm one patient rampage from slipping away myself. Sorry, but I have a four-month-old baby and a pissed-off wife at home. If we've moved into the patient warehousing business, I can't imagine sticking around very long."

The room broke into a discordance of yelling, most of the room angry with the young doctor, a few joining his cause. Dr. Hale wanted to pursue Dr. Owens's statement about Edwards. What had he done so suddenly?

"Dr. Blake, we all have lives outside of the ER, and it's not like we're sitting around useless," said Dr. Wu. "We'll implement a new triage protocol after I can meet with some of the administrators. I can't effectively shut down the ER without their input. If you choose to leave, nobody will stand in your way—but that's the end of your career here, as far as I'm concerned. We're obligated by contract to be here in the event of a disaster."

"We don't even know what we're dealing with," said the young physician.

"Doesn't matter. We're on the front lines of something big. That's all—"

Dr. Wu winced, bringing a hand to his head before continuing the sentence. "That's all we need to know."

Dr. Hale looked at Dr. Owens, who met her glance with an almost imperceptibly raised eyebrow. She scanned the rest of the faces, finding a few concerned looks, but nothing that raised any serious alarms.

"You okay?" said Dr. Cabrera.

"I'm fine. Just exhausted like everyone else…and dehydrated. Make sure everyone remembers to keep the fluids going," said Dr. Wu, still looking a little shaken by what she assumed was a sudden headache. "Are we good?"

The younger doctor raised a finger, garnering an impatient nod from Dr. Wu.

"It's going to be a long night. I suggest we restrain any of the patients that have exhibited symptoms beyond headache and fever," said Dr. Blake.

"That's more than a third of the patients," said Dr. Cabrera. "We have four sets of restraints."

"I'm sure the psych floor can lend us a hand," said Dr. Blake. "Hell, we can use duct tape. Plenty of that in the storage closet."

"We'll get sued off our asses if we start preemptively lashing patients to their beds," said another doctor. "Duct tape? What the fuck? Imagine that photo getting around the Internet."

"Exactly," said Dr. Wu. "That's why I need to talk to someone above my pay grade before we take any drastic steps."

"Fuck. Then call them up right now!" said Dr. Owens. "Duct tape is sounding pretty good right now."

"I've tried," said Dr. Wu. "Nobody is answering my calls."

The room went dead silent.

"Seriously?" said Dr. Owens.

"Yes. We're on our own until morning, with whatever police support we can wrangle," said Dr. Wu. "Dr. Hale, I'd like you to liaison with the Indianapolis PD sergeant in the parking lot. Let him see your bruised face, and make the case for a stronger police presence inside the ER tonight."

"Are the other hospitals dealing with the same thing?" said Dr. Lundy, a normally soft-spoken, easygoing member of the ER team.

"They are. Every hospital in Indianapolis is slammed. This is widespread," said Dr. Wu.

"How widespread?" said Dr. Blake.

"Citywide for sure. I don't know about the suburbs."

"Have we contacted the CDC?" said Dr. Cabrera, looking surprised by Wu's answer. "If this is widespread, it could be a pandemic outbreak or some kind of biological attack."

A few of the doctors and nurses laughed condescendingly at the doctor's comment, but most of the room remained ominously silent.

"Damn it, Larry," said Dr. Wu, grinning. "I hadn't thought of it. I'll get on the line with them right after this meeting. Maybe they can send one of their outbreak response teams or something."

Dr. Cabrera began to respond. "If this is citywide, I'd be surprised if they—"

The sound of staccato gunfire stopped him in mid-sentence. Screams from the direction of the ER waiting room catalyzed the doctors, scrambling most of them into the hallway. Dr. Wu took off for the waiting room, trailed by most of the staff.

Dr. Hale started to follow the group, but stopped when she noticed that Dr. Cabrera and Dr. Owens had paused just inside the conference room. She backed up a few steps, catching Cabrera's attention.

"In here for a second?" he said, motioning for her to join them.

She glanced furtively at the swarm of white coats and blue scrubs surging through the waiting room's doors before joining them inside the conference room.

"What's up?" she said.

"First, how are you feeling?" said Cabrera.

"Tired. Head hurts," she said. "Otherwise I'm fine."

Owens gave her a concerned look.

"Seriously. I'm fine," she said.

"Mind if I check something?" said Cabrera, producing a forehead thermometer from his lab coat pocket.

"Really?"

"Really," he said, and she immediately understood why.

Dr. Owens kept a neutral face while Cabrera pressed the thermometer to her temple for a few seconds, followed by her forehead. Moments later, the device beeped. He showed her the temperature on the LED readout before turning the screen toward Dr. Owens.

"Ninety-eight point eight. Normal," said Owens, clearly relieved.

"I figured her headache was concussion related," said Cabrera.

"That's reason enough to send you home, Dr. Hale," said Owens.

"I can manage for now," said Hale. "How many of the staff are running a temperature?"

"We don't know," said Cabrera. "Dr. Owens and I haven't found the right moment to suggest staff-wide temperature checks."

"It would be the beginning of the end for the ER," said Owens. "Not that we're moving in any other direction."

"Dr. Wu didn't look good," said Hale.

"No. He didn't. And if Wu goes, the ER will follow," said Owens. "Based on patient observation and history, I say he'll be out of commission by noon tomorrow. Maybe sooner, depending on how long he's been hiding the headaches."

"Jesus. Out of commission?" she said.

"Fever and headache will put him in a hospital bed," said Cabrera.

"If he's lucky," said Owens.

"Jesus," said Hale. "Is there anything we can do?"

"Watch your back, for one," said Cabrera. "Any of these patients can go haywire at any moment. We usually get some warning. Abusive language is a dead giveaway."

"What happened with Dr. Edwards?" said Hale.

"He fell into the *no warning* category. Probably been nursing a headache and fever for a while, but he didn't exhibit any neurological symptoms until he started beating a patient. Fortunately, he lost his shit right in front of a police officer, who stopped him cold with his Taser. We had him strapped to a gurney and out of there pretty fast."

"And nobody has any idea what's causing this?" said Hale. "It sounds like encephalitis, but I agree that it's too widespread. Rabies? Violent outbursts have been recorded with rabies."

"Rabies is a hundred times rarer than encephalitis, especially in the United States," said Owens.

"It has to be something that affects the frontal lobe," said Hale.

Owens frowned. "If we can schedule a spinal tap with anesthesiology—sooner than later—I have a friend at NevoTech that could very likely make sense of this. He specializes in this field."

"Could you do the spinal tap yourself?" said Hale.

Owens rubbed his face and squinted before slowly nodding. "I don't see why not, but I think I more or less convinced Dr. Wu that we need someone from anesthesiology to do it."

"Fuck anesthesiology. Wu's crossing his t's and dotting his i's on this one. No way he'll let you walk out of here with an official hospital sample," said Hale. "We have no idea what we're dealing with and may need to rethink our biosafety posture. All the sterile gloves and masks in the world won't make a difference against BSL 3 or 4 pathogens. The sooner you get a sample into your friend's hands, the better. If the CDC isn't responding, this might be our only way to get some answers. We'll figure out a way to get you a patient. What are the collection protocols?"

"Where did you find her?" said Owens.

"Random residency assignment," said Cabrera. "Lucky. Right?"

"Very," said Owens. "To answer your question, we'll need to time this right, especially if we don't run it through the hospital lab. Cerebrospinal fluid needs to be processed within an hour of collection, or mixed with a Trans-Isolate medium if the wait time will be longer. We don't carry the T-I medium in the ER. Ideally, my friend would be set up and waiting for the sample by the time I do the spinal tap. One of us would have to run it over to him."

"Maybe we should explore the hospital option. Sounds like a lot of moving parts," said Cabrera.

"We may have to go that route anyway. There's no guarantee my friend is in town. He travels a lot for his research. If he's here, I'm almost certain he'll want to take a look. Even if it means waiting until morning, I think it'll be worth it. He studies potential biological threats, manmade and naturally occurring. If he can't determine what we're dealing with, this might be a brand-new virus strain."

Angry voices rose from the waiting room, drawing them into the hallway.

"Shit," said Cabrera, moving hesitantly toward the double doors.

She swore to herself that she'd run in the opposite direction if she heard gunfire. They might be under obligation to stay here and treat injured patients, but nothing in her residency agreement stipulated she had to work in a war zone. Gunfire in the ER equaled cancellation of that contract. She highly doubted anyone would argue differently. As they edged toward the waiting room, Dr. Wu and two of the ER nurses burst through the double doors, followed closely by a blood-splattered police officer carrying another officer in a fireman's carry.

"Multiple gunshots!" yelled Wu. "Get trauma down here immediately!"

"On it!" yelled Cabrera, disappearing into the office next to the doors.

"Owens, emergency room one!" said Wu.

"Meet you there," said Owens, sprinting ahead and yelling over his shoulder, "What the fuck happened?"

"Guy just walked up to us, screaming his head off!" yelled the cop. "As soon as we started to walk over, he unloaded. Hit some civilians behind us, too."

Hale hated to ask this question right now, but she felt it was important. Possibly a chance to force a decision that should have been made hours ago.

"Where's the officer in charge of the police detail?" she yelled. "We need to secure the ER."

"We're about to save her life!" said Wu, stopping momentarily.

The police officer plowed past him, following Dr. Owens and the nurses.

"It's only a matter of time before this spills into the ER," she said.

He muttered a few curses before looking up at her. "Help the ER staff move the drive-by victims into treatment rooms—then lock the fucking doors. We're closed until further notice."

"Right," she said.

She took off for the waiting room to assess the situation, slipping on the floor. Nearly falling, she steadied herself and looked down at the blood-covered black and white checkered tiles. *That's a lot of blood.*

Cabrera poked his head out the office door, a phone in his hand. "Did he just close the ER?"

She took a moment to respond. "Yeah. I need to figure out how to do that."

"You need to clear the waiting room. We don't have the resources to monitor a room full of loose cannons. Then lock the doors."

Hale nodded before turning her attention toward the waiting room. How the hell was she going to shut down the ER and eject close to a hundred patients. Hale took a deep breath, the answer coming to her moments later.

"That'll work," muttered Hale, pushing the door open to the chaotic waiting room.

The only police officer visible had a patient face-planted against the wall next to the ER's wide sliding door. He was the only authority figure among a sea of desperate, deteriorating patients. She briefly considered the options, settling on the one that would solve their problem the quickest. Trying to drag the rest of the wounded through this gaggle could prove disastrous. *This is the only way.*

"Officer! We need to evacuate the ER. There's been a bomb threat," said Hale. "Everyone. Move to the exit. We've had a bomb threat."

All hell broke loose in the waiting room as patients stormed the sliding door, which opened just in time to accommodate the panicked mob. The officer released the woman he'd detained and moved out of the way, the stream of patients dragging her away. He spoke into his radio and barged through the storm of people. When he reached her, he took her aside.

"There's no bomb threat, is there?" said the officer.

"No. We needed to defuse this situation before it spiraled completely out of control," she said.

"A little late for that."

"I agree," she said, making direct eye contact with him. "The officer that was shot is with our best people right now. Trauma is on the way. She's going to make it. I need you to clear the remaining patients when this dies down, and barricade the door after we move the drive-by victims inside. The ER is closed."

Chapter Seven

Eugene Chang rolled over in bed and swiped his persistently vibrating phone from the nightstand. He'd ignored the first call, thinking the early morning caller would leave a message. It didn't happen often, but occasionally one of his colleagues around the world would get excited about a research-related breakthrough or discovery, and momentarily forget about the time difference. But two separate calls in a matter of minutes warranted his attention, however groggy that attention might be. He could count the number of times his phone had rung back-to-back on one hand; all of them had been emergencies.

When his blurry eyes came into focus on the smart phone screen, he hesitated for a moment. The caller ID read Jeff Owens, MD. It took his still-foggy brain another second to make the connection. Of course. Dr. Owens was a senior ER doctor at Indiana University Methodist Hospital. They'd met at a state disaster planning conference a few years back. Owens had kept in touch, occasionally asking for advice regarding ER policy and training related to pandemic and biological disasters. He didn't strike Chang as the type that would call at three in the morning with something that could wait, so he accepted the call.

"Dr. Chang," he said in a scratchy voice.

"Gene, it's Jeff Owens over at Methodist. Very sorry to call you in the middle of the night, but I didn't think this could wait."

"It's not a problem, Jeff. Just bear with me if I don't sound one hundred percent lucid," said Chang.

"I'm running on fumes, so I probably won't notice. I've been at the ER for thirty-seven hours straight," said Owens. "The ER has been in a maximum-overflow situation for longer than that."

Chang hadn't watched the news since he'd returned earlier in the afternoon, but he had noticed more police and ambulance sirens than usual. He could hear one in the distance right now, which was unusual for Indianapolis.

"Has there been an accident?"

Before Owens could answer, he realized that his line of thinking didn't make much sense. The sirens wouldn't still be going almost two days after an accident. His mind was still sluggish.

"Not that I know of. Why?" said Owens.

"The sirens. Seems like they've been going nonstop since I got back this afternoon. There's one going right now."

"The sirens are related to what's going on," said Owens. "Here's the bottom line. The ER is full of patients with fever, severe headaches, general fatigue, speech abnormalities, erratic behavior, catatonia or worse."

His mind raced to keep up with the list of symptoms, hoping that they were spread widely among the patients. If seen as a cluster of symptoms in a single patient, a disturbing diagnosis emerged. Impossible on this wide of a scale—unless the unthinkable had occurred. The thought of such a catastrophe cleared his mind, snapping him fully awake.

"Jeff, is this a list of what you're seeing across the spectrum of patients? Or a spectrum of symptoms seen in all patients."

"The latter. Not every symptom is present in every patient, but nearly everyone has initially presented with fever, fatigue and severe headaches. The other symptoms are spread out a little more. We're seeing a lot of speech pattern disruption and erratic behavior."

Based solely on the symptoms described, Chang's first guess would be some form of encephalitis. But in these numbers? Only a bioweapon could produce such a widespread outbreak.

"You said *or worse*," said Chang. "What did you mean by that?"

"Some patients get aggressive," said Owens.

"How so?"

"They almost all start out verbally abusive and quickly progress to physically violent. We've restrained any patients displaying neurological symptoms beyond headache."

"What are you seeing in terms of numbers for the aggressive patients?" said Chang.

"One in five. It used to be more like one in ten. My fear is that the number will continue to climb until everyone is affected."

This changed everything. Only rabies and anti-NMDA receptor encephalitis caused aggressive behavior in this percentage range, and they were both extremely rare diseases. Only two other possibilities existed. Neither good, but one was far worse than the other.

"That's a disturbingly high number, Jeff," said Chang. "Kind of narrows things down a bit unless this is a novel, contagious disease."

"It presents like herpes simplex encephalitis until patients start getting violent. And I can't wrap my head around the volume of patients. HSE in the ER is like a once-a-year diagnosis. Maybe."

"Rabies and anti-NMDA receptor encephalitis cause aggressive behavior in this percentage range, but cases of either are even less common than HSE," said Chang.

"God, I haven't seen a case of symptomatic rabies in the ER for years. Like two decades. And I've never heard of the anti-whatever thing you just mentioned."

"Anti-NMDA receptor encephalitis. It's an autoimmune disease. Very rare," said Chang.

He didn't want to bring up the possibility of the disease being a weaponized form of herpes simplex virus. Not until he'd run some tests. He wasn't sure that was even possible without clearing some serious red tape.

"So what are my chances of taking a look at some patient samples?" said Chang. "In my lab."

"One hundred percent," said Owens. "I just need to sneak a patient away to do a spinal tap. I can have one of the police officers meet you at NevoTech with the samples."

"Can you have one of your staff bring it to my apartment? A police car pulling up to the laboratory complex and delivering a package will draw attention. Security is pretty tight at the facility."

"That shouldn't be a problem," said Owens.

"Thank you. I live one block away from the NevoTech campus. I'll walk it right over and get started before the rest of the lab arrives. It's not unusual for me to arrive at five in the morning from time to time."

"Sounds like perfect timing. As soon as I hang up, I'll put my plan in motion. Probably take me an hour to steal a patient and do the spinal tap. I'll call you when the package leaves the hospital," said Owens.

"I'll be ready," said Chang.

"I really appreciate this. We're getting close to zero guidance from the hospital administration. Nobody seems to know what to do. I haven't heard word one from my boss about state CDC direction. If we had some idea what we're dealing with, I could make a strong case for moving the infected patients out. The sirens you keep hearing are police responding to violence in the city, and the police are sick, too. We're barely keeping up with what the ambulances deliver. At this rate, we'll need those beds. If not, we'll have to permanently shut down the ER."

"I'll focus all of my attention on those samples until I have something for you," said Chang.

"Thanks, Gene. I'll be in touch shortly."

Dr. Chang sat on the edge of his bed, thinking about what Owens had said at the very end of their conversation. He made it sound like the city was out of control and had been for the better part of twenty-four hours. Aside from the constant wail of distant sirens, he had witnessed nothing in the city to support the ER doctor's assessment. When he had stepped out of his apartment building to get a bite to eat, nothing had jumped out at him as abnormal.

The restaurants on Virginia Avenue hadn't been as crowded as he'd anticipated for a Thursday night, but the ever-present tipsy laughter and clinking happy hour glasses drifting onto the street from the numerous café patios felt right. People were walking and bicycling along the Indianapolis Cultural Trail, taking advantage of the late sunset and warm weather. After a while, the sirens kind of faded into the background, replaced by the bustle of Virginia Avenue's young, upwardly mobile vibe.

He'd returned to his apartment after a leisurely meal on one of those lively patios, thinking all was well in the world. Or not thinking about the world at all. A stark difference from Jeff Owens's evening. He truly wondered if it was possible for the two worlds to exist side by side. More importantly, how long would it take for enough of Owens's world to spill into Chang's, permanently unbalancing the entire system. He hoped there was a reasonable explanation for what Owens had described, and that they weren't headed for the kind of disaster he had spent a lifetime trying to prevent.

Chapter Eight

Dr. Lauren Hale turned her Honda Civic onto Virginia Avenue, barely slowing for the red light. She was in a hurry and hadn't seen more than two cars on the road since she'd left the hospital. Neither of them police cars. The police had bigger problems right now, or thousands of small problems depending on how you looked at it. Right now, everything looked normal for four thirty in the morning. The street was empty and presumably quiet. The sirens had been mostly silent when she'd retrieved her car from the parking garage. Even the ER had been eerily calm when she left. The sick had to sleep, too.

Her phone's navigation app told her Dr. Chang's address was less than a quarter of a mile away, on the left. She came up to another red light at College Street and slowed long enough to determine she was still the only car on the road. Two red lights blown in the name of science, or whatever she was doing. She was too fucking tired to ponder the question. In all truth, she probably shouldn't be driving. She remembered a *60 Minutes* segment about truck driver fatigue. The numbers cited were hazy right now, but she was pretty sure her driving was impaired at a .10 BAC equivalent based on the segment's science.

A long, four-story building loomed over the street ahead on the left. Her destination, most likely. Street-side parking had been full since she made the turn onto Virginia Avenue, so she turned into the empty parking lot of her absolute favorite breakfast spot. For the first time ever, she found a space. If only she could have made the trip two and a half hours later. Not even an ER full of raging lunatics could have stopped her from sitting down to a carrot cake waffle. It was probably for the best that the timing didn't work out. She might never leave.

Hale got out of the car and retrieved the cooler from the trunk. Owens didn't want to risk losing the samples to a carjacking. She thought he was being a little overcautious, but hadn't argued. She also hadn't brought up the fact that he hadn't once mentioned her safety. He had come out of the spinal tap single-mindedly focused on the cooler, and that was fine. Dr. Owens had probably expended the remainder of his mental focus on the delicate procedure.

Cooler in hand, she crossed the road and approached the front entrance to the apartment building. Dr. Chang appeared in the lobby and opened the door as she arrived. She was surprised by his younger appearance, having assumed he was in his mid to late fifties like Dr. Owens. Handsome and fit, Chang couldn't be more than forty. Possibly younger. It was too hard to tell in the subdued light, and she was too tired anyway.

"Dr. Hale?"

"The one and only," she said, not sure why that came out of her mouth. "Dr. Chang?"

"The one and only," he said, holding the door open.

She approached the front door, looking past him at the sleek, modernistic lobby. Definitely a few levels above her pay grade—for now.

"Sample was taken at four twelve, packaged, then run out to my waiting car," she said, holding the cooler out to him.

"Eighteen minutes. Not bad," said Chang, accepting the cooler.

Chang appeared to give her a once-over, which she'd normally find offensive. However, given her state of exhaustion, she really didn't care. All she wanted to do was get back to the ER, where Owens had promised her a few hours of sleep. Chang could pinch her ass at this point, and she'd make a beeline for her car. With the cooler delivered, sleep was her number one mission.

"Dr. Owens underrepresented your appearance," said Chang.

What? Maybe she'd make a beeline to her apartment instead, after she read Chang the riot act. Owens could make do without another doctor.

"Excuse me?" she said.

"He told me you've been awake for the better part of forty-eight hours. That you'd look like—reheated dog shit—I believe was the term he used," said Chang. "He wasn't sure about sending you out alone."

"Oh. Right," she said, nearly too exhausted to feel bad about misreading him. "I'm fine. He promised me a few hours of sleep when I get back."

"You look like you could use a few days of sleep," said Chang, stepping through the glass door and opening it wider. "Dr. Owens asked if you could crash here for a few hours. I have no problem with that."

"Here? At your place?"

The offer was beyond tempting, but felt a little odd. He seemed to read her mind.

"I'm heading right to the lab. I need to start processing these fluids immediately. You'll have the place to yourself," said Chang, nodding for her to enter. "There's a deadbolt that can't be opened from the outside."

"I didn't mean it to sound like I thought you might—"

He cut her off. "Dr. Hale, I completely understand. You can't be too careful."

A siren cut through the silence, resonating through the buildings. Red and blue flashing lights reflected off a tree across the street, quickly vanishing. Chang glanced up and down the deserted avenue as the siren faded.

"How bad is it out there?" he said.

"I'm probably not the right person to ask. This is my first trip outside the ER," said Hale. "It almost feels normal. The hospital has been a living hell for the past twenty-four hours."

"You're experiencing a form of concentration or choke-point

44

bias," said Chang. "Neither of those are official psychology terms. It's how I look at it. You're seeing a concentration of the problem because everyone with the problem has shown up at the ER's doorstep."

"It's bad, Dr. Chang. I've never seen anything like it, and neither has Dr. Owens."

"I'm not saying it isn't," said Chang. "I'm just comparing what Dr. Owens reported and what I'm seeing out here. Until his phone call an hour ago, I had zero idea anything was wrong."

"How is that even possible?" she said. "The hospital hit surge capacity early yesterday. This should be front-page news."

"The hospitals will do whatever they can to minimize the press surrounding one of their dirtiest little secrets," said Chang. "Most hospitals operate year-round at near full capacity because they have to. An empty bed doesn't generate revenue. All it takes is a severe pileup on the interstate to tie up every hospital within a twenty-mile radius. Same thing but worse happens in an epidemic or pandemic. Medical services shut to new patients very quickly."

"Do you think this is a viral epidemic?" she said.

"I should have a pretty good idea in a few hours," he said, and then held up the cooler. "So. Are you staying or heading back?"

She felt guilty staying away from the ER, where the rest of the staff would undoubtedly catch little sleep, but she didn't have the willpower to refuse at the moment. The prospect of lying down and closing her bloodshot eyes, in a clean, quiet apartment, for a few hours had no competition. The fact that her favorite restaurant was right across the street sealed the deal. She'd put in a huge order to take back to the ER when she woke up. That was how she'd make amends when she slinked back into the patient-clogged ER. Chang caught her looking over her shoulder at the restaurant.

"They open at seven. Best breakfast in town," said Chang, holding out a notecard. "The codes to this door and the apartment. Number 318."

Hale stumbled inside, the full weight of the past forty-eight hours smothering her. A quick glance around revealed a tasteful, but sparsely appointed apartment. A wall-mounted TV, couch and circular table with two chairs made up the furnishings. Definitely a bachelor pad. Like a dream, she soon found herself lying on an oversized sectional couch in a dark apartment, the thin memory of turning the deadbolt on the door slowly drifting away. A window shattered somewhere in the neighborhood, jolting her upright on the couch. She listened for several moments, finally picking up on a heated argument between a man and a woman, followed by a door crashing shut. It almost sounded like the door had been slammed inside the apartment building.

She willed herself off the couch and checked the deadbolt, not trusting that faded memory. For good measure, she wedged a kitchen chair under the doorknob, not exactly sure it would make a difference. She'd only seen this done on TV or in the movies, but it made her feel a little better. After the behavior she'd witnessed at the hospital, she wished she hadn't turned down her dad's offer to give her one of his many handguns. She'd feel a lot better with a gun.

When she got back to the couch, the argument had moved onto the street or a balcony. Hale really hoped it wasn't a balcony. She could justify sleeping through an argument, but would be on her feet in a second if someone fell to the street. Drifting in and out of consciousness through a seemingly endless tirade of slurs and foul language, she was relieved to hear a car door slam shut, followed by screeching tires. As one half of the argument sped away, the screaming intensified until it barely sounded human. One of her last thoughts before falling asleep was that the woman was smart to get out of here. The guy sounded homicidal.

Chapter Nine

Jack Harper spit a mouthful of toothpaste suds into the bathroom sink and let the water run over his toothbrush for a few seconds. He carefully put the toothbrush in the stainless steel cup on the sink counter, trying to keep it from clinking too loudly.

"Make sure you rinse the sink," Emma suddenly announced from behind the closed bathroom door.

He jumped at the sound of her voice.

"Jesus! You're like a stalker," he said. "Except I live with you."

"Yeah. I need to stalk you to keep this place from looking like a frat house," she said, jiggling the door handle.

"Hold on," he said, opening the door.

Emma stood there in gray sweatpants and a pink, oversized Indiana University T-shirt; her brownish-red hair was tied in a ponytail. She looked exactly like she did when she woke up.

"What?" she said.

"You look beautiful as always."

"Nice try. I look exactly like I did when I woke up," she said, glancing at the sink behind him. "I heard like two seconds of faucet."

"Two seconds?" he said, grabbing her by the waist and pulling her close. "Sure it wasn't three?"

"Pretty sure," she said, pressing against him.

They kissed passionately, Jack thinking that a delay in his scheduled departure time might be in order. Emma disengaged from the kiss first, pecking him on the cheek.

"Hurry up and get back," she said.

"That's it?" he said, pulling her back in.

"You don't want to keep your parents waiting," said Emma.

"They're retired," he protested.

"On a strict schedule. You don't mess with the Harpers' breakfast time," she said.

He kissed her again, nibbling gently on her lower lip before releasing her.

"Point well taken," said Jack, stepping out of the bathroom. "They tend to misbehave with low blood sugar."

"We all do," said Emma, smacking him firmly on the behind.

"What was that for?"

"Leaving me with a toothpaste-slimed sink," she said, half smirking, half frowning.

"Hey, can't keep my parents waiting," said Jack.

He grabbed his wallet, sunglasses and car keys from the corner of the kitchen counter next to the door leading to the garage. Emma appeared in the hallway past the kitchen table.

"When do you think you'll be back?" she said.

"It's seven now," he said, pausing to think it through. "I should get there about eight thirty their time. Leave around ten or eleven. I'll be back by two at the latest?"

Properly coordinating the two-and-a-half-hour trip to northwest Indiana required math. Nothing complicated, but he'd arrived an hour early on more than one occasion after failing to account for the time change. His parents lived in the one small swath of Indiana that hadn't lost its mind and gone to Eastern Standard Time several years back. That played a big part in why he hadn't left an hour ago. It was dark when he wanted to get up, which kept him pressing the snooze on his smart phone until Emma pushed him out of bed.

"All right," she said. "I'll grab some lunch for us on the way back from grocery shopping. Any requests?"

"Sushi would be nice," he said. "We haven't had Japanese since we left."

"Perfect. I'll pick up something, or I could meet you right in

Broad Ripple."

"Either way. I'll call you when I'm an hour out," he said.

"Drive safe," she said, and then blew him a kiss, which he pretended to catch and return.

She disappeared into the hallway, appearing a few seconds later.

"I was thinking about inviting some people over for drinks tonight. We can sit out on the patio all night and annoy whoever was yelling up a storm last night," she said.

Jack vaguely remembered what she was talking about, but he did recall thinking that it sounded like a vicious argument, at least an eight on a scale of one to ten. The kind of tone and language you could expect from a wife that just caught her husband cheating—and the woman was still there! As animated as it had sounded, when Emma had woken him up, it couldn't compete with a good night's sleep after a long day of travel.

"I drifted in and out. What was it all about?"

"I don't know, but it sounded serious," she said. "I thought about getting up to lock the doors."

"It wasn't Chris and Courtney next door, was it?"

"No. Sounded like a few houses down—but it was loud. It died down after several minutes, or I fell asleep. Not sure, honestly. I was pretty zonked, too," she said. "Anyone you want me to make sure to include for tonight?"

"I trust your judgment," he said before stepping into the garage.

Jack stopped his Jeep halfway down the driveway to put the top down. The forecast called for clear skies and temperatures in the mid-eighties—perfect Jeep weather. Wide rays of sunlight poked between the trees across the street, warming his face and convincing him he'd made the right decision. He'd folded the Jeep's retractable soft top into the rear cargo compartment, when his neighbor's front screen door snapped shut.

He looked over his shoulder and waved at Sam, who carried two bulging plastic grocery bags by their stretched thin handles. Jack took a few seconds to make sure the top was secure before heading over to meet his neighbor.

"No need to haul everything over, Sam!" said Jack, catching him before he'd struggled too far. "We appreciate you taking care of the mail last second like that. I totally spaced putting it on hold. Here. Let me grab that."

"It's no problem," said Sam, struggling to the contrary.

Sam strained to disentangle his hands from the handles, which left deep white lines across his palms. When the transfer was complete, the thin plastic started to dig into his own hands.

"You guys get a lot of mail," said Sam, breathing heavily.

"It's all of Emma's magazines and catalogues," said Jack.

Sam started to smile, but winced in pain instead, nearly taking a knee in the grass.

Jack dropped the bags of junk mail and steadied Sam.

"You all right?"

Sam squinted, the effects of whatever had just hit him still lingering. "Been getting these nasty headaches," he whispered. "Never had a headache outside of a hangover before. Even those weren't even close to this."

"Migraines?" said Jack. "Emma gets those every once in a while. I think it's allergy related."

"I don't have allergies. Or at least I never did before." Sam flinched again, softly grunting. "Comes in waves. I thought I could run this out to you before they hit again."

"Here," said Jack, taking Sam's arm. "Let's get you back inside. Amy's home, right?"

"Yeah. She's gonna take us over to urgent care when they open," said Sam. "She's got the same thing, but not as bad."

"Both of you with migraines?" said Jack.

"Weird, isn't it?"

"Do you think it could be food poisoning?"

"My stomach's been fine," said Sam, in between deep breaths.

"Let me check something," said Jack, feeling Sam's forehead with the back of his hand.

Jack never had much success doing the forehead-temperature thing, but the second he touched Sam's head, he could tell the guy was burning up.

"I think you have a solid temperature, Sam," said Jack. "Urgent care doesn't sound like a bad idea. Is Amy okay to drive you over? Maybe Emma can give you guys a lift."

"And get her sick, too?" said Sam. "We'll be fine. I can call a cab if it gets that bad."

"I'll have her check on you guys, either way. I'm headed up to my folks to grab Rudy. I should be back by midafternoon."

"She doesn't have to check on us," said Sam.

"If you guys haven't seen a doctor by then, I'll drive you myself," said Jack. "Even if I have to wear gloves and a mask."

Sam laughed a little, the lingering pain of a cluster headache still evident on his strained face.

"The thought of you driving us around wearing a silly mask and latex gloves is all I need to make sure we get to urgent care—on our own," said Sam, patting Jack's shoulder. "Drive safe."

"Will do," he said, starting to turn away, but remembering something. "Hey, Sam?"

"Yeah?"

"Did you hear a big commotion on the block last night? Like some arguing?"

"No. But an ambulance and a few police cars showed up around three in the morning. I couldn't tell exactly where, but it looked like three houses down from yours on that side," said Sam, pointing behind Jack.

They didn't know the couple that lived there very well. Gary and...he couldn't think of the wife's name. They were in their mid-forties from what he guessed, with no kids. Probably a good thing given last night's fiasco, especially if an ambulance was involved.

"I hope everyone is all right," said Jack. "Emma said she heard a vicious argument coming from that direction. I slept through most of it. Neither one of us caught the ambulance and police."

"Jeez, that doesn't sound good. Hate to think they had an argument that got violent," said Sam.

"Me too," said Jack, looking in that direction.

If one of them hospitalized the other, there was a good chance that both of them would be gone. One in a hospital bed. The other in a jail cell. He wondered if anyone had thought about the dogs. They had two miniature poodles that barked nonstop, but they'd been silent this morning. Jack made a mental note to check on that situation later. He had enough on his plate for now.

Chapter Ten

David Olson needed to find his ex-wife quickly. At the very least, he needed to get in touch with her over the phone. So far, his numerous calls to the three different numbers he had for her in his contacts list had gone unanswered, which was unlike Meghan. They'd had their difficulties in the past, mostly "job" related, but she'd never failed to return a call within a few hours when he had Josh, even if it meant dealing with one of David's dumb questions. Now he was starting to get worried. It had been eighteen hours since he'd left his first string of messages.

Worried about his ex, and his job. Sergeant Jackson's tone had shifted from "we could sure use your help" to "get your ass into the station ASAP" between last night and this morning. More officers had called in sick, and the department continued to get hit with an increasing number of legitimate 911 emergencies. If he could just get in touch with Meghan, he could explain the situation and work out a plan.

Ideally, she would take him back early, and he'd do an extended shift lasting until tomorrow morning. If she was out of town, he could head in this morning and stay on duty until ten o'clock tonight, scooting home to make sure Josh wasn't left alone overnight. Either way, he wanted to let her know what was going on. She got a little crazy when he went off script with their son, and he didn't need her throwing that back at him in the form of a visitation modification petition. He didn't think she'd do something like that, but why take the chance?

Checking his watch, he made a quick calculation. He could drive to her house in Fishers and back within an hour while Josh slept in. His son rarely rolled out of bed before ten during summer break, leaving him enough time to scope out her place and make it back in time to cook up some omelets. That was the plan. David wrote his son a note explaining the situation and slid it under his door, hoping it didn't get lost in the mess when Joshua stumbled to the bathroom first thing after waking up.

Why was he sweating this? The kid was seventeen years old, fully capable of fending for himself for a few hours, and he had a phone, which could apparently solve any problem in existence nowadays. Joshua could probably YouTube how to make an omelet and surprise his old man when he got back. Fat chance. He'd be lucky if the kid poured his own glass of orange juice. Meghan kind of treated him like a baby at her place, a habit he only managed to slightly rewire once a year by taking him into the forest, where mama didn't cut up the food on your plate or make a second meal because you don't like meatloaf. Who was he kidding? He was about to make the kid a three-cheese omelet with two kinds of hash browns.

Roughly a half hour later, after driving across what appeared to be a normally busy town, he pulled into Meghan's neighborhood, a tightly packed development of custom, ranch-style homes. She'd always wanted a home with the master suite on the main level so she could grow old in the home, or something like that. David always figured that would happen anyway when they moved to Florida after they retired. Most of the houses down there were one story, from what he could tell.

David drove slowly through the winding streets of the subdivision, finally spotting her house next to the community pool and playground complex. He pulled up to the curb in front of her house and idled his pickup truck forward, spotting the back end of a boxy silver SUV at the back of the driveway that wrapped around the side of the house. The boyfriend was here, with his ugly-ass, outrageously expensive Mercedes G63, or whatever the number was this year.

One hundred and fifty grand for the most aesthetically unattractive, gas-guzzling vehicle on the road. And he didn't buy any of "boyfriend's" nonsense about the thing being unstoppable in any climate or terrain. The guy lived in central fucking Indiana. The closest his SUV got to rough terrain was a muddy stretch of flat ground at one of his construction sites.

He stopped at the edge of the driveway and weighed his options. He really didn't want to see mister real estate developer. It wasn't that he was an openly bad guy, but he had a bad habit of hanging around and chiming in when they discussed Joshua. David often heard him in the background during phone calls, telling her what to say, which—as a three-time divorcé—was apparently one of his areas of expertise. Giving people domestic advice that he couldn't seem to take himself. He didn't like the guy, and if he could avoid seeing his plucked eyebrows and Botox grin, all the better.

With the truck in park, he dialed her cell number again and waited. Voicemail. Damn it. He gave her home phone a try, getting the same result. Fuck it. He was trying to do the right thing here, and if that meant saying hi to a permanently frozen face, so be it. He got out of the pickup and walked up the driveway, doing the math in his head. His ex would have had one hell of a time getting out of the garage without hitting the silver lunchbox on wheels. No way the boyfriend sat in the passenger seat and sweated her close-quarters maneuvering. Actually, why would they take her car in the first place? The housing market boom had bought her a new Lexus, but it was a base model—nothing like the marvel of German engineering standing before him right now.

A quick glance through one of the garage windows confirmed that her car hadn't left the house. Now he really faced a dilemma. If he knocked on the door, he faced the distinct possibility of encountering the two of them in their post-sex romp robes, or whatever outfit they threw on to meet his insistent knocking. David strongly considered turning around, but Sergeant Jackson wasn't going to take no for an answer for very long. The sooner he squared this away, the better for all of them.

Bracing for whatever burlesque show might appear in his ex-wife's foyer, he rang the doorbell and listened. A long minute later, not hearing any movement inside the house, he rapped on the door with his knuckles, trying hard not to sound like he was pounding. Pounding could be interpreted as aggressive. David put his ear to the door, still not detecting any kind of activity on the other side. Maybe they were sleeping. Nine twenty was a little late for adults to sleep in, by his book, but he had to consider the possibility.

He rang the doorbell several times and backed off the stoop, looking for any movement in the windows. It was definitely a stalkerish move, but he was past the point of no return here. He'd give it a few more knocks and a few more minutes before calling the Fishers Police Department. He'd ask them to take a closer look around the house, maybe kick the door in if they agreed that it was unusual enough for both cars to be here, with nobody answering. A thought hit him as he knocked on the door for the second time. Shit. They could be out riding bikes or walking. Hell, for all he knew, moneybags might have sprung a little romantic getaway on his ex, treating her to a limousine ride to the airport. Dozens of possible scenarios poured through the delayed floodgate of his mind, making him feel more like an over-reactive stalker by the second.

David stood there for a few more seconds with his hands on his hips before deciding to give up. He'd have to work something out with Sergeant Jackson. It wasn't like Jackson hadn't dealt with this problem himself over the past years. He'd divorced a few years ago, with three kids in high school. He had to know firsthand how difficult it was to balance fixed custody arrangements with often less than flexible shift work. Then again, Jackson hadn't worked rotating shifts in several years, and his wife had taken full custody of the kids, leaving his life about as uncomplicated as it gets.

He cut across the lawn, headed for his pickup truck, when the front door to the house directly across the street creaked open. A woman with disheveled hair, wearing flannel pajamas and pink slippers, stepped onto the porch and put a hand on her hip. She looked two cups of coffee short of firing on all cylinders.

"You're the ex, right?" she said.

He nodded. "I've been trying to get in touch with Meghan since yesterday. Any idea where she might be?"

The woman rubbed her head, taking a long time to answer.

"There was an ambulance and a couple cop cars here around ten last night."

"Cop cars? What happened?"

"They dragged your ex away screaming," she said.

"Wait. Who dragged my wife—ex-wife—away? The paramedics?"

"No. They put the boyfriend in the ambulance. She went away in the back of one of the squad cars."

None of this made any sense, unless Mr. Botox stepped out of line and Meghan's Krav Maga training kicked in—and didn't stop. Why hadn't she called him? He could smooth things out as best as possible with the officers he knew in the Fishers PD. Even if they had to charge her, he could make her life a little more comfortable and a lot less uncertain. Then again, she was probably worried about the custody situation. Everything came down to that after a divorce. It was a constant state of paranoia.

"He was bloody from top to bottom when they put him in the ambulance," she added.

"What? Like a bloody nose?" he said.

"No. They worked on him inside the house for a few minutes while they dealt with her. Carted him out on a stretcher with IV bags and everything. Looked like he'd been stabbed."

That couldn't be right.

"Are you—" he started.

The woman suddenly raised both of her hands to her head and squeezed the sides of her skull, grunting and groaning. A few seconds later, she dropped her arms by her sides, face still scrunched in a painful grimace.

"All right?" said David.

"Headaches," she mumbled. "Really bad. Called off work because of it."

"Well, you take care," he said, his mind about as far from this woman's problems as the moon.

As soon as he slammed the truck door shut, he dialed an unpublished number at the Fishers PD, which rang in the administrative area. He didn't expect a police officer to answer, especially if they were having as much trouble as Westfield's department, but he hoped to get someone. Anyone. After several unanswered rings, he tossed the phone on the passenger seat and started the truck. Omelets would have to wait. He needed to figure out what had happened to Joshua's mom.

Chapter Eleven

Dr. Chang swiveled his stool to face the rightmost monitor in the trio of high-resolution screens comprising his personal workstation deep inside the lab. To say that he was alarmed would have been the scientific understatement of the decade. Chang was terrified by what he saw. Remaining motionless for several minutes, he carefully reviewed the DNA analysis displayed on the monitor twice to make certain he hadn't made a mistake. He really wanted all of this to be a mistake. The implications were unthinkable.

Based on the polymerase chain reaction results, both the spinal tap and blood samples contained a human-engineered virus strain. Weaponized was a more accurate term. There was no other conclusion. On the surface, he was looking at what he had expected to find based on the symptoms described. Herpes simplex virus 1 (HSV1). HSV1 was the leading cause of herpes simplex encephalitis, a rare neurological disorder that caused severe inflammation of the brain. However, when run against his exhaustive database of previously sequenced HSV1 samples associated with HSE cases, he immediately noticed some slight variations to the DNA coding.

The virus strain in his samples would undoubtedly cause encephalitis upon contaminating the central nervous system, but the persistent difference in DNA structure suggested a sophisticated genetic engineering effort. Chang was certain that he was looking at a designer bioweapon. There was simply no other explanation.

HSV1 is estimated to be present in close to two-thirds of the global population under the age of fifty, but the vast majority remain asymptomatic their entire lives, and it's not found in the bloodstream or cerebral spinal fluid. If it were, two-thirds of the population would suffer from HSE upon initial infection with HSV1. Herpes simplex encephalitis was extremely rare, striking roughly one person in every five hundred thousand. The number of suspected cases at Methodist Hospital alone right now was statistically impossible unless every case that was projected to occur in the United States this year struck at once.

No. Someone caused this to happen—engineered it to happen—and that was the truly frightening part. Even more terrifying was the fact that he didn't have the time to fully unravel the impact of the DNA changes made to the virus. Deciphering the DNA modifications could take weeks, and he didn't plan on sticking around the laboratory past noon. Assuming Dr. Owens and Dr. Hale hadn't exaggerated the number of sick patients they'd seen at the hospital, he predicted this was just the tip of the iceberg.

HSE progressed at different rates in nearly every patient, with equally variable degrees of severity. According to the epidemiological models he'd studied regarding pandemic influenza, only a small fraction of the most severely developed cases had shown up to the hospital. For every patient that had come through the ER so far, hundreds more were out there. Chang had no intention of hanging around the city any longer than necessary. He had a place out of the city, far enough removed from the masses to weather this kind of storm. And if that failed, his suburban hideaway was a quick ten-minute drive to the Indianapolis Executive Airport. He could be in the air fifteen minutes after arriving, putting some serious distance behind him.

Before he left, he'd save the data and send it to a few trusted colleagues at Edgewood and the CDC, with a description of what the ER doctors had reported. He might even send it to a few researcher friends of his, who might have a more immediate capability to investigate the DNA changes identified by the polymerase chain reaction isolation data.

First, he needed to warn Dr. Owens. Chang dialed the doctor's mobile number and slid his wheeled stool over to a laptop on a different desk.

"Gene, I wasn't expecting a call this quick. Is that good news or bad news?" said Owens.

"I'm afraid it's nothing but bad news," said Chang. "I managed to positively identify the virus as HSV1, which means you're dealing with HSE—but I've found some persistent DNA code changes that I cannot find in any of my archived HSV1 data. This is a heavily studied virus in my field, so I'm confident that this strain has been genetically manipulated."

"Like a bioweapon?" said Owens.

"You did not hear that from me," said Chang. "Here's the bottom line. Structurally, this HSV1 variation will cause the encephalitis you're seeing. No surprise there. What I don't know is what these DNA modifications mean."

"I don't like the sound of that at all," said Owens. "What are we potentially talking about?"

"We could be looking at increased virulence, which wouldn't surprise me. Quicker replication. Faster targeting of the brain. Specific targeting of the temporal lobe. Resistance to known treatments. Increased contagiousness. I really don't know, but I suggest you and your staff take some precautions, starting with the prophylactic administration of high-dose antivirals. Acyclovir and vidarabine are good options and should be readily available in the hospital."

"Shouldn't we be giving that to the patients?" said Owens.

"Every pandemic protocol, state and federal, dictates that critical healthcare personnel are to be vaccinated first. This is the same thing. Set aside at least a two-week, daily-dose supply for you and your staff."

"I can't imagine us being here two more days at this rate," said Owens.

"It doesn't matter. If you evacuate the ER tomorrow, you can leave the stockpile behind. Just get the antivirals in your system immediately."

"What about the patients? If I can get my hands on enough acyclovir, can we make a difference?"

"Think about the standard treatment protocol if you suspect HSE," said Chang.

"I'm too tired to think, Gene. Spell it out for me."

"Sorry, Jeff. I keep forgetting what you've been through," said Chang. "Basically, you're looking at intravenous acyclovir for patients caught in the early stages of infection. I can't imagine you have a lot of that at the hospital."

"That's right. We haven't started any of the patients on antivirals because we essentially crossed HSE off the list of suspected diseases due to the volume of patients. It wouldn't have mattered, anyway. We keep a small supply for that one patient a year that shows up with symptoms. I don't even know where I'd get pills for the staff."

"You need to hit up the hospital pharmacy immediately," said Chang. "ER staff should have priority."

"Easier said than done with a hospital full of sick patients," said Owens. "Everyone working at the hospital is in direct contact."

Chang shook his head. Owens was right. There was no easy answer for this.

"Jeff, can I be really blunt with you?"

"Please."

"Take care of yourself and your staff," said Chang. "You've earned it. And upgrade your biosafety level, particularly if you're treating patients that are bleeding, spitting or coughing productively. Full face shields at a minimum. I assume you're already wearing gloves and N95 respirators."

"We are. I'll see what we can put together to upgrade our posture," said Owens. "Thanks for doing this, Gene. Can I ask you for one more favor?"

"As long as it doesn't involve working a shift in the ER," said Chang.

Owens cracked a quick laugh.

"I wouldn't wish that on my worst enemy," said Owens. "No. I was hoping you could pass what you found to the CDC. We still haven't heard word one from any of the state or federal agencies."

"The hospital hasn't been in contact with either?" said Chang.

"Not that I'm aware of," said Owens. "Then again, hospital administration has been conspicuously absent over the past twenty-four hours, and our previous ER head is now one of our patients."

"Sorry to hear that," said Chang, pausing. "I'm really surprised to hear that you haven't received any official guidance. My next call will be to the CDC. I'm sending them my analysis of the samples, too."

"Can I offer you some blunt advice in return?" said Owens.

"Of course."

"Be careful who you talk to, and watch your back. I may be falling asleep on my feet right now, but I can read between the lines. Someone planted this mess here," said Owens.

He didn't know how to respond. Owens had connected the dots, which wasn't a difficult task, and he'd made a point that Chang hadn't considered.

"Thank you, Jeff," said Chang. "In light of your advice, I think I'll route my findings through a different source. Stay in touch, and good luck."

"Same to you, Gene," said Owens. "Oh, one more thing."

"Yep?"

"Get out of the city. Patients are deteriorating rapidly. Most of them are in restraints at this point. I can't imagine what it'll be like out there in another day."

"I'm heading out very shortly," said Chang. "Stay safe."

"I'll do my best."

Chang disconnected the call and stared at his laptop screen for a moment, debating his next move. He'd take a slightly different approach to spreading the news, given the implications of what he'd uncovered. Something wasn't right with the government's response, especially at the federal level. Billions of dollars had been spent on Project Bioshield over the past few years, with much of it going to domestic detection and strategic stockpiles. He found it difficult to believe that the CDC or the state hadn't initiated emergency outbreak protocols, which would have concentrated significant diagnostic and treatment resources at the hospital level.

The more he thought about it, the less eager he was to widely disseminate the data until he knew more. The fewer links back to him, the better. Chang sent the DNA snapshot file by secure email to two Edgewood colleagues he trusted implicitly before hiding it in several locations on his computers. He'd make a few hard copies to stash inside the lab in case something far more nefarious was involved, and he needed to retrieve it. He thought about smuggling a thumb-drive copy out, but information security was tight at the lab—even for someone at his level. Leaving the source data here was the best option for now. It was one of the most secure buildings.

Glancing at his watch, he made it his goal to be on the road in thirty minutes. It might take him a little longer, since he hadn't figured out exactly how he would smuggle NT-HSE893 out of the lab. He didn't need a lot. NT-HSE893 was an experimental, once-monthly booster drug taken to prevent HSV1 and HSV2 infection, or so NevoTech hoped. His research into possible bioweapons vaccines and preventatives had unlocked the door to selling a single drug to every human on the planet, and he had access to a small quantity for use in his research—which might come in handy in the upcoming days.

Chapter Twelve

Emma Harper pushed a full grocery cart through the bakery department at Natural Foods, grabbing a loaf of sliced sourdough bread from a display next to the olive bar. Ahead of her, two shoppers milled around the prepared food section, both of them preoccupied with the salad bar. The store was noticeably empty for a Friday, especially the noon hour, when the place usually swarmed with young professionals squeezing their weekend grocery run into a lunch break.

She wasn't complaining. Still a little groggy from yesterday's travel, she'd procrastinated most of the morning, tending to one excuse after another—until she had no choice. Jack was ahead of schedule, already halfway back from his parents' house. Navigating her way past the prepared-foods section, she turned her cart toward the checkout lanes and stopped dead in her tracks. One lane was open, with nobody standing in it. She'd obviously missed that on the way in. How could they only have one lane open a few minutes before noon on a Friday?

A quick glance at her watch confirmed she hadn't messed up the time. Admittedly, she hadn't been here on a Friday in several months, so maybe she was seeing the result of the recent organic food explosion around Indianapolis. All of the supermarket chains offered a massive selection of "natural" and organic products these days, drawing customers away from Natural Foods.

Or maybe she missed something on the local news this morning?

The strip mall parking lot had been far less crowded than usual. Had the traffic been lighter? She couldn't remember, which probably meant there was nothing to notice.

Either way it didn't matter. No line at Natural Foods was a blessing—no matter what the reason. Her very pragmatic outlook changed the second she parked her cart in the entrance to the checkout aisle. The young woman standing at the register looked gravely ill. Her face was pale, almost grayish. Above her red-rimmed eyes, beads of perspiration formed a thin line across her forehead. The vacant look on her face was the worst. The woman stared past her with dead eyes for several seconds, only coming to partial life when Emma placed the loaf of bread on the conveyor.

"Sorry," the woman muttered, reaching out for the plastic-wrapped loaf.

Emma mentally cringed when the woman's hand touched the loaf. Shit. She really didn't want this woman handling her groceries. She read the woman's name tag.

"Britt?" said Emma. "Are you all right?"

Britt took way too long to respond, slowly shaking her head. "I felt a little off when I got here this morning, but I think it got worse."

"I think so, too. You really look like you should lie down," said Emma, wanting to add—*at home.*

"Most of my shift didn't show up," mumbled Britt, slowly turning the bread over to examine it. "Is this French peasant bread?"

"Sourdough," said Emma.

The woman squinted at the register screen, seemingly unable to proceed. Emma knew this was futile. She would be way better off walking out of here and hitting a different store. She'd be late with lunch, but at least their groceries wouldn't be covered with whatever flu bug had left Britt looking like a *Walking Dead* extra. How could her manager leave her at the register in this condition? Wait. Did she say most of the shift wasn't here?

"Is there a manager in the store?" said Emma.

Britt nodded her head. "The office behind the customer service desk."

"Thanks," said Emma. "Why don't you take a break for a minute? I'm going to see if I can get someone to help you."

At the very least—someone to replace you. The woman leaned against the back of the cashier enclosure and forced a smile. As Emma walked through the aisle, toward the customer service alcove, Britt put both of her hands to her temples and squeezed her head, emitting a low groan. Something was off here. She paused at the end of the aisle and glanced between the exit and the customer service desk, wavering between the two. Against her better judgment, Emma decided to do the right thing and see if she could get the cashier some help.

The door to the office behind the customer service area was open, but no signs of life materialized when Emma exaggerated a cough at the counter.

"Hello?" she said, directing her voice toward the door.

Nothing. She moved left to get a better view of the inside of the office, noticing someone behind a computer monitor.

"Excuse me?" she said in a louder voice.

"I heard you the first time!" screamed the woman behind the monitor.

"Never mind," said Emma before turning around and starting for the exit.

Definitely something off here. Maybe the home office just announced layoffs and that the store was closing. That would explain the hostility and why most of the shift didn't show up. A chair squealed along the floor in the office, followed by the sound of someone banging against something solid. Emma looked over her shoulder in time to see a woman rush through the door. She picked up the pace, focused on the automatic sliding door ahead.

"What the fuck do you want?"

Emma ignored the ensuing verbal tirade until she heard the counter's half door slam shut. She was afraid to look back.

"I'm talking to you!" barked the woman.

The voice sounded a lot closer, spurring Emma into action. She took off for the exit in a dead sprint, hoping she got to the door far enough ahead of this crazy person for the door to slide open and release her into the parking lot. Emma hit the door moments later, placing her open palms flat on the glass panel, which hadn't started to slide. By the time the door's sensor reacted, it was too late. Crazy bitch was right on her heels.

Emma darted to the left, through the express lane, the woman almost snagging her purse with an outreached hand. She made a quick decision on the other side of the lane, opting to run in the direction of the people she had seen near the salad bar instead of the previously empty produce area. Safety in numbers, she hoped. Her only other choice was to stand her ground, but this didn't hold any appeal for her at the moment. The woman had clearly blown a fuse, choosing to take it out on her.

Not wanting to scare the small group of customers, she didn't yell for help as she approached. Emma let the crazy woman advertise the situation instead. A stout, bearded guy behind the deli counter hurried down the long refrigerated display case and burst through an opening near the bakery, headed in Emma's direction. Instead of planting herself among the startled shoppers, who were slowly backing up in response to the manager's ceaseless obscenity-strewn outburst, she continued past them, headed for the one employee that seemed to have their shit together today.

"This crazy woman is chasing me!" she yelled.

"I got this," he said, barreling past her.

The man stopped several feet in front of the supposed manager, squaring off in case she didn't stop.

"Andrea! What are you doing?" he said.

The woman slowed, but continued to advance. "Get out of my fucking way!"

"Stop!" he said, pointing at her face. "Or I'll make sure you stop."

The woman came within an arm's length of the guy and halted, immediately putting both hands on her knees to take deep gulps of air. She looked up at him, her eyes immediately shifting to Emma, who hid behind a circular display of cookies. It was a maniacal look, prompting the deli guy to take a few steps back.

"What's going on, Andrea?" he said.

Her expression shifted instantly. The wild lunacy had been replaced by someone that looked frightened—and sick. Now that Emma had a moment to look at the woman, she saw the same symptoms exhibited by the cashier. Red eyes. Sweating. Exhausted looking.

"I don't know. I really don't know," whispered Andrea, who glanced at Emma with a look of humiliation. "Sorry. I have no idea…"

The man turned to Emma. "You all right?"

"I'm fine," she said. "I just wanted to let her know that the cashier looks—like she does. Very sick."

"There's been a lot of that going around," he said, keeping a close eye on Andrea. "Summer flu or something. Are you checked out up front?"

"No. I don't think the cashier can handle it. She looked like she was about to fall over."

Andrea pushed off her knees and stood uneasily. "We'll comp your groceries. It's the least I can do. I'm really sorry."

"I can pay," said Emma.

The woman's face changed again, but she didn't look quite as menacing as before.

"I didn't imply you couldn't pay," she said, partly growling.

"Andrea!" yelled the man standing between them.

"What?" she said, her voice and expression normal again. "What?"

The guy turned to Emma. "Take the free groceries. I'll walk you up and make sure everything is okay."

"Thank you," said Emma, holding back from saying more in front of Andrea.

The woman was on some kind of mental breakdown hair trigger that she didn't want to pull.

A few minutes later, with her groceries jammed randomly into thick brown paper bags, she emerged from the store shaken—but with a cart full of free groceries. Easily a two-, three-hundred-dollar score, given they had been out of town for close to two weeks.

Worth being chased by a crazy woman? Barely, but definitely not an experience she wanted to repeat. Ever. If that guy hadn't intervened, who knew what would have happened.

Emma loaded the car and sat behind the wheel, the bizarre episode finally catching up to her. All she wanted to do was get out of here. Her hands trembled, the keys on her key chain lightly jingling as she pulled them from her purse. What the hell had happened back there? The most disturbing part of the entire situation came after the guy had calmed the crazed woman down. Her facial expressions cycled between rage and calm, like she had a split personality. She'd never seen anything like it.

She started the car and drove through the mostly vacant parking lot, trying to push the woman's face out of her mind. The immediate prospect of Mexican food helped the transition. Fresh guacamole and chips from her favorite hole-in-a-wall restaurant eased all pain. A few minutes later, when she turned her car into the run-down strip mall front that housed La Cantina Roja, she cursed out loud. A black on white, red-bordered CLOSED sign hung in the window next to the door.

"Has to be a mistake," she muttered before guiding her car into the parking space right in front of the restaurant's door.

Peering through the reflected sky on the storefront windows confirmed what she suspected. No lights. No signs of an open restaurant. Bizarre. Maybe there was something to this summer flu bug idea. The Subway was open in the corner of the little mall, its yellow and white interior busy with a few customers, but nowhere near the crowd that usually jammed the preparation counter around lunchtime. No way she was eating Subway after dreaming about Mexican food. She had everything she needed to make burritos at home, anyway.

Before backing out of the parking space, she checked her text messages. Something she'd forgotten to do earlier. Only two of the four couples she'd invited for drinks and dinner tonight had responded. She'd forgotten that Angie and Scott were out East, visiting family. The other couple wasn't feeling well. Both of them, from what she could tell by the reply. She texted the two that hadn't responded, reminding them to let her know, sooner than later.

Part of her wondered if she shouldn't scrap the whole idea. She could certainly do without spending a week in bed with the flu, especially in the summer.

Chapter Thirteen

As soon as David Olson turned onto Municipal Drive, he got the strong feeling that the trip would be pointless. The Fishers Police Department building and the town-owned parking lots surrounding it were mobbed with vehicles and people. He pulled his car onto the grass off Municipal Drive and placed his Westfield PD placard on the dashboard. Next, he flipped his badge holder backward and tucked it into the pocket on his shirt. This was going to be a mess.

Walking along the road toward the station, the sound of the crowd gathered outside buzzed with anger and confusion. Hundreds of the town's citizens were here with the same kind of question. Luckily for David, he had a badge that might get him some answers. Unfortunately, it also attracted unwanted attention.

A frantic woman with a bandage taped to the side of her forehead pointed at him when he approached the main parking lot. She jogged toward him, followed by a half-dozen men and women.

"I need to find my husband!" she said. "They say they don't know where the ambulance took him, but I think they're lying. How could they not know where they took him?"

The others simultaneously started to voice similar questions. David slipped his badge fully into his shirt pocket before any others spotted it.

"I work for the Westfield PD, so I couldn't begin to help you," he said. "I'm trying to find my ex-wife."

"Is the same thing going on in Westfield?" said a tired-looking man. "I heard this was going on all over?"

"I have no idea. I just got back from vacation," said David. "Who told you that?"

"It's just what I heard from neighbors," he replied.

"I was talking to him first!" said the woman with the bandage, trying to edge in front of him with her shoulder.

"Take it easy. This will all straighten out," said David.

"I don't think so," said an older guy. "This is getting worse."

"What's getting worse?" said David.

"This," said the man, nodding to the crowds. "It's at least twenty times the number from yesterday."

"You've been here since yesterday?" said David.

"I've been back and forth trying to get answers," said the man. "My wife apparently rear-ended another car in a Starbucks drive-thru line on purpose. I don't believe that, but that's what they told me."

"You didn't talk to her?"

"They said she was too hysterical to talk to me on the phone. Asked if she was taking any antipsychotic medications. Maybe she'd forgotten to take them. I didn't understand what was going on, so I drove down here immediately. By the time I got here, they had already sent her away in an ambulance. She'd hurt herself trying to break out of her handcuffs."

"You still haven't found her?" said David.

"No. And don't even think about going to the hospitals. They're fifty times worse than this. Nobody knows shit."

"What do you mean worse than this?" said the woman next to him.

"They're completely overwhelmed. Some kind of flu bug going around, too. People in beds and cots all over the hospital...and not just in patient rooms. I couldn't get a straight answer from anyone. I'm not even sure if they're registering patients anymore."

What the hell was he talking about?

"All right. I need to get in there and see what's going on," said David, starting to walk around them.

A few of them followed him through the agitated clusters of

people, repeating the names of the loved ones and friends that had gone missing in police cars and ambulances. They gave up halfway across the lot. David felt bad ditching them, but there really wasn't anything he could do to help. He didn't want to believe what the old man had said, but the scene surrounding the police station told him it was true. There was something bigger at play here. But what?

A pandemic flu bug might explain it. A lot of people getting sick and desperate at once could panic the population, pushing enough people past their already low tolerance thresholds. If even a small fraction of them let their anger get out of control, that could be enough to overwhelm the police and EMT crews. But to this degree?

Not to mention the fact that his ex-wife was about as levelheaded as they come. Sick with the flu was one thing. Violent was another. It didn't add up.

As he got closer to the front door of the two-story police station, he was surprised by the complete absence of police officers. Not a single uniform in sight from what he could tell. Not even at the doors. He suddenly wondered if he'd made a serious mistake pushing this far into the crowd. The badge in his pocket suddenly felt like a liability.

David fought the urge to slide his hand closer to the compact pistol concealed behind his right hip. Maybe he should try a different entrance or the fenced car pool. Surely they had an officer in the lot to make sure nobody tried to scale the fence. He didn't relish the thought of flashing his badge among this many people.

Fortunately, the crowd had left enough room around the doors for him to give it a try. They appeared to have given up any hope of the police opening the doors, which would work to his advantage. Slipping through the people seated on the steps, he carefully worked his way across the concrete terrace in front of the doors. He slid his badge out of his shirt pocket and kept it concealed along the side of his thigh until he reached the door. At that point, he shifted the hand in front of his thigh and pressed the badge against the glass while knocking on the door with his other hand.

"They won't answer," said a woman behind him.

He nodded. "Have to try anyway."

"We've been doing it all morning," said another.

"And all last night," announced another voice. "They stopped talking to us yesterday afternoon. They're supposed to be on our side."

David knocked again and muttered, "Come on, guys."

"Someone needs to remind them we pay their salaries!"

"They haven't given a shit about us for years!"

"Just when we need them the most, they fucking cut us off. Vanish. What kind of crap is that?"

He rapped on the glass more insistently.

"That guy doesn't care," said a voice he remembered from the parking lot.

David glanced over his shoulder at the woman with the bandage, who stood a few people deep in the crowd. He shook his head almost imperceptibly. *Don't do it, lady. Please.*

"He's one of them."

Fuck. He kept knocking, his mind running the scenarios. Draw weapon and fire a warning shot? Draw weapon and point at the crowd? Try to make a break for it? None of them sounded good. What the hell was taking so damn long?

"You're a cop?"

"From Westfield," said the woman.

The questions came rapid fire, louder and more belligerent by the second. David didn't hear any of them. His mind focused on the rising volume of noise and the reflection in the glass door, calculating that he had another second or so to draw his weapon—if that was really what he intended to do. He wasn't exactly sure. Movement beyond the reflection, inside the building, caught his attention, and he backed up a few steps. If this wasn't a rescue, he'd just given up the remaining space between himself and the rapidly deteriorating mob.

The door suddenly opened outward, stopping halfway.

"Get inside!" yelled a gruff male voice behind the door.

David didn't need to be told twice, or the first time, actually. He squeezed through the opening, his foot getting caught as the crowd pushed against the door. A quick yank sent a flare of pain up his leg, but the foot came free and the door slammed shut. The officer turned the lock and helped him to his feet. The officer looked at least two days unshaven with dark circles under his eyes. His uniform consisted of hiking boots, jeans and a gray T-shirt—an olive drab nylon tactical vest fit snugly over his clothes. A black thigh holster extended down the side of his right leg.

"You all right?" said the officer.

"I'm good. Close call."

"I almost didn't hear you," said the officer, extending a hand. "Mark Peters."

"David Olson, Westfield PD," he said. "You don't keep anyone inside the lobby? It's getting kind of crazy out there."

Heavy pounding on the door emphasized his point.

"That's exactly why we keep the lobby empty. It just pisses them off more to see someone in here," said Peters. "On top of that, we just don't have the officers to spare."

"What if they try to breach the door or windows?"

"They can have the lobby. All of the doors leading deeper into the station are seriously reinforced, and the glass in front of the reception counter is bullet resistant. They'd have to use C-4 or a rocket launcher to get deeper into the station. It all goes back to the manpower issue. We don't have enough people to keep them out of the lobby."

"How many officers do you have at the station?"

"Five."

"Five?" said David. "Are you serious?"

"I wish I wasn't," said Peters. "We have forty-eight out on patrol out of one hundred and seven total."

David did the math. Roughly half of the force was out of commission. Peters seemed to read his mind.

"We're right at about half strength. Most of the officers missing are sick. Some are taking care of sick family members. Vacation, out-of-state training and injuries siphoned off a few more."

He couldn't believe it. No wonder Sergeant Jackson at the

Westfield station was having a cow.

"I just returned from vacation yesterday. My sergeant has been hounding me to fill some shifts, but I have my son until Sunday," said David. "That's why I'm here. I drove by her house a little earlier, and the neighbor told me my ex had been taken away in one of your patrol cars last night. I guess her boyfriend left in an ambulance. Sound familiar?"

"Sounds like every one of our calls," said Peters. "Someone ends up in the hospital. Someone ends up in a patrol car."

"She might still be here, right?" said David.

He knew it was unlikely. If the police department was getting that many calls, the station's jail cells would have reached maximum capacity long ago. Part of him was relieved. If Josh's mom was locked in a cell here at the station, he wasn't sure what he could do—or what he would do. At least Joshua would know that his mother was safe.

"We quit bringing most arrests into the station yesterday afternoon. It got to be too much to handle. We're part of a system slapped together by the county. Arresting officers bring subjects to a collection point at the public works garage out on Eller Road. A prisoner transfer bus from county makes the rounds every few hours, picking up whomever we've collected. We send them with some basic paperwork."

"To the Hamilton County Jail? How many people can they house?" said David.

He didn't think they had more than three hundred beds.

"I really have no idea how they're doing it. I'm just glad they stepped up."

The pounding at the lobby doors intensified and spread to the windows along the front of the room.

"We better get out of sight," said Peters, heading to the sturdy-looking door next to the reception window.

The officer removed a thick plastic card from one of his vest pockets and placed it against the gray, scratched-up card reader surface next to the door. A solid *click*, followed by a small blinking green light, gave him the go-ahead to pull the door open.

Once inside the station, they were met by an officer carrying an M4 rifle and wearing body armor. She appeared just as exhausted as Peters. Behind her, a large administrative space, packed tightly with workstations, sat mostly empty. A few very unhappy-looking men and women sat behind monitors, glancing around their screens in his direction.

"Everything all right out there?" she said, eyeing David apprehensively.

"Should be," said Peters. "This is David Olson with the Westfield PD. His ex-wife was processed by our department last night. He's been on vacation, so he has no idea what's happening."

"Welcome to the party," she said. "Sorry about your ex."

David nodded, still trying to process what to make of this. The whole situation sounded insane.

"I'm gonna run him through the tank area. See if she might be here for some odd reason. Then I'll turn him loose on the stacks of transfer tickets."

She nodded. "I'm headed back to the locker room to suit up. Fogelman twisted his ankle. Martinez is heading back with him right now."

"Did you talk to the lieutenant about this? We can pull their car out of the patrol rotation. Give Martinez a break until another spot opens up. We could use the help around here," said Peters. "You don't have to go out there."

"I'm not telling Harvey," she said with a stern look. "And neither are you."

"What's going on?" said David.

"That isn't an extra layer of armor under her vest. Officer Sterns here is eighteen weeks pregnant," said Peters.

"I can do the job just fine," said Sterns. "I'm barely showing."

"Yeah. Well, normally I'd agree with you, but pretty much every call leads to an altercation now," said Peters.

"Minor altercations."

"For now," said Peters.

"It's that bad?" said David. "How many are we talking about?"

Officer Sterns pointed to a cluttered table on the other side of the administrative room. Two women were sorting through a mess of paperwork, seeming to sense that they were being called out.

"The team over there can tell you. A few hundred at least. If your ex isn't in one of the tanks, the ladies should be able to find her paperwork. That's assuming it was filed. Last night was a mess."

A few hundred? Westfield didn't process that many assault cases in an entire year! Maybe two years.

"I gotta roll," she said. "Good luck finding your ex."

"Watch yourself out there," said Peters, giving her a serious look.

She gave him a thumbs-up. "I got it."

"What's going on out there?" said David.

"We have no idea. There's a flu bug going around that's hitting people pretty hard. The hospitals, urgent care clinics and doctors' offices are completely overwhelmed. The violence is probably linked, but we haven't detected any obvious connection. Not that we're putting much effort into finding one. We're one hundred percent *reactive* right now."

"This is—" started David, his phone buzzing. "Crazy."

He pulled the phone out of his pocket, recognizing the number immediately. It was about to get crazier.

"Give me a second," said David, answering the call. "Sergeant?"

"Sorry to do this to you, David, but we've initiated a crisis recall of all officers, active and reserve. If you're not here within an hour, you'll face disciplinary action. End of story."

"Give me to noon. I'm at the Fishers station, trying to find my ex. She was arrested last night. There's a good chance she's at the Hamilton County—"

"Hold on. Hold the fuck on," said Jackson. "You're at the Fishers station? Wrong station. Get your ass to the Westfield station, or you can stay there and apply for a new job. I'll give you to noon."

"I can't leave my son alone," said David.

"Your son is going to be a senior in high school. He's old enough to take care of himself for a little while. Noon. Goodbye."

"Sergeant, I need to…hello? Sergeant," he said before checking the phone's screen. "Fuck. He hung up on me."

"Sorry, man," said Peters. "Everyone's under a ton of pressure."

David uttered a few more curses. "I know. I know. It's just that I don't want to leave my son alone if it's getting that bad out there."

"If it's any consolation, most of the calls are domestics. We haven't seen much neighbor-on-neighbor violence. There's been some, but from what I've heard, it's mostly started and ended outside. No break-ins that I'm aware of. If your son stays inside, I bet he'll be fine."

"Until it starts turning into break-ins," said David. "If all of this keeps escalating, that's where it's headed."

"I wish I could say I disagreed," said Peters. "Can you leave him with someone you trust?"

"I would have left him with his mother yesterday afternoon if she'd answered," he said, raising an eyebrow.

"Point taken," said Peters. "From what I can tell, the cases don't fit any pattern based on socioeconomic background. He'd be better off buttoned up inside on his own."

"Shit," he said. "Sounds like that's my only choice? This whole thing could blow over by Monday. Be pretty stupid to throw away close to twenty years on the job like that."

Peters put a hand on his shoulder and lowered his voice. "I don't see this blowing over anytime soon, and if it keeps getting worse, like I suspect it will…"

David nodded, distracted by the faces trying to glean bits of their conversation.

"You can always show up now, while it's still generally safe out there, and pull the plug later," said Peters before bringing his voice to a near whisper. "I'm not the only one here with that plan. I'm sure you wouldn't be the only one in Westfield. There's only so much we can do…family has to come first at some point."

"It might have to come sooner than later," said David.

"Let's get you some answers, if we have any," said Peters. "Get you out of here as quickly as possible. Through the back door this time. I nearly shit my pants when I saw your badge pressed against the glass. That was a ballsy move."

"Stupid move," said David. "Not sure what I was thinking."

He'd have to do way better than that going forward. David got the distinct impression that the margin for error out there would get smaller and smaller as the days passed.

Chapter Fourteen

Dr. Chang turned his black, convertible BMW sedan off the two-lane paved road onto a tight, hard-packed gravel drive that plowed straight into a mature forest of densely packed trees. He drove in the cool shade of the impenetrable canopy of branches and thick leaves for several seconds until he reached a sturdy metal gate blocking the road. His hand extended upward, toward the bank of garage door remote control buttons on the bottom of the rearview mirror, pressing the leftmost button.

The gate slid left along its track, clearing his way a few seconds later. He eased the car forward until he was certain the gate was closing behind him. With the gate in motion again, he accelerated just enough to take the gentle curves of the forest road at a safe speed. A minute later, the BMW emerged from the trees into a two-acre tract of flat, open land surrounded on all sides by dense forest.

A shiny, two-story contemporary home with boxy lines stood in the center of the land, immediately surrounded by a well-manicured, lush green lawn. Beyond the circle of green, wide patches of tall wild grasses sat scattered between a carefully laid out arrangement of small ponds, dirt paths and empty garden beds.

Chang had bought the isolated property after the most recent bioweapons scare to serve as his bug-out hideaway from the city, or any city for that matter. The Indianapolis Executive Airport was just a few miles northwest. He could quickly fly back from a trip if something lethal surfaced, seeking refuge here until things stabilized, and if the chaos of an uncontrolled pandemic poured out of Indianapolis, threatening his safety here, he could fly somewhere else.

Of course, the project morphed from a rustic, survival hideaway to a multimillion-dollar project within a short span of time. Once he started working with an architect that specialized in self-sustainable designs, rustic gave way to modern. There was no slowing down from there. Anyway, solar panel arrays and compact wind turbines looked funny with the log-cabin-style home. That was one of many pseudo-justifications made by Chang to build his dream house.

In the end, it didn't matter. The house and property looked more suited for the cover of *Modern Home* magazine than *Modern Prepper*, but it still served the original intent and purpose—a refuge from the inevitable. A place to hide when—not if—the next global pandemic raged across the land, taking millions of lives. He had no idea if today was that day, but he wasn't taking any chances. The microscopic bug that had hit Methodist Hospital's Emergency Department wasn't fucking around.

He just hoped it wasn't contagious. His gut told him it wasn't, but a quiet voice deep in the recesses of the darkest part of his mind whispered that he was wrong. Because that was how he would have designed it. Just the thought of it gave him chills.

The gravel road cut through the center of the open land, leading to the two-car attached garage. The steel and glass garage door rolled upward, making way for a perfectly timed entrance. He edged the vehicle forward until the small green LED light mounted on the garage wall directly in front of him turned red, prompting him to stop. Perfectly situated in the neatly arranged garage, he closed the garage door and got out of the car.

A pristine black Toyota 4Runner sat parked on the shiny concrete floor next to the BMW, another bug-out purchase that kind of exceeded his original needs-based assessment. He barely drove it, preferring the much-easier-to-park-and-maneuver convertible in the city. Despite its rare use, he felt comfortable knowing it was an option. Like his plane, it gave him options. He wouldn't get far on back roads and jeep trails in the BMW in the unlikely event he had to leave by vehicle instead of his Cessna.

He'd spent a lot of money on these seemingly improbable doomsday thoughts. Amounts that most people would probably find wastefully paranoid. The same people that spent more than a thousand dollars per month for low-deductible, premium health insurance when their total healthcare costs year to year rarely exceeded one month's premium. The very same people carrying more than the minimum insurance for their automobiles year after year, despite never getting into an accident. Thousands carried concealed firearms to the grocery store in towns that hadn't seen a public murder in decades. The list went on.

None of them were wrong. It was all just a matter of perspective or, more importantly, focus. Chang had spent the past decade studying deadly pathogens. The kind developed, stockpiled and intentionally inflicted on the world by nation-states and terrorists—often one and the same. Before that, he'd researched pandemic-grade viruses. Two very costly preparedness undertakings if done right, and he had spared no expense.

Chang had long been convinced that he'd see one of these disasters in his lifetime. He just never thought he'd witness both—particularly not at one time. Despite the amount of money he'd spent preparing for these catastrophes, he woke up every day hoping it would ultimately turn out to be money wasted. The opposite, in either case, was unthinkable.

He grabbed his leather satchel from the backseat and walked in front of the SUV to reach the door leading into the house. A biometric scanner next to the door read his thumb, allowing him to punch in a seven-digit code that unlocked the sealed door. He turned the knob and pushed the door open, a current of air rushing past him as he stepped inside.

The home's forced-air heating and cooling system maintained a positive pressure environment that constantly pushed air out of the structure. It was a feature used in military vehicles and ships to prevent contamination by chemical or biological agents. Overkill for a private home, but why stop short when you were already in for a ludicrous sum of money. Aerial delivery had long been one of the preferred methods of spreading chemical and biological agents. He pulled the door shut, which required a little more effort due to the air pressure.

He now stood in a short hallway leading to what New Englanders would call a mudroom, a small separate room usually connecting the garage or side entrance to the main house. Like its name suggested, it was a place to leave muddy boots and dirt-caked outer garments before heading inside. While Chang's mudroom contained the typical arrangement of oversized shoe cubbies, numerous coat hooks and long, wide benches, it contained a feature that allowed it to serve an altogether different purpose if necessary.

The first door to the left in the hallway was a bathroom with a shower, which could function as a decontamination station in the event of a nuclear, biological or chemical (NBC) attack. He also thought it might come in handy after a long day getting dirty in the garden that would sustain him if the world collapsed, but the shower had never been used in the three years he'd built the home. The garden was still in the planning phase.

Chang removed his shoes and opened the pocket door to a kitchen gleaming with black granite counters and stainless steel appliances. He placed his leather satchel next to a small digital tablet on the oversized granite-topped island that dominated the kitchen, and flipped open the tablet. The device welcomed him with a password screen, which he bypassed with several quick keystrokes to access the home security system's control center.

At a glance he could tell that nothing notable had occurred on the property while he had been gone. The forest-based sensors had no human incursions to report. Combined input from motion and thermal sensors had confirmed a dozen or so deer passages. Nothing out of the ordinary at all. He often woke up to the sight of deer in the clearing. He'd calibrated the system to account for them.

Likewise, the three-hundred-and-sixty-degree sensor and camera feeds covering the open field indicated that nothing had approached the house from the forest. Sensors inside told a similar story. He suspected as much, since any indication of a home break-in or human breach of the forest perimeter would have been remotely reported to his phone immediately upon detection. Another warning would have been provided when he pressed his thumb to the biometric scanner in the garage. Opening the tablet and checking the specifics was more a habit than necessity.

He highly doubted it would ever become a necessity. In three years the system had registered one human breach of his property. A group of teenagers had cut a hole in the livestock fence surrounding the forest and partied for a few hours, leaving behind a mess of beer bottles and cigarette butts. He'd mended the fence and posted a NO TRESPASSING sign at the point of the breach the next day, leaving the kids to wonder how he'd discovered their secret. His message must have been received. The midnight parties didn't continue.

Chang closed the tablet and opened the mostly empty refrigerator behind him, removing a bottle of sparkling water. He'd order a same-day delivery of produce and other grocery items from one of the local supermarkets. If he placed the order soon, the groceries would arrive in time for him to prepare dinner. If not, he'd be putting together a freezer meal. With that thought in mind, he made his way to a spacious office toward the front of the house.

Floor-to-ceiling windows gave him a view of the forest and clearing northwest of the house when seated at his desk. Part of the driveway had been visible when he walked into the office. The office was noticeably devoid of personal pictures or knickknacks, beyond the diplomas on the wall behind his desk and the select landscape pictures he'd enlarged and framed for the walls flanking the windows. Galapagos Islands. Machu Picchu. Patagonia. The few exquisite places he'd taken the time out of his hectic professional career to see. As stark and beautiful as the photos looked on his walls, they were a constant, ironic reminder of what he'd sacrificed for his career—a family of his own to share these beautiful memories. One of these days, he kept telling himself.

He activated his desktop computer and waited a few moments for the system to boot up. After he ordered the groceries, he'd do a little digging through a few of the classified archives he could access through his confidential arrangement with Edgewood and the CDC. He'd remembered something from a hushed conversation with a few of his Edgewood colleagues over dinner. He vaguely knew what they were talking about, but the topic must have been highly classified. The discussion ended just as abruptly as it had started, leaving him with nothing more than the scattered information he'd previously assembled about the thwarted U.S. bioweapons attack in 2008 and its link to a far more nefarious attack in Russia.

He still hadn't heard from any of his trusted contacts at either organization, which struck him as odd. He'd reach out to them again. Chang found it hard to believe that they didn't already know about the growing problem in Indianapolis. Checking his phone again, he confirmed that he hadn't missed a call in all of the excitement of getting out of the city. Highly unusual. He was at ground zero of something clearly significant.

Was it possible Indianapolis had somehow remained below the CDC's radar? He couldn't see how. The government had spent billions of dollars on sophisticated detection and reporting systems over the past decade, for the sole purpose of giving disease response teams the critical jump needed to identify and prevent a possible infectious disease outbreak.

On top of that, several private initiatives had emerged in the wake of recent disease scares to augment detection efforts. Given what Dr. Owens and Dr. Hale had reported, CDC headquarters should be at code red. Even the World Health Organization should be well aware of the problem by this point, even if they didn't advertise it.

Chang opened the search browser's favorites folder and navigated to the CDC website, first checking the Flu Activity and Surveillance page. Based on his examination of the spinal tap sample delivered by Dr. Hale, this certainly wasn't the flu, but initial reports from area hospitals would more than likely be filed as suspected influenza due to the rapid nature of the outbreak. He didn't find anything fitting the pattern of an influenza outbreak centered on Indianapolis.

A few minutes later, after searching every other possible location for signs of an outbreak and finding nothing, he leaned back in his chair and took a deep breath. Something didn't add up, or maybe the CDC had already discovered what they were truly up against and had decided to delay the release of any information until they could muster an appropriate response. That was entirely possible, especially given the public panic that would ensue at the first hint of the word *bioweapon*.

A quick check of the World Health Organization's Global Outbreak Alert and Response Network surveillance page yielded similar results, which didn't surprise him. If the CDC wanted to keep a lid on this for public safety reasons, the WHO would cooperate—at least temporarily. It was very possible that the WHO had detected the outbreak anomaly first, through their Global Public Health Intelligence Network (GPHIN).

GPHIN utilized a sophisticated, Internet-based data collection system to check publically available media sources for reports of disease outbreaks. Very often, informal sources of information provided the first hints of a new outbreak, prompting the immediate deployment of WHO response teams. A simple mention of overrun emergency rooms on any of the Indianapolis area's news station websites should trigger an alarm, prompting CDC notification.

Chang clicked on the link for the International Scientific Pandemic Awareness Collaborative (ISPAC) website, wondering if they would follow the CDC's lead. By far the most generously funded private organization dedicated to outbreak detection, the ISPAC had developed an epidemic intelligence network rivaling, if not exceeding, the capability of the CDC and World Health Organization.

They fielded their own investigative teams and had developed a comprehensive social media and news network crawling system to identify disease outbreaks at the grass roots level. The information collected was shared with the CDC through a standing, reciprocal agreement, with the one caveat being that the ISPAC remained independent. That said, when ISPAC leadership didn't see a conflict jeopardizing public safety, they cooperated across the board with the CDC. He wondered if this would be one of those cases.

HTTP ERROR 500 (INTERNAL SERVER ERROR)

He hit the link again, getting the same result. The site was probably overloaded. Something big was definitely going on, possibly in more than one city. He tried the University of Minnesota-based CIDRAP (Center for Infectious Disease and Research Policy) website.

HTTP ERROR 500 (INTERNAL SERVER ERROR)

"Wow," he muttered, clicking the mouse again and receiving the same message on the screen.

Chang spent the next minute cycling through a half-dozen different private or university-sponsored sites reporting live disease surveillance, coming up with the same internal server error message. Unconsciously, he clicked on the CDC site again, and the screen displayed the Atlanta-based agency's homepage. Shaking his head, he restarted the computer, convinced something was wrong on his end. He knew better, but he did it anyway. Slightly panicked, he checked his phone while the computer whirred. Nothing. Not even a text.

When the web browser loaded, he checked each of the sites saved in his "Outbreak Surveillance" favorites folder, coming up with the same result. As a scientist, he couldn't rule out the remote possibility that exceedingly high traffic had simultaneously overwhelmed every private and university-sponsored site. He navigated to a site that assesses website activity and typed each website's domain name, verifying that the sites were down. Not busy, but down—hard. What were the odds that every private site was crashed, but the CDC site was up and running without a glitch? Chang shook his head, knowing the answer.

He dug through his top desk drawer for the remote control to the flat-screen TV mounted next to the office door. Chang wasn't sure the batteries in the remote were still good. He hadn't used this TV in over a year. Clicking the power button on the slim remote, he was rewarded with a red light in the bottom right corner of the TV, followed by a source input screen. A few more button pushes got him to a national cable news network. He stared at the screen long enough to determine that the situation in Indianapolis hadn't made the headlines.

His next stop was a twenty-four-hour local news channel feed, where he suffered through an extended weather forecast and a north suburb school referendum story before finally catching a previously recorded segment about the impending catastrophe. The caption at the bottom of the screen read INDIANAPOLIS AREA HOSPITALS HIT WITH LATE SEASON FLU OUTBREAK.

A reporter stood a considerable distance from what Chang recognized as the Sidney and Lois Eskenazi Hospital, a modern steel and glass structure near the Indiana University-Purdue University city campus. A few police cars with flashing lights sat parked in front of the main entrance, superimposed in front of a thick crowd of people.

"We just learned this morning that Eskenazi Hospital has joined the long list of hospitals and urgent care clinics to close their doors to new arrivals, a situation likely to fuel the growing unrest that has gripped the city. Little is known at this point, but an anonymous source at Methodist Hospital has confirmed that their hospital has been struggling to keep up with the rapidly rising number of sick patients for close to forty-eight hours. City and state representatives have pressed the mayor's office for alternative options, but so far, Indiana Department of Health officials have not responded. Hospital administrators across the city have been similarly quiet, making no public statements."

He didn't like the sound of that at all. Nobody in any official capacity on any level was talking about this? Something about this entire situation reminded him of a very unofficial story he'd heard from a colleague at Edgewood. He wasn't sure why it rang that bell, but couldn't shake the thought that the circumstances were similar.

"Indianapolis area police and fire departments have confirmed that they are overwhelmed by an inexplicable surge in domestic calls involving serious injuries. A paramedic on the northeast side of the city was quoted as saying that 'the whole

city seems on edge, and it doesn't take much anymore to push anyone over it.'
What does this mean for Indianapolis and its suburbs? We don't know, but stay
with us for the latest updates as the situation develops, or visit our website at
www.latestnewsIndy.com."

Chang checked the website, not the least bit surprised to see
HTTP ERROR 500 (INTERNAL SERVER ERROR). Interesting.
The easiest and arguably most vulnerable source of news external to
Indianapolis had been cut off. Without pausing, he typed a
combination of letters he'd never expected to type again in his life.
There was no point. It was only a rumor at this point, and a
completely unverifiable one at that. He'd never seen the evidence,
which had supposedly only surfaced once, on Reuters, before the
website crashed and stayed crashed for two weeks.

Worse yet, the crashes weren't limited to the Internet. Several
Reuters correspondents and editors met with accidents or suddenly
quit their jobs over the same time period. The story became so toxic,
literally, that nobody would touch it. It had become Russia's
Tiananmen Square, except it was rumored to be about a thousand
times worse, and nobody could or would confirm it. Whatever
happened had been worth killing over and continuing to suppress
with a dedicated cyber-slash operation.

He pressed enter and shook his head.

No results containing your search terms were found.
Your search – **Monchegorsk** *– did not match any documents.*

The Russians had made an entire city disappear in the supposed
aftermath of a devastating bioweapons attack against the city's water
supply. To this day, the area was closed off, and nobody within the
Russian government acknowledged it. He couldn't help wonder if the
information blackout developing in Indianapolis was a similar effort
by the U.S. government.

Chapter Fifteen

David Olson removed his Glock 17 service pistol from a small shelf-mounted safe in the walk-in closet and tucked it into the retention holster on his right hip. The pistol went into the safe when he got home after a shift and didn't come out until he went back on duty. He kept his off-duty pistol, a more concealable Glock 19, with him at all times when this pistol was locked in the safe.

There was no official requirement to lock up his primary service weapon. He just liked the ceremony of it. Changing of the guard. With the pistol fit snugly in his duty holster, he placed his off-duty weapon and a spare magazine in the safe, leaving the door partially open for his son. He didn't think Josh needed to be walking around the house with the pistol, but he wanted his son to have quick enough access if things got any stranger out there.

David stopped in front of the mirror on the way out of the bathroom and double-checked his uniform and patrol rig. Everything looked in order. A quick glance at his watch told him he was pushing the time. He had eighteen minutes to pull into the station and report for duty. It didn't leave much wiggle room, especially if he ran into a problem en route or right outside the station, like the Fishers municipal building.

Halfway down the stairs, he called out to his son. He didn't have time to search the house, and he had important instructions to pass along. It could be a while before he returned. He planned to do everything in his power to get back by midnight, but he knew how these things worked. If the situation on the streets was getting worse, like the officers in the Fishers station had indicated, the likelihood of signing out for the night was slim to none.

Josh responded from the kitchen, drawing David deeper into the house. He glanced around as he walked down the center hallway. Windows everywhere. Josh might be better off hanging out in the basement when it got dark. People would be drawn to his house, knowing he was a cop, which would put Josh in a bad spot if it looked like someone was home. He needed to be reporting for duty right now like a damn hole in the head. His son was a capable young man, but whatever was going on out there was something different. He could feel it.

He found his son eating toaster waffles at the kitchen island, thumbing through his smart phone.

"Sorry about the omelets, buddy," said David. "I owe you a Denny's run or that fancy place your mom takes you."

"It's fine, Dad," said Josh. "You don't want to lose your job over a few omelets."

"Not just any omelets," said David.

"I'll survive," said Josh.

He opened the refrigerator to survey its contents. Leftover pizza boxes, a plastic tray of precut vegetables, a tub of ranch dip, a brick of cheddar cheese and a carton of eggs. The freezer didn't add much to the equation. An oversized bag of hash browns, three frozen pizzas, an opened box of waffles and several bags of mixed vegetables that had been in the freezer for longer than he cared to admit. A bounty by bachelor standards—but not a sustainable amount of food.

He'd been too tired yesterday to shop for the entire week, so he'd focused on getting through the weekend with Josh. Now he really wished he'd taken another twenty minutes and loaded up the fridge. Before closing the door, he quickly inventoried the beers. A full six-pack of Heineken and three loose Coronas. Joshua snapped his eyes away from the refrigerator when he turned around.

"I count nine beers," said David.

"Dad."

"Just making an observation."

Joshua started laughing.

"What?" said David.

"Nobody steals beers from their parents. It's too easy to notice," said Joshua. "They raid the hard alcohol bottles a little at a time so it's not obvious."

"I don't have any bottles of liquor," said David.

"Then you don't have anything to worry about," said Joshua before getting back to his plate of circular waffles.

He couldn't help but laugh at that. The kid had a point.

"All righty then," said David. "Here are the rest of the ground rules."

Joshua looked at him funny, like he'd been taken off guard. "Ground rules?"

"Yeah. Things are inexplicably weird out there, so I need you to play along with me on this."

"Okay," said Joshua, still eyeing him skeptically.

"I need you to stay inside and stay away from the windows. No exceptions. When I drive out of here, I want everyone to think this house is empty. We'll shut all of the shades now and keep them that way."

"Wouldn't it be better if everyone thought you were home? If people think you're gone, they might try to break in," said Josh.

"I don't think we're at the point of people breaking in, but if people are scared about what they're hearing on the news, they might come by to see if I have any inside scoop. I don't want to put you in the position of having to answer the door. Especially if there's some flu virus spreading. Better they think the house is empty."

"What about the lights at night? You can tell they're on with the shades shut."

"That's the second bit of bad news. About an hour before sunset, I want you in the basement. Grab some spare blankets from the hallway closet upstairs and nail them up to cover the windows in the finished part of the basement."

"Like use real nails?" said Joshua.

"Whatever it takes to get them tight against the windows. Use two blankets folded over on each window, if that's what it takes. The window wells are below ground level, so if you put a thick layer up and keep the lights to a minimum down there, I think you'll be totally good to go. I'll leave the alarm in alert mode, so you'll hear a double beep on the panel down there if any of the exterior doors or windows are breached."

"Do you really think it's that bad out there?" said Joshua.

"You saw the news, right? It's already pretty bad," said David. "If there's a pandemic flu going around, this could get way worse. People will get desperate."

"What do I do if someone tries to break in?"

"Hide and call the—" started David, remembering the situation in Fishers. "Call me. I'll make sure someone gets out here fast."

His son didn't look very convinced by the plan, and frankly, David had little faith in it either. He wasn't sure why he'd even said it.

"Here's what you do. Before you retire to the basement for the evening, grab the Glock 19 from the gun safe in my closet. I left it open for you. Bring it with you into the basement and keep it close by, but don't take it out of the holster. There's a round in the chamber. You pull the trigger and it goes off. Understood? If someone breaks in, you follow my original instructions. Hide and call my cell phone. Do not go investigating. The pistol is an absolute last resort. Understood?"

"Yes," said his son, completely serious.

"About eight o'clock, you should be fed and ready to barricade yourself in the basement. I keep a spare set of keys in the same safe with the pistol. One of those keys locks the basement door from the inside. Make sure you lock that door. If you get hungry after hours, grab an MRE from my survival stash."

Joshua nodded. "What about Mom? What if she shows up or calls?"

David hated to double-down on his lie, but saw no other option. He was already up to his neck in it, having told Joshua that it looked like she had gone away for the weekend. He was afraid to tell him anything different. The kid might get a bad idea and rev up one of the old motocross bikes for a very ill-conceived search and rescue operation.

For now, he needed Joshua to believe that his mother was safe. It bought him another twenty-four hours to square away the situation with his police department, so he could watch over his son twenty-four seven. She wasn't "due back in town" until tomorrow evening, when David had originally agreed to bring him back. He had no idea what he'd tell Joshua tomorrow night.

"If your mom shows up, call me immediately."

"I can let her in, right? I mean, with the flu and everything, do you think it's safe?" said his son.

"You know your mother. She wouldn't do anything to put you in danger. If she shows up, I'm sure she's fine. Just let me talk to her first. She might not know about the outbreak."

"Okay."

"What else?" said David.

Joshua shook his head. "I think that's it. Be careful out there."

"I will," he said.

David gave his son a one-armed hug, ruffling his hair after he let go. He planned on being more than just careful out there. He was all Joshua had left right now.

"Be good and stay out of sight. Keep your phone charged, too. I'll check in with you every few hours."

"When do you think you'll be back?"

"I don't know. I'm going to try for tonight. If that doesn't fly, sometime in the morning—whether I have to quit or not."

David's eyes caught the microwave clock. Shit. There was no way he was going to make it to the station by noon. Sergeant Jackson would just have to wait a few more minutes.

Chapter Sixteen

Eugene Chang paced back and forth at the far edge of an elaborate slate patio, pausing occasionally to check his phone for voice messages or emails. He was beyond frustrated and scared at this point. The sun hung low on the horizon, and he hadn't received a single return message from any of his Edgewood colleagues. He could understand why his CDC contacts might choose to remain incommunicado, but not Stan Greenberg or Christine Bell. Unless he'd totally misread the political and bureaucratic situation at Edgewood, there was no excuse for their silence. Not in light of what Chang had discovered and passed along to them.

The two researchers had dedicated the bulk of their professional careers to preventing the very disaster now unfolding in Indianapolis. The only possible excuse he could imagine was the detection of a nationwide bioweapons attack that triggered some kind of government-wide gag order. Jesus. Maybe that was it. It would certainly explain the simultaneous crashing of every website the public might use to learn about the virus.

The concept behind controlling information at the outset of a bioweapons attack had some merit, regardless of the inherent ethical dilemmas. Keeping the public in the dark long enough to mobilize an initial containment response gave the government a better chance of slowing or stopping the inevitable panic-induced exodus from the hot zone. Keeping infected victims from vanishing to points unknown was one of the most effective strategies for combating a lethal virus outbreak. The longer the government could delay mass panic, the better for everyone—outside the hot zone.

Sadly, the tactic condemned the blackout area to accelerated casualty rates. A tragic consequence deemed to be an acceptable compromise to prevent or reduce the geographic expansion of an outbreak hot zone. There was no good answer in the face of this kind of disaster. People would die in great numbers. It was just a question of containing those deaths to the smallest area possible.

The Russians had supposedly quarantined the entire city of Monchegorsk, systematically killing the sick population or anyone that protested. He doubted they had started out killing, but with thousands of sick and deranged patients, it had probably just evolved as the easiest and most effective tactic available to an army unequipped for a major medical disaster. He wondered if the same thing could happen here. He hoped not.

Chang glanced at his phone again, thinking that it would only be a matter of time before cell service was disrupted, at least temporarily. Then entire server networks—all while they worked on establishing and enforcing quarantine zones.

That thought got him wondering if he should call Jeff at the airfield and postpone the mechanic's proposed repairs to the left wing. He wasn't overly worried about finding himself trapped in a quarantine zone, since his house was well outside Indianapolis, but it couldn't hurt to be ready for a quick departure. Airfields would be priority quarantine targets. The repairs could wait. He called the number he'd entered in his phone's contact list yesterday and hoped Jeff hadn't gotten to the repair yet.

"Jeff Simmons, Montgomery Aviation."

"Jeff, this is Eugene Chang."

"Hey, Dr. Chang. Funny you should call. I just took the wing apart. Well, not the whole wing. You know what I mean," said Jeff. "I got it all ready to make the adjustment. I should have it done by the end of the day tomorrow. Maybe earlier."

"You're going to hate me for this, Jeff, but I really need the plane back in one piece, ready to fly as soon as possible. I know it's getting toward the end of the day, and Friday at that, so maybe tomorrow morning? I'm really sorry about this. I will most certainly pay for the time you've already spent and the time tomorrow morning."

"It's no trouble at all, Dr. Chang. Seriously. My wife's got something going on at the church this evening, so she won't be home until late. I'll put your plane back together after we shut down. Technically we stop services at sunset, but I usually wait another fifteen minutes or so in case someone fell behind on the flight plan and was hell-bent on making the airfield. Shouldn't take me more than an hour after that. Ten thirty or so, and I'll be done."

"Jeff, I can't have you staying that late," said Chang, hoping Jeff didn't change his mind.

"I don't mind at all. I already ate a sandwich for dinner. We're getting ready for a bunch of Friday afternoon flights to return. This is normal for me when I work the back end of Friday. That's why my wife volunteers at the church."

"Well, I really appreciate it, Jeff. Something came up that might take me right back out of town."

"Anything related to that craziness down in Indy?"

Chang was caught off guard by the question, unsure why Jeff asked it. He couldn't possibly know what Chang did for NevoTech. He wasn't even sure if Jeff knew he worked for NevoTech. It had to be a mostly innocent question, tainted by Chang's own knowledge of the situation. But how did he answer his question like someone who didn't know a lethal bioweapon had been released? He was about to lie, when he remembered the NevoTech parking sticker on his windshield. Damn. Better to tell a half-truth.

"Quite possibly. I do some consulting work outside of NevoTech on vaccines. Looks like a late season flu outbreak in Indianapolis. Really late. As in—unusual," he said, hoping to leave it at that.

"Hit Cleveland, too."

"What?" said Chang.

"I had a guy fly in a few hours ago to visit his brother in Fishers. Said Cleveland was kind of a mess. I can tell you this. He sure as hell didn't know Indy was in the same boat. If his brother's family hadn't been waiting in the lounge, I think he might have headed right back to Ohio."

"Interesting," said Chang. "Have you noticed anything odd in your neighborhood, like the police coming out more often? People seem to be really freaking out over this flu."

"Nearest neighbor is a half mile away. I live just outside Sheridan on Route 38. Nothin' but farmland out there," said Jeff. "Never could stand neighborhood livin'. Everyone up in your business and everything."

"You may be onto something, Jeff. Between you and me, I'd stay put this weekend unless you're working. The farther from Indianapolis you stay, the better."

"Hell, I haven't been down to Indy in years," said Jeff, pausing for a moment. "Hey, I gotta let you go, Dr. Chang. They're stacking up on us. I'll have your bird fixed up good by eleven at the latest."

"Thanks, Jeff. Let me know what I owe you."

"Will do," said Jeff, and the call disconnected.

Chang turned toward the house, thinking about Cleveland. Two cities now. A coordinated attack meant a massive government response. At a minimum, it would involve a full-scale National Guard mobilization in each state impacted, along with the Guard units in neighboring states. If the number of cities hit stretched National Guard assets too thin, Department of Defense-backed deployments might be considered. An emergency session of Congress would be called to legislate a temporary exception to the Posse Comitatus Act. Failing that, the President would authorize the implementation of whatever nationwide contingency plan existed for this kind of attack.

He considered something Jeff had said about Cleveland. The pilot that arrived had no idea Indianapolis was a mess because Cleveland was under a similar media blackout, and his relatives conveniently forgot to mention it or didn't know. Shit. He knew how to determine which cities had been attacked. The solution was so simple he'd overlooked it.

Chang was back in his office and on the computer in under a minute. Thirty minutes later he had a list of cities under complete

HTTP ERROR 500 (INTERNAL SERVER ERROR) lockdown.

Indianapolis, Indiana
Fort Wayne, Indiana
Cleveland, Ohio
Columbus, Ohio
Cincinnati, Ohio
Louisville, Kentucky
Milwaukee, Wisconsin
Des Moines, Iowa
Minneapolis, Minnesota
St. Louis, Missouri
Detroit, Michigan
Pittsburgh, Pennsylvania
Nashville, Tennessee
Memphis, Tennessee

The pattern was obvious. The Midwest had been hit with a coordinated attack. He needed to get out of the region as soon as possible and join the disaster response effort from the outside. Way outside. America's heartland was about to go into lockdown, and if he stuck around for too long, he ran the risk of trying to explain his way out of a FEMA camp. No. He'd pack up the SUV with supplies and head to the airport at first light. He could be in Atlanta before noon. Same with Baltimore.

Chapter Seventeen

Jack Harper took a long sip of his second mojito of the evening, tasting Bacardi more than anything else. He scratched the top of Rudy's neck, just behind one of his ears, causing the chocolate lab to lean into the plastic patio chair. Another sip of the drink only bolstered his growing buzz. Emma stepped through the open patio door, carrying an oversized plastic bowl of tortilla chips and a container of salsa. He held his cup up and nodded.

"I think you forgot the rum," he said.

A nearby siren broke the early evening quiet, stopping Emma in her tracks.

"Still not strong enough for me," she said before putting everything down on the low glass table in front of their chairs. "I'll be right back."

Emma disappeared into the house, presumably to get her drink— not that it would likely help the situation. His wife looked like she could use a Xanax prescription at this point. The sirens had been going nonstop since he'd returned with Rudy in the early afternoon, compounding the stress she felt after being attacked at the grocery store. He barely believed her, not that he was questioning her story. It simply didn't jive with his personal experience.

He'd been hit with some serious bugs before, all of which either put him on permanent stakeout in the bathroom or made him feel like curling up in a ball and sleeping for an eternity. What on earth could cause someone to get ragey like that? The local news said some kind of flu outbreak had hit the city pretty hard, straining police and emergency medical response efforts. He'd fallen victim to seasonal flu a few times, which had knocked him flat on his ass. Knocking someone else on their ass had been the furthest thing from his mind. He didn't get it.

There was some mention of rising tensions in some neighborhoods, leading to confrontations with the police and multiple arrests, which would explain the constant barrage of sirens—but not what happened to his wife. Given the incident and the neighborhood's new background music, they decided against walking up into Broad Ripple for dinner, instead opting for a "quiet" evening in the backyard. Now he was thinking they would be better off inside, with the doors and windows closed. His wife returned with her drink and a small blue bowl, which she placed in front of him.

"Look at you with the fresh guacamole," he said.

"The least I can do for the man that promised to make dinner."

"I did?"

"Grilled fajitas, if I remember correctly," she said.

"I think you just made that up," said Jack.

"Maybe."

She settled into the Adirondack-style chair next to him and gulped close to half of her drink. "These are kind of strong."

"Just slightly," he said, taking her hand. "How are you doing?"

"Better. I think," she said, squeezing his hand back. "I'm kind of glad nobody could make it tonight. With everything going on, I could use a quiet evening."

"Not exactly quiet," he said, reaching for a chip.

"It can't go on all night," said Emma.

A barrage of yelling erupted somewhere in the neighborhood, followed a moment later by the squeal of tires. A car roared by their house, the urgent sound of its engine quickly fading down the street.

"I don't know. Could be a long night."

Jack wished he hadn't said that. Emma had started to ease up a little after sitting down. Now she looked as stiff as a statue in her chair.

"Everything will be fine, Emma," he said, leaning over to kiss her cheek.

"I know. It's just all so bizarre. Right?" she said. "Or am I just too jumpy from the most dissatisfying grocery run ever."

"Ha! I think you're understandably jumpy after that," said Jack, pausing to take a sip of his 80 proof cocktail. "And the situation out there is pretty damn bizarre."

"Do you think we should leave for a couple of days?" she said before shaking her head. "Sorry. I'm overreacting."

"It's not out of the realm of possibilities, but things would have to get pretty bad for us to leave," he said. "Where would you want to go? Another cruise?"

She laughed. "I was just thinking we'd scoot up to your parents' house, but I'm not opposed to a cruise—or a trip to Vegas."

"Don't tempt me. I'm always up for Vegas," he said. "Though I'm not sure how we'd manage to take more time off after being gone from NevoTech for close to two weeks."

"I'm sure we're fine right here," she said unconvincingly.

"We'll keep the option open," said Jack. "We can be up at my parents' place in a few hours."

"They didn't have any of this going on up there?" said Emma. "If it's a seasonal flu thing, it should be everywhere."

"Not that I could tell. They certainly didn't mention anything," said Jack. "I didn't hear any sirens."

"Maybe you should call them. See if they've heard anything? They watch the news religiously."

"Right now?"

She shrugged her shoulders. "I don't mind. I'll even start chopping up veggies for the fajitas."

"Sounds like a fair trade," he said before pulling his phone out of his pocket.

Emma munched on a few chips and finished her drink while he dialed his mother's mobile number and waited. She picked up right before he was about to hang up and try the home phone.

"Hi, Jack," she said. "Miss us already?"

"Very funny, Mom. I wanted to ask you something."

"Do I need to take you off speakerphone?" she said.

"Hey, son," said his dad. "Plotting my demise again?"

"I was raised by two comedians," said Jack. "Except I don't remember the two of you being this funny when I was a kid."

"We were under a lot of strain trying to boot the three of you out the door," said his mom. "I meant to say 'trying to raise you to be responsible young adults.'"

He turned to Emma, who had started toward the patio door. "I swear they're like two completely different people after retirement."

She smirked and shook her head.

"That's what happens when the burdens of life are lifted," said his dad, laughing at his own joke. "Everything all right down there?"

"Yeah. I think so," said Jack, not sure how to pose the next question without sounding crazy. "Has there been anything on the news up there about Indianapolis?"

"We never hear about Indy up here. It's all Chicago news," said his dad.

"Right. Is anything odd going on in Chicago? Like a flu outbreak?" he said, pausing to take a quick drink. "We're getting some strange reports down here, and there's nothing but sirens in the distance. It's been like this since I got back."

"It's pretty quiet up here," said his dad.

"There was something on the news about a late season flu making the rounds on the south side of Chicago," said his mom. "But it's like a war zone there already."

Before his dad could launch into a discourse about the ever-rising homicide rate in Chicago, he steered the conversation back to the flu.

"Right," said Jack. "Did the news give any specifics?"

"Not really. Just said that the ERs are filling up pretty quickly with flu cases," said his mom. "Is this what's happening by you?"

"Sounds the same, but I think we're a few days ahead of Chicago. The ERs around here stopped taking flu patients," said Jack.

"What? Wait a minute," said his dad. "What do you mean they stopped taking patients? When has the hospital ever stopped taking patients?"

"I don't know, Dad, but it's all over the news here. That's why I asked if you'd heard anything about Indianapolis. I can't imagine this not making the national news."

"It didn't, unless I completely missed it," said his mom. "We watch a lot of news."

"I know," said Jack. "Well, I just wanted to check in with you. Let me know if you hear any more out of Chicago. We're going to start watching the cable networks to see if anyone is talking about this outside of Indy."

He waited a few seconds for a response, hearing nothing.

"Mom? Dad?"

Silence.

"What's up?" said Emma, stepping onto the patio.

"I think they hung up on me," said Jack.

"Wouldn't be the first time."

"True."

He touched the phone's screen, illuminating it. *CALL DISCONNECTED.*

"Definitely hung up on me," he said, redialing his parents.

The screen lingered for a moment, displaying the phone number and the word *CALLING* before abruptly changing to *CALL FAILED.* He tried again, getting the same screen.

"That's weird," he said. "The call failed."

"Failed?"

He checked the cell reception indicator at the top of the screen, noticing that indicator was SEARCHING. The Wi-Fi fan had also disappeared.

"Looks like my phone dropped the network. Wi-Fi is out, too. What about yours?"

"Hold on a second. It's inside," she said.

Jack powered the phone down and restarted it, hoping for the best. While he waited, Emma walked out of the dark house, stopping a few steps away.

"No cell service. No Wi-Fi," she mumbled.

"Yours too?"

"Yeah. This can't be right. We should still have Wi-Fi," she said. "The power is on."

His phone finished restarting, moments later giving him the same result. He got up from the chair and started for the house.

"Do we have our landline hooked up? I can't remember," he said.

"I'm pretty sure we do. It was free to keep it," said Emma. "I don't think we have a regular phone in the house. I threw away the box with the cordless handsets last year."

She was right. They hadn't used the landline for close to two years. He stopped and finished the rest of his drink.

"Shit. This is probably nothing. I'll mix up another round of slightly less potent mojitos," he said, turning to face the glass table with their appetizers. "We'll sit back and enjoy your guacamole before I make dinner."

A single distant gunshot echoed off the trees, causing Emma to drop her finished drink. The thin highball glass shattered on the patio, sending pieces in every direction.

"You okay?" he said, grabbing her hand.

"Yeah. Just startled me."

"I say we move the party inside," he said.

"I couldn't agree more," said Emma. "Grab the broom and dustpan from the kitchen. I'll keep Rudy out of the glass."

"I don't think you have to worry about him," said Jack, nodding at the sleeping dog. "He looks pretty comfortable."

"Not a care in the world," she added. "Must be nice."

"I'll grab the broom and pan," he said. "Are you good being out here by yourself?"

"I'm fine," she said, letting go of his hand. "It's not like the neighborhood has gone crazy. That's not the first gunshot we've ever heard. This *is* Indianapolis."

Inside the house, Jack took a quick detour through the family room to check on something. He turned on the flat-screen television and cable box, making sure the TV was set to cable. *NO INPUT.* Exactly what he didn't want to see. How could the cable be down, too? Before returning to the kitchen, he made sure the front door was locked and that the garage bay was closed. With no Internet, cable TV or phones, he was pretty sure the neighborhood would see some crazy tonight.

Chapter Eighteen

David Olson slowed the Ford Interceptor SUV as they approached Maidenfield Road, where the 911 call had originated. If his partner spotted a crowd on the street, they'd approach from a different direction or abandon the call altogether. Westfield police officers had been attacked twice tonight responding to calls, which the department now strongly suspected to have been fake 911 emergencies. Both attacks had led to gunfights with multiple citizens situated in different houses, requiring backup units to extract the ambushed officers.

By this point, both David and his partner had agreed to avoid taking any unnecessary chances. Given what they'd witnessed and experienced firsthand over the course of their shift, it was understood that simply showing up in the same neighborhood of the call posed a risk—but they still had a duty to protect the legitimate citizens of Westfield. They'd respond to calls, applying every possible caution on the approach and during whatever encounter unfolded.

"This is Maidenfield coming up on the right," said David.

His partner, Robert Bower, leaned forward and craned his head to get an advance peek at the unfolding scene. He'd known Bower for a number of years and felt comfortable riding with him in the patrol vehicle. He hoped Bower felt the same about him. Neither of them had ever been on a two-officer patrol before today.

"Can you point the light across the hood?" said Bower.

"Yep," said David, using his left hand to position the light.

"That should work," said Bower. "I can already see someone standing in the middle of a yard. More than one person."

David stopped the car at the intersection and triggered the light, adjusting it until Bower told him to stop.

"I have three adult males and one female adult. Nothing suspicious or aggressive about their posture or response to the light. What do you think?"

Two of them pointed at the house next door, which didn't look any different than the rest of the homes on the tightly spaced block. Porch light on. Lights on inside. Door shut. Nothing out of the ordinary at all.

"The neighbors look legit?" said David.

"Look normal enough from this distance, but they could be packing Uzis for all I know."

"Nobody uses an Uzi anymore. You're a few decades off," said David.

Bower laughed. "Yeah. *Miami Vice* days. Now they dual wield Glock 19s with extended mags." He'd seen his son do this playing a video game.

"*Call of Duty*," said David. "My son used to play it."

"My two boys still do. I've tried to explain to them how it's not possible to fire two automatic pistols at the same time and hit anything, but they don't seem convinced," said Bower, getting serious again. "The two ambushes occurred on empty streets. This feels legit enough to check out. You concur?"

He took one more look at the street, not seeing any reason to disagree.

"I concur," he said, activating the police lights and turning the steering wheel hard to the right.

Bower clicked the radio transmitter attached to his tactical vest. "Unit Eight approaching four one five on Maidenfield."

Dispatch responded briefly. "Copy, Eight."

A few moments later, they pulled up to the address given to them by dispatch. The people started to move in the direction of the patrol vehicle, but Bower kindly asked them over the Interceptor's megaphone to stay put. They complied, which was a good start to the call.

"You do the honors," said Bower. "I'll cover you."

Bower raised the M4 rifle off his lap, keeping it below the line of the windshield or door windows.

"Yep," said David, opening the door.

He stepped onto the curb, leaving the door open in case he needed to make a quick departure. It also gave his partner an unobstructed view of the house in question. After taking a few steps toward the neighboring yard, he activated his flashlight and directed its beam at the group waiting for him.

"Can I have you form a line and lift your shirts a few inches above your waistlines?" said David, purposefully keeping his other hand away from his pistol to avoid spooking them. "We've had some strange encounters tonight. I just need to do a quick visual for weapons."

The group immediately complied with his request. Another good sign.

"Do a quick three-sixty, and we're good to go," said David.

He watched their waistlines closely, seeing nothing that concerned him.

"Sorry about that. Been a strange night," said David before deactivating his flashlight and approaching the group. "Who called 911?"

"I did," said a normal-looking guy in jeans and an oversized Colts T-shirt. "Their boy banged on our door. He was yelling about the mom beating up his dad with a baseball bat."

"The mom?" said David.

"That's what he said," said the guy.

David's mind immediately thought about his ex-wife. Would she have attacked Joshua instead of her boyfriend if he hadn't taken their son on the camping trip? Until right now he hadn't considered that possibility. What the fuck was happening out here? He needed to stay focused. They had a raving madwoman inside the house, possibly holding her husband hostage.

"Where is the boy now?" said David.

"He's inside our house," said the guy, nodding at the home immediately to their left. "My wife is treating his injuries. Mostly scrapes on his arms and face."

"Does he need emergency medical attention?" said David. "EMS is strapped tonight, but if you think he needs it, I'll make the call."

"I think he'll be fine. I don't know about the dad, though."

"We'll cross that bridge when we get there," said David. "What about the rest of you? What's going on?"

"My husband and I live across the street," said a young woman in pajamas.

"We heard the commotion," said the husband.

The other guy, an older man dressed in knee-length shorts and a white tank top, added that he lived directly across the street and heard yelling.

"Did any of you see anything?" said David.

"I saw Marcie chase the kid halfway across the lawn before turning back and slamming the front door shut," said the older guy.

"We just heard the yelling," said the young woman, holding her husband's arm. "It was really freaky."

"It's not the first time we've heard some strange shit," said the older guy. "There was some kind of big argument in one of the backyards on the street behind me. Doors slamming. Not sure what the hell happened."

"What about the dad inside the house?" said David, focusing on the next-door neighbor. "The boy told you he had locked himself in a bathroom?"

"Right. Upstairs. Master bathroom," said the neighbor.

"He just left the boy to fend for himself against the mother?" said David.

"I don't know. It sounds like things went bad really fast."

David nodded. "Any guns in the house?"

Nothing had come up registered through the town for the address or any of the names associated with it—not that it really made a difference. Only concealed-carry permit holders were required to be on record. There were probably a thousand unrecorded firearms for every concealed-carry permit in the state. Maybe more.

"All right. I need all of you to go back inside your homes. We'll take it from here," said David. "No matter what you hear inside the house or in the yard, do not go outside to investigate. And whatever you do, keep the kid inside."

The young woman turned to the neighbor. "We'd be happy to help you with Kyle while they sort this out. I'm a licensed clinical social worker. I've worked with kids before."

"We could use the help right now. We're dealing with a ten-year-old and a six-year-old, too. We don't have enough hands to keep them away from the windows," said the neighbor.

"Sounds like a plan," said David. "Remember. Stay inside."

Several seconds later, he was back at the Interceptor. "Ready to go inside?"

"Not really," said Bower. "What did they say?"

"Nothing we didn't already know, except that the kid has a bunch of scratches on his face and arms, and his mother chased him halfway across the yard before going back in the house."

"It's really the mom?" said Bower.

"That's what I said. Old man across the street confirmed it."

"Maybe the dad went after the kid, and mom got protective. Took a bat to him, then chased after the boy."

David shook his head. "I don't know. Why would the mother stop and go back inside?"

"None of this makes sense," said his partner.

Bower got out of the SUV and shut the door before walking in front of the vehicle to join him. David retrieved the keys and locked the Interceptor. The last thing they needed was for someone to take off with it, stranding them out here. Several attempts to steal or break into department vehicles had occurred over the past forty-eight hours.

"Front or back?" said Bower, slinging the rifle over his shoulder.

Department policy strictly prohibited officers from carrying service rifles into personal residences, but given the circumstances, they had chosen to interpret that policy to mean carrying the rifle in a ready-to-immediately-shoot condition. Not that it would take Bower long to put the rifle into action. He'd flipped it around in one swift motion several times tonight when things heated up.

"We pretend to walk around back, then hit the front. Together," said David, having no intention of splitting them up.

"Damn right, together," said Bower.

"I kick the door in. We move upstairs quickly and carefully, with me in front. You're watching our backs."

"Works for me."

"Call it in," said David.

"Dispatch, Unit Eight. Both officers entering home on Maidenfield."

"Copy, Eight," replied the radio.

They walked up the driveway, keeping a careful watch on the closed curtains above the side-loading garage. When they reached the corner of the garage, they drew their pistols and slid along the front of the house, staying below the home's windows. After stepping up onto the concrete front porch, they stacked up next to the door and listened for a few seconds—hearing nothing inside. He hated this part.

"Ready?" whispered David.

Bower tapped his shoulder, prompting David to step in front of the door and land a hard, boot-bottom kick next to the door handle. The door blasted inward a few inches, immediately stopped by a secondary locking device.

"Shit," he muttered, stepping a few feet back.

It took him less than a second to identify a chain lock above the handle as the culprit. He squared off against the door and kicked as high as he could, snapping the chain and launching the door against the inside wall. David moved swiftly into the living room, sweeping his pistol across the room and stopping on the entrance to the kitchen directly in front of him.

The side of a stainless steel refrigerator faced him, covered in business cards and handwritten notes held up by magnets. Beyond the refrigerator, a long black counter extended to the far corner of the kitchen. He tried to visualize the space beyond the doorway, but without seeing the rest of the kitchen, the mental exercise was useless. It didn't matter. They were going straight upstairs to the master bathroom. Searching the rest of the ground level would just give whoever was hiding upstairs more time to come up with a plan to ambush them.

"Cover the kitchen," he whispered, shifting his aim to the top of the stairs.

Bower moved behind him, aiming into the kitchen, as David stepped toward the bottom of the carpeted stairway next to the kitchen door. The house was entirely too quiet given what had transpired here ten minutes ago. He started up the stairs, constantly shifting his aim between the railing banisters above his head to the top of the stairs. When his head reached a point about a foot below the level of the second floor, he paused and turned to Bower, who was right behind him.

"I'm gonna do a quick peek topside," said David.

Before Bower responded, gunfire exploded through the banister's white spindles. A searing pain creased David's forehead, followed by a hammer blow to his upper back, which knocked him flat against the stairs. Bower let out an agonized scream as bullet after bullet cracked above and around David. He jerked his head upward in time to see a pistol emerge between the spindles. Instead of trying to squeeze off a shot at the blurred figure behind the pistol, he hurled himself down the stairs, bringing Bower down with him. Several more bullets snapped past them, the gunman frantically trying to hit them from a hopelessly odd angle.

The gunfire stopped as soon as they crashed into the family room, a tangled mess of bloodied arms and legs. David caught movement at the top of the stairs and raised his right hand, relieved to see that it still had his pistol. A woman dressed in gray sweatpants and a pink V-neck T-shirt stood above them at the top of the stairs, holding a pistol and a silver aluminum baseball bat. The slide on the pistol was locked back, indicating that she had expended the entire magazine—a fact that appeared completely lost on her.

He rolled off his partner and straightened out on his back, holding the pistol in a two-handed grip above his midsection. Malevolent eyes glared at him beyond the pistol's sight picture, leaving little doubt in his mind what would happen.

"Drop the gun! Drop the bat! Stay where you are," he yelled.

"Fucking shoot her," groaned Bower. "She's gone."

He'd give her one more chance.

"Last—" he started, when the woman broke into a sprint down the stairs with the bat raised over her head.

David's first shot went a few inches wide, striking the wall behind her head. Fuck it. He aimed center mass and pressed the trigger repeatedly, her body jerking left and right. Bower's gun joined the shooting frenzy by the time she got three-quarters of the way down the stairs. Within the span of several seconds, the two officers fired a combined total of thirty-four hollow-point bullets at the crazed woman, most of them hitting her in the torso or arms.

The woman slowed under the hail of bullets, blood spraying the carpet and walls all around her, before she teetered backward against the stairs. David lay there frozen, the gun's barrel smoking at the end of his hand. He'd never seen anything that devastating happen to a human being—not even in a movie.

"Fuck," muttered Bower. "What the hell was wrong with her?"

"I don't know," said David. "Can you reload?"

"Negative. My arm is fucked," said Bower, grunting the words.

"Hold on," said David, then reloaded his pistol.

He depressed the pistol's slide release, chambering a round, and pushed himself up. A quick scan of the family room and kitchen revealed no additional threats. Bower's empty pistol remained pointed toward the stairs, a small pool of blood soaking the carpet under his left shoulder. From what David could tell, his partner had been hit in the upper arm. The bleeding didn't look urgent, but he wasn't a paramedic. Bullets had a strange way of causing unseen damage.

"Lay your pistol across your chest," said David. "I'm going to drag you deeper into the living room."

David holstered his own pistol and gripped the drag handle on Bower's tactical vest with both hands, pulling him across the thick carpet and stopping in the middle of the sparsely furnished room. He wanted to get them away from the doorway leading to the kitchen, and any more lethal surprises. His next job was to get Bower an ambulance.

"Dispatch, Unit Eight. Shots fired at 2322 Maidenfield. Request backup and immediate medical response. Officer down."

"Officer down at 2322 Maidenfield. Request all available units to assist. Diverting EMS," said the dispatcher. "Eight, who got hit, and what's the status?"

"It's Bower. He took a bullet to the upper left arm," said David. "I can't tell how bad overall."

"Copy. Stand by," said the dispatcher.

While he waited for a response, he examined the arm. Could be a through and through, but it was impossible to tell without tearing away the sleeve. He started to search Bower's belt for a utility knife.

"Keep an eye on the stairs," grumbled Bower, gripping his wrist.

"Right. Right," said David, aiming his pistol toward the stairs. "How are you doing?"

"Hurts like a motherfucker, but I think I'm good," said Bower. "You took one to the forehead, by the way."

"What?" said David, touching his forehead.

His hand came back smeared with blood.

"I feel fine," said David. "How bad is it?"

"Barely bleeding. Looks like it just grazed you. Lucky son of a bitch. A half inch over, and they'd be cleaning your brains off the wall," said Bower, grimacing. "Gonna be one hell of a scar, though."

He could live with a scar.

The radio squawked. "Backup and EMS en route. Closest backup unit two minutes out. EMS five minutes out."

David responded, "Eight copies. We're stable for now. Look for us inside the front door to the right, on the floor."

"Copy. Passing that to responding units. Hang on, Eight."

He took his hand off the radio transmitter and steadied his pistol, which was visibly shaking.

"You should check on the dad," said Bower. "If she had a gun, he might be in worse shape than me."

"I'm not going anywhere, Rob. You're stuck with me until backup arrives. They can unfuck the rest of this situation."

"What was she thinking?" muttered Bower.

"Something was wrong with her," said David. "She looked at me with a hatred I've never seen before. Like I'd been her personal tormentor for life, and this was her chance to settle the score."

"Fucking crazy," said Bower.

A police siren wailed in the distance, getting louder by the second. He couldn't help but think about his ex-wife. Was this what had happened to her? She just turned into a homicidal maniac and tried to kill her boyfriend? David shook his head. He was heading home after this. Joshua was his top priority now. His only priority. And he didn't care if it meant the end of his career. If things kept moving in the direction they'd seen tonight, it wouldn't matter. The Westfield Police Department would be swallowed by an unstoppable wave of violence.

Chapter Nineteen

Emma Harper sat holding her husband on the kitchen floor, listening closely for any more signs of chaos outside. Someone had thrown a sizable garden rock through one of their front windows while they were eating dinner, which kicked off an endless string of mayhem outside. Gunshots, nearby and distant, could be heard every ten to fifteen minutes now. The screaming and yelling had become background noise to the ceaseless call of police sirens. Tires screeched and cars raced up and down the street. Shattering glass didn't even cause them to look up anymore. It sounded like a riot had broken out nearby, but every time they peeked through their shades, the street didn't look any different than any other busy Friday night in a Broad Ripple neighborhood.

A gunshot startled both of them. This time, it sounded like it came from their block. An inhuman screech followed.

"That's it. We're out of here," said Jack, standing up. "We'll head to my parents'."

"I don't think it's a good idea to go outside, Jack," said Emma. "Maybe we should stay here until it's light out again. Leave when we can at least see what's going on around us."

A distant, staccato burst of gunfire paused their conversation. Emma took a deep breath and exhaled, trying to calm an overwhelming sense of panic. They had no idea what was happening around them. Every method of communication available to them had been cut off, leaving them figuratively and literally in the dark. They had chosen to turn off all of the lights in their house to avoid attracting attention.

"It's getting worse out there. I'm afraid if we don't leave now, we might not get another chance," said Jack, now pacing. "Or a mob might break into our house. I don't know. I just want to get out of here."

Jack was starting to scare her. He never freaked out about stuff, to the point where he came off as cluelessly laid-back. If Jack was this worried about their situation, they needed to get out of here.

"Then we go," said Emma. "We can be on the road immediately. We both have spare clothes at your parents'."

Her husband looked deep in thought.

"Honey?"

"Let's pack up as much food, water and other survival stuff as we can in the Jeep," said Jack. "Who knows what the situation will be in northern Indiana. It wouldn't take much to empty the stores in a panic."

"We don't have any survival gear," said Emma.

"I mean like our hiking stuff. We can turn our backpacks into those bug-away bags that all of the preppers talk about.

"Bug-out bags," she said, smirking.

"Right. They're supposed to be good for seventy-two hours out in the wild," said Jack. "You start organizing the food. Use all of those paper bags with the handles. I'll put together the bug-out bags."

"Lights?" said Emma, looking around the house.

She could see her way around the house, but it would be a lot easier to organize their supplies with the main house lights on.

"I don't think it's a good idea. Dig out the flashlights," said Jack, looking around the kitchen. "Where's Rudy?"

"He was here a minute ago," she said.

Jack walked over to the kitchen door, muttering a curse. "I forgot to shut the dog door. He must have slipped out. I'll grab him and load up his dog food."

While her husband went into the backyard to retrieve their sleeping dog, Emma laid out their flashlights on the kitchen island

and tested each one. Half of them needed batteries, which she kept in the same box as the flashlights. She'd changed the batteries in two of them when Jack stepped back inside the house without Rudy.

"Are you sure he's not in the house?" said Jack.

"No. At least I don't think so," she said before calling out to their dog in her silly voice. "Rudeeeeee! Come here, boy, boy! Rudeeeeee! Want a treat! Get in the car!"

The house remained silent, which was highly unusual. Rudy didn't always come running, but they always heard the tags on his collar jingle when they called. She called him again, exaggerating her doggy voice. Nothing.

"He wasn't outside?" said Emma.

"I looked everywhere."

"What about the hole we fixed? He's always trying to re-dig that when we're not looking. I knew he was being a little too quiet out there. The neighbors had a barbeque going."

"Shit. You're right. Damn dog is clever," said Jack. "Let me grab one of those."

She handed him one of the freshly charged lights, and he took off into the dark backyard again. With the flashlights finished, she started to stack the cans of food in their pantry on the counters. After her third trip back and forth from the pantry, she opened one of the kitchen drawers and removed a can opener, placing it on top of one of the piles, just in case they needed to open some on the way up to Jack's parents. She couldn't imagine how or why that might happen, but felt compelled to bring it.

With the cans organized, Emma turned to the four-quart, airtight dry food bins containing loose beans, rice, grains and oatmeal. She lined all eight of them up next to the cans and returned to the pantry to start on the packaged food. They had a ton of stuff like crackers, oatmeal and pasta in assorted-sized boxes. None of it very practical on the road, but the plan was to transport it up to Jack's parents' in case the stores were emptied. She turned around with an unbalanced load of food packages, unexpectedly running into Jack. Most of the packages clattered to the floor.

"Damn. I didn't see you," said Emma. "You scared me."

Jack just stood there looking through her, seemingly in a daze.

"Jack, are you okay? Where's Rudy?" she said, taking a step back.

"We have to leave immediately," he whispered, still looking spaced out.

"Why? Where's Rudy?" she said.

He locked eyes with her, a deep sadness filling them. "We need to go now."

Emma tried to push past him, but he grabbed both of her upper arms and yanked her back. She tried to shake free, but he held her tightly, almost hurting her.

"What happened to Rudy!" she screamed.

"Shhhhhh," he hissed. "Someone might hear us."

"What the fuck are you talking about?" she said, trying to shake free again with no success.

"Trust me, Emma, like you've never trusted me before. We need to go. I'll grab our packs and a few other things from the basement. Shove as much of this stuff into bags as you can and be ready to drive out of here in two minutes. It's that bad."

Her lip started to quiver, tears flowing immediately. Jack hadn't answered her question about Rudy. He looked directly at her, barely holding back his own tears.

"Rudy—" he started, shaking his head involuntarily. "He's gone. We have to go."

"What happened?"

He continued to shake his head for a few seconds before swallowing hard. "Do you trust me?"

She nodded, barely able to muster a response. "Yes."

"Do not go into the backyard. Do not look for Rudy," he said. "I need to go into the basement, but I can't leave you until I know one hundred percent that you will not go into the backyard."

"Is he in the yard?" she said.

"Emma!" said Jack, his voice rising slightly. "He's not in the backyard. Promise me you'll stay inside. Please."

She tried desperately to process what he was saying, or more instructively—not saying. He still hadn't said what happened to Rudy, so he clearly didn't want to tell her. Finally grasping that, she was able to think clearly.

"Promise," she said.

He kissed her forehead and let her go. "Two minutes. Something is irretrievably wrong with the world outside this house. Lock the slider and start loading up the Jeep."

"Okay."

"I love you, Emma," said Jack. "I won't let anything happen to you."

She didn't know how to respond to the last part of his sentence, so she went with the obvious. "I love you, too."

Jack quickly kissed her lips before heading to the basement door. He disappeared before she could say anything, leaving her alone in possibly the most uncertain moment of her life. She glanced at the open patio slider, afraid to walk over and lock it. She didn't trust herself to stay in the house.

"Nothing good will come of that," she muttered, forcing herself to walk to the garage to grab a stack of paper bags.

Emma frantically filled several of the sturdy bags before Jack returned from the basement, shouldering both of their hiking rigs. He stopped next to the kitchen island and placed a small unfamiliar box on the granite surface. She directed her flashlight at the box, perplexed by the label.

50 Rds .38 Special
150 GR Full Metal Jacket

"Is that some kind of ammunition?" she said.

Jack pulled a dark pistol from his right pocket and set it on the island next to the box. "Yep."

Emma didn't know much about firearms, but she knew enough to determine that it was not something they typically saw on TV shows. In other words, it wasn't the semiautomatic kind with a magazine you inserted into the grip. It looked like a revolver. Where the hell did he get something like this? She wasn't as mad as she was curious.

"I didn't realize we had a gun in the house," she said.

"It's my grandfather's service pistol. My dad passed it on to me. He never liked firearms. I kept it as an heirloom, mostly."

"I thought your grandpa retired from the water department," said Emma.

"He did. Twenty years as a cop. Twenty years with the water department. Double pension," said Jack. "They had a decent racket going on in the city."

She shook her head, forming a reluctant smile. "Have you ever fired it?"

"No. Never fired a gun in my life," he said, lifting the pistol from the island and pointing toward the family room.

"Careful," she said. "Is it loaded?"

"No," said Jack, one-handedly working some kind of magic that opened the pistol's cylinder.

"You look like you know what you're doing."

"I play with it from time to time. Never loaded it, though," he said.

"Do you know how to load it?" she said.

"Seems fairly straightforward," he said.

"I'll fill up the Jeep," said Emma. "You figure out what to do with that."

Jack pressed the cylinder back into the pistol with his free hand and pulled the trigger; a deep metallic *click* filled the room.

"That's it," he said. "I think."

"Except you have to load it."

"Right," said Jack, glancing at the patio slider. "You didn't lock the door?"

"I didn't trust myself."

"I don't blame you," he said, finally turning to face her. "Let's get out of here, Emma."

He finally sounded normal again, or as normal as someone could sound under the circumstances.

Chapter Twenty

Joshua Olson paused at the top of the basement stairs, holding the key to open the deadbolt in one hand and his dad's Glock 19 in the other. He knew he should stay in the basement, but someone had rung the doorbell several times throughout the evening, and he could still hear voices outside the western-facing basement windows. Something big had gone down nearby about a half hour ago.

It had started with a bunch of screaming and yelling, which sounded a little like the way his parents argued before the divorce— but twenty times worse. He was pretty sure some of the neighbors intervened, because he heard at least four or five other raised voices. The police showed up about ten minutes later, the squawking of their radios clearly identifiable above the heated voices.

Just a quick peek. Five minutes at most. Well, maybe a little longer. One of the frozen pizzas kept calling his name. He'd get that started first and be back in the basement in fifteen minutes. He unlocked the deadbolt and put the key in his pocket, opening the door slowly. Aside from the faint sound of voices outside, the house stood quiet, only the faint hum of the refrigerator detectable from the doorway.

He waited a few more moments to be sure before stepping gingerly onto the hardwood floor in the foyer hallway. He wasn't sure why he was tiptoeing. Nobody could see inside the house through the shades, and they certainly couldn't hear him walking around. As long as he didn't make any ridiculously loud noises, like drop the pizza pan, his presence should go unnoticed.

Joshua shifted the pistol into his right hand, mindful of the trigger, and headed deeper into the house, making his way to the stairs. Moving from room to room on the second floor, he'd get a three-hundred-and-sixty-degree bird's-eye view of the neighborhood. The trees and bushes around the ground floor obscured too much of the street. He started with his bedroom, located at the front, northwestern corner of the house, which should give him the best view of the incident next door.

After laying the pistol on his desk, he edged up to the window next to his bed and lifted one of the horizontal blinds a half inch—just enough to see outside. A cluster of five people stood in the driveway of the house across from his next-door neighbor. He could hear their voices, but couldn't decipher what they were saying through the closed window. Nearby porch lights cast enough illumination for Joshua to determine they were all men, but he couldn't identify them individually. None of them looked like a police officer. Whatever had happened here was finished.

One of the men appeared agitated, his voice rising above the others'. He looked in the direction of the Olsons' house and pointed repeatedly. Moments later, they were headed diagonally across the street—toward Joshua. Crap. Now he had to make a choice. Scurry into the basement or hang out up here until they left. He chose to stay put and lay in bed.

Waiting for the doorbell to ring, he suddenly remembered that he'd left the door to the basement open, casting light into the foyer hallway. If any of the guys approaching the house right now had been to the door before, they'd notice the change. Stupid. Joshua shot out of bed and ran down the carpeted stairs, easing his footfalls as best as possible without slowing down. He reached the open basement door just as a flashlight hit one of the front door's frosted sidelights, quickly shutting it before crossing into the dining room. He sat on the floor, out of sight of the front door, and caught his breath.

The doorbell chimed, startling him. He pressed against the wall, making sure his feet were tucked in far enough behind the wall. Not that it mattered. They couldn't see that well through the frosted glass, especially when the house was dark. He glanced across the hallway at the basement door, seeing little more than a dull glow underneath. The towel he'd placed underneath it from the inside probably eliminated all light, but he didn't think it would be a problem. It wasn't something that stood out, even sitting right across from it.

An insistent, hard knock on the front door followed the doorbell. He didn't like the way the knocking sounded. More like a fist pounding than a neighbor knocking politely. Did they see the light? Or maybe catch a blurred shadow moving inside the house while walking up to the door? No way. He could barely see his own way through the house. A second solid thumping against the door gave way to muffled voices on the front porch. Even though the men were right on the other side of the door, he couldn't catch an intact conversation. What he did manage to separate from the noise froze him in place.

The response was mostly muffled, but ended in, "Well, we can't just break in and take them."

Take what? The three men talked over each other for a few seconds before a voice Joshua thought he recognized broke through the din.

"We need to protect the neighborhood somehow. The cops can't get here fast enough."

Shit. Joshua understood what they wanted. Guns. The swift realization brought on a panicked awareness. He'd left his dad's pistol upstairs. Part of him wanted to dash up the stairs and retrieve it, but he knew that would likely give up his carefully crafted deception. He stood up and leaned as close as he dared to the edge of the dining room.

"We need guns if the police can't stop these people."

What people? Neighbors? His dad had said things were getting dicey out there, but could it be that bad?

Another round of pounding caused him to pull back.

"Dave! You in there!" said the familiar voice, pausing for a response. "Joshua! It's Mr. Aleman from across the street. We just need to talk to your dad!"

Mr. Aleman was a good guy, from what Joshua remembered—always throwing neighborhood parties and barbeques. He really wanted to answer Aleman and get some information about "these people," but his dad would be pissed enough to know he'd ventured upstairs after dark. Opening the door and chatting with the neighbors represented an entirely different level of "not following instructions." Not only that—they wanted guns. Badly enough to knock on a police officer's door. His best course of action was to sit here quietly until they went away, then make his pizza. Actually, he could get a head start on that right now.

Ignoring their continued pleas and knocking, he slipped into the kitchen through a separate doorway and preheated the oven to 425 degrees. He liked his pizza crispy. Standing in the kitchen, farther removed from the voices, he took out his smart phone and checked his text messages. Nothing from his dad for an hour. He'd received a call or text every thirty minutes until about 9:30. The hour-long gap left him with an uneasy feeling. He typed a message and pressed send.

Dad, just checking in. Something happened next door. Mr. Aleman at our door with a few neighbors. All is well. You?

His phone rang a few seconds later, the screen illuminating the kitchen. Joshua fumbled to answer his dad's call, finally pressing the phone to his ear.

"Dad?"

"Where are you right now?" said his dad.

"I'm…uhhhh. Well, I wanted to get a better picture of what's going on next door, so—"

"So you went upstairs?"

"Yes."

"Presumably with my handgun?"

"Yes."

"I need you to get downstairs immediately," said his dad.

He peeked down the foyer hallway from the kitchen, seeing a flashlight just beyond the front door.

"Mr. Aleman and two other neighbors are still on our porch," said Joshua.

"Do they know you're there?"

"No. I closed the door to the basement, and I got into the dining room before they reached the door," said Joshua, knowing he was just digging his hole deeper.

"How did you know they were on the way?"

"I was in my room," said Joshua. "It has the perfect vantage point!"

"You might want to lower your voice," said his dad. "Where are you now?"

"I'm in the kitchen."

"All right. Stay put until you know for a fact they're gone. You might have to sit there on the floor for a while. The shades covering our patio slider don't go all the way to the bottom, so it's possible for someone outside to spot you if they decide to look inside every door and window."

He'd forgotten that. Damn.

"I'll stay put. I'm cooking up another pizza," he said, immediately regretting the statement.

"I'm gonna pretend I didn't hear that," said his dad.

"I figured since I was already up here—"

"Not making it any better, Joshua."

"Right. Sorry," he said. "When are you coming home? Mr. Aleman said something about stopping *these people*. I don't know what happened next door, but it really freaked out our neighbors. What do you think he meant by *these people*?"

A long pause ensued. When his dad answered, he sounded exhausted.

"I don't know, Josh. All I know is everything is going to shit out here."

"Are you coming home now, Dad?" he said, frightened by his dad's remark.

"Soon. I need to get checked out by the paramedics. Our last call got a little rough."

He could tell his dad was holding back most of the story.

"Are you okay?" said Joshua.

"I'm fine. A little scratched up, but that's it."

Joshua didn't believe a word of it. His dad sounded like he'd seen a ghost.

"That bad?"

Another long pause.

"Just get in the basement and stay there until I get home. Lock the door. I honestly have no idea what's happening out here. People aren't acting right. Mr. Aleman might sound normal, but it's no guarantee."

"What?" whispered Joshua. "What do you mean?"

"I don't know, but you can't trust anybody. Understand?"

"Yes."

"How long until your pizza is done?" said his dad.

"I didn't put it in the oven yet."

"Can you live without it?"

"Yeah. I can crack open an MRE or something from your survival stockpile," said Joshua.

"Speaking of the stockpile, if you're looking for something to do other than creep around the house, making pizzas and attracting the neighbors' attention, I have a job for you."

"Yeah. Sure."

"There's a fully loaded backpack next to the gun safe—"

"Your bug-out bag?"

"Right," said his dad. "I want you to make a second pack for yourself. Take the first one apart and see what you need. I have duplicate supplies on the shelves. While you're out and about in the house, grab two pairs of the pants from your room. Hunting or hiking pants with lots of pockets. A few pair of underwear and T-shirts. One waterproof shell from the closet by the garage. Socks. All that kind of crap."

"I got it, Dad," said Joshua. "Do you think we'll need to leave?"

"I really don't know, buddy," said his dad. "But I want to be ready to drive out of here at a moment's notice if necessary. When I get home, we'll carry the rest of the supplies upstairs and load the truck. I have a lot of stuff down there. Enough to get us by for several weeks."

"What about Mom?" said Joshua.

He'd called and texted her hourly since his dad left for his shift, not completely convinced by his dad's explanation. She'd never ignored his calls for this long, even on trips. There was more to that story than his dad was telling him.

"If we decide to leave town, we'll make a run over to her house to see if she's back," said his dad. "There's only so much we can do before we need to get out of here."

"We can't leave without her."

"We won't. If she's here, we'll bring her with us, even if it means bringing jackass with us."

Joshua stifled a laugh. He really didn't like his mom's boyfriend either. The guy perpetually oozed self-importance, occasionally pausing long enough to fake a little interest in Joshua's life—and his mother's, it seemed. He didn't understand what his mother saw in the man, but she seemed happy overall, which was all that mattered. She'd been through several obviously frustrating relationships since the divorce, all abruptly ending with late night telephone tirades. Most of the single dudes around his mom's age were complete dickheads. At least that was how they treated his mom.

"Stay safe, Dad," said Joshua. "I'll start working on the gear when Mr. Aleman leaves."

His father didn't respond.

"Dad?" said Joshua, hearing no response. "Dad? You there?"

He examined the phone's screen, seeing the word *SEARCHING* where he should see a solid three reception bars. Joshua waited for the indicator to change, thinking there must have been a quick glitch with the cell tower a few neighborhoods away. While he stood at the kitchen island, waiting, he sent a quick text to his dad. He remembered learning that text messages often got through when cell service was unavailable or busy, because it took a fraction of the data to transmit.

A minute later, his dad hadn't replied. A small message had appeared under his text. *UNABLE TO DELIVER*. What the hell was going on? He sent the text again and walked to the edge of the doorway leading to the foyer hallway, checking the front door. The flashlight was gone, and so were the voices. He'd give it a few more seconds and dash upstairs to get his dad's pistol. After seeing that his second attempt to send a text message failed, he stepped into the hallway and made his way upstairs.

Joshua grabbed the pistol from his desk and tucked it into the waistband of his cargo shorts, debating whether to take another look through the blinds. There was no point. He was heading back into the basement after the pizza was done. No way he was going to sit down there and eat one of those nasty MREs when he could have pepperoni pizza.

Back in the kitchen, he opened the freezer door and removed the pizza, quickly shutting the freezer. He started to tear open the cardboard box in front of the stove when a beam of light hit the refrigerator, followed by a firm knock on the patio slider's thick glass panel.

"I told you. Someone's in there!" said a voice, which sounded clear through the glass.

Joshua crouched below the level of the kitchen island, quietly placing the pizza box on the floor. He'd screwed up big time. The neighbors had circled around to the deck. Now what?

"Josh! It's Mr. Aleman. Is that you in there?"

What were the odds that they'd go away if he just stayed silent? Probably not very good, but then again, what could the neighbors possibly do? There was no way they'd break in. Not a cop's house, even if they knew he wasn't home. Right? He wasn't sure. Now at least two of them were knocking on the glass door.

"We just want to get some information about what's going on out there! People are starting to migrate out of Indianapolis. The Cadys next door to you had a break-in. Three guys walked here from the west side of the city. Come on, Josh. We know you're in there."

His dad said not to trust anyone, but Aleman sounded reasonable enough. Agitated, but not crazy. He just didn't see them going away anytime soon.

"Hold on!" yelled Joshua, and the knocking stopped.

He stood up and tucked the back of his shirt between the pistol's grip and his body so he could easily grab it if things went wrong. Standing to the side of the wide patio door, he pulled the drawstrings, raising the blinds above his head, before flipping the deck lights on. He peered around the wall, seeing that they'd backed up to the deck's railing. Satisfied that they weren't trying to bust right into the house, he unlatched the glass door and pushed it open a few inches, realizing he'd forgotten to lower the security bar into place earlier. It shouldn't have budged at all. Another screwup on his part. What else had he forgotten? Deeper in the house, the alarm panel beeped twice, acknowledging that the door was open.

He recognized all of them right away with the light. Mr. Aleman nodded with a smile, holding both hands out in a gesture of neutrality. Mr. Roscoe stood in the middle with his arms crossed, a friendly enough look on his face. He lived on the other side of the Cadys and had probably been the one to call the police. The man on the left was Mr. Pavram. The Pavrams had introduced Joshua to Indian food a number of years back when his parents were barely still together—hosting them for dinner. It was the last time they did something like that as a family. Things had deteriorated at home soon after, and nothing was the same again.

"Good evening, Joshua," said Pavram. "Hope we didn't scare you."

"Sorry about hiding," said Joshua. "My dad was very specific about me staying out of sight."

"That's because your dad is a smart guy, Joshua," said Mr. Aleman. "Does he know what's happening?"

Feeling comfortable about the situation on the deck, Joshua opened the door several more inches.

"I just spoke with him. He really doesn't know what's going on, but it sounds like things are out of control up in Westfield. He really just wanted me to stay hidden in the basement until he got home."

"When is he coming back?" asked Roscoe. "We could use a law enforcement presence around here."

"He doesn't know. The department was hit hard by this flu bug thing, so he's pulling overtime," he said, stretching the truth a little.

"That's the thing we can't figure out. Everyone that works in Indianapolis is sick with something, but it's not the flu," said Aleman. "The only thing this bug has in common with the flu is a high fever and headache. I've Googled it. If this was a late season flu or, God forbid, a pandemic flu, the symptoms would include coughing, chills, body ache—all the usual stuff you feel when you're sick. This is something different."

"I guess. I don't know. My dad is just doing his job," said Joshua. "It sounds like a mess out there. What happened next door? I heard you say something about *these people.*"

"A group of three scumbags broke into the Cadys' house while they were eating dinner. Jimmied their patio slider latch," said Aleman. "Make sure you put up the security bar. That's how those assholes managed to break into the Cadys'. Just jiggled the damn latch, apparently."

"Is everyone all right?" said Joshua.

"Yeah. They ran upstairs with the kids and locked themselves into a bedroom while the guys tore the place apart. They didn't put up much of a fight when the police showed up. Lots of yelling, but that's about it. They said Indianapolis was like a scene out of the *Walking Dead.* I had to look that up. Zombie show."

Mr. Pavram spoke up. "We've watched it from the beginning. Completely depressing, but addictive."

Aleman and Roscoe gave him a funny look, which caused Joshua to laugh. He loved the show.

"What?" said Pavram, winking at Joshua. "I have to know what's going to happen with Rick. He's like one of the family at this point."

"I really have no idea what he's talking about," said Aleman, laughing along anyway.

Roscoe shook his head. "I'm trying to picture you and Mrs. Pavram watching a zombie show."

Pavram shook his head. "Oh, no. She won't watch. Too scary for her. I have to DVR it and stay up late."

They all shared a brief laugh until the gravity of the situation pulled them back to reality.

"Can you ask your dad to give me a call when he gets in?" said Aleman. "Having him around will give the neighborhood some peace of mind. Everyone is scared. Especially with people migrating out of Indianapolis."

"Sure," said Joshua. "Did the police take the people away?"

"Of course," said Aleman. "I mean...they drove away with the guys. Why?"

"I don't know. My dad made it sound like the police have their hands full with calls like this."

"Man, that's not good," said Roscoe.

"No. It's not," added Pavram. "If they can't incarcerate these kinds of violators, they'll probably just drive them to the town limits and shoo them away."

"I'm sure they'll do more than *shoo* them away," said Roscoe.

"I don't think so," said Pavram, sighing. "Zionsville is only a mile and a half west of here, and Westfield is a few blocks north."

"They wouldn't take them north," said Aleman. "My bet is they'll take them south."

"Maybe so, but where do you think the Westfield Police Department will take their violators?" said Pavram. "Carmel is south of Westfield. What comes around, stays around."

"Goes around," said Aleman.

"However you say it," said Pavram. "I think we might all need to take Joshua's father's advice and barricade ourselves inside."

"We're better off forming a neighborhood defense," said Aleman. "Safety in numbers. We all keep an eye out and spread the word if more people appear, so everyone has some warning. Then we call the police."

Joshua glanced back at his phone on the kitchen island. "My

phone lost cell service a few minutes ago. I couldn't get a text to go through either."

"What?" said Aleman, digging his phone out of his pants.

"The kid's right," said Pavram. "My phone says *SEARCHING*. That's not a good sign."

"I was talking to my dad when the call went dead. My phone said the same thing. *SEARCHING*."

"Shit. This is bad," said Roscoe. "I need to get home."

"Fuck," muttered Aleman. "Me too. Joshua, please ask your dad to stop by when he gets back. In the morning or something. He'll probably be wiped out from his shift. We'll make him breakfast. Seriously. You're invited, too, of course. We're going to need his help to keep the street together."

"I'll let him know," said Joshua. "Even though he's gonna be pissed at me for this."

"I'm sure he will, but we'll change his mind with a hearty breakfast. I appreciate your honesty. You're a good kid. Always have been," said Aleman. "We'll let you get back to hiding or whatever you were doing. Frozen pizza, perhaps?"

Joshua nodded. "Busted."

They all laughed for a few moments.

"Your secret is safe with us," said Aleman. "Make sure you install the security bar after you shut the door."

"I will," said Joshua. "Thank you. And sorry for hiding earlier."

"Sounds like we should all be doing the same until tomorrow morning," said Aleman.

The three men disappeared after stepping off the deck and out of the light's illumination arc. Joshua flipped the light switch, returning the backyard to darkness. He wondered if that was such a good idea, with burglars prowling the neighborhood, and turned the lights back on. He'd do the same with the front porch light, now that the neighborhood knew the house wasn't empty. He should have listened to his dad.

Chapter Twenty-One

David Olson stared at his phone, annoyed with the dropped call. He pressed redial, immediately getting *CALL FAILED*. Really? The word *SEARCHING* appeared at the top of the screen. He needed this like a hole in the head right now. His son was prancing around the house, making pizzas, attracting the entire neighborhood to their house, and now it looked like he was going back out on patrol.

Getting shot in the head while standing next to your partner, who also took a bullet, only got you a ten-minute break—after the paramedics finished bandaging your head. At least they sent him back to the station, where he could let his guard down for a while. He'd felt like a target in the Interceptor, even when the streets were empty and quiet.

What he really wanted to do was go home to his son. From what he guessed, there were hundreds, if not thousands of individual time bombs, like the crazy-wife shooter tonight, waiting to go off out there. David was rapidly approaching a serious decision point. Maybe he'd already reached it. Right now, he just wanted to talk to his son, and his phone was still screwed.

"Anyone else having phone issues?" he asked the half-filled briefing room.

Tired faces looked up, some of them already with phones in hand. The others dug through their pockets for their devices.

"This piece of shit just cut off a call to my husband," said Jody Price, an officer with a few more years on the force than David.

"Looks like it's searching for a cell tower."

"Mine did the same thing," said David. "The call failed when I tried to call my son back."

"I thought my flip phone finally crapped out on me," she said, shifting in her seat. "Your son's home alone?"

"Yeah. All alone on such a wonderful night," he said, not attempting to disguise his displeasure with that fact.

She shook her head. "You should be home with your kid."

"Isn't he a senior in high school?" grunted an officer slouched in his seat, arms folded and head rested against the back of the chair.

"Something like that," said David.

"Then he's fine," said Mitch Grimes, not moving any part of his body besides his mouth.

"You really think so?" said David. "I just got back from a call where a mother beat her husband half to death with a baseball bat, then turned it on her kid. She capped off the night by unloading a pistol on Bower and me."

"Then you have nothing to worry about," said Grimes.

"What do you mean by that?" said David, knowing exactly what he meant.

"I mean you don't have to worry about your wife."

"Fuck you, Mitch!" yelled David, abruptly getting up from his seat.

The other officer nearly fell out of his seat, trying to scramble to his feet.

"Take it easy! Both of you!" said Price, already on her feet. "We've got enough problems—out there. Sit the fuck down."

David reluctantly lowered himself, shaking his head and glaring at Grimes the whole time.

"We all have family at home, Dave. You're not the only one hanging on by a thread," said Grimes, taking his seat, but remaining upright and alert.

He was right. Everyone was in the same boat, walking the line between duty to the job and duty to home. Inevitably, each and every officer here would have to choose between the two. It wasn't a matter of *if*—more like *when*—and David planned on making that decision sooner than later. Until then, he planned on playing it even safer than before.

"Sorry, Mitch. This got me a little freaked out," said David, touching the bandage taped to his forehead.

"Just a little?" said Grimes. "You got shot in the fucking head."

They all shared a quick laugh.

"Yeah. I guess I did."

"My phone's screwed, too," said Grimes, raising his voice. "What the fuck is going on out there?"

Sergeant Jackson appeared in the briefing room doorway, carrying a clipboard and a phone. "I'll tell you what's going on. Nothing good."

"Thanks for the news flash, Sarge," said Price.

"It gets better," said Jackson, pulling a chair next to the podium normally used for shift briefings. "I hope you don't mind if I sit. It's either that or risk falling on my face. How is everyone feeling? Don't answer, David. By the way, Officer Bower is expected to make a full recovery."

"Back on the frontlines tomorrow?" said David.

"Very funny," said Jackson. "Not my fault that little scratch didn't qualify you for a hospital bed."

"Nine-millimeter scratch," said David.

"And we're thankful that's all it turned out to be," said Jackson. "Seriously."

"Sarge, I've been on for thirty-eight hours with no break," said Grimes.

"I'm pushing thirty hours," said Price.

The three other officers in the briefing room expressed similar sentiments. David suddenly felt a little guilty. He was just coming up on twelve hours—nothing compared to thirty.

"That's why I pulled the five of you in here, plus David. I can't put an officer that just got shot in the head back on patrol. That would make me look bad," said Jackson.

David laughed with the rest of the officers. It sounded like he had something different in mind for them, which was interesting.

"Don't get all laugh-happy yet. I got good news and bad news," said Jackson. "Bad news is that nobody is going home."

"Shit. You gotta be kidding me?" said Grimes.

"I wish I was," said the sergeant. "The good news is that you won't be going back out on patrol. Not for a while. Actually, I wasn't done with the bad news."

"You're killing us here," said Price.

"Turns out that some of the speculation about this being a flu pandemic must be true. The National Guard is setting up a quarantine perimeter around Indianapolis, using the 465 Interstate. They'll block all of the entrances, underpasses and overpasses, while patrolling the highway and some of the street areas around it. It's far from a perfect system, so the state will form a secondary containment line to grab anyone that manages to slip through the 465. Part of that secondary line cuts right through Westfield. Route 32."

"We're gonna have the National Guard running around here?" said Grimes.

"Don't knock it. We could use the help," said Price.

David stayed quiet. Something wasn't right about this. The flu pandemic was only part of the problem. A quarantine would do nothing to halt the epidemic of violence erupting for no apparent reason in homes across town. Or was it all connected, and the "flu pandemic" was something altogether different? Something government health officials were keeping quiet. The thought pushed him off the fence. He would head home to Joshua when the opportunity presented itself.

"It won't be the National Guard. They're focusing all of their resources on the 465 quarantine. This isn't confirmed yet, but I heard that a Brigade Combat Team from the 10th Mountain Division is on its way to the Grissom Air Reserve base up in Kokomo. I keep hearing midnight as an arrival time, but I'm not sure if that means arrival here or up at Grissom."

"Regular Army units?" said Grimes.

"That's what they're saying," said Jackson. "Hey, that's a good thing. They'll have a lot of experience with roadblocks and containment procedures. When they get here, I'm going to integrate each of you with whatever units they decide to place in Westfield. You'll help them identify vulnerable approach routes to Route 32 and keep me notified of anything that might impact our neighborhood patrols. Should be easy liaison work. I'd be shocked if you couldn't find time to catch up on some sleep."

"Do we have any information about rules of engagement? Stuff like that?" said David. "It's a pretty big deal to deploy military units like this. Who do they report to? Are they putting together field hospitals, too?"

"Dave, you know just as much as I do right now. I'm just trying to get ahead of this a little so we don't get blindsided when an infantry battalion shows up," said Jackson. "I'm sending all of you up to the Hamilton County fairgrounds. Everything for the county will be coordinated from there. A sheriff's department friend of mine said that's the focal point. FEMA. Homeland. CDC. 10th Mountain. They all have people there right now, trying to sort out this mess. I want you there to make sure they don't make more of a mess for us in Westfield."

"10th Mountain is already there?" said David.

"Maybe a half-dozen soldiers. Officers and enlisted," said Jackson.

David nodded. He was familiar with the concept. "It's an ADVON party."

"That's it. That's what he said," said Jackson.

"Advanced Echelon. The rest of the brigade won't be far behind," said David. "This is a serious combat unit, by the way. We can expect heavily armed vehicles, like uparmored HUMVEEs and MRAPs. They'll probably come with an aviation element, too. Black Hawk helicopters and Apaches. This isn't going to be a small presence."

"Well, it sounds like you're the man for the job. You know this stuff better than I do," said Jackson. "The head wrap might cause a few double takes, but it looks like we've found our head liaison. No pun intended."

David pretended to laugh, thinking about one thing. How the hell was he going to get out of this? He had no intention of getting roped into this any further. He might be able to get some answers about his ex-wife up in Noblesville, but the trade-off wouldn't be worth it. Even if he could find her, there was nothing he could do to help her. Time and time again tonight, he'd seen exactly what she'd likely become. A violent, raving lunatic. Her fate was in the county's hands, or whoever was in charge of this mess now. He suspected the federal government had taken control of the situation through some closed-door session of Congress or some kind of emergency executive order. He might never know.

What he did know was that the deployment of regular military units on U.S. soil represented a seismic shift in government response, from assistance to containment, and he had no intention of getting caught inside any kind of quarantine zone—regardless of whether he was wearing a badge. Local law enforcement might not even be recognized by federal military units.

He'd return home as quickly as possible, without drawing too much attention, and get Joshua past the Route 32 containment line before it became impassable. Preferably before the helicopters arrived. Helicopters would be the biggest problem. He knew the area well enough to slip through on foot, but he couldn't hide from thermal imaging sensors.

Jackson dismissed the group so they could clean up and grab a few minutes of downtime before heading out. While they filed out of the room, David approached Jackson with an idea.

"Do you want us to take two cars up?"

The sergeant winced. "I don't know if I can spare the vehicles."

"We could do one patrol car, so we look official, followed by a personal vehicle," said David. "We can use my pickup. Plenty of room to haul back some gear if the county's giving out goodies."

"Not a bad idea," said Jackson. "You're in charge of this little expedition. Make it happen."

"Roger that, Sergeant," said David.

Jackson focused on David's head for a second. "You really got lucky out there, didn't you?"

"That's what everyone keeps telling me," said David. "I'm starting to believe it."

"I wish I had enough ballistic helmets to go around," said Jackson. "I don't even have one for each car."

"Bower and I left it in the backseat. Figured we'd both take the same risk."

"Yeah. That's what everyone has been saying," said Jackson. "Maybe the army will loan us some helmets. We are on the front lines, after all."

"No doubt about that," said David. "Sergeant?"

"Yeah?"

"What are they going to do with people trying to get past the quarantine line?"

"I don't know for sure, but my same contact at county said there's been initial talk by the FEMA and CDC people about suitable locations for refugee and quarantine camps. This is some serious shit," said Jackson.

"No kidding," said David, nodding. "Well, I'll get the show on the road, so to speak."

"Make sure everyone takes a handheld," said Jackson. "Cell service is down. We're looking into that."

"We'll bring radios."

He let Jackson walk out of the room, lingering far enough behind to avoid getting caught up with the rest of the newly formed team. Price waited for him down the hallway. When everyone was out of sight, she spoke in a lowered voice.

"You're not going to the fairgrounds, are you?"

He shook his head. "I need to get home. Something is really off with all of this. Cell service is down. We have a combat brigade inbound at any moment. People are going crazy in their homes and trying to kill their own family members. And nothing we're being told holds water. Pandemic flu, my ass. I'm getting Joshua past that quarantine line before it's too late."

"How do you plan to get out of this liaison detail?" she said, sounding interested in joining him.

"Jackson wants us to take one police vehicle and one personal car up to Noblesville. I volunteered my pickup," said David.

"Well played."

"Thanks," he said. "What about you?"

"I think I'll ride shotgun in your pickup if that's all right with you," she said reluctantly. "Bill thinks we should pack up Ethan and head to Michigan to stay with his parents. You know my son is in a wheelchair."

"No. I know he has muscular dystrophy and had trouble walking, but I didn't know he was in a wheelchair now. Sorry," said David.

She shrugged her shoulders. "It is what it is. He can walk on his own a little bit, but he just recently crossed the line between getting around on his own two feet and needing a wheelchair. He's safer in the chair, but it complicates things."

"I imagine," said David. "Actually I can't."

"I had thought about sending Bill with Ethan right now, and I'd join them later," she said. "But now I'm wondering if this might be my last real opportunity to get out of here. Plus, I worry about Bill driving late at night with Ethan. We don't know if this rage virus is isolated to Indianapolis."

"Did you just say *rage virus?*"

"Yeah. That's what I think this is. Like rabies or something similar. I know it sounds crazy, but what other explanation is there? This isn't just a bunch of people getting freaked out about crowded hospitals and empty grocery store shelves like the news makes it out to be. People are trying to kill each other for no apparent reason, and they're making no secret of it. I've worked this job for twenty-one years, and I can count the number of public murders on this thumb," she said, sticking her thumb toward his face. "Until tonight. By the time the clock strikes twelve, I'm going to need to borrow a hand to keep count."

"A disease like that isn't normally contagious. Not wildly contagious, at least," said David.

"I have no idea. I just want to get the hell out of here," she said. "Get my son and husband out of here."

"All right," he said. "You live in Noblesville, right?"

She nodded. "I'm southeast of the town center, in a newer development close to 146th."

"Which side of 37?"

"East," she said, grimacing. "If you get me across the White River, I'll walk the rest of the way."

"I can probably get you farther than that. Would it help if I took you farther south on Allisonville Road?" said David. "Unless something changes, I'm headed in that direction anyway."

"I'd go all the way to 116th if I were you," said Price. "When we break off from the lead car, they'll report us immediately. You want to be as far away from Westfield as possible."

"I live a quarter mile from the Westfield border. They know where to find me. I'm hoping they have bigger fish to fry."

"Me too. I live pretty damn close to the fairground," she said. "I was excited by the idea of heading up there, until Jackson said the 10th Mountain Division was headed our way."

"It's going to get really crowded up there," he said.

"We're heading to Michigan as soon as I step through the door."

"Then that's it," said David, looking around at the station walls. "All of this for nothing, I guess."

"I have a feeling we've just seen the tip of the proverbial iceberg out there," said Price. "In forty-eight hours, nothing will be the same, and all of this will be gone anyway."

David didn't detect an ounce of exaggeration or drama in her voice. She really believed what she'd just said—and so did he.

Chapter Twenty-Two

Jack Harper scanned the road ahead of the Jeep, trying not to be lulled into complacency. Their departure from the neighborhood had miraculously gone down without incident. They'd seen a number of inexplicably bizarre things on the way out of the Broad Ripple area, but nothing immediately threatening.

The number of people outside surprised him, particularly given the ever-present sirens and increasingly frequent gunshots. His first instinct when the gunshots sounded closer was to go inside. He assumed that was pretty normal, but that didn't seem to be the case on the streets. People were everywhere, like they were headed to a block party or a street festival on Broad Ripple Avenue. Not only that, something felt off about many of them.

Some people walked sluggishly, like they were in a daze. Others walked fast, but with glitchy body movements. A good number lay on the ground near houses or sat curled up against trees and porches. Some just stood in place, displaying a wide variety of repetitive motions. They saw a few runners screaming wildly as they careened through yards and climbed over the hoods of cars.

None of it explained what he'd seen in their neighbor's backyard. That had been the depraved act of a lunatic. He didn't want to think about it. He especially didn't want to talk about it with Emma. Mercifully, she hadn't asked about it again. He had no words to describe what had happened to their dog. For now, it would have to remain unspoken. He needed to stay focused on the task at hand. Once they were on Interstate 65, cruising north at eighty miles per hour, he might have the mental bandwidth and the clarity to discuss it, but only if Emma wanted him to.

The traffic light down the street turned yellow, and Jack lightly applied the brake in anticipation of stopping.

"What are you doing?" said Emma.

"Stopping at the light. Why?"

"I think you should run this one," she said. "I don't like the look of this area."

Michigan Road had always looked pretty run-down along this stretch. The road presented one run-down strip mall after another, linked together by a vacant, dilapidated mega-store of some completely defunct brand. Jack couldn't remember the last time they had driven this way.

"I'd hate to get pulled over," said Jack.

"Are you kidding?" said Emma. "I'd love nothing more than to see a cop right now, even if it means a ticket."

"The police have been conspicuously absent from the streets," he said, speeding up. "Along with cars."

"It is close to eleven at night," she said. "But yeah. It's a bit creepy."

He cruised through the empty intersection, noticing a commotion in the gas station on the corner. About a half-dozen people, men and women both, had gathered around the front door of the station, a similar number of cars stopped at the pumps or pulled into the parking lot facing the door. Emma leaned over to check the fuel gauge.

"We have enough to make it all the way to my parents'. Barely," he said. "Plus the half gallon in the lawn mower can. I was planning on siphoning the gas out of your car, but—" He went quiet, realizing where this conversation might lead.

Fortunately, Emma either didn't catch on or purposely didn't pursue it.

"You were going to siphon gas?" she said, with a joking voice.

"Yeah. Is that so hard to imagine?" he said. "I'm a regular MacGyver."

"Not familiar with that one," she said. "What were you going to siphon the tank with?"

"I don't know. I was going to cut a length of garden hose," said Jack, squeezing her knee. "Any more questions?"

"I just never understood how that worked. Seems more like a good way to get a mouthful of gas than anything else," she said.

"I honestly couldn't tell you," he said. "It just does."

They drove in silence for a few more minutes before another traffic signal appeared in the distance. The light turned red as they got closer, a few cars speeding through the intersection. Headlights appeared beyond the intersection. Good. It was actually nice to finally see some signs of civilization. Maybe the whole world hadn't gone crazy after all.

"I think I need to stop for this one," he said.

"I don't know. If nothing's coming from either direction, I'd blow through it."

"What street are we coming up on?" said Jack.

"The last intersection was Seventy-First."

"We're not far at all from the 465. A couple minutes," said Jack. "The turnoff for Interstate 65 is a few miles beyond that. Keep your fingers crossed."

He slowed enough to watch for intersection traffic, seeing nothing that posed even the remotest risk for a collision, before continuing through the red light. The occupants of the car stopped at the light on the opposite side of the intersection watched them speed by.

"Looked like a family with kids," said Jack.

"It was. Not sure why they'd be heading south."

"Maybe things aren't that bad up here," he said.

"I hope not," she said.

Michigan Road turned into one continuous strip mall after Seventy-First Street, with a stoplight every five hundred feet. The street-side edges of the parking lots became more and more packed with cars and people as they drove north. The east-west roads bustled with a steady flow of traffic, making it impossible to run the traffic lights. Far ahead, a long stream of steady brake lights extended as far as he could see, appearing to take up both sides of the four-lane road. Jack glanced in the rearview mirror, noticing a few headlights farther south. Without knowing it until now, Jack and Emma appeared to be part of a slow dribble of traffic heading out of Indianapolis. Why more people weren't fleeing was kind of baffling.

"Looks like some kind of backup," said Emma.

"Yeah. I don't like the idea of getting caught up in that," said Jack. "We could be here all night if there's an accident blocking the road."

"I'm not familiar enough with this area to come up with a bypass," said Emma, tapping the phone in her hand. "And my phone is still useless."

"Don't bother with that anymore," said Jack. "I think I'll turn us around and take Seventy-Ninth. It has to connect with the 465 at some point."

"What about Eighty-Sixth Street? I know that would give us a lot of options."

"It looks like that traffic jam extends past Eighty-Sixth," said Jack. "It'll take a while to get to Eighty-Sixth. And I'm seeing a lot of people sitting in cars in the parking lots around here. Like they're waiting for something."

"I don't like this," said Emma.

"Me either. I'm pulling a U-turn," said Jack, easing the Jeep into a one-hundred-and-eighty-degree turn on Michigan Road.

They passed two cars headed north before arriving at the Seventy-Ninth Street traffic light. With no cross traffic in sight, he rolled through the red light onto the westbound road, not exactly certain it would lead directly to the 465. Logically, it had to intersect the interstate loop at some point not very far from here, but he couldn't guarantee Seventy-Ninth Street fed into an on-ramp. A few seconds later, the Jeep's headlights unveiled a loose line of cars blocking the road. He slammed on the brakes and shifted the Jeep into reverse.

"What's wrong!" said Emma, looking up from her phone.

"Roadblock," he said before speeding backward and turning the wheel.

Jack had them headed back toward Michigan Road within moments. He'd caught a glimpse of people lurking off the side of the road near the barricade while he backed up, but the scene had gone dark when he turned. He had no real idea what that had been about. Neighborhood blockade? Trap? Now what?

"What about the other side of Michigan?" said Emma.

He needed to think about it, but he didn't have much time, and there was no way he was slowing down until he got back to Michigan Road. It looked like some kind of setup to rob them. If it had been a neighborhood security checkpoint, the people would have been more visible.

"Uhhh...the numbered streets run in an east-west grid pattern. We're bound to hit a north-south road. I guess we turn north on something we recognize, like Towne or Ditch. The Chases live off Towne," he said.

"That's right," said Emma. "But Towne doesn't connect with 465."

"I know. I don't think any of the north-south roads between here and Meridian connect with it," said Jack. "I can't imagine Meridian being any better than what we saw up ahead. Our best bet is to work our way to the other side of the 465 on smaller roads. Find Route 421 again. From what I remember, we can take that all the way up to northern Indiana."

"I'd rather be on an interstate," said Emma.

"I'm pretty sure we can get to the interstate from Route 421," said Jack. "We can stop up in Carmel and buy a map. I was stupid thinking we could rely on our phones for navigation. Seemed like a sure thing."

Jack drove through the green light at the intersection, checking his rearview mirror to make sure none of the cars at the roadblock had followed him.

"Jack!" screamed his wife.

A hard jolt immediately followed, knocking the steering wheel out of his hands and slamming his chest into a rigid seatbelt. The Jeep spun ninety degrees to the right and came to a stop at the far edge of the intersection. Jack sat there for a few seconds, his foot jammed against the brake, before the gravity of what happened finally sank in. He glanced around, making sure they were far enough out of the intersection to avoid another collision, before taking the transmission out of gear and setting the emergency brake.

"You okay?" he said.

Emma nodded, a dazed look on her face. "I think I'm fine. Holy shit, that was close. They were coming right at me."

He opened his door to activate the roof light so he could look her over. "I'm so sorry, Emma, I didn't see them coming."

"They didn't have their headlights on," she said in a low voice.

She looked all right, which was what he expected. The vehicle that hit them had clipped the back of the Jeep, spinning them around violently without damaging the passenger compartment.

"You look all right," he said. "I'm going to check on the other car really quick."

Emma's eyes widened. "Jack!"

His car door flung open and a pair of hands tried to yank him out of the driver's seat; his seatbelt held him in place. He instinctively reached for the glove box to grab the revolver, but the violent tugging continued, preventing him. His wife leaned over the center console and grabbed his arm, trying to keep him in the seat.

"The gun," he hissed, feeling his body start to slip through the seatbelt.

Emma let go of him and opened the glove box, exposing the revolver's wooden grip.

"They have a gun!" yelled his attacker before lunging across his chest to get at the pistol. "I need some help!"

He slammed the man's head against the steering wheel, the horn blaring. The sweaty attacker clawed at Emma, pulling one of her hands away from the glove box before she grabbed the pistol. Jack pushed forward on the guy's head even harder before punching down on his flailing arms. The desperate move gave Emma enough time to grasp the pistol, which she pressed flat against the passenger door, out of the man's grasp.

Before he could tell her what to do, the passenger-door window shattered, the face of a hammer coming through. Jack squeezed a hand free to take the pistol from her, but the man pinned against the steering wheel started thrashing ferociously. In his peripheral vision, he saw the passenger door open.

"Stop! Just stop!" screamed Jack. "You can take—"

A deafening gunshot stopped everything. The guy between the steering wheel and Jack's shoulder reversed direction, tumbling backward out of the Jeep. Emma stopped screaming. The horn stopped blaring. He turned his head slowly, expecting to find his wife dead and a gun pointed in his face.

Instead, Emma sat flat against the passenger seat, staring forward; her hand extended straight out of the open car door—holding the pistol. A tendril of smoke rose from the weapon's shaking barrel. A figure lay flat on its back beyond the door, one of its feet twitching. Jack reached over her and pulled her arm inside the Jeep, gently taking the pistol out of her hand. She started to look toward the body, but he tilted her face back.

"You don't need to look," said Jack, then leaned across her lap and pulled her door shut.

A loud bellow erupted outside the Jeep, followed by screaming. "What have you done! What have you done to my boy!"

Jack glanced over his shoulder to see a shadow cross behind the Jeep.

"We need to go, Emma," he said, putting the pistol back in the glove box, but leaving it open.

He released the emergency brake and shifted into first gear, easing his foot off the clutch while pressing the accelerator. The Jeep barely moved, feeling anchored to the street. The damage done by the crash had been far worse than he'd initially thought. Shit. Now they had a massive problem. Jack scanned the intersection, seeing a number of people approaching the accident scene. He tried to drive the Jeep again, getting little response. The rear tire must be totaled, along with the rear axle. The Wrangler was a rear-wheel-drive vehicle—unless he put it in four-wheel drive!

Jack gripped the smaller drive stick next to the manual transmission and shifted it from two-wheel drive (2WD) to four-wheel low (4WL). He was rewarded with more forward motion when he hit the accelerator, but it was clear that he was just dragging the rear tires at this point.

"Fuck!" he yelled, hitting the steering wheel. "We have to leave the Jeep behind."

He engaged the emergency brake and yanked the stick out of gear.

"What?" said Emma.

"Get your pack, and let's go. Right now," he said, grabbing her before she opened the door. "Wait."

He took the pistol out of the glove box and opened his door, stepping onto the street. The crowd wandering toward them from the Marathon station on the corner stopped when he rushed around the front of the Jeep—presumably having noticed the pistol. Jack swiftly moved up the passenger side, opening the door for Emma. The man that had moments ago tried to pull him from the Jeep and beat him to death was on his knees next to the figure lying on the street—crying.

"Don't look," he whispered to Emma through the broken window. "Get your pack and stand in front of the Jeep."

She nodded and got out of the Jeep, opening the back passenger door while he put himself between Emma and the remaining attacker.

"What about the rest of the stuff? The water. Food," she said.

"We have everything we need for now in the packs," he said over his shoulder.

The man looked up at him. "You killed my son. And my wife."

"Your son tried to kill my wife with a hammer. You tried to pull me from the Jeep," said Jack. "You ran a red light and hit me."

"I never saw you."

"You didn't have your lights on," said Jack.

"No. You burned through a red light and killed my wife."

"What are you talking about?"

The man didn't answer. Instead, he pointed north, past the Jeep. Jack walked to the back of the vehicle, instantly seeing what had happened. The sedan that had hit them sat facing the Marathon station, forty-five degrees off from its original direction. A dark lump lay several feet in front of it, bent at an unnatural angle. Jack looked back at the man, who hadn't moved.

"You hit me," said Jack, wondering if that was true.

He'd been so panicked after fleeing the roadblock—maybe he'd made a mistake. No. The light was green. He was sure of it. Or was he?

"You killed everything I had in the world," the man said, lifting his head. "I should kill you."

Jack didn't know how to respond. Regardless of who was to blame, the guy had lost his wife and son—within the span of minutes. Arguing blame was pointless.

"Does your car still work?" said Jack.

"What does that matter?"

"Saint Vincent Hospital is a few blocks away," said Jack, pointing down Seventy-Ninth Street. "You take this road and make your first left. The hospital is on the right. They have a level-one trauma center. Get them over there. You never know."

"My son has a bullet hole in his forehead," said the man. "My wife's neck is bent at a ninety-degree angle. No hospital is going to fix them."

Jack started backing up, watching him closely. When the man put his hands on the street and pushed himself off his knees, into a crouch—he knew what would happen next. He cocked the pistol's hammer, keeping the weapon by his side, and stood next to the open rear passenger door. He didn't have to wait long. The man charged him, head down, moving way faster than he had anticipated.

He brought the weapon up, one hand instinctively wrapping around the other on the wooden pistol grip. The pistol bucked forcefully in his hands. In the dim red glow cast by the traffic light, he didn't wait to see if the first bullet connected. He brought the pistol back on target and pressed the trigger again, better prepared for the recoil this time. Jack fired the weapon two more times in rapid succession until the man careened into the rear corner of the Jeep and slumped to the street—groaning.

"What did I do?" muttered Jack, the pistol still pointing at the motionless heap.

"Jack, we need to go," said Emma. "People are closing in on us."

Jack slipped his free hand through the shoulder strap of the backpack waiting for him on the backseat and hiked the overloaded pack onto his shoulder. He tucked the pistol into his front pants pocket before sliding his other arm through the remaining strap and tightening the pack's retention system. With the pistol back in his hand, he joined Emma in front of the Jeep's hood. A quick glance around confirmed his wife's concern. Several groups of people edged closer, some yelling out to them.

"Did you get the bullets?" she said.

"Shit. They're still in the glove box," he said, returning to the front passenger door.

He grabbed the small box of .38 Special ammunition and dumped the rounds on the front seat, quickly stuffing them in his pocket.

"Start walking," said Jack.

They didn't make it far before the yelling turned overtly hostile.

"You can't just shoot people like that and leave!" said someone in the group approaching from the Marathon station.

"Where the fuck do you think you're going?" yelled another.

"They got some serious supplies!" he heard behind them, looking back to see a small cluster of people peering into the back of the Jeep.

"What did they take with them!"

Jack urged Emma forward, keeping a close eye on the Marathon station group. They were the closest and could easily take him down. He had two bullets left in the gun and didn't dare try to reload in front of them. At least he thought he had two bullets left. He really had no idea how many he had fired.

"How many bullets did I fire?" he whispered.

"I think three," she said.

"Let's pick up the pace," he said. "Can you jog with that on? Just for a little bit?"

"Do I have a choice?"

"Not really. We need to get as far away as possible from this intersection."

"I'll be fine," she said, gripping his arm. "That guy is getting a little close."

Jack pointed the pistol at a twentysomething, short-haired guy that had broken out of the Marathon station pack.

"Don't point that thing at me," said the guy.

"Then step the fuck back," said Jack. "And stay the fuck back."

His words had an immediate effect.

"Ready?" he whispered in Emma's ear.

She nodded, and they picked up the pace, though it hardly qualified as jogging. The packs weighed them down significantly. They'd rushed out of the house so quickly, he hadn't taken the time to sort through any of their gear, and they'd stuffed some of the food cans into the exterior pockets. Not the best idea, but it was easy food they didn't have to cook. They had some dehydrated camping food in each pack, but he hadn't inventoried the packs since their last backcountry hiking trip—last fall.

"This sucks," she said.

"I know. We'll have to rearrange the packs and ditch some of this crap after we get the hell out of here," he said, and guided her to the left. "Let's walk on the shoulder so we can get off the road quickly if we need to."

"Looks like nobody is following us," she said, slowing down a little.

He looked over his shoulder and saw a large crowd gathered around the Jeep, but no figures headed west. The stretch of road under the Harpers' feet was dark, but he still wanted to put a lot more distance between them and the intersection before stopping.

"We have to keep going," he said.

"I know," she said.

They fast-walked silently, breathing heavily and grunting, for about ten minutes before Jack decided it was safe for them to take a break to reorganize their gear. The traffic light behind them was no longer visible, and he could see a blinking red light in the distance ahead of them, which might be one of the roads they could take into Carmel.

"I think we can stop now," he said, dropping his pack onto the side of the road.

"This shouldn't be that hard," said Emma, doing the same. "We've hiked from sunup to sundown before, up and down hills."

"It's not the packs or the jogging," said Jack. "It's what happened back there. Like a giant shot of adrenaline. Let's get back from the road."

Jack grabbed both of their packs and guided them across a shallow sloping, empty drainage ditch to a thick constellation of bushes a third of the way up the yard from a dark house. He didn't see any signs of life in the one-story home, but he picked a spot between the bushes that gave them cover in every direction. He set the packs on the ground and lay down next to Emma, who had already flattened herself on the prickly, pine needle dirt.

"I just want to lie here for a few minutes and not think about any of this," she said.

"So do I," he said, taking her hand in his.

Jack lay there with her, staring up at patches of the night sky visible between the dense tree canopies—unable to shake any of the terrifying images he'd seen over the past hour.

Chapter Twenty-Three

Dr. Chang sat at a stone table on the patio with his laptop open, making annotations on a paper map with a pencil. Facing the back of his house so the patio lights wouldn't cast a shadow over his work, he added San Diego to the growing list of outbreak cities. When cellular service and his home's Internet connection had failed earlier in the evening, he'd retrieved his satellite phone and mobile hotspot rig from the basement survival station and set up a satellite Wi-Fi connection. He was back to work in no time, connecting the insidious dots as they appeared.

He'd uncovered a second wave of outbreaks, using a concentrated string of keyword searches on dozens of search engines. Finding the news had been tedious work, since the top search engine sites had been systematically scrubbed of reports related to the outbreaks. He caught a few digital sniffs on some of the more obscure search engines, piecing together a disturbing trend.

More than a dozen major cities had reported flu outbreaks over the past twenty-four hours, mostly confined to high-crime areas like the Southside of Chicago, southern Atlanta or East Los Angeles. The affected geographic zones around San Diego conformed to this analysis. National City and Chula Vista, two cities bordering San Diego to the south, had been the epicenter of reports coming out of the area.

He examined the map, which he'd torn out of an unused road atlas and taped back together. Beyond the previously identified

Midwest cluster, he strongly suspected similar outbreaks in parts of Chicago, San Francisco, San Diego, Los Angeles, Boston, Atlanta, Denver, Philadelphia, Hartford and Seattle based on available local reports. From a big-picture, geographic perspective, no obvious pattern like the Midwest cluster jumped out at him. If only he could get in touch with Stan or Christine to discuss this. One thing was certain—they were staring down the barrel at a bioweapons attack. The conclusion was inescapable.

Chang surfed back to Stan Greenberg's Facebook page more out of habit than hope. He had Christine's page open in a tab as well. He didn't know why. Neither of them could be classified as prolific Facebook users. Most of their activity consisted of garden-variety family posts. He took a quick look at Stan's page, seeing the post about the Greenberg family's annual Outer Banks gathering for the thirtieth time. He was about to shut the tab, when he noticed something different. A misspelling in the first sentence.

Certain that it hadn't been there earlier, Chang clicked "read more" to expand the post, which he admittedly hadn't bothered to do before, because Stan had a tendency to ramble. He read the entire post, finding fifteen mistakes, which was very unlike his friend. Staring at the mistakes a little longer, he grinned.

"Can't be that easy," he muttered, pulling a scratch pad in front of him.

He wrote the numbers 0 through 9 in order, followed by the letters A through I beneath each corresponding number. It was possibly the simplest cypher imaginable, which left him with little hope. Greenberg would get more complicated than this. Right? Chang ran the cypher, coming up with a numeric string he recognized to be a satellite phone number. 8816 was the Iridium prefix. Unbelievable.

Fingers trembling, he keyed the digits into the phone and pressed SEND, hoping he wasn't too late.

"Took you long enough, Gene," said a familiar voice. "I thought they might have grabbed you already."

"You picked one hell of a place to hide your message," said

Chang. "I can't imagine anyone reads your full-page vacation rundowns. No offense."

"None taken. That's why I put it there," said Greenberg, pausing long enough that Chang thought the connection had been severed. "Great to hear your voice, Gene. I can't even begin to tell you."

"Where do we even begin, Stan? I'm at a complete loss. This is unmistakably a bioweapons attack."

"I concur," said Greenberg matter-of-factly. "The coordinated appearance and widespread nature of the attack suggests a state-sponsored attack. It's too sophisticated to be anything else."

"I assume you have an idea who's behind this?"

"I did—until early this morning," said Greenberg. "Turns out Ockham's razor can be misleading, particularly if you don't know most of the story."

"This is related to Monchegorsk," said Chang.

"That's what I thought, and in a sense, it is related—indirectly," said Greenberg. "This isn't the Russians or one of their proxies. Frankly, I'm not sure I believe the information in my possession, though it would certainly explain things."

"Inside job?"

"That's what my new friends say," said Greenberg.

"Where are you, Stan?" said Chang.

"I honestly have no idea," said Greenberg. "Forest and mountains all around. That's about all I know, or I'm allowed to say."

"Who are these new friends?" said Chang, growing less and less comfortable with the call by the second.

"I guess I shouldn't call them friends, yet. The jury is still out," said Greenberg. "They managed to thwart my kidnapping this morning, though I suppose it could be the other way around. Hard to say."

"How can you trust them?"

"I don't really have a choice at this point," said Greenberg. "Where did you manage to hide? Don't tell me the actual location."

"I didn't really hide, Stan," said Chang. "I mean, I'm not at my apartment, but this place isn't exactly a secret."

He heard some hushed voices in the background of the call.

"Gene, you need to get out of there. Anyone with even the slightest research-side knowledge of the Zulu virus has been taken out of circulation, as my friends put it."

"What does that mean?" said Chang. "I've never heard of the Zulu virus."

"I assume you sent me a DNA snapshot of it this morning," said Greenberg. "A modified version most likely."

"HSV1 with indeterminate modifications. I left the lab as soon as I confirmed it. I wanted to get out of the city," said Chang.

"I don't blame you," said Greenberg. "Based on what I know about the virus, the disaster unfolding in Indianapolis will reach a tipping point tonight or tomorrow, and only get worse from there. Do you know about the other cities?"

"I put together a map based on information blackouts—" started Chang.

"I told them you were clever," interrupted Greenberg.

"Right. The Midwest was hit hard, and it's starting to show up in larger cities," said Chang. "I had to use a satellite data link. They cut cell service and Internet."

"Of course they did. Did you send the DNA snapshot to anyone else?"

Chang wasn't sure he should answer that question. He still had no idea if the group that "rescued" Greenberg was friend or foe. It was safer for everyone involved to assume the worst until proven otherwise. He must have paused for too long.

"I understand why you'd be hesitant to answer that," said Greenberg. "Here's the thing, and I don't know how to say this without just saying it. Christine left me a text message this morning. A single word. *RUN*. I haven't heard from her since."

"She might have gotten away, like you," said Chang, careful not to confirm whether he'd sent her an email.

"Let's hope for the best, but assume the worst. If she's fallen into the wrong hands, your call may have been intercepted," said Greenberg.

"I didn't call until late in the morning."

"Well, then maybe there's still hope. They may have disabled her phone by then to prevent it from being tracked."

"How is that hopeful?"

"Hopeful for you. I'm not optimistic about Christine, and neither are my new acquaintances," said Greenberg. "I'd get as far away from your current location as possible."

"Then what?" said Chang. "Where do I go?"

"Now might be a good time to take your plane and head to Canada," said Greenberg. "Explain your situation and ask for asylum. Give them the DNA data you sent to Edgewood, along with a file I'm about to upload. Everything you ever wanted to know about Monchegorsk, Russia, but were afraid to ask."

"Stan, I don't have the data with me," said Chang.

"What do you mean?"

"I mean I didn't smuggle it out of the lab," said Chang. "Too risky."

"Shit. This isn't good," said Greenberg.

"There's no shortage of samples available," said Chang. "Not to be flippant about it."

"True, but I suspect that research scientists familiar enough with HSV1 to make the kind of assessment you made this morning will be in short supply soon. Nobody goes through this much trouble to let a few pesky scientists stand in the way."

"Is that you talking or your new friends?"

"Both," said Greenberg. "And speaking of these friends, they really think you should be on your way. Call me using this number when you're safe. Hopefully out of the country."

"You might want to take your Facebook post down," said Chang.

"Already done."

He checked his laptop screen, immediately noticing the change.

"Slick," said Chang. "Almost too slick."

"They're serious about getting their hands on that data and someone that can explain it," said Greenberg.

"Have you told them what I do for NevoTech?"

Chang continuously apprised Stan of his progress on NT-HSE893, the HSV1 vaccine, which had been one of the main reasons for their initial partnership. The government was interested in a rapidly deployable treatment regimen to counter an HSV1-based bioweapon, and NevoTech was interested in selling a once-monthly booster drug to hundreds of millions of customers worldwide. It represented a win-win situation for the population, and he felt good about his work on the vaccine.

"I have," said Greenberg. "They said it's too late at this point. Nothing can stop this cataclysm. My file should be available for download through your sat phone. Don't waste your time reading it now. Get somewhere safe and call me."

With the call disconnected, he let Stan's words sink in. Cataclysm might be an understatement. This would be more like an apocalypse. Millions of Americans were likely infected, with no hope of recovery—their humanity stripped away slowly by the disease—until nothing was left.

Chapter Twenty-Four

Eric Larsen woke from a sound sleep, his brain slow to register the insistent rapping at his door. He peeked at the digital alarm clock next to his bed. **11:29 PM**. The knocking continued. *Another mobility drill. Wonderful.* Before he could form the words to answer his staccato summons, the door flung inward, a set of keys dangling from its knob. Larsen covered his eyes with a hand; the hallway's blazing lights silhouetted the figure in the doorway.

"Don't hit the lights, please," said Larsen.

The room's overhead lights flickered momentarily before bathing the room in a dull, institutional fluorescent glow.

"Thanks," he muttered, reaching for the lamp on his nightstand. "Kill the lights. I got it."

"No can do," said the man they called the *grim reaper*. "The colonel wants all teams dressed and assembled in the pit within five. First bird rolls in twenty-five minutes."

Right after this drill, he'd remove the translucent plastic ceiling panels and yank the light tubes. Larsen had made that same promise before, always opting for sleep instead. He apparently hated losing sleep more than the lights.

"Got it," said Larsen.

Larsen's feet hit the thinly carpeted floor, his hands reaching for the pair of tactical cargo pants crumpled on the chair next to the nightstand. With his pants secure, he rushed into the hallway, knocking into Laura Ragan. Ragan held firm, bouncing him into the doorframe. Somehow she was already dressed, complete with drop holster.

"Walk much?" she said, brushing past him. "And put a shirt on. You know—so you sort of look like a team leader."

"Didn't your mom teach you not to run inside?" he said, smirking.

Ragan mumbled an obscenity about his mother and shook her head while knocking on one of her teammates' doors. She was all business with Larsen, if not a little hostile, which suited him fine. He wasn't here to get chummy with anyone. He was here to collect an easy, oversized paycheck that had fallen into his lap.

Almost too easy. One month locked down in the middle of nowhere Indiana, followed by a few days of sustainment training. Then one month off with his wife and baby daughter, playing outdoors in the Colorado Springs area. He'd have the house paid off in three years, plus enough money in savings to pay for his daughter's college. Not a bad gig at all, as long as one of these odd-hour shakedowns didn't turn out to be the real thing. The Department of Homeland Security had created the unit with the worst-case scenario in mind. If one of their drills turned out to be real, something big and bad had gone down on U.S. soil.

Larsen walked calmly to the room next to his and pounded on the door. A few seconds later, the door opened to reveal a fully dressed, towering, muscular black guy. Randy Dixon, the team's second in command, took one look around and shook his head.

"Does everyone but me sleep in their clothes?" said Larsen.

"Fly's down, man," said Dixon, nodding at his pants. "How long and where?"

"The pit. Four and a half minutes," said Larsen, adjusting his zipper status. "I'll wake Peck. You get Brennan. Meet at the entrance to the southern stairwell in three."

"Got it," said Dixon.

Four minutes and twenty-seven seconds later, Larsen's team filed into the sunken auditorium and sat in the closest empty row to the front—behind the rest of the unit. A few dozen members of the unit watched them settle in, disapproving eye rolls and head shakes heralding their arrival. Larsen raised his hand in front of his face, glancing at his watch with exaggerated interest before lowering it and mouthing, "Fuck you," to his audience. He had zero patience for these poseurs.

The man standing in the shadows next to the auditorium screen moved forward into the light. Warren Cooper, aka the colonel, pressed the keyboard on the computer station next to him. He was about as real a colonel as the bearded gentleman featured on the side of a KFC bucket. An imaginary title bestowed upon him by his staff, from what Larsen guessed. It didn't really matter. He was the senior Department of Homeland Security official at the compound. Everyone's boss.

The floor-to-ceiling screen next to Cooper illuminated, displaying the aircraft manifests. Shit. It was going to be a long day. A Cat One alert put the entire unit in the air. Drill or no drill, it was a big fucking deal.

"There you have it. Category One deployment," said Cooper. "I want to report wheels up on our last bird within twenty minutes. Sooner if possible."

"Any indication if this is a drill?" said one of the team leaders, who had moments ago cast him a condescending look.

Larsen couldn't resist. The guy had been an asshole from day one. "What do you think, Ochoa?"

Ochoa's entire team cast murderous glares at him as muffled laughter filled the auditorium. Cooper pressed onward like the verbal exchange hadn't occurred.

"Get to your aircraft. Mission details will be delivered before the aircraft start to taxi. Good luck. God speed. Hope to see you all back here shortly."

Cooper said the same thing every time, betraying nothing. A fact some of his colleagues appeared unwilling or unable to grasp. In the seven months Blue Team had spent in active status on the base, they had also done the same thing—every fucking time—until they received their mission packets. Zero variation.

Most of the time, the packet instructions told them to debark the aircraft and report back to the auditorium. Drill completed. Sometimes, the initial instructions outlined their kit requirements, and the aircraft took to the sky. They'd change into the required gear, still unaware of their detailed mission parameters, and wait for the aircraft commander's permission to open the next set of instructions. Typically, those instructions informed him that the aircraft was headed back to Grissom Air Reserve Base for landing and debark. Twice in his career with the unit, they had been instructed to egress from the aircraft in flight, over the airbase, putting their wingsuit and parachuting skills to the test.

He studied the screen for a few seconds while the rest of the room scrambled for the exit to the tarmac. Zombie, his team's call sign, was manifested with Specter, Banshee and Vampire on aircraft three. Wonderful. Specter was Ragan's team, and Vampire was Ochoa's. Two of his biggest fans. At least they'd have plenty of room to stay out of each other's way. They'd been assigned to one of the C-130Es.

Larsen slowly got up from his seat, making eye contact with Ochoa, who was bunched up with the rest of the teams trying to squeeze through the double doorway. The team leader sneered, clearly on the verge of spewing another ill-conceived comment or insult.

"Take your time, Larsen," said Ochoa.

"Hurry up and wait. Takes less than a minute to get to the flight line," said Larsen, tapping his watch. "Keep my seat warm if you don't mind."

"I'll take a dump in your seat! That'll keep it warm!"

Ochoa and his team laughed, a few of them adding that they'd warm up all of Larsen's team's seats.

"The C-130 has sixty-four seats. I count sixteen of us on the manifest. How many shits are you planning to take?"

Everyone inside the auditorium started to laugh, including Cooper.

"You can go fuck yourself!" blurted Ochoa. "We're all wondering why the fuck you're even here."

"Because someone has to check your math from time to time,"

said Larsen before turning to his own team.

"You better watch your shit!" yelled Ochoa.

The guy had horrible impulse control, which was probably why he got booted from the Dallas PD. Actually, he didn't get kicked off the force. Just suspended—for the third time in his five-year tenure as a patrol officer. Larsen guessed he'd landed the job here because of his brief stint with Dallas SWAT. Everyone here had some kind of paramilitary experience.

"I'll start watching mine when you start counting yours," said Larsen. "Correctly."

Ochoa's half-cocked response got lost in the laughter.

"You enjoying yourself?" said Dixon.

"Not really, but he tees himself up—and he's a dickhead."

"We *all* have to live with that dickhead, and his disciples."

"Very true," said Larsen. "Sorry for stirring him up. Everyone else good?"

Jennifer Brennan gave him a thumbs-up. She still looked half-asleep, which was a good thing considering the fight he had just picked. She and Ochoa most definitely didn't mix. Brennan had "gently" kicked him in the testicles during a volleyball match after he got a little too gropey with her along the net. She didn't take shit from anyone, which made her a good fit with Larsen's less demanding leadership style. He assumed that was why he hadn't been kicked in the balls—yet.

The fourth member of the team, James Peck, was a different story altogether. He presented an alert, but disinterested look—like always. It was no secret that Peck wanted to transfer to a different team. The disapproval heaped on Larsen by the other team leaders got under his skin.

Unfortunately for both of them, Peck's skillset as the team's communications and technology specialist was the most difficult and expensive to replace. Unless another ComTec from the unit was willing to swap places, the only way he could get off the team was to resign, or get Larsen fired. He kept a constant eye on Peck. The former Ranger had started to hang out with the likes of Ochoa and other prominent haters, who undoubtedly encouraged the divide.

"You good, Peck?" said Dixon.

"I'm here," said Peck before shuffling away.

His team filed out of the auditorium last, entering a long, well-lit corridor resembling a school hallway. Metal doors stenciled with team names flanked each side. Each room served as an individualized team staging and preparation area, mostly used for regularly scheduled training missions and team meetings. All of the equipment and gear cases they would find in their assigned aircraft had been packed in these rooms.

The deep buzz of powerful turboprop engines reverberated inside the cinder-block structure, intensifying as they approached the open door to the airfield tarmac. When the team ahead of them vanished into the darkness beyond the door, leaving them alone inside the hallway, Larsen was hit by the bizarre urge to turn back. The feeling passed just as quickly, but it was the first time he'd ever felt that way before. He'd never experienced the proverbial "bad feeling" about any operation or mission before, even with the SEALs. He let out a quick laugh.

"What's up?" said Dixon.

Larsen wasn't one of those superstitious pre-mission ritual types at all, but he had no intention of informing his team "he had a bad feeling about this one."

"Nothing. Just thinking how much it would piss off Ochoa and Ragan if we walked to the aircraft," said Larsen.

Peck shot him a disapproving look, which almost convinced Larsen to do it. Instead, he stepped onto the shadowy tarmac and broke into a jog toward the third aircraft in the line of darkened behemoths.

Chapter Twenty-Five

Emma Harper dropped her lightened backpack on the gravel next to the road and took a few deep breaths. They had decided to forego turning north on Township Road, the first intersection they reached after the car accident, because they saw nothing but brake lights ahead—again. The last thing they wanted to do was wade through more of the ugly humanity they'd so far encountered on their short journey. The decision made sense, but it added distance to their trip, and Jack seemed hell-bent on making up the time by moving as fast as possible.

She didn't mind the pace. The sooner they got out of Indianapolis, the better, but there was no way they could keep this speed going for too much longer. Jack assured her they would only have to keep moving like this for another hour at most. They were almost out of the mayhem, he said, though she wasn't altogether convinced. Interstate 465 was their goal.

For some reason, they viewed the six-lane ring road around the city as a perceived barrier of safety. Probably because everyone did. The city on the other side of 465 was one of the safest communities in the country, aggressively patrolled by a robust police force vested in keeping the premier suburb safe from the expanding drug violence in Indianapolis.

Carmel, Indiana, was one of those places where upwardly mobile families with young kids moved for *better schools* and *home owners association* guaranteed property values. It was where you moved when you grew out of walking to the closest bar and grabbing a drink on the patio after work—on a Wednesday. They weren't that grown up yet. Not even close. But right now, all she wanted to do was get across the 465 and set foot in that holy Mecca of grown-ups.

"This looks better," she said, staring up Ditch Road.

Brake lights illuminated the night ahead, but not in the same concentration as either of the previous two roads. Jack put his arm around her and pulled her close, just breathing her in. She loved when he did that. No words. Just the love of her life taking it all in.

"Don't breathe too deeply. I didn't wash my hair today," she said.

He laughed. "I don't care. You always smell like you under those expensive haircare products. That's all I'm after. You."

"I think I need you a little more focused on the task at hand here," she said, quickly kissing his cheek.

"I suppose," said Jack, placing his pack on the ground next to hers. "How are you doing?"

Emma wasn't ready for this conversation. She wasn't sure why, but it didn't feel right. It wasn't that she needed more time to digest what had happened at the intersection, or what might have happened to their dog. Her focus was simply somewhere else. Like about a mile north of here, far enough away from Indianapolis to feel somewhat safe.

"I'll be doing a lot better when we get out of here," she said before taking a long sip of water from the CamelBak hose extending from one of the pouches on her backpack.

Jack nodded, his face grim but understanding in the sparse light of the half-moon night. "We'll be inside Carmel within thirty minutes."

"If they let us in."

"I don't think that's going to be a problem," said Jack.

She wasn't sure. Why were there traffic jams on every northbound road? Street traffic was negligible. Something wasn't right up ahead.

"Let's just take it slow until we know," she said. "And keep that pistol completely hidden."

Jack had quietly and discreetly reloaded the revolver during their brief stop to rearrange the backpacks. She'd let him do it without saying anything, appreciating the gift of silence. Neither of them wanted to talk about what had just happened. On top of that, they'd had more pressing business—cutting down on the weight of the contents of their backpacks.

Since it was seventy-eight degrees and muggy, they'd decided to ditch the sleeping bags and stick with the waterproof bivy sacks. Each pack contained a fleece liner and a pair of thermal underwear pants, which would keep them warm enough. They also ditched the tent, which had been in Jack's pack. He'd taken most of the canned food in exchange. Both of them had discarded most of the spare clothing stuffed in the packs, retaining socks and underwear. They'd retained the basics. Water filter, basic first aid kits, spare socks and food. Sufficient to get them far enough to call Jack's parents.

They drank water and rested for a few minutes before resuming the march north. Halfway to the intersection of Ditch Road and Eighty-Sixth Street, Jack stopped without warning, grabbing her arm.

"Is that a military vehicle?" he said.

"I can't see that far. You have the binoculars in your pack," said Emma, stepping behind him and patting his backpack. "One of these pouches. Where am I looking?"

"Right side," he said, turning his body to make it easier for her.

Emma unzipped the pouch and removed a small pair of binoculars, scanning the intersection. She couldn't be sure, but it looked like a Humvee sitting under the traffic light on the near side of Eighty-Sixth Street, big machine gun and all. Things must be getting really bad in the city.

"I think it's a Humvee," she said, handing him the binoculars. "Maybe we should avoid the intersection and cut through one of the neighborhoods we've passed."

"What's to say it's any different here than in our neighborhood?" he said. "I feel better in the open."

Jack was right. The neighborhoods would be darker, with too many hiding places. They were way more exposed on the main streets, but that worked both ways. Nothing could sneak up on them. Emma just didn't like the idea of getting too close to those machine guns. She knew logically that they posed her no threat under these circumstances. They probably weren't even loaded. Still, just seeing one deployed on a street in her city gave her a sinking feeling.

"I agree," she said. "I still think we should avoid the Humvee."

"They might have some information," he said.

"I don't want to get caught up in anything. That's all I'm saying," she said, adjusting her backpack straps. "Ready?"

"Ready," he said, taking a few steps ahead of her.

They'd walked a few paces apart since lightening the backpacks, Jack up front, with Emma trailing. This allowed Emma to focus on watching their backs while Jack focused on everything ahead of them. She had no idea if it really made a difference, but Jack had rightly pointed out that you didn't see soldiers patrolling side by side, holding hands.

As the intersection drew closer, their hopes of an easy walk into Carmel drifted further away. The cars lined up on the road were blocked by the Humvee, unable to turn onto Eighty-Sixth Street. A larger military vehicle resembling a truck blocked Ditch Road past the intersection, mostly obscured by the darkness. Soldiers had formed a rough perimeter around the road junction, mingling with pedestrians. The whole affair looked harmless enough, but from a distance, it was clear that the soldiers had orders to keep vehicle and foot traffic from heading north.

The sound of a megaphone echoed off the strip mall storefronts as they got closer. Emma couldn't make out the words, but it didn't sound like the kind of repetitive yelling you heard at a street protest. Had to be the soldiers giving directions or passing along information.

"Looks like we can get close enough to figure out what's happening, without getting too close," she said.

Jack mumbled something before raising the binoculars. A few moments later, he lowered them and shook his head.

"I think they're blocking Ditch Road," said Jack. "To all traffic. Shit."

"We'll find another way," said Emma. "They can't wall off the city. There aren't enough soldiers to guard the entire 465."

Her husband nodded. "Let's get close enough to hear what they have to say. Figure it out from there."

Half of the cars had pulled into the opposing lane and driven past them by the time they reached the outskirts of the blockade. They wandered off the street and into a mostly empty CVS parking lot to listen to the soldier with the megaphone. Clusters of people and families—some with backpacks, others with nothing—populated the outer edges of the lot, focused on the soldiers milling around the intersection. Jack led them to the front of the dark store and leaned against the glass next to the automatic sliding doors. Nobody paid any attention to their arrival. Emma lowered her pack to the concrete sidewalk and sat against it, listening to the soldier reading a script from a clipboard.

Please keep your distance from the intersection, and do not approach the National Guard soldiers manning their checkpoints. We have several soldiers circulating through the crowd to answer your questions.

Effective immediately, all traffic north of this intersection and along the adjoining sections of Eighty-Sixth Street has been restricted by emergency order of the governor. This applies to pedestrian and motorized traffic. Interstate 465 has been declared a federal quarantine boundary by the Department of Health and Human Services, creating the Indianapolis Quarantine Zone. The governor has authorized the full use of the Indiana National Guard to enforce this boundary.

Guard elements will be deployed at all major intersections and on-ramps leading to the 465, in addition to overpasses and underpasses. The interstate will be heavily patrolled. I can't stress how important it is that you take this seriously. Anyone found attempting to breach the federal quarantine boundary will be apprehended and transported to a consolidated release point—inside the quarantine zone.

About a dozen CRPs have been identified throughout the city, and they all have one thing in common, they're nowhere close to the 465 boundary. One of them is the Indiana State Fairgrounds. That's about five miles from here. You do not want to get sent to one of these, so please don't try to get across the 465.

"We're getting across the 465," stated Jack, a little too loudly.

A guy in cargo shorts and a T-shirt, standing with a few other men at the edge of the parking lot, turned his head. He said something to the other men, who all nodded and spoke softly before the man started walking toward Jack and Emma. Jack's hand shifted slowly behind his thigh, seeking the pistol. Halfway across the short stretch of asphalt, the guy raised his hands.

"Sorry. I didn't mean to spook you," said the guy. "I live a few blocks from here, in a neighborhood on the off-limits side of Eighty-Sixth Street. Well, it's not really off-limits. I mean, they haven't stopped anyone from crossing the road. They don't have the manpower. The 465 is the real boundary. They're just trying to keep as many people from approaching the interstate as possible. We've walked up and down Eighty-Sixth, checking out the situation, and they're only at the major intersections like Township, Ditch and Spring Mill."

"How long have they been set up here?" said Jack.

Emma grabbed Jack's hand and pulled herself up.

"About an hour. We heard a bunch of trucks pull by and ran out to see what was going on," said the man. "We have a neighborhood watch set up, hidden out of sight; that's how we heard them. Mostly Humvees and those big troop transport things with the canvas tops."

"Does anyone know what's going on in the city?" said Emma. "I know there's some flu supposedly going around, but that doesn't explain the need for this quarantine thing."

"Quarantine boundary zone," said the man. "I'm Fred, by the way."

"Jack and Emma," said her husband, nobody reaching out to shake hands.

Fred shrugged his shoulders and sighed. "We can't figure it out either. Cell service is down. Internet is down. Everything's down, but the power grid is still up. Something doesn't add up. Where did you come from?"

"Broad Ripple," said Jack.

"What's it like down there?" said Fred. "We've been hearing some strange stories. Something happened at one of our neighbors' earlier tonight, but they all left. Never came back."

Emma looked at Jack, not sure where to begin or what to say. He'd obviously seen something far worse than anything she'd witnessed. The intersection was another story altogether. She paused long enough for her husband to get the hint that she didn't want to talk about any of it.

"It's hard to say what's going on. The gunshots are a constant now. That really picked up tonight, which is a big part of why we left. Police sirens nonstop. People roaming the streets all over—acting kind of glitchy," he said, glancing at Emma.

"Glitchy?" said Fred.

"I'm not describing it right. The people we saw outside just didn't look right. Like they were slow or maybe stoned. Some looked stalled out. I don't know. We had a few police calls in the neighborhood," said Jack.

Thankfully, her husband skipped any and all reference to Rudy. She wasn't ready to hear what happened, even though she knew it was probably the most telling piece of information he could pass along.

"Damn. We've heard a few gunshots, but nothing like you're describing," said Fred. "You guys didn't walk from Broad Ripple, did you?"

"No," said Jack. "We got into a very unfortunate accident at Seventy-Ninth and Michigan. We walked away unscratched, but our Jeep was trashed—not that it looks like it would have taken us any farther than Eighty-Sixth Street."

"Walking is your only way out of here now," said Fred. "Where are you headed?"

"My folks live a few hours north of here," said Jack. "We're hoping to walk far enough in that direction to get cell service again. Get them to drive down and pick us up."

"That would work," said Fred, nodding approvingly. "Shoot. I thought we might be fine here. We live in a pretty nice neighborhood. No gates around it unfortunately, but it's pretty well tucked away. Once word gets out that the city is under quarantine, it'll be every man for himself—or herself."

"It's bizarre," said Emma. "You don't quarantine a city for the flu. Like you said, something doesn't add up. We're getting out of here while we can—if we can."

"Yeah. Sounds like the 465 is locked down hard," said Jack.

"Come here," said Fred, motioning for them to follow. "I just want to show you Eighty-Sixth Street."

Emma picked up her pack and slung it over one shoulder, shrugging her shoulders. Jack took her hand, following Fred to the street.

"Take a look east," he said, pointing in the opposite direction from the soldiers. "Nothing. No cars. No military vehicles going back and forth. The 465 is the same except they have, like, one Humvee cruising back and forth between off-ramps. That's what Jay said."

Emma stepped onto the empty road, confirming Fred's claim. She thought she might be able to see the next set of stoplights, way out in the distance, but couldn't be sure. Jack did the same, walking into the middle of the nearest lane.

"Nothing," stated her husband before heading back. "Who's Jay?"

"One of the guys with me," said Fred. "He just got back to us about five minutes before you showed up. He drove through the neighborhoods and found a quiet spot overlooking the interstate. Said it was like five minutes in between patrols."

"How hard is it to get to the 465 taking the back roads?" said Jack.

"Not hard at all. I'd say you're looking at a mile-long walk. I can give you directions and let you cut right through our neighborhood, which will save you a ton of time."

"Do you think it's safe in the neighborhoods?" said Emma.

"Our street is always quiet, and it's isolated," said Fred. "We have Williams Creek on one side and a bunch of quiet, wooded streets on the others. There are some big apartment complexes between us and the 465, so that could be different. Jay didn't seem to think anything was amiss."

"Is there any way Jay would be willing to drive us to a point where we can cross?" said Jack. "I know that's asking a lot."

"We can always ask him," said Fred. "Come on."

A few minutes later, they were in the backseat of Jay's Pathfinder, headed away from the intersection with Fred. They turned into Fred's neighborhood less than a minute after that, stopping in front of a gate.

"I thought you didn't have gates," said Emma.

"We don't have a fence around the whole neighborhood. I wish we did," said Fred. "This just keeps the cars out. Won't do a lot of good when everyone starts pouring out of the city."

"I don't think you'll see a lot of action here. It's tucked away nicely," said Jack.

"Yeah. But if the National Guard blocks the main roads, people will start looking for cracks in the wall."

"We didn't see a lot of people leaving," said Emma. "I think most of them are sick."

"How did the two of you avoid this mystery bug?" said Jay, a hint of suspicion in his voice.

"I don't know. We just got back from a two-week vacation yesterday," said Jack.

"Whatever is going around must have hit while you were gone," said Fred.

Had it all been a matter of timing? Would they be stumbling around the streets with the rest of their neighbors right now, shooting off Jack's gun, if they hadn't gone on vacation?

"This is a very nice neighborhood," said Jack.

Emma looked up, taken aback by the size of the brightly lit, palatial homes. Nice was an understatement. Cut into a backdrop of mature trees and manicured yards, long driveways connected sprawling mansions to the street. To the left, moonlight reflected off the calm water of a massive pond with homes on the other side.

"We're kind of partial to it," said Fred.

"I can see why you don't want to leave," said Emma. "I think you should turn the lights out."

"We debated that," said Fred. "Jay and I agree with you. Not everyone feels the same way. Frankly, most of our neighbors are in denial. You've met the entire contingent that thinks we need to be a little more proactive about what's happening."

Emma thought about it for a minute. "At least you have the National Guard close by, blocking the major approaches."

"The question is *for how long?*" said Fred. "I'm strongly considering a trip north. A few of us are."

"I wouldn't wait too long," said Jack. "If you saw what I…what we saw, you'd agree. Something is horribly wrong down in Indy."

"Might be a good time to try what I suggested," said Jay.

"I wouldn't be opposed to it," said Fred.

Emma elbowed Jack. She wasn't sure what they were talking about.

"What's up?" said her husband.

"We're going to do you one better," said Fred. "How would you like a ride across the 465?"

"Is that a good idea?" said Emma.

"What about the center median?" said Jack. "I'm pretty sure that's a concrete barrier."

"There's a gap in the median for state troopers or local cops to make U-turns," said Jay. "It's almost a straight shot across from one of the apartment building parking lots. No problem for an SUV."

"It'll be a test run," said Fred. "Over and back just long enough to drop you off. Even if they spot us from one of the overpasses, there's no way they can respond quickly enough to catch us."

"I don't know," said Jack. "Bullets travel a lot faster than cars. Just saying."

"I hear you," said Fred. "That's why I want to leave sooner than later. Before they reach the point where they're no longer kindly apprehending and relocating city refugees."

Emma couldn't imagine the situation deteriorating to a point where the National Guard was shooting at people. Then again, she still didn't know what Jack had seen in their neighbor's yard. Why Rudy disappeared. She might feel differently if she possessed that knowledge.

Jay drove them around the pond, the road continuing its lazy arc around the water. She didn't see how they would get out of the neighborhood. The road looked like it winded back to the gate. Jack noticed the same thing, shifting in his seat to free up access to the pistol.

"Hang on," said Jay. "We're going to do a little off-roading."

They grabbed the roof handles as Jay turned into a driveway and maneuvered the SUV around the house, slowing to squeeze through the headlight-illuminated trees.

"This is my house, in case you're curious," said Fred.

"I was hoping it was one of your houses," said Emma.

"My backyard abuts some common property along a street in the neighborhood behind us," said Fred. "That street connects with the back roads leading to the interstate."

The SUV emerged from the bushes onto Pickerel Drive before taking them on a short, twisty ride on the local roads to an apartment community backlit by the interstate. Jay turned off the headlights as they approached the first of three buildings that lined the 465. He turned the vehicle into the second building's front parking lot, creeping between the buildings to the back. They narrowly fit between a concrete dumpster corral and an open-sided, covered parking structure, stopping on a short stretch of flat grass with scattered bushes. The gap in the median sat directly in front of them, separated from the SUV by a low wire fence.

"See," said Fred. "It's almost a straight shot."

"What about the fence?" said Jack. "I don't think you want to crash through that. Looks flimsy enough, but you never know."

"I checked it out," said Jay. "Little more than a half-gone cattle fence put up years ago to keep toddlers from running onto the interstate. Two minutes with a bolt cutter and a hacksaw."

"I hear something coming," said Fred. "Back up."

Jay eased the SUV back into the parking area behind the building, and they all got out to peek around the brick dumpster corral. Several seconds later, a Humvee rolled slowly by on the eastbound side. Fred returned to the SUV and handed Jack a bolt cutter. He held a hacksaw in the other hand.

"It'll turn around at Meridian, so this is the short part of its back and forth run," said Fred. "We'll get the fence down and wait for it to pass again."

"Are you sure you want to do this?" said Jack. "I'd hate to ruin this route for you, or even worse—get you caught."

"If we're going to get caught, I'd rather get caught without my family in the car," said Fred. "Plus my wife isn't convinced we need to leave, yet."

"Neither is mine," said Jay. "It'll be a while before we leave, and there are other places to cross."

"If you change your mind," said Jack, "we can do this on foot."

"We'll be fine," said Fred.

A few minutes later, they had cleared a section of fence wide enough to fit two vehicles, in case Jay and Fred needed to make a less than precise, high-speed return to the parking lot. With the work finished, Emma and Jack waited in the idling SUV with Jay for Fred to give the signal, which came shortly after they got situated. Fred sprinted to the vehicle, jumping into the front passenger seat and slamming the door shut.

"They just passed, heading west," said Fred.

As Jay brought the SUV to the edge of the highway, Jack handed his binoculars to Fred.

"These might help," said Jack.

"Perfect," said Fred, scanning each direction for several seconds. "Looks clear in both directions. I can see the Ditch Road and Ninety-Sixth Street overpasses, but I can't tell if anyone is watching."

"Only one way to find out," said Jay.

The Pathfinder sped across the eastbound lanes and cruised through the gap in the median. Emma stared out of her window, praying that Jay was right about the Humvee's patrol pattern. When they crossed the westbound lanes, she saw a pair of red brake lights in the distance, beyond the Ditch Road overpass. The SUV rolled over the concrete shoulder and came to a rest at a shallow angle to another cattle fence. She looked past Jack, through the passenger window, still able to see some of the Ninety-Sixth Street overpass.

"Damn. I thought we'd be out of sight," said Fred, opening his car door and illuminating the cabin with the interior lights. "Shit! Kill the lights."

Jay cursed profusely, fumbling with the dashboard controls until the cabin went dark. Emma and Jack hopped out of the SUV immediately after it went dark, making their way to the fence. Fred followed, carrying the same tools they'd used to cut the other fence.

"I don't know how much time we'll have, or if it's even a good idea to cut a hole here," said Fred. "If they saw us, they'll investigate. I screwed up with the interior lights."

"I didn't think of it earlier, but what about the brake lights?" said Jack. "If they didn't see the inside lights, they had to see those."

"That's why we parked at an angle," said Fred. "They might see the reflection off the ground, but that's the best we could do. I guess it doesn't matter. Help me cut a hole, and we'll get the hell out of here. Emma, do you mind keeping an eye on the interstate?"

"I can do that," she said, taking the binoculars from Jack.

Emma passed Jay, who waited in the driver's seat for a quick getaway, and took up a position at the back of the Pathfinder. The brake lights were gone, and she didn't see anything that resembled a squat, dark shape heading in their direction. The overpass in that direction didn't show any activity from what she could tell. The National Guard roadblock had probably been assembled in front of the overpass. Her assessment of the eastern approach was the same. It didn't look like they'd attracted any attention.

"Emma!" said Jack. "Time to go."

She paused in front of Jay's window. "Overpasses look clear. The roads, too. I think you have a viable escape route."

"Thanks," said Jay. "Safe travels."

"Thank you for getting us here," she said before joining Jack and Fred at the fence.

"Ditch and Ninety-Sixth intersect at a roundabout just past these buildings. Watch yourself there. I can't imagine you'll have any problems beyond that."

"We'll stick to quiet neighborhoods," said Jack. "Less chance of running into the authorities."

"Probably best," said Fred. "Take care, guys."

"You too. Don't wait long to leave," said Jack.

They shook hands and Jack and Emma took off, hiking toward the perceived safety of the city's northern suburbs—situated behind the federal quarantine boundary.

"We made it," said Jack, giving her a quick hug.

Automatic gunfire rattled in the distance behind them.

"I hope so," said Emma, picking up the pace on her own.

Chapter Twenty-Six

Dr. Chang took a last look at the jam-packed rear cargo area of his 4Runner and ran his mental checklist. The bulk of his cargo consisted of food, enough to last two weeks. He'd added two prefilled heavy-duty plastic jerry cans, giving him a total of ten gallons of potable water before he had to use one of his portable filtration units. He was tempted to leave one behind, since each can weighed forty pounds and his Cessna's maximum payload was around seven hundred pounds—fully fueled.

Two water cans plus his bodyweight represented more than a third of the aircraft's current payload. Chang guessed that the rest of his gear weighed around three hundred pounds. He wouldn't know for sure until he got to the hangar. Montgomery Aviation kept a scale in each hangar to help with payload calculations. If his total payload exceeded six hundred pounds, he'd consider leaving one of the cans behind. Pushing the maximum weight made for a protracted and sluggish takeoff, a problem he didn't want this morning.

He planned to load up the aircraft and sleep in the hangar, setting his wristwatch alarm for 5:30 AM. That would give him thirty minutes to freshen up and roll the aircraft out of the hangar for a 6:00 AM takeoff. Sunrise wasn't until 6:18 AM, but he should have more than enough light on the horizon by that point to guide him down the runway.

Satisfied that he hadn't forgotten anything critical, he shut the rear hatch and got in the driver's seat, ready to flee. Chang could barely believe he was leaving. He'd designed this house with exactly this type of disaster in mind, and one phone call had taken all of that away—turning him into a fugitive. At least he had the plane.

With the plane, he could fly anonymously over the border pretty much anywhere and land at any local airport, dealing with Canadian customs officials later—if they even bothered to show up. More than likely, he'd have to seek them out. His biggest challenge was deciding where to fly. The easiest and most direct route to Canada took him below Detroit, over Lake Erie. He could be over the border and on the ground in less than two hours. Of course, that would also be the most obvious route. Thinking about what Stan Greenberg had said, he was strongly considering a more northerly route, toward Minnesota and the long U.S.-Canada border.

He'd identified several airfields in Minnesota that were well within range. Bemidji Regional Airport stood out as a top-notch facility, where he could take some time to refuel and narrow his choice of Canadian airports. Chang probably wouldn't make a flight plan decision until morning, after giving Greenberg a quick call to see if anything had changed.

Chang opened the garage door and backed into the driveway, stopping to activate his home's sophisticated security system using his cell phone. He'd hooked his satellite phone to a magnetic, roof-mounted antenna, turning his hotspot satellite rig into a mobile Wi-Fi hotspot. The more he thought of it, in light of Greenberg's revelation, the less he thought he should use the cell phone, even with the location services disabled. He was certain it could be tracked regardless. When he got to the airport, he'd take the battery out of the phone, if possible, or destroy it if not. He had a noncellular data-equipped tablet and a laptop he could use to access the Internet.

He drove carefully through the forest, the tight gravel road scary enough during broad daylight. He slowed when his headlights disclosed two red reflectors flanking the road, inching forward until the motion detector activated the gate. When he reached the main road, he turned north and sped toward the airport, his mind on the outside chance that Jeff hadn't put the wing back together.

Chang knew that was highly unlikely, especially given Jeff's exceptional work history, but he couldn't get the bug out of his head. If the plane wasn't flyable, he had a decision to make. Wait around for Jeff to show up in the morning and finish the job, or drive out of town. As much as he didn't want to leave the plane behind, he was leaning toward the road-trip option.

Endless rows of soybean plants and cornfields flanked the road. The dark outline of a warehouse appeared above the corn, which meant he was approaching Route 32. The airport lay in the darkness beyond the sea of soybeans. During the day, the white hangar that held his plane peeked above the green plants. He passed a yellow "stop ahead" sign and started to slow. The four-way stop was just ahead.

He sensed something was wrong before his headlights fell on a makeshift wood barrier blocking the intersection. The stop sign that normally sat atop a tall metal pole on the right side of the road had been removed, now attached to the center of the hastily made obstruction. Several heavily armed figures clad in helmets and body armor stood on each side of the road, one of them walking forward with a hand held out, signaling for him to stop. Chang complied, bringing the SUV to a stop well in front of the soldier—or whatever he was.

Three soldiers jogged up to his vehicle, triggering their rifle lights when they drew even with the front doors. Chang instinctively raised a hand to block the light, immediately placing it back on the steering wheel. No sudden movements. Bad things happened when you made sudden movements. He closed his eyes, the lights searing through his eyelids.

Everything went dark, and he heard a hard knock on the driver's side window. He opened his eyes to see a soldier holding a gloved hand to the glass, his rifle lowered. The soldier signaled for him to lower the window, which he did immediately, breathing in the humid central Indiana air.

"How are you doing tonight, sir?" said the soldier in a thick Boston accent.

"Well enough," said Chang, glancing over his shoulder.

The other two soldiers slowly walked down the side of the SUV, directing their rifle lights into the backseat and cargo compartment.

"Unfortunately, I can't let you pass through this intersection right now. We have orders to turn all traffic back. Really sorry, sir."

"Why? What's going on?"

The soldier glanced over his shoulder, nodding quickly. "We're enforcing the outer quarantine boundary. Route 32 straight across into Noblesville. Michigan Road is our western boundary, so just in case you're thinking of heading that way—you'll run into the same thing."

"Wait. When did this go into effect?" said Chang.

"About an hour ago," said the soldier.

"Can't you let me by? I mean, seriously, how many cars have even come up this road in the last hour?"

"You're the first," said the soldier, starting to look like he was thinking about making an exception.

"I just want to head north. Away from Indianapolis, as you can imagine," said Chang.

At this point, he would skip the airport if they let him through, and avoid any more patrols along Route 32. He studied the soldier's uniform, looking for any indication of his unit or rank. Three chevrons and something under it—a rocker. One rank above sergeant. It was all coming back.

"Staff Sergeant, right?" said Chang.

"Staff Sergeant Andrews, 10th Mountain Division," he replied.

"Regular army?" said Chang. "How bad is this?"

"I honestly don't know, sir. But it has to be bad. I've never seen anything like this," said the staff sergeant.

"Please, Staff Sergeant," said Chang, sighing. "Let me through. I won't say a word. I'll just disappear. I don't want to go back."

The soldier thought about it hard, but eventually started shaking his head.

"I'm really sorry, sir. My orders are crystal clear. I can't let you pass. We're dealing with a quarantine situation."

"Then why aren't you wearing a respirator? Or a biohazard suit?" said Chang.

"We're part of the rapid deployment battalion," said Andrews. "We don't even have vehicles."

"Don't you find that odd?" he yelled, immediately regretting the outburst.

"I think it's time for you to head back the way you came, sir," said the soldier.

"It probably is," said Chang. "Sorry for yelling at you. It's just all very frustrating."

"I understand, sir," he said. "The best I can offer you right now is to tune in to one of the local emergency broadcast frequencies or local news broadcasts. FEMA and DHS are coordinating some kind of medical response, which will hopefully be implemented as soon as possible."

"Sounds good," said Chang, wanting to scream at him.

"All right. We'll get out of your way and let you turn around."

How nice of you. Chang feigned a smile before raising the window, waiting for the soldiers to stand clear before turning the SUV around. Things were far worse than he thought. There was absolutely no way that a regular military unit could get here that fast, even rapid response elements, unless the federal government knew days ago that there was a problem. Not a chance.

Significant resources had been dedicated over the past several years to improving early response protocols for pandemic outbreaks and bioweapons attacks, but nothing on the kind of scale that would put regular military units on roadblocks this quickly—and without proper biohazard gear. That was the other thing. There was quarantine for medical purposes, and there was geographical containment. These soldiers were equipped for the latter.

Time for plan B. The problem was that he didn't have a plan B. He hadn't anticipated a containment boundary this far out of Indianapolis. There was no reason for one as far as he was concerned, unless the government suspected or knew the virus was contagious. He really hoped that wasn't the case. The outbreak would go from a worst-case scenario to something unimaginably catastrophic.

He had to get out of here. As he sped back to his house, the rough outline of a very risky plan materialized. A nearly hopeless plan in light of what he'd just seen. Then again, what other choice did he have?

Chapter Twenty-Seven

Dr. Lauren Hale stood inside the emergency room's ambulance delivery doors, waiting for the inbound ambulance. Gunshot wound to the pelvis and a chest stabbing, both picked up in the same neighborhood—all one block over from her apartment. Indianapolis had descended into pure chaos from all reports, the city's emergency services on the verge of a complete collapse.

Yelling and panicked cries for help echoed off the blood-smeared walls behind her; the rooms and hallways of the once pristine state-of-the-art emergency facility reduced to little more than a battlefield triage site. Hale stared at herself in the reflection of the sliding glass door. She looked more like a butcher than an ER doctor, her light blue apron and scrubs splattered with blood and gore. She lowered her respirator and glanced furtively over her shoulder, a self-preservation tic she'd developed over the past twenty-four hours.

She shouldn't have to worry about being attacked inside the ER at this point. All of the self-ambulatory virus patients had been removed earlier in the day after Dr. Cabrera was nearly stabbed to death by one of the infected in a treatment room. That was what they called them now. Infected. A delirious woman brought in with a chest and face full of birdshot pulled a steak knife out of her boot while Cabrera was checking her vitals, jamming it into his gut several times before an orderly caved her skull in with an IV stand.

The delivering paramedics had mistakenly identified her as a victim instead of one of the infected. It hadn't been the first mistake resulting in violence, but it had been the last. The new protocol ordered by Dr. Owens required all injured patients registering a temperature upon admittance to be immediately restrained, treated and removed as soon as possible from the ER. The new system had worked so far.

A pulsing red light reflected off the trees lining the intersection, growing brighter by the second. Hale pulled the respirator back into place over her nose and mouth and lowered her splatter glasses. Moments later, the ambulance raced into view, speeding toward the hospital. She could tell right away that it wasn't going to make the turn. The police officers barricading the entrance to the ER parking lot sensed the same thing and slowly started to back away from their vehicles.

The ambulance barreled into the intersection, tires screeching, as the orange and white truck teetered on two wheels for a few agonizing seconds before crashing onto its right side. Sparks trailed the ambulance as it skidded across the pavement and slammed into the curb, coming to a crunching halt that sounded like a bomb blast inside the ER doors. Hale had her swipe card in hand, ready to open the doors and run outside, when Owens yelled from the hallway behind her.

"What the fuck was that?"

Owens was covered in blood from head to toe, having repeatedly handled the most severe cases brought through the ER doors. Only his gloves and respirator were clean, indicating he was ready to take the worst case offloaded from the ambulance.

"Ambulance took the turn too fast and crashed on its side," she said. "I'm going out to help."

"No, you're not," said Owens. "We have a strict protocol in place. EMS delivers patients with a police escort through these doors. That's it."

"Come on, Jeff. The paramedics are going to need help, too," she said, raising her hand to the card reader.

"Damn it," muttered Owens before pointing at her. "You watch your ass out there. Any sign of a shit storm, and you get your ass back inside."

"Got it," she said, swiping her card.

She stepped into the night, immediately hearing a not-so-distant-sounding gunshot. The single blast was answered by several rapid shots, also nearby. The police officers jogging toward the ambulance stopped and drew their pistols, scanning the streets. One of them leveled a military-style rifle in the direction of the gunfire. Maybe this wasn't such a good idea. Hale ran across the parking lot toward the police car blocking the western entrance.

The sound of heavy vehicles reverberated through the parking lot, intensifying the closer she got to the street. Just before she reached the police car, a column of armored military vehicles emerged between the buildings. She stopped in the middle of the lot and watched this bizarre sight unfold.

The first vehicle, which she now recognized to be a Humvee, pulled even with the police car blocking the eastern access point, its machine gun turret swiveling in a slow arc as if an unseen enemy might ambush them at any moment. A soldier got out of the front passenger side and approached the police standing in front of the squad car.

"Dr. Hale!" yelled one of the officers near the crashed ambulance. "What do we do here?"

She glanced in his direction, but her attention was mostly focused on the line of Humvees. Beyond them, she could see larger trucks.

"Dr. Hale! I think everyone in the back is dead!"

The soldier and police officers shook hands, each retreating to their vehicles. A moment later, the police car backed out of the way, allowing two Humvees to pull into the parking lot, before returning to its original blocking position. The remaining Humvees drove past, stopping at nearly equidistant intervals on the streets surrounding the emergency room parking lot, their turrets facing outward.

"Dr. Hale! What do we do!" screamed the officer.

She turned to him. "Bring whoever looks like they'll survive into the ER."

"What?" he yelled. "How the fuck am I supposed to do that? I'm not qualified to make that kind of decision!"

"Just figure it out!" she snapped, returning her attention to the soldiers getting out of the Humvees near the ambulance entrance.

"What's going on?" she yelled, drawing their attention.

She jogged toward them, worried that they might smash the glass in if they couldn't immediately gain access. A few of them already appeared to be trying to separate the doors.

"I can let you in!" she said. "Just hold on!"

One of the soldiers stepped out of the group to meet her. He was dressed in full combat gear, like something she'd expect to see in a war zone. Ballistic helmet fitted with a night-vision device. Body armor covered his torso, pelvis, shoulders and neck. Full ammunition pouches attached to his body armor. Thigh holster. He truly looked like he was geared up for a battle—and maybe he was. The soldier reached over the rifle slung across his chest to shake her hand.

"Major Nick Smith, 2nd Battalion, 151st Infantry Regiment, Indiana National Guard," he said, looking her up and down. "What the hell happened here?"

"It's been a long few days," she said. "What's all this?"

"I have orders to secure the hospital and remove all patients," said Smith.

"What?" she said. "Remove them to where?"

"Some kind of quarantine facility where they can separate the sick patients. I have close to a hundred trucks and school buses standing by for the evacuation. I'm supposed to start moving them out of here immediately," said Smith.

This didn't sound right. They could do that right here. Hale couldn't think of any reason why they'd need to clear the hospital of everyone. Removing the infected made sense on some levels, but not the entire patient population. She decided not to protest too strongly. For all she knew, they planned on removing the staff, too.

"Most of the hospital's patients are either too sick or too injured to be transported on a bus," said Hale.

"We'll do what we can to accommodate the different patient

types," he said.

"You have to keep the infected patients restrained," she said. "Otherwise you'll have problems."

"What's the ratio between the *infected*, as you call them, and the rest?" said the major.

"Ten to one in the whole hospital? That's what I've heard," she said. "About one in five in the ER?"

"Why the difference here?" he said.

"Because we've moved most of them out," said Hale. "They kept attacking the staff."

"Jesus," said Smith. "What is this?"

She shrugged her shoulders. "It's a living nightmare, Major. I hope your soldiers are prepared for this."

"Me too," he said. "I need to get inside and coordinate with hospital administration."

"Hospital administration is gone. We haven't heard from them in over twenty-four hours."

"Who's running the hospital?" said the soldier.

"Doctors. Nurses. Other staff that decided to stick around. There's no centralized decision-making point."

"This just keeps getting better," said Smith.

She swiped her card and punched in a short code. The door slid open, remaining in that position.

"I disabled the security feature. Your soldiers can come and go," she said.

"I guess we'll start with the ER. Who's in charge here?"

"Dr. Owens. Last I saw he was in one of the surgical suites. Take the first right inside these doors and keep going. You'll see it past a circular nurses' station," she said. "I should probably help the police move those accident victims inside."

The soldiers took off down the hallway, their boots pounding the linoleum floor and gear clacking as they ran. Hale walked calmly down the hallway straight in front of the sliding door, ducking into the room where she'd seen Owens a few minutes ago. He stood just inside the room, his arms folded.

"What was that all about?" said Owens. "They're not going to be happy to find out you lied."

"They're here to clear the hospital," said Hale. "All of the patients, sick or not, on military trucks and buses. Immediately. It doesn't sound right."

Owens stared at her for a second. "No. It doesn't. Here's what you're going to do. You're going to walk out that door and disappear."

"I'm not going anywhere," she said.

"No time to argue with me," said Owens. "You either leave now on your own, or you leave on one of those buses. That's where this is headed. My guess is they're doing a clean sweep of this place. Staff included."

"I have nowhere to go," she said. "The two coming in on the ambulance were picked up a block away from my place. If the 465 rumors are true, I don't really have any options."

"What about Dr. Chang's place? You said that was pretty secure," said Owens. "He gave you the codes to get in, right?"

Hale fished through her scrubs, feeling the worn, folded card in her front pocket. "I don't have my keys or purse."

Owens pulled a set of keys from his pocket and held them out to her. "You don't have time. Plus, my car is in the lot right across the street. Lot L. Rank hath its privileges."

"I can't take your car," she said. "What are you going to do?"

"You know what they say about the captain, right?" said Owens.

"I'm too tired for riddles."

"The captain always goes down with the ship," said Owens. "I'm going to warn the others. If I get out of here, I'll find Chang's place. I have the address in my phone."

"I'll walk," she said.

"You won't get very far out there," said Owens. "Take the fucking keys, Lauren. They probably figured out you lied by now."

She swiped the keys from him, not sure what to say.

"You can thank me later. Get out of here," said Owens, grabbing her arm and speed-walking toward the ambulance entry.

When they reached the open doorway, Owens turned, looking over his shoulder at her and mouthing, "Go!" A commotion broke out at the far end of the hallway, a nurse gesturing wildly at a cluster of soldiers. Lauren passed the soldiers standing around the entrance, nodding politely before breaking into a jog and eventually a sprint—never looking back. There would be plenty of time for guilt later.

Chapter Twenty-Eight

David Olson started pressing his garage door opener as soon as his house came into view after turning the corner. He wanted to slide the truck inside the garage and avoid any possible downtime on the driveway. The last thing he needed right now was a chat with the neighbors. He was friends with all of them, but now wasn't the time. The trip to Noblesville had taken far longer than expected, mostly because advance elements of the 10th Mountain Division had arrived from Grissom Air Reserve Base ahead of schedule, jamming the roads in and around the city.

The only good thing to come of it was being cut off by a convoy of Humvees headed south. He'd actually enabled it to happen by slowing down when he saw a Humvee edging toward the road. The driver took the bait, lurching onto the street in front of him, followed by a dozen more armored vehicles. By the time the last vehicle in the convoy turned down the road and Olson got moving again, the Westfield patrol car was nowhere in sight.

Since the other Westfield officers wouldn't suspect anything for a while due to the unexpected and lengthy interruption, David drove Price all the way to her house instead of dropping her off at a point that would have required a thirty-minute walk. The rest of the trip had been smooth sailing, with the exception of a Carmel Police Department checkpoint on 116th Street. Carmel PD officers asked a few questions and took a look in the back of his pickup, but the uniform and badge got him through with very little scrutiny.

His garage door started rising a little later than he would have liked, forcing him to slow his approach to time it perfectly. The pickup pulled into the driveway and rolled into the garage, the door closing before he shifted into park. He took the keys out of the ignition and stepped onto the concrete floor, keeping a close eye on what he could see of the driveway for shadows. When the garage door stopped and he was certain nobody had slipped inside, he unlocked the door to the house and opened it a few inches—triggering the alert beep that his son would hear in the basement.

Unable to call Joshua and let him know he was coming home, he'd have to be careful entering the house. He pushed the door open all the way while standing aside in case his son had once again decided to disregard his request to stay in the basement. When no gunfire erupted, he stepped into the house and called out.

"Josh! It's me, Dad!"

He didn't sense any immediate response.

"Josh! Where are you? It's Dad!"

Shit. Where was he? He shut the door behind him and locked it, waiting for his son to respond. Nothing.

"Dammit, Josh! Where are you?" he screamed.

A rumble sounded beneath the floor, and David drew his service pistol. He took a few more quiet steps into the dark house, keeping the weapon pointed high to avoid reflexively shooting his son if he suddenly appeared.

"Josh! Answer me!"

"Dad?" answered a muffled voice.

A few moments later, David heard footsteps coming up the basement stairway.

"Dad, I'm coming up!"

He holstered his pistol and walked into the main hallway, stopping near the basement door. After a heavy *click*, the door opened, light pouring into the house. His son stood sleepy eyed for a moment at the top of the stairs before his eyes darted to the bandage on David's head.

"Dad, what happened?"

"No big deal. Cut my head on some broken glass."

David grabbed his son and hugged him.

"Why didn't you answer right away? Scared the crap out of me."

"I finally fell asleep," said Joshua. "I never heard the alarm beep. That's a little scary."

David squeezed him tighter for a few seconds before letting him go.

"I didn't expect you to stay awake all night. Actually, I hope you got a little rest. We need to get out of town and head north."

"I got the second pack ready and moved the fifty-gallon plastic bins next to the stairs. All of the water, too. I didn't realize you had everything so organized down there," said Joshua.

"There's been a little change of plans," said David. "Let's head downstairs. We can't use the truck. We have to walk out of here."

"What? Why?" said Joshua.

"Shut the door and lock it," said David. "Things have gotten really bad out there. Worse than I originally thought."

David found all eight plastic bins lined up in a neat row, labels facing forward.

CAMPING1

CAMPING2

FOOD—PRIMARY

FOOD—SECONDARY

CLOTHING—WWX.

CLOTHING—CWX.

MEDICAL/COMMS/MISC.

SURVIVAL

A dozen five-gallon water cans stood upright behind the bins. The only things missing were the weapons and ammunition. Speaking of which. He glanced around the room, spotting the Glock 19 in its concealed-carry holster next to a few dirty plates and glasses on the circular table in front of the couch. He'd help Joshua attach the holster and position it for the journey. His son stepped into the basement, behind him.

"So we're not taking any of this?" he said.

"We'll pick through these and bulk up the packs," said David.

He'd thought about it on the drive back. They'd strip down several MREs, keeping the main course, side dish and cracker. Anything densely caloric. One of the larger medical kits would be good insurance against a serious injury. He could attach that to his own tactical vest. A few small propane tanks and a one-burner stove would make boiling water and cooking a lot easier in the long run. He'd add a small lightweight aluminum skillet to one of the packs. He anticipated living off the land for a little while. Better fishing tackle and an extendable rod with an attachable reel would come in handy for that. Plenty of retention ponds and small lakes with edible fish in central Indiana. He didn't think he could add much more than that without tying an extra bag to one of the packs.

"They're already pretty bulky," said Joshua.

"Each of us will carry a rifle and ammunition, too," said David. "Infantry Marines lug around two to three times what we'll be carrying. This'll be good for you."

"I'm more worried about you," said his son jokingly.

"This old man carries twenty-five pounds of gear around every day," said David. "And don't even try to convince me your school backpack counts."

They laughed for a few seconds before David brought them back on task.

"I'll start prepping the weapons and ammunition. Rig you a tactical vest. We'll need more pistol magazines. A few knives and flashlights," said David. "Then we'll figure out what we can stuff into the packs without killing ourselves. Right now, you could help out by opening all of the MREs in the bin labeled FOOD—PRIMARY. Separate all the main courses, side dishes and anything else that's food."

"Okay," said Joshua, nodding. "Dad?"

"Yeah?"

"Why can't we take your truck?" said Joshua.

"Two reasons. One, the 10th Mountain Division, a regular military unit, has taken up positions along Route 32, forming some kind of quarantine blockade."

"You're a cop. They'll let you through," said his son.

"Maybe. Maybe not. That's the second reason. I left without permission," said David. "I've seen some things tonight that defy explanation. When I heard they were forming a quarantine zone north of here, I didn't want to take any chances that we might not be able to get out. And I didn't want you to be here alone."

"What do they think is going on?" said Joshua.

"That's the problem," said David. "Everyone is big on orders, but short on answers. They're either hiding something, or they really have no idea. Either way, we need to get as far past the Route 32 blockade as possible."

"How?"

"I think we should head northwest and find a quiet spot to cross. They can't cover the whole thing. We just have to be careful. Stick to cover," said David. "I'll get us past them."

"Then what?"

"We keep going until we get cell phone service. I have some friends up north," said David. "Worst-case scenario, we find a nice pond or lake and live off the land for a while. We'll be fine."

"What about Mom?" said Joshua sullenly.

"Still no word. My guess is her flight back was cancelled. Part of the quarantine," said David. "We'll figure it out when we get cell phone service."

"We had service yesterday and this morning," said Joshua. "She didn't answer. She always answers."

"I can't explain it, Josh. Everything is beyond messed up," said David. "We'll find your mother later. Right now, we need to focus on getting out of here. I want to be walking out of here in less than an hour. You good?"

"I'm good, Dad. Promise."

David sighed, putting a hand on his son's shoulder. "We'll find her. Just not right now. I promise."

Joshua brightened for a moment, nodding.

"Let's get to work," said David.

He watched his son for a moment, painfully aware that he had to face the consequences of that lie at some point in the near future.

Chapter Twenty-Nine

Jack Harper checked his watch. It had taken them a little over two hours to walk five miles. Not a bad pace, even with the hide-and-seek they played with cars along the road. Mostly police cars in a hurry. He leaned his head against the tree, his eyes drifting shut. Not yet. They didn't have far to go. He rubbed his face and took a deep breath. A light buzzing sounded in his ear, and he waved his hand next to his head. The mosquitos had found them.

"You still awake?" he said, nudging his wife's shoulder.

"Barely," she croaked. "I could sleep right here."

It wasn't such a bad idea. They were just outside their friend's neighborhood, hidden in a thick roadside stretch of forest that didn't seem connected to a house. They could move deeper into the forest and find a flat enough spot for their bivy bags. Might even be safer than the neighborhood. He swatted his arm, unable to see if his hand had connected with whatever had bitten him.

"I'm not opposed to the idea," he said.

"I'd rather sleep in Deanne's screen room," said Emma. "The mosquitos will eat us alive out here. I can smell standing water somewhere close."

"You want to get moving?" said Jack. "Sounds quiet enough around here. I can't imagine we'll attract much attention at two twenty in the morning."

"Yeah. I'm starting to get a little too comfortable here, even with the mosquitos."

Jack pushed off the ground far enough to use the tree to lift him the rest of the way. He took Emma's hand next and helped her up. Shouldering their packs, they walked out of the forest, keeping an eye out for headlights. So far tonight, avoiding trouble north of Interstate 465, outside the quarantine zone, had been fairly straightforward. They crossed the road one at a time, something he'd seen in a movie, and walked together on the sidewalk toward the entrance to their friend Deanne's neighborhood.

"You sure you remember which house?" said Jack. "I don't want to get shot breaking into someone's screen porch. Mosquitos aren't that big of a deal."

"It's the second right inside the neighborhood. I'll recognize the house. It's almost at the end of the cul-de-sac, on the left. There's a forest behind them."

"Too bad we can't get inside," said Jack. "They might have Internet access or a landline."

"We're not breaking into Deanne's house," she said. "Anyway, cell service is still out, even up here. It must be more widespread than we thought."

"I'm worried it might be a statewide problem. Then what?" said Jack.

Emma's pace slowed a bit, the weight of his statement figuratively and literally weighing her down.

"How far is it to your parents'?" said Emma.

"About a hundred and fifty miles," said Jack. "At this pace, allowing for some slowdown, it would take us about seventy hours to walk that distance. Assume we can go for sixteen hours a day, which I think is a stretch; we'd be on the road for four and a half days. That's best-case scenario. Add weather. Detours for safety. Water procurement. Five to six most likely."

"What's your point?" said Emma. "I feel like you're working up to something."

"Well, given the state of emergency right now, I don't think it would be too out of line for us to borrow one of Deanne's cars. I mean, we can drive to my parents', make contact, and then drive the car back."

His wife didn't pause. "No. We're not breaking into her house, and we're certainly not stealing a car."

"We'd return it immediately," said Jack.

"And repair whatever window or door we broke to get in?"

"Keep it in mind."

"It's already out of my mind," said Emma.

"Just saying," said Jack.

"I'm not breaking into my friend's house," muttered Emma.

"I thought it was out of your mind."

"It is," she said.

"We'll see."

Like the other neighborhoods they'd passed on Towne Road, every exterior light on the houses glowed bright, almost like nothing was wrong just a few short miles south. Maybe it was a citywide strategy to discourage crime. He could see that being the case, because it certainly had a chilling effect on him as they strolled down the sidewalk at two in the morning. He felt distinctly out of place and on display. The mosquito-infested forest wasn't looking so bad right now.

"Which house is it?" said Jack.

"About five houses down on the left."

"About five houses? I thought you knew which one it was," said Jack.

"I don't count the houses and turn when I visit," she said. "I'll know it when I see it."

Jack didn't like the sound of that. From what he could see from the main road leading through the subdivision, the builder had offered three home plans, with not much variation in the front-facing design. Not a problem during the day, when you could easily differentiate siding and brick colors, but at night—every other house looked pretty damn similar.

"Do you know her address?" said Jack.

She stopped on the sidewalk. "Seriously?"

"Seriously. We can't be creeping into someone else's backyard."

"I have it in my phone."

"Please double-check," said Jack. "I'm not trying to be a jerk."

"Well—you're getting there," she said, pulling out her phone.

While she scrolled through her contacts list, Jack heard a *click* somewhere nearby. He glanced around, not finding the source of the sound. Emma must have heard it too, because she was doing the same thing.

"Hurry up with that address," said Jack. "Let's keep walking. I got us covered."

They made it several steps before a voice called out from the right.

"Are you guys lost?"

Emma slowed, and Jack whispered, "Keep moving."

Jack scanned every inch of the house and the bushes as they walked by, unable to determine where the voice originated.

"You should turn around. We've had enough trouble tonight," said the same voice.

Jack figured it out this time. A ground-floor window on the house next to them had been raised a few inches, along with the shade. Unless the guy was hiding in the bushes like a lunatic, the window had to be his lookout post. He put himself between Emma and the house, just in case they were in a shoot-first-and-ask-questions neighborhood. It sounded like they'd already had a few problems.

"We're not looking for trouble," said Jack. "We're friends with Deanne, a few houses down on the left. We're going to camp out in her yard and head out in the morning. No trouble at all."

"Deanne's out of town," said the voice.

"Yes. We know that. She's in Myrtle Beach, visiting her in-laws," said Jack.

"I don't know anything about where she is," said the voice.

"Well, we do, because we're good friends," said Jack.

Emma whispered, pulling at his arm, "There's another one."

Jack turned his head. A man carrying some kind of long gun stood next to the house directly across the street, a few feet from the corner of the garage bays.

"Keep moving," he said. "The guy to our right won't be able to see us if we keep walking."

"How does it help us with the other guy," she said.

"I don't know," whispered Jack.

Jack heard the familiar sound of a garage door opening. *Shit. Here we go.* The garage door to their right was already a quarter of the way open. He would have told Emma to run, but the figure across the street had taken a more active stance with his rifle.

A man ducked under the garage and stood upright, pointing something at them. Jack didn't think it was a pistol, though he couldn't tell for sure in the sketchy light.

"Stop right there!" said the man.

Jack complied, pulling Emma behind him. "Seriously. We're not here to cause trouble. We're getting the hell out of Indianapolis. Simple as that. We'll be on the road in the morning."

Emma whispered very quietly in his ear, "That's not a gun. It looks like a Nerf blaster wrapped in tape or something."

His wife had far better sight than him, so it was entirely possible.

"Are you sure?"

"Definitely," she said. "And I'm pretty sure the guy across the street is holding a broom handle. If it's a gun, it's a Revolutionary War flintlock."

"You're awesome, Emma," he said, stifling a laugh.

"Time to go!" said the guy standing in front of his open garage.

Jack was done at this point. If it had been a real gun, he would have been diplomatic, eventually turning around and finding a nice spot in the woods somewhere—away from this crazy shit. Since that wasn't the case, he decided to go with a less subtle approach.

"Dude, that's a Nerf gun," said Jack. "I can see the tape on it."

"It's real," said the man, with zero confidence.

"No, it's not," said Jack. "And the guy across the street is carrying a broom handle—or a rake. We're not here to cause trouble. I promise you that."

"We have guns in the neighborhood trained on you right now," said the man, in a shaky voice.

"No, you don't."

"The guy next to your supposed friend is a cop," said the man, pointing two houses down. "You stay in the Chases' backyard, and you'll deal with him in the morning."

"Good. It'll be nice to talk to someone with answers," said Jack. "And an understanding of the law."

"I doubt he'll be up for any of your nonsense."

"Odds are that we'll be gone before he wakes up," said Jack. "Like I said, we're pressing north."

Emma nudged him and whispered, "See if he has phone service or Internet."

"Do you have any phone service?" said Jack.

"What?" said the man. "Why?"

"My parents live a few hours north. If you have a landline or Internet service, we could get in touch with them. They'd come get us right away."

"We're not stupid," said the man. "Nobody is letting you in their house."

"Then let me jump on your Wi-Fi," said Jack. "I can do that from here."

"I'm not getting any Wi-Fi signals," said Emma.

"You won't. We lost everything about four hours ago," said the man. "How do you know the Chases?"

"I know her from NevoTech. We both work in the finance department," said Emma.

"Are you going to put the Nerf gun down?" said Jack.

The man lowered the plastic gun and took a few cautious steps toward them. "Sorry about that. We're doing our best to keep an eye on the neighborhood. We had a violent break-in earlier. People walking up from Indy."

"I promise you we're not here to break into any houses," said Jack. "We're just looking for a relatively safe place to crash out until first light. The Chases' screen porch sounded more appealing than the forest. I'm Jack, by the way. This is my wife, Emma."

"Travis," he said. "That's Spencer across the street. Pretty sure that's a broom handle."

"It is!" yelled Spencer. "I'm going back in if everything's all right."

Travis gave him a thumbs-up before turning his attention back to the conversation. "How far have you travelled?"

"Broad Ripple," said Jack. "We had a Jeep, but lost that in an accident at Seventy-Ninth and Michigan. Been on foot ever since. Not that the Jeep would have made a difference."

"What do you mean?"

"The 465 has been turned into some kind of quarantine boundary zone—patrolled by the National Guard."

"What?" said Travis. "You're not serious."

"I wish I wasn't," said Jack. "They've set up blockades a few blocks ahead of any on-ramps, overpasses or underpasses. We managed to sneak across the interstate between vehicle patrols."

"This is fucking insane," said Travis. "The whole 465 is a quarantine line?"

"That's what the National Guard soldiers at Ditch and Eighty-Sixth said. The whole thing."

"What the hell is happening in Indianapolis?" said Travis.

"Nobody knows," said Emma. "But it's more than just a flu thing, like the news suggests."

"We're not even getting the news anymore," said Travis. "Spencer has a TV with an antenna. Nothing."

"It's almost like an information blackout," said Jack.

"Blackout," repeated Travis. "What if the power goes next?"

Jack honestly hadn't thought of that. He wasn't even sure if that was possible on a wide scale. What were they talking about here? Some kind of conspiracy? Even if that was the case, cutting the power would have a disastrous impact on the National Guard's efforts to enforce the 465 quarantine. Or would it? The soldiers all wore night vision. Jesus. Cutting the power might actually make it easier for them!

"That's why we're getting as far away from here as possible," said Jack.

"Sounds like we need to give this some serious thought, too," said Travis.

"I don't think it's a crazy idea. At least until things settle down," said Jack, wanting to add *if they ever settle down.*

"Jack, I need to lie down," said Emma.

"All right," he said to her, turning back to Travis. "We're going to crash in the Chases' screen room, then take off in the morning. Are we good?"

"We're good. Try not to make much noise," said Travis. "The police officer that lives next door got back about forty minutes ago from his shift. I have no idea what he'll do if he finds you there."

"We'll be discreet," said Jack. "Good luck, Travis. Let's hope this all goes away soon."

"Until a few minutes ago, I thought this was a temporary glitch. You know—a momentary panic. Now I'm not so sure," he said. "Safe travels tomorrow."

They continued down the sidewalk, crossing the street in front of the Chases' house. Emma confirmed the address, and they walked up the driveway, slipping around the house into the backyard. Jack looked at the murky forest, seriously wondering if they might be better off hidden in the foliage. He wasn't worried about Travis or any of the neighbors. They seemed harmless enough, and they clearly didn't have access to any firearms. Jack was far more concerned about the home invasion Travis had mentioned.

It wouldn't be long before hundreds, if not thousands of people slipped past the 465, all of them desperate to get the hell out of the greater Indianapolis area. Jack and Emma hadn't been the only people heading north, but they'd only seen a few other groups. Not enough to convince him to hide out in the forest.

They found the screen porch unlocked, not that it would have taken more than a few seconds to cut through the screen and flip the latch—another reminder that the screen room provided a false sense of enclosure and security. Jack knew the forest was the better option, but the wide cushions on the L-shaped couch in front of him sang a more compelling siren song. He could already feel himself drifting to sleep.

"You gonna move?" said Emma, gently nudging him in the back.

He shook his head, still standing in the doorway. "I think I fell asleep standing up."

"I don't care where you sleep at this point," said Emma. "As long as it's not between me and that couch."

Jack stepped out of the way and held the door open, making room for Emma, who dropped her pack and plopped onto the closest section of the couch. He shut the screen door gently, lowering his own pack to the concrete floor.

"That's it?" he said.

"Yep. Too tired for all of the formalities. Love you. Good night," said Emma before turning on her side.

"Sure you don't want to slip into your bivy bag?" he said.

"I'm good," she said, raising her head. "Give me a kiss."

He pressed his lips against her cheek. "Sleep tight. Do you want me to set an alarm?"

"Not really," she said. "We'll wake up with the sun."

"Or to one of the neighbors," said Jack. "Hopefully not the cop next door."

"We'll be fine," mumbled Emma.

Jack locked the screen door, for what it was worth, and took a seat on the other side of the sectional couch. He dug through his pack, removing a fleece jacket that he unzipped and placed on top of Emma. She always woke up cold. Leaning against the cushions, he took a long sip from his nearly empty three-liter CamelBak. They'd need to spend some time at one of the neighborhood retention ponds in the morning, filtering water and refilling their hydration bladders. It wouldn't take too long, since their Katadyn filter could treat close to two liters per minute.

He swung his feet up onto the couch and moved one of the outdoor pillows under his head, immediately starting to fade away. Jack twitched a few times, waking himself from the inevitable slumber, each time sinking a little deeper into sleep. He jarred awake again, this time from something else. A noise somewhere close by in the neighborhood.

Jack nudged Emma's foot, trying to rouse her from what he

hoped was a shallow sleep. She murmured something before going quiet again. He raised his head to a point where he could see out of the room, catching some movement in the police officer's backyard. Two figures walked off the deck and stopped on the grass, adjusting oversized backpacks. Both men. One looked distinctly younger than the other. He guessed that was the police officer's son.

Both of them carried rifles, their shapes unmistakable. These weren't broom handles. He was sure of that. After a few moments, they set off for the woods, disappearing into the dark mass of trees behind the row of houses. Why the hell would they do that? Maybe he was too tired to think it through, but he could only come up with one reason right now, and it didn't bode well for anyone.

"Emma," he whispered, shaking her arm.

Her eyes fluttered open, focusing on him for a second before closing.

"Emma," he said, putting a hand gently over her mouth and pinching her.

"Owww," she said, her voice muffled by his hand. "What the hell?"

"Sorry," said Jack. "The cop next door just left. He had someone with him. Looked like an older teenager. They walked into the woods with huge backpacks—and rifles."

"So?" she said, trying to keep her eyes open.

"Why would they be leaving on foot?" said Jack.

"How do you know it was the cop if you couldn't really see them?"

"Who else would it be?" said Jack. "That's the house Travis pointed to. I think he knows something nobody else knows."

"Who? Travis?" she said, still out of it.

"No. The cop," said Jack. "He just got back from his shift, and now he's hiking out of town? He knows something nobody else knows."

"Like what?"

"I don't know, but I think we should follow him," said Jack.

"Two guys armed with rifles?" said Emma, sounding a little more lucid. "I don't think that's a good idea."

"We'll follow them from a distance. A long distance," said Jack. "They're walking for a reason. What if there's another quarantine line out there? A police officer would know about it. They could guide us through it."

Emma rubbed her eyes and took a deep breath. "You're serious, aren't you?"

"I'd lie back down and go to sleep if I didn't think this was an important opportunity," said Jack.

"I hate you right now," said Emma, cracking a thin smile. "But I still love you."

Jack kissed her forehead. "Trust me. Those two know what they're doing. We just keep our distance and everything will be fine."

He hoped.

Chapter Thirty

Eric Larsen scanned the aircraft's cargo hold, making his best assessment of the other teams. Specter, led by Ragan, and Banshee, led by Webb, were outfitted the same as his team. Standard MultiCam pattern, which was typically used in non-arid, forested or "green" climates. This meant they would stay out of urban areas, more than likely operating on the peripheries of the suburbs, making a onetime foray into housing areas to secure their objective.

They fielded what he considered a light combat load consisting of plate-carrier vests fitted with a reduced number of rifle magazines and equipment pouches. It was a streamlined kit that sacrificed a significant degree of ballistic protection for unhindered movement and agility.

Their weapons load-out reflected the same. HK416A5s with eleven-inch barrels—fitted with EOTech holographic sights and AN/PEQ-15 Advanced Target Pointer/Illuminator/Aiming Laser (ATPIAL). Compact enough to use in close-quarters combat and street situations, but not suited for longer-range battlefield engagements. Not that they expected any.

Unless society broke down en masse, he couldn't envision a scenario in which any of the teams would ever need to use firearms to accomplish their missions. Better safe than sorry, he supposed, and from what he'd seen during dozens of "full dress" drills with the unit, this was the heaviest load-out provided to the teams.

Their job was to protect high-value individuals (HVI) critical to the nation's continuity of operations plan in the event of a widespread attack or disaster. Essentially, it was an expensive and dramatic form of high-value babysitting dreamed up by someone in Washington, D.C.—with way too much time on their hands.

Vampire team, Ochoa's band of misfits, was the anomaly on board the aircraft. They were dressed in street clothes, carrying nondescript, medium-sized backpacks containing nearly all of their mission gear. They'd been a bit secretive about their load-out for some reason. Larsen mostly attributed it to Ochoa being a defective asshole, but maybe there was more to it. He'd seen a few Vampire team members pull MP7 submachine guns from the preloaded packs, along with long suppressors. By his best guess, Vampire was headed into either an urban or densely packed suburban environment.

Nobody knew, of course. None of the teams had received their final orders. The customized kits were their only indication of what the mission might entail—if this was even a real mission. It wouldn't be the first time they'd geared up and stood at the aircraft's ramp, ready to jump into the night. Hell, they'd even jumped before—their navigation system directing them to a drop zone back on Grissom Reserve Air Base. Tonight felt different to Larsen. He couldn't say why, but he had the distinct feeling that this was the real deal.

"Any updates?" said Randy Dixon, his head pressed to the nylon jump-seat strap next to him.

"Nothing," said Larsen. "As usual. The kit is our only hint."

"Kind of overkill on the weapons," said Dixon.

"A little," said Larsen. "But who knows what we're jumping into. We're the last resort—when the situation on the ground has deteriorated beyond a certain point."

"And what point is that?" said Dixon.

"No idea," said Larsen. "I assume we'll find out shortly."

"Or we'll turn around and head back to Grissom. Like always."

"I can think of harder ways to make six figures," said Larsen.

"Good point," said Dixon.

Larsen nudged Jennifer Brennan with his foot. She lay on the metal deck in front of them, her head propped on her backpack.

"What?" she snapped.

"Just making sure you're awake," said Larsen.

"It's three in the morning," she said, her eyes still closed.

He smiled and shook his head. "Fucking rogue's gallery is what I got."

Dixon laughed. "All but Pecker-head."

Larsen looked over at James Peck, who had taken a seat on the deck with Ochoa's team. Peck was a problem. Not a mission-failure kind of problem, but a thorn-in-the-side type. Something none of them needed, especially in a critical position on a high-stress mission. He'd tried to get Peck reassigned, but the process of removing or reassigning a member of the Critical High-value Asset Security (CHASE) program required documentation. Lots of documentation. The kind he wasn't used to dealing with.

As a SEAL platoon commander, Larsen had nearly complete authority over the composition of his team. He didn't handpick them from scratch, but if he didn't think one of the officers or enlisted men was a good fit with the rest of the platoon—end of discussion.

Unfortunately, few of those safeguards seemed to be in place here. Ochoa was a prime example. He could think of others. That said, most of the members he'd gotten to know were pretty squared away. Former cops, Marines, soldiers and federal agent types—all willing to abide by the most restrictive set of security rules he'd ever come across. He had to remember that. There were only a few rotten eggs in the bunch.

Unfortunately, one of them was assigned to his team. Actually, he wasn't a shit bag. James Peck had deployed twice with 1st Battalion, 75th Ranger Regiment to Afghanistan and had been awarded a Bronze Star with valor during a two-day-long operation in the Korengal Valley. Larsen had initially been thrilled with Peck's assignment, but the honeymoon didn't last long. He'd have to keep a very close eye on Peck.

"He's the literal definition of rogue," said Larsen. "What is Ochoa shit-talking about now? How he got booted from the Dallas PD?"

"Suspended," said Dixon. "Unfairly from what I heard."

"You mean from what he's said?"

"Of course," said Dixon, shaking his head. "That's why he quit. They kept suspending him for no reason."

Brennan started laughing. "Yeah. That's pretty normal. Three suspensions in five years."

They all laughed at that, drawing looks from Ochoa's team and Peck. Ochoa cocked his head, something stupid about to pass through his lips.

"Telling more fag jokes, Larsen?" said Ochoa.

Peck laughed with Ochoa's crew, and even some of Ragan's team joined in. He knew he should let it go. Nothing good would come of responding—but he just couldn't pass up another opportunity to shut this asshole down. Yelling over the aircraft's engine noise, Larsen delivered his retort.

"No. We were just trying to figure out how you got suspended from the Dallas PD," said Larsen, Ochoa's smile vanishing, "three times in five years. That's gotta be a fucking record!"

Ochoa hesitated before opening his mouth again. "And what's so funny about that?"

"Nothing at all. Pretty fucking disturbing, actually," said Larsen.

The cargo bay lights shifted to a monochromatic red before Ochoa could respond. Showtime. Or fake showtime. Didn't matter either way. They'd treat it the same until the moment the drill was stopped. Larsen was about to call Peck over, but the former Ranger was already on his way. He might be a surly asshole, but it never got in the way of getting things done. He was thankful for that. When Peck arrived, Larsen got them working on the second part of their kit.

"Suit up for the drop," said Larsen. "I'll synch DZ data when everyone is ready."

The aircraft's loadmaster, a wiry guy draped in a flight suit, walked down the center of the cargo hold with a handheld scanner. He stopped next to Larsen's team and ran the scanner over the electronic lock attached to each of the remaining unopened Pelican cases. The locks clicked open, allowing them access to the rest of their gear, which would consist of the parachutes.

"No oxygen. Regular altitude jump. Square rigs," said Dixon.

Larsen gave Dixon a thumbs-up while he activated the team's CTAB (command tablet). The rugged military device had a built-in satellite antennae for receiving mission updates and connecting to the MILSTAR battlefield information network. He could download local maps, access real-time satellite imagery and conduct mission-related research using the tablet. Most of that would be included in his mission download anyway, but planners couldn't think of everything.

The main screen told him *ZOMBIE MISSION PROFILE UPDATED*. He glanced around, seeing the other team leaders doing the same thing. At this point, none of the team leaders were allowed to communicate with each other. Their missions were considered separately classified operations. TOP SECRET. In fact, the team leaders weren't allowed to brief their own teams regarding the objective until they hit the ground. The only information he could share was the drop zone location, which he would upload to the heads-up displays (HUD) integrated into their helmets.

Larsen pressed the screen, activating the mission packet. The first thing he did was click the OBJECTIVE tab, checking out the drop zone (DZ). Interesting. The primary DZ was located twenty miles north of the center of Indianapolis, in Westfield. He zoomed the satellite image in on the DZ, seeing that it was located in the middle of a forest—in a small clearing that contained a single house. Precision landing. An alternate DZ had been designated a quarter of a mile southeast of the clearing, on the edge of what appeared to be a sprawling farm. He noticed a small regional airport two and a half miles northwest of the primary drop zone, wondering if that would be the extraction point.

He clicked on the High Value Individual (HVI) tab within the OBJECTIVE screen, where he was shown a name, several identifying pictures and a few lines of information pertinent to the mission.

MISSION TYPE:
LOCATE/SECURE/PROTECT/TRANSPORT.

HVI: EUGENE CHANG. PICTURES PROVIDED CURRENT.

-NO PRIOR MILITARY SERVICE OR SIMILAR DOCUMENTED TRAINING.

-HOME LOCATED AT PRIMARY DZ OWNED BY EUGENE CHANG.

-HOME STRONGLY SUSPECTED TO BE SECURED BY ALARM SYSTEM.

-EXTERNAL MOTION DETECTORS SUSPECTED.

-NO KNOWN FIREARMS ASSOCIATED WITH EUGENE CHANG.

-TEAM WILL REMAIN ON-SITE WITH HVI AND AWAIT INSTRUCTIONS.

-HVI MAY NOT BE AT RESIDENCE.

-IF HVI NOT PRESENT, TEAM WILL REMAIN IN PLACE AND AWAIT INSTRUCTIONS.

The intelligence package didn't include any information betraying why the HVI was considered important enough to be secured by a CHASE team, and it didn't matter. They treated each mission the same.

Larsen cleared the tablet screen, sliding it into one of his reinforced cargo pockets. He'd secure it into a specially designed compartment on his parachute equipment rig just before the jump. With the tablet and its data secure from prying eyes, he joined the team, helping them don their MC-4 Ram Air Parachute Systems. When every member of the team, including himself, was secure in an MC-4 rig, they attached their custom drop bags.

Each drop bag contained a preloaded backpack based on the wearer's specialty, case-protected night-vision gear and a padded sleeve for a rifle. The bag was worn in front of the parachutist, attached to the MC-4 rig, and would be manually released shortly before landing. Ideally, the bag would come to the end of its line several feet above the ground and gently lower to the earth with the parachutist.

With the drop bags attached and their rifles stowed inside, he pulled his Jump HUD goggles over his face and toggled a rubber button under the center of the goggles. A green display appeared at the bottom of his right eye, flashing the words *NO INPUT*.

"Let's get the goggles synched," said Larsen before removing the CTAB from his pocket.

While the team adjusted their goggles, he pressed his thumb to the biometric reader on the bottom right corner of the device and activated the screen. He was the only member of the team that could activate the tablet while he was still alive. If he was killed or permanently incapacitated, the tablet could be unlocked if all three remaining members pressed their thumbs to the reader in a predetermined sequence only known to Dixon, at which point only Dixon's thumbprint could unlock the device from that moment forward. There was no contingency procedure to transfer command if Larsen and another member of the team were killed at the same time. He presumed the people that came up with this system had a reason for that.

He pressed the COMMS tab and selected HUDSYNCH, finding four devices designated *zombieHUD*. A few seconds later, the tablet indicated that the *dzdata-zombie* had been synched to the small navigation units attached to the Jump HUD goggles. The data in his own display changed, in addition to the appearance of a small green arrow, which pointed to the DZ.

ALT8200 : HDG340 : DIST40.3 : DIR355

Altitude eight thousand and two hundred feet. Heading 340 or sharply northwest. Distance to DZ was forty point three miles. Direction to DZ 355, or almost due north. Based on a quick calculation, they were nearly twenty miles south of Indianapolis, heading north. Three to four minutes away. If any of this was real.

"Everyone got the feed?" he said, getting a positive response from everyone.

"Helmets on," said Larsen before fastening his own into place.

He looked around the cargo bay for the loadmaster, who was headed in his direction.

"Is Zombie all synched up?" said the loadmaster when he reached him.

"System says we're a go," said Larsen. "Team reports positive feed."

"All right," he said. "Secure your CTAB and stack up behind Specter. First jump is in two minutes."

Larsen nodded and turned to his team, who all acknowledged what the loadmaster had said. After stuffing the CTAB in a hip pouch attached to his tactical vest, underneath the parachute harness, he triggered his communications headset. "Final radio check."

After everyone responded using their headsets, he led them to the ramp. They waddled with the drop bags banging into the front of their legs, and formed a two by two column behind Ragan's team. When all teams were in place on the nonskid deck, the lighting shifted to a deep blue and a single red light appeared on the jump-status panel next to the loadmaster station. A moment later, the ramp started to lower, the smell of fresh air rushing through the cargo hold.

The loadmaster stopped the ramp when it was flush with the deck, creating a level walk for the parachutists. Beyond the edge of the ramp, clusters of lights dotted the distant, murky darkness. It still wasn't too late for them to call this off. If the ramp closed right now, he wouldn't be surprised.

The light turned green, the loadmaster immediately giving Ochoa the hand signal to jump, and Vampire team walked slowly forward—vanishing into the night. The light turned red again, and the aircraft gently roll to port, the heading in his HUD changing from 340 degrees to 260—almost due west. Less than two minutes later, Specter joined the night.

This wasn't a drill, or they would have dropped both teams in the same location. Maybe. This could be the most elaborate drill yet. He wouldn't know for sure until they hit the ground and secured Chang. Possibly not even then. That was the bizarre thing about these missions. Information was kept to a bare minimum, almost to the point where they could execute an entirely real mission and still think it was a drill, especially if the disaster or national crisis triggering the CHASE team deployment was a distant terrorist attack. Unless there was some nearby sign of trouble, how would they know? Once again, it didn't matter. They'd do the job regardless of the bigger picture. That was the deal.

Chapter Thirty-One

Larsen watched the DIST and ALT numbers in his Jump HUD, making minor adjustments to his body posture to get as close to the drop zone as possible at one thousand feet AGL (above ground level). That would give him more than enough time to locate the clearing in the middle of the trees and steer his parachute for a precise landing. Since the sky was clear and the moon was close to full, he should have no problem identifying the drop zone without the aid of night-vision devices. If planners had predicted a problem, his helmet would have been pre-fitted with the night-vision goggles that sat in a hardened case within his drop bag.

At an altitude of two thousand feet, he'd closed the distance to the DZ to a little over a thousand feet. With more than two hundred free-fall parachute drops under his belt, he could track through the air at a one-to-one glide ratio, which meant he'd reach the parachute deployment point directly over his objective.

As the numbers rapidly decreased, Larsen was certain that he could see the drop zone below. It was hard to miss. A lightened square patch in the middle of a sea of dark treetops. He'd overshoot it a little, but that wouldn't matter. When his altitude read one thousand feet, he deployed the parachute, the MC-4 harness yanking him unforgivingly when the parachute filled with air.

Instantly going from one hundred and thirty feet per second to fourteen felt like a simultaneous gut punch and wedgie, the violent shock of it one of the most welcome thrashings of your life. It meant your parachute worked, which was especially important at one thousand feet above the ground, where you didn't have much time to deploy the reserve chute if something went wrong.

He grabbed the toggles above him and took control of the parachute, turning in the direction of the drop zone, which was a few hundred feet behind him. The parachute responded immediately, setting him on a course to intercept the forest clearing. He'd likely have to spiral lazily around the DZ several times once he was directly overhead so he didn't stray too far from the clearing and find himself in an undesirable situation. Wind changes. Thermal rises. All kinds of unpredictable last minute nonsense would thwart a careless approach. The wind was predicted to be light, but he'd spent enough time in the Midwest to know that the wind rarely cooperated.

Larsen glanced upward, relieved to find three dark, square shapes above him, headed in the same direction. As far as he was concerned, the hard part was over. The drop zone was wide enough to accommodate a simultaneous landing, which was the default plan he'd discussed on the aircraft. A minute and a half later, he skimmed the treetops along the southern edge of the clearing and toggled the brakes, slowing his rate of forward and downward motion. He released his parachute drop bag and drifted steadily toward the northern side of the field. The drop bag grazed the field, tugging gently on his harness and letting him know he was moments from hitting the ground. He flared his parachute moments later and landed smoothly on his feet, jogging forward to avoid the deflated parachute.

He immediately turned and saw that the rest of the team had landed, each of them on their feet and moving to get away from their parachutes. It had been a textbook drop and an excellent start to the mission.

"Zombie, status report," he said into his headset, immediately getting a positive reply from everyone.

"Copy. Secure parachutes and gear up. Looks like we didn't wake anyone up."

The house in the middle of the clearing was completely dark, inside and out. Examining it for a few seconds, he seriously doubted anyone was home. He would have expected to see something inside, like an oven light or bathroom light. The outside wasn't promising either. He didn't detect any exterior uplighting or a porch light.

"Looks like nobody's home," said Dixon over the radio net.

"It does look pretty dark," said Larsen. "We'll know in a few minutes."

Larsen detached his parachute from the MC-4 shoulder harness points and gathered the billowing material into a pile. He then removed the entire harness system and crudely stuffed as much of the parachute as he could into the now empty main parachute compartment. Satisfied that the parachute wasn't going anywhere immediately, he retrieved his drop bag and pulled his rifle out of its sleeve, checking it over for any obvious damage. He didn't expect any, but it was better safe than sorry when it came to your primary weapon.

Night vision was next. He unsnapped the hardened case and removed a pair of AN/PVS-14 monocular night-vision goggles. Within seconds, he'd attached the night-vision device to the mounting bracket on his helmet and activated its green-scale, light-intensified image. A quick sweep of the house showed no light sources beyond moonlight reflecting off the solar panels and windows. He jogged to Dixon, who had just snapped his night-vision goggles into place.

"Looks completely dead," whispered Larsen.

"That's a bummer," said Dixon.

"Depends on how you look at it," said Larsen. "If this is a drill, then the world isn't coming to an end."

"Or it's coming to an end," said Dixon. "And you were sent to the wrong place."

"Good point," said Larsen before raising his night-vision goggles. "Gather the team on me. I'm going to report our status."

Dixon patted him on the shoulder and took off, heading for Brennan, who appeared to be struggling with her night-vision mount. While his second in command squared away the rest of the team, Larsen took the CTAB out of his hip pouch and pressed his thumb to the biometric reader. The device automatically calibrated to the available light, giving him just enough illumination to read the screen without shining a light on his face that could be seen by the enemy. Of course, anyone using night vision could see the screen from a mile away, which was why he would never use it in the open under hostile conditions.

When the screen activated, he immediately saw a high-priority flag, which meant something had changed. He shook his head, guessing CHASE HQ had just received new intelligence verifying that Chang was not here. Even more likely, it was a message confirming that this had been a drill and providing RTB (return to base) instructions.

Before chasing down the new information, he opened the PROGRESS tab and pressed TEAM LANDED, followed by PRIMARYDZ and NOCASREP. Team landed at primary DZ with no casualties to report. He wasn't a big fan of the CTAB's push-button mission-reporting system, but had to admit that it kept things simple, and with hundreds of CHASE teams deployed simultaneously around the country—he assumed—it was probably the only reasonable way to keep track of it all. And he could always call via satellite phone if he encountered something the software planners hadn't programmed into one of the screens.

The reply to his status update arrived instantly.

ZOMBIEXC33 STATUS UPDATE RCVD
IMMEDIATELY ACKNOWLEDGE MISSION UPDATE

"Okay. Okay," he muttered. "Let's see what's so important."

He read the message twice, thinking he had misread it the first time. What the fuck was this?

MISSION TYPE CHANGED
MISSION TYPE: CAPTURE/KILL
-CAPTURE ONLY IF SITUATION PRESENTS NO RISK TO TEAM

-HVI LIKELY ARMED
-HVI LIKELY AWARE OF MISSION

CAPTURE/KILL? Did he miss part of their training? At no point during his year tenure in the CHASE program had he heard of CAPTURE/KILL being a mission type. This was beyond bizarre. He was familiar enough with the designation from his SEAL days. It was the kind of label slapped on a high-value enemy target in the general area of operations when headquarters didn't want to come right out and say "kill this motherfucker if you see him."

Larsen opened the MISSION tab, still seeing the original profile, with the change next to it. He clicked through the photographs, shaking his head. Something was really off with this. How did the mission change that quickly? No more than fifteen minutes had elapsed since he'd first received the mission data synchronization. Now this Chang guy was suddenly armed and aware of his team? That was one hell of an intelligence shift, and he didn't buy it.

A hand patted his shoulder, startling him. Brennan settled in next to him, cradling her rifle.

"Shit. Am I not supposed to see that?" said Brennan.

"It's fine. I need to give everyone a good look at the HVI," said Larsen. "Meet Eugene Chang."

Brennan raised her NVGs. "I don't think he's home."

"Neither do I," said Larsen.

"Do you think it's a drill?"

"My gut says no. It would be the most elaborate drill to date," said Larsen. "And I'm not getting any orders to stand down. We're going in."

Dixon and Peck arrived, ready to proceed. Larsen paused for a second, carefully considering what to say. Since he had no intention of killing Eugene Chang, he'd omit the new information. They'd proceed like nothing had changed and "secure" Chang. Locate. Secure. Capture. Same result. Different word. If at any point things got dicey, he'd order the team to stand down and take up positions to observe and protect. That was standard procedure if an HVI refused to comply with a CHASE team's orders. Nobody would suspect he'd modified the orders. Since he controlled the mission data, he controlled the mission.

"Take a quick look at Eugene Chang," said Larsen. "Shouldn't be too hard to identify. Mission is to locate, secure, protect and escort. No firearms on record. Possible alarm system and external motion sensors. Not sure if the sensors are linked to the alarm or just external lights. I see some floodlights mounted under the roof overhangs. I suspect the front is the same."

"We could use the suppressors and shoot out the lights," said Peck.

Not wanting to immediately slap down the ridiculous idea and piss off Peck even more, Larsen went with a more diplomatic response.

"I thought of that when I first saw the house," said Larsen. "But we're looking at a half-dozen light fixtures. Each with two lights. That's twelve bullets passing through the house. I don't think we can risk the outside chance one of those bullets hits Chang or convinces him he's under attack. We're gonna scare the shit out of him as it is."

Peck nodded. "I hadn't thought of that. Though I doubt it would matter. The house looks empty. Even for three thirty in the morning."

"That's why I'm thinking it doesn't matter," said Larsen. "I'll range ahead and see what's up with the lights. If Chang is there, I'll make contact with him and explain the situation. If he doesn't answer, we'll enter the house."

"I'll move the team into the high grasses while you investigate," said Dixon. "Just in case."

"Better safe than sorry."

Chapter Thirty-Two

Soaked through his clothes with sweat and swatting bugs continuously, Chang started to seriously regret his decision to hike to the airport. The backpack he'd previously assembled as a bug-out bag, based on the combined input of several prepper websites, had seemed like a good idea riding shotgun in his Toyota 4Runner. On his back, the straps digging into his shoulders and the weight pulling him off balance with every uneven step, the pack felt like a horrible idea. He only had himself to blame, of course. He'd never walked more than twenty feet with the pack before, and that was after heaving it onto one shoulder and setting it in the corner of his safe room.

Less than two hundred yards into his journey, not even five percent of the way to the airport, according to his GPS unit, all Chang could think about was discarding items from his backpack that had taken him weeks to decide belonged in it! On top of that, it didn't help that he was out of shape. Not horribly unfit, but enough to make hauling fifty pounds of survival gear through a thick forest difficult.

He paused for a moment, leaning against a tree to take a sip from the CamelBak he'd never used before. The water had a rubbery taste, which was to be expected for a brand-new bladder. He hadn't rinsed it prior to filling it from the sink tonight. All of his gear was brand new, unused and untested. Chang had no doubt all of it would work. It was top-of-the-line stuff, no expense spared, but even the best gear was borderline useless if you didn't know how to use it. He shook his head at the thought and pressed on in the dark, wondering if that pair of night-vision goggles he'd considered purchasing for around four thousand dollars would have made any difference. Probably not.

After several more minutes of trudging through the trees and thick forest growth, he stopped to check his GPS unit, encouraged that he'd travelled another hundred yards. Seven percent of the way there! Ha! At this rate he'd be there long after sunrise, with little hope of sneaking into his hangar and executing his plan. He assumed the airport was heavily guarded. It simply had to be. Technically, it sat inside the quarantine boundary, but every plane that took off represented an immediate quarantine breach. It would be guarded, and approaching it during the day would be risky.

The cell phone in one of his vest pockets buzzed. Maybe cell service had been restored! Chang wasn't sure how that helped him, but just the thought of it excited him. He retrieved the phone and opened the message center, finding an alert notification from his home security system. Had he forgotten to close a door? Maybe to the patio? He hoped not. There was no way he was backtracking at this point.

He opened the home security center application on his phone and investigated the alert notification. The long-distance motion sensors covering the clearing behind his house had been triggered a few moments ago. How could something trigger the sensors in the clearing without being detected in the forest? Chang glanced in what he thought was the direction of his house, unable to make out anything through the dense trees and darkness.

He waited for the system to analyze the data and give him a clearer picture of exactly what had set off the motion detectors. The system gave him a preliminary answer moments later. Four objects had "appeared" halfway between the house and the edge of the clearing behind his house, spread out evenly in the backyard. What the hell could this be? It was almost like someone had dug four tunnels and popped up out of the ground. No sense in guessing. It was time for a closer look.

Chang navigated on his phone to the camera controls and selected one of the night-vision-capable units facing the backyard. The green image that appeared nearly caused him to topple over. Two of the "objects" were in view, and it was immediately clear how they had appeared without triggering the forest sensors. They had parachuted into the clearing.

The figures gathered what looked to be some kind of square rig parachute used by Special Forces soldiers. He'd seen this type of precision-maneuvering parachute at the various military air shows he'd attended since starting his flying career. He took control of the camera and panned it to the left, seeing two more figures doing the same thing. Paralyzed by fear, he stared at the screen, barely able to comprehend what he was seeing. They had come for him, just like Greenberg had warned. He cupped a hand over the screen, cutting down on the light reflecting off his face. Couldn't be too careful.

A few minutes later, the four figures gathered together in a small group, appearing to dig through the squat rectangular bags they had hauled from their original drop locations. He zoomed in on the group, squinting at his phone. It was hard to tell in the grainy night-vision image, but it looked like a few of them had removed rifles from the bags. The others donned backpacks and attached night-vision goggles to their helmets. When they were finished with the bags, all four of them had rifles.

The weapons were slung across their chests, like soldiers on patrol in the news clips from Iraq and Afghanistan. He wasn't sure if that was good or bad, but at least they weren't pointing at the house. The soldier leading the group took out some kind of digital tablet, the screen illuminating his face green in the night-vision camera. The leader pressed the tablet several times, studying whatever it told him, before the rest of the team gathered around him.

He considered his options. He could continue toward the airport, hoping that the team sent to kill or capture him didn't come to the same conclusion. Chang hadn't exactly concealed the fact that he'd just been in the house. Half-empty glasses. Food wrappers in the trash. The truck filled with survival gear. Both cars still in the garage.

It wouldn't take long for them to figure out he'd recently departed on foot. Then what? They call the 10th Mountain Division and tell them to secure the airport? His pilot's license wasn't a secret, either.

Chang cursed under his breath, unsure what to do, until a crazy idea hit him. Bat-shit crazy as some might say, but entirely possible and relatively risk-free. Even if it didn't work, he was no worse off than he was right now. He had to give it a try. If it worked, Greenberg's new friends might be able to make some sense of who was behind these attacks.

Chapter Thirty-Three

Sitting against a thick tree trunk in the forest a few hundred yards north of his house, Chang monitored the four-person team with his smart phone. After gathering together briefly, three of them sprinted for the nearest cluster of ornamental grasses while the remaining team member walked toward the back patio—holding the tablet by his side. Based on the soldier's interaction with the rest of the team and his willingness to approach the house alone, he assumed this was the team leader. Chang studied him carefully as he continued toward the house, neither of his hands touching the rifle slung across his chest.

Who the hell were these people? At first he had assumed they were some kind of assassination team, but now he wasn't sure. They didn't act like one, or how he expected one to act. Then again, what did he know? Four heavily armed assassins probably wouldn't consider Chang any kind of threat, and maybe that was what he was seeing reflected in their attitudes. Either way, he wasn't going anywhere near the house. Not until his trap was sprung.

Hands slippery with sweat, he quickly navigated to the security system control panel and disabled the exterior, motion-sensor-activated lights. Next, he shut down the home's positive pressurization system and remotely unlocked the mudroom door facing the rear of the house, leaving the sliding doors locked. Chang didn't want to make it too easy or obvious. If he did this right, not only would he get his house back, he might get some answers.

Chapter Thirty-Four

Larsen reached the edge of an elaborate stone patio, a point where the motion detectors couldn't possibly miss him. He could see the sensors attached to the lights. It was starting to look more and more like Chang hadn't been here for a while. Why else would you leave the exterior lights off? At the sliding door, Larsen kneeled and looked inside, cupping his hands around his face. The interior was completely dark except for moonlight entering from the floor-to-ceiling windows. He lowered his night-vision goggles and pressed the front lens opening against the glass, forming a seal with the rubber.

He had a clear view to a kitchen, seeing nothing out of place on the spacious kitchen island or counters. Everywhere he looked was the same. Like nobody lived in the house, or whoever lived there was a meticulous neat freak. Larsen tried to move the patio slider, unsurprised when it didn't budge. He looked down the side of the house toward the garage, seeing a door without a window just beyond the patio.

"Dix, move the team up to the house. I don't see any signs of life inside. I think we'll pop open the door by the garage."

"Copy. Moving the team up."

Larsen walked along the house, stepping down off the patio and approaching the door. He crouched next to the entrance and waited for the team to arrive, examining the nearest light fixture. This one was different than the others. He stood up to get a better view, surprised to see a camera installed above the lights. The camera was pointed right at him, which made sense, since it covered the back door. He wondered if the cameras were deactivated, too. The team arrived in a tight formation, stacking up along the stone wall behind him.

"No window?" said Dixon, staring at the door with a perplexed look.

"I know. It's a little strange," said Larsen. "But I don't see any windows on the garage, either. It doesn't matter. We'll keep kicking doors down until we get inside the house. Be absolutely sure it's empty. If this isn't a drill and something really fucked is going on out there, Chang could be playing it really safe. Making it look like he's not here. We have to assume he's here until we determine otherwise. Peck, you want to do the honors?"

"Fuck yeah," said Peck, standing up and moving next to him.

Larsen shifted his rifle into the ready position and nodded at Peck, who stepped in front of the door and gave the kind of front kick that could cave a man's chest in. The door, however, didn't budge, and Peck toppled into the bushes behind him.

"Motherfucker!" yelled Peck. "That door is solid steel. Jesus!"

"Shhhhh," said Dixon. "Quiet the fuck down."

"What does it matter?" said Peck, getting back to his feet. "Nobody's home."

"You want to hit it again?" said Larsen. "Or are we looking at a demo charge? You hit that thing harder than hard, and I didn't hear it give at all."

"It didn't," said Peck. "It's solid as fuck."

Larsen tapped the door with the barrel of his rifle, immediately understanding the problem. Peck was right. It was metal, and not the kind of hollow metal doors they used in new home construction these days. This was solid metal.

"Brennan, blow it open," said Larsen.

Brennan slid along the group and crouched next to the door, making a quick assessment.

"I think you're looking at multiple deadlocks on this side," said

Larsen. "The door didn't budge at all when Peck hit it."

"Might be easier to break one of the glass sliders, honestly," said Brennan. "Sure as hell would be a lot quieter."

"Peck?" said Larsen.

"It would be my pleasure," said Peck, taking off in a dead sprint.

"Dix, make sure he doesn't cut himself," said Larsen.

They trailed Peck and Dixon, catching up when Peck stopped long enough to wrestle loose a softball-sized piece of smooth decorative stone from a granite slab display. Larsen was thinking more along the lines of hitting the glass with a rifle stock, but he supposed this would work, too. Peck picked up speed again and hurled the stone like a shot put at the patio slider. When it bounced off the glass and thudded across the patio, leaving little more than a scratch on the glass, they all stood there for a moment—completely baffled. Larsen knew what was coming next.

"Time for the heavy artillery!" yelled Peck, raising his rifle.

"Stop!" said Larsen. "Do. Not. Fire. You'll kill one of us or yourself with a ricochet."

"Why the fuck does this house have bullet-resistant glass?" yelled Peck, still aiming at the slider.

"Safe your weapon," said Larsen.

"It is safe," said Peck. "As long as I'm not pulling the trigger, it's fucking safe. What the fuck is this?"

"Let's get back to the door," said Larsen.

"I mean, who the fuck has a bulletproof, solid steel door constructed house?" said Peck.

"It doesn't matter," said Larsen. "We gain entry, and we search high and low for Mr. Chang. My guess is he's not here."

Back at the garage door, Brennan started to unpack her explosives kit.

"What if we can't demo the door?" said Dixon.

"Don't say that," said Larsen.

"Seriously, though."

"Then we report the situation and take up positions around the house. Keep the place secure," said Larsen, grabbing the doorknob in front of him for no real reason. "Nobody said this would be straightforward."

He turned the doorknob effortlessly and pushed the door inward, shaking his head as it swung open. That bad feeling vibe was back—a lot stronger this time.

"You've gotta be kidding me," said Dixon.

"Fucking idiot forgot to lock the back door," said Peck, walking carefree toward the opening.

"Peck!" said Larsen, putting an arm across the door to stop him. "Chill the fuck out."

Peck shot Larsen a murderous glare, slowly stepping back from the threshold of the house.

"We clear the house as a full team. Safeties engaged," said Larsen. "We'll clear the second level first and work our way down. Stack up, Brennan, Peck and Dixon. Watch your sectors."

They entered the house and stopped in a small slate-tiled room with cubbies for shoes and a row of hooks for hanging jackets. A long bench took up the wall just inside the door they'd opened. The room was empty besides the furniture.

"What's up with that door?" whispered Larsen.

While Dixon examined the door, Larsen took a few more steps into the room. A bathroom with what looked to be a half shower was located next to the door leading to the garage. He couldn't see into the house from the room; a wood-paneled door blocked his view. Could be a titanium-reinforced door for all he knew. The house seemed to be full of surprises.

"You ain't gonna believe this," said Dixon.

"Peck, watch the door to the house," he said, pointing Peck in the right direction. "Brennan, clear the bathroom."

He slid by the two operatives and joined Dixon at the door.

"Watch this," said Dixon.

He turned the latch on the inside of the door, above the doorknob, and six four-inch-deep-by-one-inch-thick bolts smoothly extended past the edge of the door. He examined the metal doorjamb, finding six steel-reinforced slots. Dixon reached around the outside of the door and turned the doorknob, returning the slots to their original positions flush against the edge of the door. The system was power driven, not purely mechanical, from what he could tell. Larsen didn't know what to make of it. The lock seemed disabled now. He looked around for a keypad, finding nothing.

"Bathroom clear," reported Brennan.

"Copy that," said Larsen, grabbing Dixon's arm. "Jam the door open."

He didn't like the idea of motorized locking mechanisms. If something went wrong, they could get trapped inside the house, especially if every door was constructed like this. They certainly weren't shooting their way through the windows. He was starting to seriously wonder who they were dealing with here and if the mission change reflected a legitimate danger to his team.

Once Dixon had wedged a flare under the door, pressing it against the wall, they continued the search. Keeping Peck in place watching the entrance to the main part of the house, he moved the team to the garage. Just inside the door, they located a biometric scanner and a keypad, which presumably prevented access from the garage. Like the door they'd used to enter the house, the garage door featured the same bolts and locking mechanism.

They found two vehicles inside the garage. A BMW convertible and a Toyota 4Runner. The third garage bay housed a serious riding mower. They scoured the garage for Chang, coming up empty, as he expected. On the way out of the garage, Dixon grabbed him by the arm.

"Engine's warm," said the former Marine staff sergeant.

Larsen pressed the exposed skin on his wrist to the hood, feeling the warmth. The vehicle hadn't been used minutes ago, but it had definitely been used within the past couple of hours. This changed everything. Or did it? They had been sent to secure and protect Eugene Chang, and there had never been any reason to assume he wasn't here.

Shit! He wasn't in the house! That was why the back door was rigged to open from outside? He'd left for some reason, but he hadn't gone far. Or did he somehow get word that a team was coming for him? Maybe he was watching them from the forest? Or he left the door open to lure them into an ambush? Too many variables had crept into the equation at this point, along with far too many assumptions.

It was time to start eliminating variables, the easiest one being the house.

"We clear the entire house. If we don't find Chang, which I suspect we won't, we'll lie low and wait. My guess is he's outside," said Larsen.

Dixon nodded, along with Brennan, who whispered, "What about Peck?"

"Keep this between us right now," said Larsen. "He's itching to shoot something. We clear the house first."

Chapter Thirty-Five

Chang watched the team methodically clear his house, room by room, starting with the upstairs. From what he could tell, they were good at their job. They'd discovered that his 4Runner was still warm from the aborted trip to the airport. They'd spent enough time examining the back door to figure out that the locking mechanism had been deactivated, though he was pretty sure they didn't understand how the system worked. They'd closed it before moving out of the mudroom, leaving some kind of device on the floor. He assumed it was a motion sensor, which meant they suspected he was outside the house.

They were probably sweeping the house so they could claim some secure space, and man, were they taking their time. Time he didn't have. If his plan at the house didn't work, it was back to slogging it toward the airport—and a very risky plan that required skills he didn't possess. If the house plan worked, it would buy him time and possibly a way out of this that didn't require him to spend the rest of his life as a fugitive. The team in his house didn't look like an assassination squad. If he could talk to them, he was sure he could work something out.

He fumbled with the phone to switch camera views, almost dropping it, as they gathered in the hallway next to the L-shaped staircase descending into the great room, careful not to move the camera. He'd almost blown it when the team leader scurried from the patio slider to the garage door. The camera had followed him the whole way, fortunately pausing in a natural position watching the back door. Originally, it had been pointed outward, guarding the expansive clearing behind the house.

The team moved in unison down the stairs, their rifles covering every direction. They were definitely spooked. Prior to encountering the solid steel back door, they hadn't paid much attention to their weapons. When the team reached the great room, they cleared the obvious hiding spaces, making their way to the adjoining office, where they spent a considerable amount of time searching the bookcases and cabinet drawers below them for secret passageways— he presumed. When they exited the office and started for the unexplored areas across the great room, he broke out in goose bumps. If they continued searching the house using the same tactics, there was no doubt his plan would work.

Chapter Thirty-Six

The search had been textbook so far, everyone doing exactly what they were trained to do. Interestingly, they had found no signs of anyone having been here for a long time. No ruffled bedcovers. No water in the showers. No water in the sinks. Empty trash bins. Whoever had driven the 4Runner back hadn't spent much time in the house.

They moved through the kitchen, Larsen opening all of the under-counter drawers to find the garbage. He discovered a dual trash bin drawer containing two empty water bottles in the recycling bin and a microwave burrito package in the other. He removed the frozen burrito package, noting some condensation on the inside of the package. There was no doubt someone had been here, and he was starting to suspect it might not be Chang.

He wasn't sure why, but the bare-bones pattern of use they'd uncovered didn't fit the mold of someone that spent a considerable amount of time maintaining the grounds outside the house. The riding mower had told an interesting story, leading him to other discoveries.

The mower showed frequent use, a thick layer of grass collected on the outer edge of the blade cover. The gas-powered weed trimmer showed similar wear and tear, the strings worn down to a few inches and in dire need of replacement. The garden tools looked well used, a few of them still caked in dirt, and several yard waste bags sat filled with dried leaves, signs of a final spring cleanup. From what he could tell, none of the flower beds or bushes held any leaves left over from fall.

Whoever lived here did their own yard work, suggesting a far more frequent and permanent presence than two water bottles and a frozen burrito. For a moment, he had the most paranoid thought that an assassin might have arrived earlier, somehow given the codes necessary to enter the house and make use of the SUV to search the surrounding communities for Chang. He dismissed it as far-fetched until it suddenly dawned on him how bizarre his own job and mission would sound to anyone outside the program. As far as he was concerned, anything was possible in this world.

A few closed doors remained, one of which likely led to a basement, although he hadn't seen any windows or window wells that would suggest a lower level. Given the vast square footage of the house, he wouldn't be surprised to discover that the house had been built without one. He couldn't imagine a single person needing any more space.

They moved out of the kitchen and entered the central foyer, stopping at the first door. Brennan pulled the door open, revealing a staircase leading to a basement. So much for his original theory.

"Wedge the door," said Larsen.

Brennan removed a small security wedge and jammed it under the door. The wedge could withstand several solid hits before dislodging. Two hits and it sounded a high-decibel alarm. He would have left one in the mudroom door, but there was no space between the door and doorjamb. With the wedge in place, he signaled for Dixon to lead the team through the final unexplored door, his mind busy trying to piece together the scattered puzzle he'd encountered since hitting the drop zone.

"Eric, you need to see this," he heard through his earpiece.

Larsen walked through the door, not sure what to expect. What he found took him completely off guard. It was the last thing he thought he'd find in this house, but it suddenly made perfect sense. The bullet-resistant glass. Impenetrable doors. Sophisticated security system. Solar panels. And now a room stacked with food, water, medical supplies and survival gear. Chang was some kind of high-end doomsday prepper on top of whatever else landed him in the CHASE database—at the receiving end of a CAPTURE/KILL order.

He stood in place only a few feet into the room, unsure he wanted to go any farther. A vault-like door sat against the wall to his right, easily four times as thick as the back door to the house. If that thing closed and locked, they'd never get out of here. No. He'd stay right here. In fact, he'd drag one of the fifty-gallon plastic bins off the shelves and block the doorway.

"Check this shit out," said Peck, pulling open a hinged circular hatch to expose a dark hole in the concrete floor.

Dixon raised his night-vision goggles and pointed his rifle into the hole, triggering its side-mounted light.

"Sweet Jesus," said Dixon. "Looks like a bomb shelter or something."

Morbid curiosity got the better of Larsen, and he started toward the hole, getting halfway there before a mechanical hum reached his ears. Shit. No. He reversed direction, lurching toward the vault-like door, which had already swung shut with surprising speed. His fingers reached the edge of the door as it sank flush with the steel wall. They were trapped.

Chapter Thirty-Seven

Chang set his house as the next GPS waypoint and took off running, leaving the overstuffed backpack behind. If he needed it again, his GPS track could lead him back to it. He stumbled a few times, miraculously tumbling headfirst onto the soft forest floor instead of into an immovable tree trunk. After one too many close calls, he slowed to a fast walk, moving as quickly as he dared through the nearly pitch-black forest.

He held the GPS unit in one hand and the smart phone in the other, keeping himself pointed toward the house while monitoring the situation in the safe-room bunker. Chang needed to get back fast before the team tried anything drastic. He couldn't think of any way they might escape, short of using explosives, which would be catastrophic for the team and likely render the bunker's contents and equipment useless.

He'd designed the two-story bunker complex to be self-sustaining, even if the solar panels failed. A dozen micro-hydro generators, each no larger than eighteen inches wide, were connected along various lengths of the piping used for the home's geothermal energy system, and connected to the home's massive battery storage banks. The batteries could run the air filtration system, well and geothermal pumps, keeping the entire system going in the face of a disaster that killed the electrical grid and somehow managed to take out the solar panels.

The closed-loop system wasn't one hundred percent efficient.

Slowly, the electricity required to run the geothermal pumps and any other systems in the bunker would outstrip the power created by the micro-hydro generators, depleting the batteries. To combat this, he had four micro wind turbines installed at various locations on his property, each connected by cable to the backup electrical system. Even if two of the turbines failed, the remaining two turbines would create enough power to keep the system running perpetually. That was the theory, which wouldn't matter one way or the other if the team set off any explosives in the bunker.

All he could do now was watch and pray that they didn't overreact. He needed the home security tablet to talk to them. The phone could be used to monitor and control the different systems, but it was designed for remote use. The tablet served as the primary in-home control unit, additionally allowing the user to listen or speak to intruders in any room of the house. He could sit in his closet and inform an intruder in his kitchen that the police were on the way, or activate a series of lights in the house that might convince an intruder that he was on his way downstairs with a shotgun. Once he got the tablet, which sat in a drawer in the kitchen island, he could try to talk them down.

The GPS unit said he had one hundred yards to go, but he still couldn't see the house or clearing. He triggered the exterior lights in front of the house, a bright aura penetrating the forest in front of him. With the GPS now stowed in his pocket, he broke into a run, using his free hand to feel for trees. When he broke into the clearing outside his house, the situation on the phone screen looked dire. The team was engaged in an argument, which he guessed centered around blasting their way out of the room. It just wasn't possible, and he had to let them know before they tried.

Chapter Thirty-Eight

Larsen was pretty sure he'd have to subdue and restrain Peck shortly. The guy was losing it, repeatedly aiming his rifle at the walls and threatening to shoot his way out of the room, which was dangerous for everyone—not to mention plain stupid. Based on the thickness of the door, nothing in their possession was likely to breach the walls. They might have a chance of creating some kind of shaped charge to blow through the door they found in the basement level, but he wasn't sure, and the last thing he wanted to do was create an explosive shockwave that couldn't escape the enclosure.

The blast's overpressure would kill them instantly, no matter where they stood. He doubted closing the hatch between levels would make much difference. With nowhere to go, the blast would break through the weakest point, which looked like the hatch. Same result. Everyone dead.

"Peck, we are not using explosives," said Larsen. "End of discussion."

"Then how the fuck are we getting out of here?" said Peck, his finger on the trigger of his rifle again.

"We're not going anywhere at the moment," said Larsen. "Command will send a team to investigate when we haven't reported. Four teams jumped over Indianapolis. I guarantee one of them was a backup."

"What if we're the backup?" said Peck.

That didn't even make sense. They'd found Chang's name on paperwork and files in the office. The guy owned the house. How often he used it was a different question.

"We're not a backup team," said Larsen.

"How do we know?" said Peck. "You keep that stupid tablet hidden from us all the time. For all we know, this Chang guy is dangerous. Maybe they wanted us to remove him from circulation. He led us in here like mice to cheese, then locked us in!"

"We locked ourselves in," said Larsen. "That's how safe rooms work. This one was designed to shut by itself after someone entered. Can you imagine trying to close that door with a home intruder chasing you? As soon as I stepped all the way in, it shut."

Peck stood in front of the door, shaking his head and muttering something unintelligible. Shit. He was going to do it. Larsen moved his right hand slowly across his thigh, waiting for enough noise to conceal the sound of the Taser holster unsnapping. He glanced furtively at Dixon, who nodded imperceptibly.

"Damn it, Peck! Get your finger off that trigger!" yelled Dixon, giving him the cover he needed to unsnap the holster.

"Someone has to do something," said Peck, the rifle coming up a little more.

An unfamiliar voice filled the room, the sound originating from the back of the room.

"Mr. Peck, I wouldn't do that if I were you."

Peck reacted predictably, aiming his rifle past them, the barrel pointing at Larsen's head for a fraction of a second. They all ducked, yelling at him to safe his weapon.

"Who the fuck said that?" demanded Peck, shifting his aim back and forth along the back wall.

Crouched on the floor below the line of Peck's aim, Larsen said, "My guess is Eugene Chang. And he's not in the room. Please safe your rifle before you get someone killed."

"He's right, Mr. Peck. On both counts. You can't shoot your way out. The bullets would ricochet off the steel until they hit something softer. I'd hate for that to be one of you," said Chang.

"Eugene Chang, my name is Eric Larsen. I'm part of a team sent to protect you. I have no idea why you're important or what is going on in the greater world that requires us to protect you, but I assure you that is our only purpose here. I was woken up a few hours ago and put on a plane with no details about you or my mission. I only learned your identity and the location of this house about thirty minutes ago. You didn't appear to be home, so we accessed the house, or you let us in on purpose—to lead us here."

"Jesus. He doesn't need to know who we are. He just needs to let us out of here," said Peck, pounding the door next to him.

"That's not going to happen until I get some answers," said Chang. "And don't even think of trying to blast your way out with explosives. The steel enclosing the upstairs safe room is designed to survive an F5 tornado. It's bullet resistant well past fifty caliber. In fact, I was told that it could withstand a hit from a handheld rocket launcher. Sounds a bit like salesmanship overkill to me, but either way, I'm pretty sure you'll end up killing yourselves by detonating explosives—on either level."

"Mr. Chang, what can I do to convince you that we mean you no harm?" said Larsen.

"First, you can show me your orders," said Chang. "I assume you have them stored on your tablet thing?"

"How the hell?" muttered Dixon.

"I've been watching you since you landed," said Chang. "I was warned that someone might come for me at some point, but I never expected it to come by parachute."

"Where are you?" said Brennan.

"I'm actually right outside the safe-room door," said Chang.

"Once I see the orders, you drop all of your weapons down the hatch and close it," said Chang. "I can lock the hatch remotely, but I can't move it like the door."

"I told you he locked us in here," said Peck. "He ain't who we think he is."

"Peck, please."

"So if we disarm, you'll let us out of here?" said Larsen.

249

"He'll mow us down the second we throw our weapons down the hole," said Peck.

"I don't own any weapons," said Chang, "aside from a few survival knives."

"We'll toss our weapons," said Larsen. "I can live with that."

"First I need to see your orders," said Chang. "I have no doubt any of you could break my neck with little effort."

"See. This makes no sense," said Peck. "Why would he want us to toss the weapons after checking out the orders?"

"Mr. Peck, you're the reason I want all of the weapons well out of reach if I open this door. You look like you want to shoot someone," said Chang. "In fact, I'm starting to seriously question what I could possibly gain from any of this."

"Jim, hand me your rifle and pistol," said Larsen.

Peck turned to face him, but didn't make a move to disarm. "So now we're on a first-name basis?"

"Just do it, Peck," said Dixon, unslinging his own rifle. "Brennan. Everyone."

Larsen unclipped his rifle from the one-point sling and started to walk over to the open hatch. Brennan was doing the same. The quicker they got the weapons down the hatch, the better. There was no way Larsen could show Chang the tablet, not with anyone still armed. He was quite certain that Peck would attack him.

"Mr. Larsen," said Chang, "I'm not opening the door until I see your orders. You can hold the screen up to the camera in the front corner of the room, across from the door."

He glanced in that direction, seeing a black dome camera mounted in the corner.

"You could probably hold up the tablet from there. I can zoom in pretty far," said Chang.

"Let's get all the weapons down the hatch first," said Larsen, turning to face Dixon and Brennan.

Dixon furrowed his brow slightly, indicating that he didn't quite track Larsen's logic. Brennan looked uncomfortable with the order, but continued to comply, although a little slower than a moment ago.

Fuck. He had to disable Peck before they killed each other.

"Just show him the tablet," said Peck. "Just a minute ago you were giving him a blow by blow of our mission. Show him the tablet; then we toss our weapons."

"I'm sorry," said Dixon. "Are you the team leader now?"

"Might as well be. Ochoa is right. This guy can't get the most basic shit right," said Peck. "Tablet. Then weapons. Simple. Right, Mr. Chang? Whoever the fuck you are."

"Mr. Peck is right. I need to see your orders. Once I confirm you're not here to murder me, we'll meet face-to-face, without guns. Guns make me nervous," said Chang.

Larsen wasn't sure how he was going to do this without either getting half if not all of them killed or dooming them to this prison. The first thing he needed to do was incapacitate Peck. Unfortunately, Peck was on edge, his rifle gripped in both hands. He had the weapon pointed toward the floor, but there was no way Larsen could draw the Taser and fire it before Peck unloaded on them. Judging from the amped look on Peck's face, he had no doubt that was what would happen. He needed more time and an opening.

"I can't show you the orders, Dr. Chang," said Larsen. "I can't even show them to my team. The information is highly classified and everything in this unit is compartmentalized—for a reason."

"Suit yourself. Lucky for you, there's at least three years of food split between the two levels. The sink down below is serviced by a well. Air filtration is self-sustained. You'll be fine until they send someone to look for you."

"Show him the tablet," said Peck. "Fuck all this classification shit. The mission's straightforward. Locate, secure, protect and escort. Obviously something's going on out there that put you on this list. Am I right?"

"There's been a major bioweapons attack," said Chang. "Multiple cities. You didn't know this?"

"We're kept in lockdown on base for a month, waiting for a CHASE mission. One month on. One month off," said Larsen.

"What's CHASE?" said Chang.

"Critical Human Asset Security," said Larsen. "We secure and protect assets critical to national security in times of crisis. You would not have heard of the CHASE program. It's like a doomsday contingency. Continuity of national operations level."

"And now that you disclosed top secret information in front of all of us," said Peck, "I see no reason why you can't show him the orders on the tablet."

"We'll say this was the only way to accomplish the mission," said Dixon quietly.

Peck had backed him in a corner, so he decided to go the honest route, which would for all practical purposes sound like the lying route to some of them. At this point he didn't see another option. Chang would either believe him or not, and Peck would either follow Larsen's orders to disobey the update or he'd kill Peck. He had no idea what Dixon and Brennan would do, but he didn't think they'd go along with what was obviously an illegal order.

"I'm going to show you both sets of orders," said Larsen, removing the tablet from his hip pouch.

"Both sets?" said Peck.

"Mr. Chang, can I ask you a question first?"

"I suppose so. It's Gene. Dr. Gene Chang."

"Dr. Chang, do you have any reason to suspect that your life is in danger? I mean outside of whatever it is you normally do for a living," said Larson, not finding the right words.

"I conduct pharmaceutical research in a field related to bioweapons," said Chang.

"Fuck," muttered Larsen.

"What the hell does this have to do with anything?" said Peck, closing the distance between them.

"What did you mean by two sets, Eric?" said Dixon.

Peck stopped a few feet in front of him, rifle pointed away, but his finger near the trigger well.

"How can there be two sets?" said Peck.

"I received an update to the original mission order when we hit the drop zone," said Larsen. "I disregarded it because it's unlawful and has zero to do with our job."

"I'll be the judge of that," said Peck, lunging to grab the tablet.

A brief struggle for the tablet ensued, ending with Larsen shoving Peck back a few feet. Peck's rifle came up, and before Larsen could react, Brennan pushed by and jammed her pistol under Peck's chin.

"Drop your rifle, or I'll blow the top of your motherfucking head off," spat Brennan. "I'm tired of your shit."

"You're gonna pay for this, bitch," said Peck, remaining rigid.

The barrel of Dixon's rifle inched forward in Larsen's peripheral vision, aimed at Peck.

"Stand down, Peck," said Dixon. "Right the fuck now."

Larsen instinctively took a few steps back and raised his own rifle.

"Peck, this situation is fucked, but we need to pull together," said Larsen. "We don't kidnap or kill. Bottom line. Either the new orders are a mistake, or the CHASE program has been bullshit from the start."

A disturbingly calm look spread across Peck's face.

"The other team leaders were right about you."

Larsen removed some of the slack in his trigger, the barrel aimed at Peck's head. This would go down at any moment.

Chapter Thirty-Nine

Chang backed away from the safe-room door despite the fact that nothing could possibly hurt him from the inside. He knew this logically, but the scene unfolding inside defied logic, and it didn't look like he'd get a chance to process it. The maniac called Peck seemed hell-bent on immediate violence. He considered saying something to Larsen, who seemed reasonable enough, if not a bit conflicted, but decided against it. His words echoing through the room would only serve as a distraction from a peaceful result. This Peck guy was beyond reason.

He bumped into the wall behind him, startled by its sudden intrusion, but never taking his eyes off the tablet screen. With three weapons pointed in Peck's face, he felt sure the standoff was over. No sensible person would try to buck those odds. It was suicide. Pure and simple. What Peck said next froze Chang in place. Something about the statement was final.

"The other team leaders were right about you."

And that was it. Metallic bangs and muffled screams sounded beyond the door as his tablet's speaker transmitted automatic gunfire and yelling. He watched in horror, his view briefly obscured by the smoke from their weapons. When the thin haze cleared, he took a quick breath. All four members of the team lay on the blood-splattered concrete floor. He could barely believe what he was seeing. His eyes focused on the digital tablet next to Larsen, not that it really mattered anymore. Chang believed the man had fully committed to disobeying his orders. He could tell by the exchange in the room. They'd been duped on some level. Even Peck had expressed disbelief.

He watched his tablet for a few more seconds, looking for signs of life, but nobody moved or made a sound. What a miserable waste. There was no point to opening the door. He had everything he needed now, including the knowledge that some faction of the government wanted him dead. Stan Greenberg had been right. He was about to shut down the tablet when Larsen moved. The man pushed himself up with one arm and rolled over onto his back, surveying the room and shaking his head.

Chang activated the lights inside the safe-room and opened the door. He peeked around the corner, exposing as little of his head as possible.

"Dr. Chang?" he heard, the voice sounding like Larsen.

"Yes," he said, not sure what else to say.

"I need some help. It's Larsen."

"Is anyone else alive?" said Chang.

"Peck's dead. No doubt about that. Dixon is gone. Brennan—I don't know about Brennan," he said.

Chang stepped inside the room, the sharp odor of gunfire barely covering the smell of blood. He actually had no idea what either smelled like, but could differentiate between two smells he'd never experienced before—neither of them good. Peck lay in front of the door, knocked back by multiple gunshots. His helmet lay upside down in the corner of the room under the camera, a trail of brains and blood extending from his head to the helmet. The top of Peck's head was gone, exposing a bright red mess. Chang fought against a strong gag reflex, forcing himself to look at the ceiling, which was splattered with blood.

"Jesus," he gasped, closing his eyes.

"Take shallow breaths," said Larsen. "You'll be fine. Look at the back of the room, past my voice. Just walk to me."

He lowered his field of vision to Larsen, who sat up, covered in blood.

"Are you hit?" said Chang.

"Multiple times," said Larsen. "Right in my chest plate. I probably have a broken rib or two, but I'm fine."

Chang's eyes started to drift downward.

"Look at me, Gene. Only me," said Larsen. "Let's move Brennan out of here. She still has a pulse."

He nodded, taking short breaths and moving forward. When he reached Larsen, the soldier, or whatever he was, extended a bloodied hand.

"Help me up. I feel like I've been hit by a truck," said Larsen.

Chang took his sticky hand and pulled him to his feet. Larsen leaned over and grabbed the blood-smeared tablet.

"I need you to see this," said Larsen, navigating to the MISSION tab.

He toggled between the two sets of orders, leaving the screen on the CAPTURE/KILL update. A pop-up box next to the update stated: ACKNOWLEDGE UPDATE IMMEDIATELY. Larsen hadn't acknowledged the order yet.

"I don't know what the hell this is, or why my command structure would think I'd comply with the order," said Larsen, straightening himself out. "You never really answered my question earlier."

Chang knew what he was talking about. "You never really asked the right question."

Larsen grinned, nodding. "Why do they want you dead?"

"Because I know what's happening out there, and I'm in contact with similarly qualified experts who are convinced our government is behind it."

"The bioweapons attacks?" said Larsen. "Why would the government be behind it?"

Chang shook his head. "I don't know, but this is too coordinated and widespread to be anything short of an inside job. At the very least, it's a sophisticated, state-sponsored attack. It's too big for a few decentralized terrorist cells."

The woman behind Larsen groaned but remained unconscious. Larsen kneeled next to her, searching for the wound. His hands stopped at her right pelvis, pulling back the bottom of her camouflage jacket to reveal a small hole in her pants, which was swamped with a dark red stain. A wide, thick pool of blood spread around her in a circle. "She's bleeding internally," said Larsen, muttering a few curses under his breath before continuing. "Judging by the blood loss, it's arterial. She's done unless we can get her to a level one trauma center shortly."

"We could drive her to a hospital. Saint Vincent's has a level one trauma center," said Chang.

Larsen removed one of his gloves and reached inside the collar of her tactical vest. He took his hand out after several seconds.

"Her pulse is extremely faint," said Larsen. "She's gone."

Chang refrained from agreeing. He had no experience in the matter and didn't feel it was appropriate to condemn one of Larsen's colleagues to death. His eyes darted to Dixon, curiosity getting the best of him. It wasn't as bad as he thought it would be, but the image would likely never go away. Two tightly spaced, small red dots were visible on his upper right cheek under his eye. He glanced away, trying unsuccessfully not to imagine the damage done beyond those tiny holes. Peck's fate left little to his imagination.

"Is there a way to make sure she remains comfortable if she wakes up?" said Chang. "Morphine or something?"

"I'll take care of it," said Larsen. "Let's meet outside in a minute or so."

Chang left him alone to take care of his dying team member. He sat against the wall directly outside the safe room, trying not to glance inside. Peck's vacated skull was partially visible on the ground. He scooted to the right until it was no longer visible. When Larsen emerged, he carried two rifles, a night-vision-equipped helmet and a headset with a handheld radio. He kneeled next to Chang and placed the helmet next to him before removing several rifle magazines from his cargo pockets.

"We'll get this comms rig and helmet fitted right; then I'll show you the basics for the rifle," said Larsen.

"I don't like firearms."

"If we're going to survive, you need to know how to use this," said Larsen, with a sympathetic face. "No two ways about it."

Chang wasn't about to argue. The worst had been confirmed, and he wasn't about to go down without some kind of fight. Not after two of Larsen's colleagues had taken a deadly stand on his behalf. Plus, he might have more to offer the fight ahead than he'd originally thought. Greenberg seemed to think so. He'd do his best to enlist Larsen into the fight. At this point, Larsen didn't appear to have a better option. He certainly couldn't follow whatever protocol he'd arrived here thinking would protect either of them. Larsen was as much a lone wolf as Chang now. He took the rifle and slung it around his shoulder before stuffing a few of the magazines in his pockets.

"I've only fired a rifle once in my life, and I think it was a .22. One of the camps my parents took me to," said Chang.

"We'll get you better acquainted with the rifle later," said Larsen. "I want to get moving as fast as possible. Three other teams jumped into the area. I have no idea what happens if I don't acknowledge my new orders. Worst-case scenario, headquarters assumes I went rogue and hunts us down."

"What's the best-case scenario?"

"They assume my team was taken out before we could acknowledge the orders—and hunt us down," said Larsen. "We need to get as far from here as possible. The 4Runner looked fully stocked with the kind of gear we could use."

"We can't go north," said Chang.

"What?" said Larsen.

"10th Mountain Division has roadblocks set up a few miles north of here, along Route 32," said Chang. "Part of the Indianapolis quarantine zone. I don't think we'll have much luck trying to drive out of here."

"Indianapolis is under quarantine?" said Larsen. "From the bioweapons attack?"

"That's what everyone is being told," said Chang. "I've heard firsthand that things are out of control in the city. Thousands are infected with a virus I've spent the past several years trying to thwart."

"Jesus," said Larsen. "How widespread is this?"

"I could show you if we had some time. Explain the whole thing," said Chang.

Larsen hesitated. "I think our best course of action is to get clear of the house."

"Because of the other teams?" said Chang, and Larsen nodded.

"What happens if you acknowledge your orders now and say I'm not here?" said Chang.

"I've already delayed responding for too long," said Larsen.

"Make something up," said Chang. "Do they have any reason to doubt your report?"

"Maybe. Maybe not," said Larsen. "Frankly, I have no idea who I really work for anymore."

"How long would it take the reserve team to get here?" said Chang.

"It depends where the reserve team was dropped," said Larsen. "If headquarters wanted them here quickly, they'd commandeer a vehicle."

"My assumption is that they'll drive to the front gate and proceed on foot, or pick a point along the perimeter and do the same. Correct?"

"That's how I'd do it," said Larsen.

"Then we'll have plenty of warning," said Chang. "I have sensors everywhere, extending from the perimeter to the house. That's how I knew you arrived by parachute."

Larsen pulled the tablet from the pouch attached to the side of his vest and gave it a long look.

"I guess there's no harm in trying," said Larsen before pressing the touchscreen several times. "Done."

"Do they give you any indication of what's going to happen?" said Chang.

"Not usually. Information sharing is sparse at best," said Larsen, turning the tablet so Chang could see it. "Case in point."

Chang read the response line. OBSERVE ALL APPROACHES TO HOUSE AND AWAIT FURTHER INSTRUCTIONS.

"That's it?"

"That's headquarters getting chatty," said Larsen. "What do you have to show me?"

"In my office," said Chang, motioning for him to follow.

Chapter Forty

Larsen stood next to Chang, with his arms folded, studying the map laid out on a spacious desk. The scale of what the map represented was mind-boggling. Twenty-six cities had been affected, if Chang was right—or he wasn't lying about everything. Larsen had no way to prove Chang right or wrong. He was essentially cut off from the outside world; his only method of communication limited to a useless tablet.

Fortunately, Colorado Springs was not on Chang's list of doomed cities. He had no way to warn his wife. All cellular and Internet service to the greater Indianapolis area had apparently been severed. Or had it? Chang's cell phone indicated NO SERVICE, but the house was in an isolated area. Cutting the Internet to the house was as simple as disconnecting a wire.

"How sure are you that this is confined to Denver?" said Larsen. "My family is in Colorado Springs."

"I can't say one hundred percent," said Chang. "The Midwest cluster appeared first, followed by the major cities. Almost like two waves spaced closely together, but far enough apart to allow the virus to fester in the smaller cities for a few days before widespread news coverage was unavoidable. It's a lot easier to shut down coverage of Indianapolis than Chicago or Los Angeles. It's also far easier to infect a larger percentage of a smaller city's overall population. The attacks in the major cities seem to have hit densely packed areas, which will produce similar casualty numbers, but not affect the entire city. Initially. That said, unless there's a third wave of attacks targeting smaller cities, Colorado Springs should be safe."

"Won't the virus spread?" said Larsen.

"It shouldn't. Used as a bioweapon, the virus in question would theoretically be distributed in the water supply or by some kind of similarly widespread transmission method. We're talking a variation of the herpes simplex virus, which can be highly contagious in extremely close contact, but doesn't spread like influenza. The affected area would remain limited to the reach of the distribution system. Colorado is far enough away from Denver that your wife should be safe."

"You keep using the word *should*," said Larsen.

"Once again, I can't be one hundred percent certain. I got a close look at the virus in question at my laboratory, but I didn't have the time to study its genetic modifications. If one of those modifications changed its contagiousness markers—all bets are off. But even then it would be a very slow burn, like a flu outbreak. The real danger with this virus will come from the infected themselves."

He didn't like the sound of that at all.

"What exactly does this virus do?" said Larsen. "In plain English."

"It exploits an extremely rare and devastating aspect of a normally harmless virus," said Chang. "Nearly everyone infected with this modified strain of herpes simplex will develop herpes simplex encephalitis, a merciless and unpredictable infection affecting the central nervous system."

"Can it be treated?"

"Yes. Immediate treatment with high-dose, intravenously administered antivirals has shown some promise, but it's still fatal in close to thirty percent of treated cases."

"Intravenous treatment? That's not likely to be available on even the smallest scale."

"Right. And treatment needs to commence very early, or the death rate is close to seventy percent. And that's not the worst part."

"I can't see how it gets worse?"

"It's really the perfect bioweapon," said Chang. "And I don't say that with a shred of admiration. It's perfect because the survivors don't really survive. The infection destroys the temporal lobe, causing permanent, crippling neurological damage. Of course, that doesn't happen immediately. The victim will suffer from a progressively worsening spectrum of cognitive and behavioral decline. Violence and lack of impulse control is common in untreated and treated patients. Imagine an entire city population infected by this. Thousands of citizens becoming violent at once."

Larsen stared at the map, trying to make sense of what Chang had just said. It didn't take him long to conclude that there was no sense to be made of it. The United States faced an unmitigated disaster.

"I don't see how the government could effectively respond to this," said Larsen.

"The real question is *how does the government humanely engage and manage tens of thousands of irreversibly brain damaged and potentially violent citizens packed into one tight geographic area?*"

"They can't," said Larsen, shaking his head.

"That's exactly why this is the perfect bioweapon. There's no way to do it without taking draconian measures," said Chang. "It's why I've spent the past six years trying to come up with a way to prevent it. We were getting very close at NevoTech. I can't help think that the timing of this attack is related."

"You were on the verge of creating a vaccine against this?"

"We were in phase two trials," said Chang. "It looked very promising."

"And your vaccine would have prevented this bioweapons attack?" said Larsen.

"It was an oral preventative treatment for herpes simplex one and two, which would double as a preventative measure against a herpes simplex-based bioweapon."

Larsen's mind immediately flashed to his family and the possibility of vaccinating them against this madness.

"This has been tested?" said Larsen.

Chang nodded slowly, hesitating to answer.

"You took some with you when you left the lab," said Larsen, "didn't you?"

"Yes."

"And the data on this virus?"

"No. I couldn't risk smuggling the data out. It's stashed in the lab," said Chang.

"And you think our government is behind all of this?" said Larsen.

"It makes sense on too many levels to dismiss at this point," said Chang. "At the very least, it's a splinter group within the government. I'm not the only one with that opinion."

He couldn't afford to get bogged down in the conspiracy details right now. They had more pressing matters to consider and solve.

"Exactly why do they want you dead?" said Larsen. "You say you know what's going on, but it won't be long before the conspiracy theories start flying and virus test results are made public. What do you know that everyone else won't in a few days?"

"I'm one of a handful of people that have extensively studied the potential use of HSV as a bioweapon. With the research and data in my lab, plus what I have stored up here," he said, pointing to his head, "I could conclusively prove that the level of sophistication required to modify and reengineer this virus far exceeds the capabilities of just about every nation and organization in existence beyond our own—and maybe Russia. Other scientists with the same level of expertise and knowledge have similarly disappeared. *Taken out of circulation* was the phrase used by the only colleague I've managed to reach."

"Then we need to get you out of here. You're obviously important—and a serious threat to whoever is behind this attack," said Larsen.

"I'll take you up on the offer. I'm pretty sure I used up all of my luck here," said Chang. "I'm very sorry about your friends."

Larsen grimaced. "You never know when things will go sideways in my line of work."

"I never thought the same could be said about mine, but I

suppose that's all changed now," said Chang.

"Everything has changed, if you're right about all of this," said Larsen.

"I can't thank you enough for offering to help me get out of here," said Chang. "I'm sure you have enough on your mind as it is."

"I think we can make this work for both of us," said Larsen, hoping Chang understood what he meant.

He could tell by Chang's look that the message was received.

"How many doses do you need?" said Chang.

"Three. If you can spare that many. Two if you can't. I don't care about myself."

"Wife and child?"

Larsen nodded.

"How old is your child?"

"Daughter. She's fifteen months," said Larsen.

"I smuggled adult doses out of the lab, but you can break them in half. That should be fine for that age. The only real side effect is a little upset stomach and possibly diarrhea."

"I'll take whatever you can give, Dr. Chang. Thank you," said Larsen. "So I guess the question now is *how the hell do we get you out of here?* Off-road it with the 4Runner? Do you have any knowledge of the area's back roads?"

Chang shook his head. "I don't."

"Then we hike out of here," said Larsen. "Take our time and evade patrols."

"What would you say if I told you I was an experienced pilot, with a plane waiting in a hangar nearby?" said Chang. "I could fly us pretty much anywhere, using this map to avoid any possible quarantine zones."

Larsen could barely believe it. Flying to Colorado beat the hell out of Larsen's plan, and it meant less exposure to any authorities. Private, domestic air travel could be fairly anonymous if done right. "Can we drive to the plane without hitting the roadblocks?"

"No. But it's only about two and a half miles away."

"Then I'd say we better get moving."

They made several steps down the hallway, when Chang's security tablet illuminated, chiming an alarm.

"What is it?" said Larsen.

"Two people just entered the southeast corner of the forest surrounding the house," said Chang.

Larsen shook his head. "It's too soon for another team to get here."

Chang didn't have an opinion about the matter. He was completely trusting Larsen's assessment and judgment about the capabilities of the other teams. Larsen thought it over for a few seconds before rubbing his face.

"Kill the lights out front," said Larsen before removing a long, thick cylinder from a sleeve on the side of his backpack and attaching it to the barrel of his rifle. "If this is a second team, I can take them down in the forest before they know what hit them."

Chapter Forty-One

Joshua Olson walked cautiously across the invisible forest floor, keeping a close eye on his father, who was about twenty feet ahead. He made sure he didn't snag a boot on a tree root or anything else that might tumble him to the ground. His dad walked point, and Joshua was following his lead. They had travelled next to each other in the open, on the streets, walking as fast as they could stand with the heavy packs, but when they reached the cattle fence at the edge of this vast forest, his dad had changed their tactics.

It was nearly impossible to see very far in the forest, so he wanted them spread out, allowing their senses to react separately to their surroundings. Something his dad missed in the distance, Joshua might catch, and vice versa. They'd moved slowly, stopping long enough to listen for movement. The cattle fence just outside the forest led his dad to suspect they might be coming up on a house hidden inside the woods. He would have diverted them around it, but the trees extended as far as he could see in either direction, and his dad wanted to keep them moving in a northwesterly direction.

According to their GPS unit, Little Eagle Creek was about three-quarters of a mile ahead. Once they crossed the creek, they would be travelling near the 10th Mountain Division's western quarantine boundary. His dad planned to hike parallel to the road at that safe distance until they ran into Finley Creek. The creek ran under Route 421, representing the safest way out of the quarantine zone he could identify.

His dad knew the spot where Finley Creek crossed the road. Heavily wooded on both sides, he said they could avoid aerial detection, day or night, but eventually it would become a popular crossing point for refugees—and a focus for the soldiers. His dad wanted to get across tonight, before the 10th Mountain Division started to plug all of the possible gaps in their containment line.

He shifted his rifle to the other shoulder. "This thing," as he now called it, was really starting to bother him. His dad wanted him to take something with a little more range and power, so he'd given Joshua the M1-A1 Scout Squad rifle, a modernized, shorter-barreled version of the M14. With the scope and twenty-round magazine, it weighed significantly more than the AR-15-style rifle his father carried. On top of that, the M1-A1's basic shoulder sling put it at an awkward position along his side, where it was constantly bumping away at his hip. His dad's rifle was in a comfortable three-point sling over his vest, basically hanging across his chest. Maybe at some point they could trade off. He couldn't imagine walking for days with "this thing."

Joshua eased between the two trees his father had passed through moments ago, careful not to let his rifle bang against either. When he caught sight of his dad's shadowy form again, his dad was crouched low, holding up a fist. Joshua immediately unshouldered the rifle and lowered to a crouch, listening intently to the forest around him. He didn't hear anything beyond the usual insect noises and occasional flutter in the leaves above. After several seconds, his dad slowly and silently joined him.

"We're being followed," his dad whispered. "I definitely saw two people back in the neighborhoods before we broke into the fields. I thought I saw them a few times after that, and I'm pretty sure I saw them again just now. Just barely. It's hard to see anything in here."

"They're probably doing the same thing we're doing."

"Probably," said his dad. "Which worries me. They could blow it for us at the creek, or earlier."

"They've been pretty quiet," said Joshua. "I haven't heard them."

"They do have that going for them," said his dad. "Let's lie low for a few minutes. See what they do."

Joshua placed the rifle on the ground next to him and lowered himself to the forest floor, facing the path they had just taken. His dad lay down next to him, staring through his rifle scope at the murky forest in front of them. Joshua kept his rifle next to him, uncomfortable with the idea of similarly using his scope as a pair of binoculars. The thought of pointing his rifle at the people following him didn't seem right. He supposed it was fine. There was no way for the rifle to accidentally discharge. It just seemed weird to him to sight-in on someone like that.

"Dad, can you get the binoculars out of my backpack?" he whispered. "Right side pouch."

"Hold on," said his dad. "I can see them."

Joshua froze, willing himself deeper into the musty forest floor. He put his hand on the M1-A1 and pulled it in a little closer. "What are they doing?"

"Nothing. That's the problem. They seem to have stopped because we stopped," said his dad. "I think one of them has a pair of binoculars."

"What do you want to do?" said Joshua.

"I want to see what they do," said his dad. "But we don't have the time. They might sit there all night. I'd go back and have a chat with them, but I can't tell if they're armed. Hate to get shot by a nervous Nellie."

"I could walk ahead. Bring them to you," said Joshua.

"That's not a bad idea," said his dad. "Not a bad idea at all."

Chapter Forty-Two

Jack Harper searched frantically through his binoculars. The two men they had followed since leaving their friend's neighborhood had stopped for a few minutes before taking off again—at a much faster pace. He didn't figure that out until the last person in the group, the younger one, nearly vanished from sight, the cop already long gone. It was the first time he couldn't see both of them through the binoculars, even if they just appeared as shadows in the distance. Now he couldn't find either of them. Wait. There! He nudged Emma.

"I got the kid again," he whispered. "Let's go."

"They have to know we're following them," she said.

"That's my guess. They're trying to lose us without making it obvious."

"Maybe we should back off," said Emma. "Make our own way. We can keep going in this general direction. See where it takes us. They've pretty much stayed on the same course. At least I think they have. It's almost impossible to tell."

Jack took a step forward, putting his hand on a tree. "That's the problem. We don't have a compass. No location services on our phone. We're literally walking in the dark. We'd have to go back to using roads."

"It worked fine before," said Emma.

"Until we run into a roadblock," said Jack, stepping between the two trees he'd seen the cop and kid behind earlier. "They know something we don't."

Emma followed him through. "Or they're headed for someone's house, kind of like we were earlier."

"Then we'll move on by ourselves," said Jack, turning to make sure she was still right behind him. "We need to pick up the pace."

A blinding light filled his eyes, causing him to raise one of his hands to his face. The other went to his right hip.

"Both hands in the air," said an authoritative voice. "That hand moves another centimeter toward your hip, and you're a dead man. Ma'am, both hands in the air."

Jack raised his hands immediately, struggling to see past the burning light. He could barely keep his eyes open. Once he caught a glimpse of a rifle barrel next to the light, he put himself between the light and Emma.

"Ma'am, I need you to step to your left. Into the light," said the voice. "Sir, do not move. I understand that you want to protect your wife, but the best thing you can do for her right now is keep your feet planted. Nod if you understand."

He nodded, hearing his wife shuffle to a spot next to him.

"We had no intention—" started Jack.

"Before we get to that, let's have a look at your right hip," said the voice. "Very slowly turn left."

"It's a .38 revolver," said Jack.

"Still need to see it," said the voice.

Jack turned slowly to face his wife, who stood wide-eyed with her hands pointing skyward. She glanced at him, a look of complete panic on her face.

"Ma'am, you're going to be fine," said the voice, seeing the same face. "Sir, very slowly lower your right hand and pull your shirt up. I can't see the revolver. In case you're curious, I'm holding a semiautomatic rifle. No matter how many times you've practiced drawing and firing that revolver, you will not get it clear of your holster before you're dead. Understood?"

"Yes," he said. "It's my grandfather's service weapon. He was an East Chicago cop."

"Plenty of time for that later," said the man. "Let's see the revolver."

Jack carefully and deliberately lowered his hand to the edge of his T-shirt and lifted it to expose the pistol.

"With two fingers, pinch the grip and drop it at your feet. At no point should your hand come toward me."

He felt for the wood grip without looking, squeezing it firmly between his thumb and index finger before lifting it out of his waistband and dropping it at his feet. For a fraction of a moment, when his fingers let go, he thought the pistol might discharge, getting them both killed. When it thudded softly against the forest floor, he audibly breathed a sigh of relief.

"Kick it over," said the man.

He did what he was told.

"Any more weapons?"

"I have a small folding knife in my back pocket," said Emma.

The light vanished. "I think we're good. Take a seat. I'm not going to hurt you."

"How do we know that?" said Jack.

A less intense light exposed the man's face, one of his hands holding a small flashlight. He was older than Jack by about ten to fifteen years. Tan face with crow's feet extending past the corners of his eyes. Deeply wrinkled forehead above greenish-brown eyes. The other hand held a gold and silver badge.

"Officer David Olson, Westfield Police Department. Sorry about the drama, but you were following us," he said, directing the light back at them. "What's your story?"

"Jack Harper," he said.

"Emma Harper," said his wife. "Officer Olson, sorry if we freaked you out."

"Please call me David."

"Okay. David, we met a few of your neighbors, who happened to mention you were a cop."

"They told you that?" said David.

"They threatened us with it," said Jack.

272

"We're friends with the Chases. Your neighbors. Our hope was to spend the night in their screen room and take off at first light, but we saw you and your—" said Emma, pausing.

"My son," said David.

"We saw you and your son take off from your house. Jack assumed you knew something we didn't, and that's why we followed you."

"We just want to get as far north as possible. The 465 is locked down by the National Guard," said Jack. "Once we get cell service again, I can have my parents drive down to pick us up. They live a few hours' drive in that direction. They'd be happy to give you a ride, too. Where are you headed?"

David paused longer than Jack expected, almost as if the question had taken him by surprise.

"I just want to get past the next quarantine boundary," said David. "The 10th Mountain Division has secured Route 32 north of here and Route 421 west of here. I was going to cross 421 somewhere past the airport and keep going north. I figured the farther west and north we travelled, the fewer soldiers we'd encounter. I hadn't given much thought to what comes after that."

"I knew it. There's another quarantine line," said Jack, thinking more about what David had just said. "The regular army is here?"

David nodded slowly. "Yeah. Something big happened down in Indianapolis. Here too, I think. People just started losing their minds."

"We came up from Broad Ripple," said Jack. "The same thing happened down there. Craziest shit you ever seen. But it was everywhere. It's pretty quiet up here."

"You were down there?" said David. "South of the 465? How did you get out?"

"It wasn't that hard," said Emma. "They have the roads barricaded, but anyone can get across the 465 if you time it right."

"They've put all of their manpower at the on-ramps, underpasses and overpasses, where the bulk of the people show up," said Jack. "We only had to deal with one Humvee on the 465, and it was as predictable as the sun."

"How bad was it down there?" said David.

"Apocalyptic," said Jack.

"What do you mean by that?" said David.

"It means everyone is acting fucking crazy," said Jack. "Stumbling around with vacant looks on their faces. Running around vandalizing shit like lunatics. Gunshots every minute. Sirens nonstop. It was insane."

"What happened to Rudy?" said his wife.

The question momentarily short-circuited his mouth. He tried to say something. Anything. But nothing came out. He obviously knew she hadn't forgotten about it, but he'd kind of pushed it as far back in his head as possible. Hoping it would come up in a quiet, unrushed conversation a few weeks after everything had settled. He truly didn't know what to say, even if he could form the words.

"I want to know," she said. "I need to know."

"Who's Rudy?" said David.

Jack detected an increased tension in the police officer's voice. He could understand why. The way his wife posed the question, Rudy could have been someone Jack took for a walk and never came back with. He took a shallow breath and answered, "Rudy was our dog."

"What happened to him?" said David.

Jack shook his head slowly. "I don't want—"

"I need to know, Jack," said Emma. "I need to know what we're up against out here. What's really wrong with everyone."

"I can't, Emma," said Jack. "Please."

"Jack, I'm not taking another step until you tell me," said Emma. "I know he's dead. I just want to know what happened."

He glanced at David, whose face had lost the rough edge it had come into the conversation with. In fact, he looked like he'd rather be anywhere but here right now. Exactly the way Jack felt.

"Tell me," said Emma. "Please."

Jack swallowed hard, tears already welling. *Fuck!*

"He was on their grill!" said Jack. "Already dead."

Dead silence engulfed the group, broken a moment later by a new voice from the forest.

"Nobody moves. I have all of you covered," said the voice.

"What the fu—" started David.

"Kill the light and let the rifle fall to the ground. I can see you in the dark, too. One fuckup and the whole group goes down—plus the guy you have about fifty yards northwest of here. That's an easy shot. I'll be on my way in about three seconds."

The forest went dark, leaving Jack to guess what they had walked into following Officer Olson.

Chapter Forty-Three

Eric Larsen kept his rifle trained on the cop, the bright green laser centered on the man's chest. He'd been a little slow to follow his order to let the rifle fall, indicating an attitude problem. He tolerated the delay because the cop had to unclip the rifle from a three-point sling to make it happen, and because he wasn't the enemy. Still. He wasn't taking any chances. When the rifle hit the ground next to the cop, Larsen noticed the handle of a revolver at his feet.

"Kick the revolver away," said Larsen.

When the cop didn't immediately comply, Larsen fired a suppressed bullet past his head.

"That wasn't necessary!" yelled the cop.

"I need you to take me a little more seriously," said Larsen.

"Message received," said the cop, kicking the pistol away.

"I heard part of your conversation," said Larsen, addressing the couple but keeping his eye on the cop. "Sorry. I don't know what else to say about it."

"There's not much else to say," said the husband. "I'm Jack Harper. This is my wife, Emma."

"And I'm David Olson, Westfield PD," said the cop.

"You're a little out of your jurisdiction, Officer Olson," said Larsen.

"Just David. I'm getting out of here while that's still an option. My son is the guy northwest of us. Please don't hurt him."

"Your son is fine," said Larsen. "He doesn't appear to be aware of me."

"Well, you snuck up on us pretty good," said David. "Are you the landowner?"

"Nope. Just a concerned party," said Larsen. "Needed to check you guys out before I moved on."

"I can't see you," said David. "But I get the impression you're more than just a concerned party."

"More like a none-of-your-concern party," said Larsen.

"Funny," said David.

"Do you know what's happening out there?" said Emma.

"I go where they send me," said Larsen.

"I know what's going on," said Chang, appearing from behind a nearby tree.

"Jesus. How many people are out here?" said Jack.

Larsen shook his head. "You were supposed to hang back where it's safe, Dr. Chang."

"These people are safe. I could tell by the surveillance feed," said the scientist. "They're trying to get out of here just like you and me."

"That doesn't mean they're safe," said Larsen.

Chang cracked a red chemlight and tossed it between the Harpers and the cop.

"Damn it," muttered Larsen.

He raised his NVGs and stepped forward, keeping his rifle at low ready, still not sure what the cop, or any of them, might do. Chang moved next to him.

"I really think we should head back to the house," said Larsen. "They might be infected."

"They don't look or act infected," said Chang.

"I may not be a world-renowned virologist," said Larsen. "But even I know that what you said is complete nonsense in the virus world."

"You have a point," said Chang. "I have a thermometer back at the house. If they're not running a fever, I can't imagine any scenario in which they're infected. The virus was most likely released two to three weeks ago."

"Released?" said Jack. "Like a weapon?"

"That's what I suspect."

"What the hell are you talking about?" said David, taking a few steps forward.

Larsen tensed, ready to raise his rifle. "This is a bad idea, Chang. Time to go."

"Wait a minute," said the police officer. "You think this is a bioweapons attack?"

"That's what I suspect," said Chang. "I work in a related field, which is why this gentleman has been assigned to protect me."

And then ordered to kill him.

David studied Larsen for a moment, no doubt seeing the blood sprayed on his tactical vest. The cop kept a tight poker face—betraying nothing.

"We need to keep moving," said David, directing his comment at the Harpers. "The quicker we're out of here, the better, especially if doctor doom over here is right about this being a bioweapons attack."

"Dr. Chang. Eugene Chang."

"David Olson. Officer David Olson. Westfield police."

"Why are you leaving on foot?" said Chang.

"Sounds like he left without telling anyone," said Larsen.

"That's part of the problem," said David. "The bigger part is the brigade combat team from 10th Mountain Division that will fully arrive by midday, reinforcing the outer quarantine boundary around Indianapolis. I'd like to be gone before the bulk of that brigade arrives," said David.

"I ran into a roadblock a few minutes north of here," said Chang. "Just soldiers."

"The vehicles and helicopters will be here soon. Hundreds of them," said David. "All equipped with highly sophisticated sensor equipment."

"What's your plan to get out of here?" said Chang.

"Head northwest from here and cross under Route 421. Put as

much distance as possible between ourselves and Indianapolis," said David.

"I have a better idea. Gather up your weapons and call your son over," said Chang.

David whistled sharply, repeating the sound three more times. His son responded with the same number of whistles.

"He's on his way over," said David. "What's your better idea?"

"You're coming with us."

"Whoa! What do you mean we're coming with you?"

"Chang," said Larsen, shaking his head vigorously, "not a good idea."

"We're going to bring them," said Chang, "if they want to come."

"We don't even know if they're infected!" said Larsen.

"We can figure that out at the house," said Chang. "It's on the way."

"Bring us where?" said Jack.

"I have a Cessna Stationair at the Indianapolis Executive Airport a few miles northwest of here. If we ditch most of the gear we're carrying, I can take off with everyone," said Chang.

The plan wouldn't work with six people. Sneaking into a presumably guarded hangar and taking off under fire would be dicey enough with the two of them, but six was impossible. On top of that, tripling their weight would mean a long takeoff. Twice as long on the runway as a target. Bringing them along would severely jeopardize their chance of success.

"Are you crazy?" said Larsen. "This is way too many people. The 10th Mountain Division will have a presence at the airfield."

"We're all headed in the same direction anyway," said Chang. "They can decide if they want to get on the plane when we get there. The last place on earth anyone wants to be is inside this quarantine zone."

"I can attest to that," said Jack. "Indianapolis is on the brink of complete collapse."

"The suburbs aren't in great shape either. My department is probably one shift away from falling apart. I took a bullet to the head on my last call," said David, removing his ball cap to reveal a bandage. "Just grazed me."

"You said you cut it on some glass," said the cop's son, appearing in the red light.

"I didn't want to stress you out more than you already were," said David. "This is my son, Joshua."

"Please excuse me if I don't shake hands," said Chang. "I've invited you and your father to fly out of here on my airplane."

"That sounds awesome," said Joshua.

"Really bad idea, Chang," repeated Larsen. "I can't stress this enough."

"Your objection is noted," said Chang.

Larsen shrugged his shoulders. Chang didn't fully grasp how this might play out. If they reached the airfield and Larsen determined it was impossible to get six people on the plane without jeopardizing his own escape—one or more of these people weren't getting on that aircraft.

"How far can you take us in the plane?" said Jack.

"I plan to head north. I could land near your parents' house. Officer Olson, I can put you wherever you'd like as long as it's on the way north."

"Count us in," said Emma, glancing at her husband, who nodded in agreement.

"We'd really appreciate it," said Jack. "You can drop us off wherever we can get cell service. My parents will drive down and get us."

"Jack, I have a satellite phone. You can call them when we get in the air and let them know you're on the way," said Chang. "I'll still take you all the way."

"That would be incredible," said Jack. "Thank you."

"Officer Olson?" said Chang.

The deep thumping of helicopter rotors echoed through the forest.

"I'll hold off on making a final decision until we get a look at the airport."

"Fair enough," said Chang.

"Larsen?"

He nodded, not sure what he was agreeing to. Larsen's thoughts lingered on the mention of a satellite phone.

"Dr. Chang," said Larsen, "can I use your phone?"

"Sure. As long as you don't plan on calling your headquarters," said Chang, smiling nervously at a joke nobody else could understand.

"No. I need to call my wife and warn her," said Larsen. "I don't know how far these people will go once they discover what I've done."

"Certainly," said Dr. Chang, handing him the phone.

"What's going on here?" said David. "Who is this guy?"

While Larsen dialed his wife's cell phone, he heard Chang's response.

"He's my only hope of surviving the night, and I trust him implicitly."

The last part of Chang's sentence hung in the air like an anvil as he waited for Caroline's voicemail to pick up.

Chapter Forty-Four

Emma Harper waited a few seconds, after Dr. Chang and his bodyguard stepped through the door next to the patio, before turning to her husband.

"I don't like this Larsen guy," she whispered. "Did you notice the blood on his vest and sleeves?"

"I saw it," said Jack. "Something's off."

"Maybe we should leave," said Emma.

"We're all going in the same direction—"

"Supposedly," said Emma, turning to David Olson. "What do you think? You had to have noticed the blood."

"The blood *and* his latest generation gear," said David. "He's not private security. My guess is government or military, but like you said—something is off."

"If Larsen was sent by the government or military, they wouldn't need to sneak out of the quarantine zone like the rest of us," said Emma.

"Exactly," said David. "Judging by the blood, something went wrong somewhere. I find it hard to believe Larsen would have been sent alone."

"You think he killed his own team?" said Joshua.

"I don't know what to think," said David. "All I know is that I'm going to keep a very close eye on Larsen. I suggest you do the same. Let them take the lead on the way to the airfield."

"I didn't like what Larsen said about the airfield being guarded," said Jack.

"Neither did I," said David. "And judging from the frequent helicopter sounds, I'm not optimistic about the plane-ride option. The airfield would be a logical place to land helicopters."

"Whatever you decide at the airfield, we'll follow," said Emma. "I trust your judgment."

"So do I," said Jack.

"You don't even know me," said David.

"No offense, but we're low on options," said Emma, suddenly laughing at her bluntness.

The rest of them laughed, too, even if it was nervous laughter more than anything.

"I guess we're all in the same boat," said David. "If the airfield is a bust, we'll keep going. I can keep us out of sight, even during the day. It'll be slow going, but eventually we'll get a cell signal. Did you bring food with you?"

Jack nodded. "We did. Enough for a few days. Plus a water filter."

"Perfect," said David. "We'll be set in case we have to hide out during the day tomorrow. Once we get farther away from the quarantine zone, we'll make really good time."

"Maybe Chang will let us use his phone to call my parents," said Jack. "We could give them a rendezvous point that we can easily reach within twenty-four hours."

"I didn't want to say anything earlier, but I'm not so keen on using Chang's satellite phone," said David. "If Chang and Larsen are on the run and that phone somehow falls into the wrong hands, those wrong hands will have a record of your parents' number. If they're on the run from the government? All bets are off. We fly far enough out of here to get a cell signal and part ways."

"They're coming," said Joshua.

A few moments later, Larsen emerged holding two rifles and what looked like a few sets of helmet-equipped night-vision goggles. Chang pushed past him.

"I have a forehead thermometer," he said. "We can confirm what

I already suspect. That none of you are infected."

Less than a minute later, the Olsons and Harpers had passed Chang's test, showing normal temperatures.

"Emma and Jack, do you mind if I ask you a question?" said Chang.

"I suppose," said Emma.

"Eric overheard—"

"Larsen. Please," said the bodyguard. "Unless you want to give them my address and social security number, too."

Chang rolled his eyes. "Larsen overheard you say something leading him to believe that everyone in your neighborhood showed signs of infection," said Chang. "Is that true?"

"More or less," said Jack. "I didn't come across everyone, but the neighbors on both sides were sick, and nearly everyone we saw on the streets looked glitchy. We didn't stick around long."

"One of our neighbors cooked our dog," blurted Emma.

"Eric mentioned that," said Chang. "I'm very sorry."

Emma wanted to cry, but it wasn't the right time. She cleared her throat and wiped her eyes.

"I don't think we would have escaped if we'd stayed much longer," she said.

Chang nodded sympathetically, glancing at Larsen before continuing. "It sounds like the problems in the suburbs are a symptom of people getting infected in the city, which makes sense given the way a virus like this would be unleashed. If Indianapolis was attacked through the water system, the most likely method of virus distribution, anyone that worked in Indianapolis and lived in the suburbs would be infected. Anyone visiting the city and drinking water at a restaurant or friend's house could also get infected. Everyone living in the city or affected area would be infected. So— how did you avoid infection?"

"I don't know," said Emma. "We've been on vacation."

Chang's eyes widened. "When did you leave?"

"We got back yesterday from a nine-day cruise to the Caribbean," she said.

"Interesting," said Chang. "I've been out of town on business for ten days, and I'm not sick either. I work at NevoTech, as you know."

"I was just about to say that," said Jack.

"Ten days," muttered Chang. "That's nearly half the time I had expected."

"What do you mean?"

"This isn't the first time a virus like this has been used on a city population," said Chang. "I was under the impression things didn't get this bad for three weeks in that case."

"This has happened before?" said Larsen.

"Yes. In Russia. A city on the Kola Peninsula, south of Murmansk," said Chang.

"An entire city?" said David. "I think I would have heard of that. Sounds like a Chernobyl-level event."

"Apparently it was," said Chang. "But all traces of it have been effectively erased, and travel to the area is forbidden. The Russian government completely denies it. I received a data pack tonight from a friend that knows the story, or what's left of the story. I haven't reviewed it yet, but I think it will shed some light on what is going to happen here and everywhere else the virus was released."

"Everywhere else?" said David.

"Twenty-six cities by my estimation," said Chang.

"Good heavens," said Emma. "What happened to the city in Russia?"

"Nobody really knows," said Chang. "Early bootleg footage indicated a brutal military crackdown, followed by a systematic extermination of the population."

"With that final thought in mind," said Larsen, "can we take this show on the road? I'd like to get the fuck out of the quarantine zone. Does anyone disagree?"

After everyone immediately indicated they were ready to get moving, Larsen handed the rifles to Emma and Jack.

"I just need you to carry these for now," said Larsen. "Emma, I have a helmet with night vision for you. David, the other set is for you."

Emma took the helmet, which felt wet. She dug through her pocket for a small flashlight and directed the thin beam into the helmet, expecting to find it coated with blood. It looked like water from what she could tell. The night-vision goggles dripped water, too.

"Why are these wet?" said Emma.

"You don't want to know," said Larsen.

"I'm tired of people telling me that," she said. "Why are these wet?"

Larsen turned to her and put his hands on his hips. "Because I had to wash them out," he said. "Someone's brains got blown out wearing that helmet. You can pass it along to your husband."

"I'll wear it," said Jack.

"I'm fine," she said. "As long as he washed it out properly."

"I may have missed a few of the smaller pieces," said Larsen.

The thought of putting on the helmet disgusted her, but she wasn't about to give Larsen the satisfaction of intimidating her. She placed the wet helmet over her head and snapped the soaked chinstrap in place, thinking the night couldn't get any worse.

Chapter Forty-Five

David Olson lay at the edge of a cornfield, roughly two football fields away from the Indianapolis Executive Airport's main tarmac, observing the airfield activity through binoculars. He didn't like what he saw. Several helicopters sat on the massive concrete tarmac, rotors turning while ground crews moved between them, presumably engaged in refueling.

Two of the helicopters were Kiowa scout helicopters, each equipped with mast-mounted sights (MMS)—a sophisticated sensor package located above the main rotors. MMS gave the crew sweeping three-hundred-and-sixty-degree thermal imaging. He was more concerned about the MMS system than the machine guns attached to the weapons pylons. One of those helicopters hovering several hundred feet in the air could scan a massive area for heat signatures. They'd have to be extremely cautious whenever they heard a helicopter nearby.

Three Black Hawk helicopters descended out of the night sky to land on the wide taxiway just beyond the tarmac. They didn't stay for long, each helicopter disgorging a squad of heavily equipped soldiers before rising and disappearing into the darkness. A small convoy of vehicles comprised of four Humvees and a canvas-covered five-ton truck raced across the open concrete taxiway to pick them up, ferrying them to points unknown in the immediate area.

The longer they sat here, the worse their chances of slipping out of the quarantine zone. They'd already wasted too much time sneaking around the runway to get into a position to effectively observe the business end of the airfield. Time they could have spent hiking west, toward Finley Creek. Now he didn't think there was any way they could reach Route 421 before dawn.

The crossing was still a good mile from here, and sunrise was a little more than an hour away. The eastern horizon was already showing signs of lightening. In thirty to forty minutes, it would be bright enough to see without night vision. They needed to make an immediate decision. If the airfield was a no-go, they could get to Finley Creek and wait for sunset, or try a day crossing if road patrols were as light here as the Harpers claimed Interstate 465 had been a few hours ago. He liked the Harpers, and adding two sharp people to the group enhanced their chances of escaping.

David crawled backward, settling in next to Jack Harper. This close to the airfield, he didn't dare stand up. The corn plants were only four feet tall at this point in June. He looked around for his son, not seeing him. Emma was on the other side of Jack, but Joshua was gone.

"Where's Josh?" he said.

"He crawled off toward Larsen and Chang," said Jack.

David didn't like the thought of his son far from his side, especially with Larsen around. He still didn't fully trust the man. He seemed more mercenary than government agent.

"How long ago?"

"A few minutes," said Jack. "What does it look like out there?"

"The airfield is bigger than I expected. I saw several large buildings, mostly hangars," said David. "Looks like the 10th Mountain Division set up a FARP right in the middle of it, though."

"FARP?"

"Forward arming and refueling point," said David. "At some point tonight, they flew in bladders of aviation fuel. Probably used Chinooks for that. They'll refuel any helicopters ferrying troops to the quarantine boundary. I've seen Black Hawks and Kiowas so far. Everything done in the dark, which means this is a pretty slick operation. Everyone is using night vision."

"That doesn't sound good," said Emma, who was on the other side of Jack.

"It's not," said David. "I mean, I don't think we'll have any trouble getting to Chang's aircraft unobserved. His hangar is on the western edge of the complex, which looks really quiet. I just don't know how he'll get the plane onto the runway. The main tarmac he'd have to cross to reach it appears to be the center of flight operations. I have to imagine the soldiers down there would put an end to that escapade pretty quickly."

"Sounds like we might be better off skipping the airport," said Jack.

"I don't know. At this point, we're not getting across the 421 before sunrise," said David. "And I just watched three helicopters offload a platoon of soldiers. They're beefing up the number around here pretty quickly. If Larsen comes up with a reasonable plan to pull this off, I think it's worth a shot. If his plan involves blowing that place sky-high and killing soldiers, he can do that by himself."

Chapter Forty-Six

Larsen shook his head imperceptibly behind the powerful rifle scope, not wanting to scare Chang. No way they could pull this off without blowing something up. He passed the M1-A1 back to the cop's son and rolled onto his back, taking in the night sky through the cornstalks. He just didn't see any other way to do it.

"Thanks for the look," he said. "Did your dad teach you how to shoot that? It's one hell of a rifle."

"I've fired it a few times," said Joshua. "I'm basically lugging it around in case we need it."

"Your dad used something like this before?" said Larsen.

"Something similar," said Joshua. "He was a Marine designated marksman."

"Really?"

That might come in handy if he'd kept his shooting skills intact.

"How long ago?" said Larsen.

"Close to twenty. He got out before the first Gulf War."

Not likely to be the kind of useful he'd need to make this job easier. Still. He'd keep it in mind. He didn't like seeing Kiowas on the tarmac. One well-placed shot could disable their mast-mounted sights.

"Joshua, right?"

"Yes."

"Can you drag your dad up here?" said Larsen. "The Harpers too. Quietly. We need to figure out how we're going to pull this off."

"I'll be right back," said Joshua before slithering away.

"Can we pull this off?" said Chang. "It looks awfully busy. Helicopters and trucks coming and going. I don't see how."

"I was having a hard time seeing myself, but I see it now," said Larsen. "There's no guarantee it will work, but it's a simple plan, and in my experience—simple works best."

"Why do I get the feeling I'm not going to like this?" said Chang.

"Trust me. Nobody is going to like it," said Larsen.

He backed up far enough into the cornfield to still see the airfield, but give them a little concealment in case anyone did anything stupid. He'd been on operations with veteran SEALs who triggered a rifle light at the wrong time. It could happen to anyone at any time, and now would be a really bad time. When everyone had crawled into place around him, he started with an honest assessment of their chances. Better to get that on the table up front.

"I have a plan that can work," said Larsen. "I give it a fifty-fifty chance."

"Jesus," said David. "Vegas odds."

"Better than Vegas odds. Just slightly," said Larsen.

"I think we've wasted enough time here," said David. "We could have been past 421 already, or pretty close."

"You're making a big assumption about the 421," said Larsen.

"I know we can't take crossing it for granted, but it's better than fifty-fifty."

"No. I'm talking about the assumption that you'll be home free after the 421," said Larsen. "My guess is they'll patrol all the way to Interstate 65. They might not have the manpower yet, but you saw the Kiowas. They can cover a lot of ground."

"We can take our time," said David. "Thermal imaging is far from perfect."

"I'm just making sure you thought it through," said Larsen. "If my plan works, we'll be well past the quarantine line before you get beyond the western end of this cornfield. Granted, you will undoubtedly get to the end of the cornfield. Beyond that, with those Kiowas flying around, there's no guarantee of anything. Not that I'm promising a walk in the park here."

"Let's hear it. If it starts with blowing up a helicopter, we're walking," said David.

"It starts with blowing up—one of the fuel bladders."

David cocked his head, which gave Larsen a little hope that he had the Marine hooked.

"Won't that end up blowing up the helicopters?" said Chang.

"No. Not unless they've completely fucked up down there," said Larsen. "Based on what I've observed, this crew knows what it's doing. I wouldn't expect any less from the 10th Aviation Regiment."

"We create a distraction?" said David.

"Sort of," said Larsen. "Our biggest problem down there is the refueling zone. They put it smack dab in the middle of the big tarmac, blocking Dr. Chang's taxi path. I have no doubt I can get Chang to his hangar undetected, and with all of the rotor noise down there, they'll never hear his hangar bay open or his engine start. However, once that Cessna rounds the corner of the hangar and starts taxiing toward the tarmac, all bets are off."

"I can maneuver in and around them," said Chang. "There's enough space."

"In the dark, with night-vision goggles?" said Larsen.

"That'll be the least of his problems," said David.

"Exactly. The refueling group is armed, as well as the helicopter crews. There's a squad providing light security. I don't think we'd make it to the tarmac," said Larsen. "Which is why we need to clear it, and nothing will clear it faster than a suspected fuel system malfunction. If one of those bladders goes sky-high, they'll detach the fuel hoses and launch every helicopter immediately. That's when we'll roll through, hopefully under the cover of thick smoke. Once we hit the main taxiway, we're home free."

"With a bunch of helicopters overhead," said David. "Two of them with highly sophisticated surveillance sensors."

"That's where you come in," said Larsen. "I heard you might be handy with the M1-A1."

"I told him you were a designated marksman," said Joshua.

"Sorry. I shouldn't have said anything."

"That's okay, Josh," said David, his head turning to Larsen. "I'm not killing anyone down there."

"I'm not asking you to shoot anyone," said Larsen. "I just need you to put a bullet or two into each MMS if the helicopters are still there when this goes down. Can you do that from here?"

"Not a problem," said David.

"Then that's it," said Larsen.

"That's it?" said David.

"Pretty much. You'll stay here with your son and the Harpers. Chang and I will sneak down to the airfield. I'll do my thing and he'll do his. If all goes well, we'll pick you up on the taxiway next to this cornfield. Chang said he can take off using the taxiway, so we'll be in the air a few seconds after pickup."

"That easy, huh?" said David.

"Everything and anything can go wrong, David. You know that," said Larsen. "This way, if it goes wrong on the tarmac, only my journey and Dr. Chang's ends early—assuming you knock out the Kiowa sensors before they get airborne. I can't imagine you'll get far with every helicopter in the area on high alert."

"As soon as the fuel bladder goes up, I'll take out the mast-mounted sights," said David. "Even in the dark, they kind of make easy targets."

"Music to my ears. A man—or woman—that doesn't doubt their shooting skills," said Larsen. "So is this it? Are we all in? Harpers?"

"I'm in," said Emma.

"We're in, then," said Jack.

"Joshua?" said David.

"I say we do it, Dad."

"Then we do it," said David.

"For the record, this is a fucking crazy plan," said Larsen. "I have made that clear already, right?"

"Abundantly," said Jack.

Larsen laughed. "All right. Let's go over it again and get this rolling. Time, tide and formation wait for no man—and that sun is coming up whether we like it or not."

Chapter Forty-Seven

Olson followed Chang's and Larsen's dark shapes through his scope as they sprinted the short distance from the edge of the closest cornfield to the western hangar. He wasn't concerned about them being spotted, because the largest building at the airfield—a behemoth three-story, curved-roof hangar at the southern edge of the airport complex—stood between Chang's hangar and the refueling helicopters. Nobody at the airfield had a clear line of vision to them, and once they reached the hangar, only a sentry patrolling the western side of the vast complex might run into them. They were as safe as they would be on this mission.

When they vanished behind the long hangar, he shifted to the helicopters, sighting in on one of the Kiowas' mast-mounted sights. The distinct, ball-shaped sensor stood several feet above the main rotors, an easy target at this range. The trick would be hitting each sensor ball twice, at the very least. Three times would be preferable. The ball was at least three feet in diameter, containing two forward-facing optical lenses. One of them housed the thermal imaging system, and he didn't know which. Neither did Larsen. The plan was for him to hit each ball as many times as possible, spreading the bullets evenly between the two helicopters before they took off. Hitting them in the air would be nearly impossible.

He had sighted the scope for two hundred yards, so he'd have to adjust his point of aim for the longer distance. It wouldn't be a big adjustment, but at night, with a blazing inferno in the background, he might not be able to tell if his rounds were on target, and he wouldn't have much time to make up for missed shots. Joshua would have to help him with that. Lying next to him with the binoculars, his job would be to look for any sign of a hit once he started firing. Sparks. Obviously shattered lenses. Sharp noise from debris hitting the rotors. Anything.

His son would also be keeping an eye on the small security team's whereabouts, along with any stray members of the ground crew, while Larsen planted an explosive charge on one of the bladders. David wore the spare communications rig that Larsen had produced. Interestingly, the handheld radio had been smeared with blood, too.

Something serious had gone down before they met Larsen and Chang in the forest, and neither of them had been keen to discuss it. He just hoped it wasn't the kind of secret that would come back to bite them later. David had privately told his son to keep a close eye on both of them. He had no reason to trust them, but they needed each other. If the plan worked, they'd get farther out of the quarantine zone in ten minutes by air than ten hours on foot.

"What are you seeing?" said David.

"From what I can see, the entire refueling team is busy with the helicopters," said Joshua. "A few members of the security team are spread out along the perimeter of the tarmac, the rest are between the tarmac and the bladders. I don't see how Larsen is going to blow one of those up without killing some of them."

"He'll figure out a way to give them a warning or something," said David, not really believing his own words.

In fact, he was starting to feel like he'd been duped by Larsen. David wasn't questioning the man's assessment of the situation on the airfield or their chance of success, he was questioning Larsen's true motive for putting him behind a rifle scope, with a clear view of the tarmac. He should have seen it earlier, but Larsen had played him well. He'd placed all of the emphasis on taking out the Kiowas' sensors, distracting him from the obvious problem at hand—the thirty-plus soldiers at the airport. There was no way Chang's aircraft was getting to the taxiway without some shooting, and Larsen couldn't cover the entire tarmac by himself.

"That son of a bitch," muttered David.

"What?" said Joshua.

"Nothing. Just mumbling to myself about our whole situation," said David. "Never in a million years."

"We're gonna be okay, right, Dad?"

He patted his son on the shoulder. "We'll be fine. I won't let anything happen to you."

"Or you," said Joshua. "I don't think we're going to see Mom again."

"What makes you say that?" said David. "She's out there somewhere. Hopefully she got the word that Indianapolis was a mess and stayed clear. We'll find her when we get out of here."

"I appreciate you saying that, Dad," said Joshua. "But she wasn't answering her phone or messages long before cell service was cut."

"She mentioned taking a trip with what's his name. Maybe they took off for one of those all-inclusive deals down to Cancun."

"I don't know. I think you know more than you're telling me," said Joshua.

"I promise we'll do whatever we can to find her," said David. "Right now I need to stay focused on getting you out of here. You need to stay focused on your job."

"Dad?"

"Yeah?"

"One of the sentries started walking to the big building," said Joshua.

"Probably taking a head break," said David before pressing his transmitter.

"Larsen, we have one sentry headed for the big hangar. We'll let you know when he reappears."

"Copy that," said Larsen. "We have the hangar door open. The plane looks good to go. Chang is ready to start her up. Just to make sure. We'll shut her down once everything checks out. Keep an eye on the field for a reaction."

"Copy. One more thing, Larsen."

"Send it."

"Four members of the security team have situated themselves between the tarmac and the bladder farm," said David. "They'll be crispy critters if you send that fuel sky-high."

"Got it," said Larsen, pausing a few seconds before continuing. "I have an idea, but you're not going to like it."

"What else is new," said David.

"If they don't move on their own, you might have to start firing a few seconds before I set off the fuel. The soldiers will scramble for the tarmac at the first sign of gunfire," said Larsen.

"Or they'll guard the fuel," said David.

"Trust me. Nobody will want to be anywhere near that fuel in a gunfight," said Larsen.

"Good point. We'll keep an eye on it."

"Chang just started the engine. Any reaction?" said Larsen.

"Stand by," he said before turning to Joshua. "Chang just started the plane. Check for a reaction. Anything different with security or the refueling crew."

"I didn't hear it," said Joshua.

"Neither did I."

He scanned with his rifle scope, not seeing any obvious reaction. They watched for several seconds, coming to the conclusion that the noise from the rotors on the tarmac had drowned out the Cessna's engine.

"Larsen, I'm not seeing any kind of reaction from the soldiers. We didn't hear it either," said David.

"Perfect. I'm going to have Chang shut down while I run my errands," said Larsen.

"Give the sentry some time to do his business and rejoin the others," said David.

"Let me know as soon as he rejoins the others," said Larsen. "I'm going to get in the best position to sabotage one of the bladders."

"You'll have to clear some open space to do that," said David.

"I'm counting on my old college arm."

He gauged the distance from the closest building to the bladders.

That was going to be one hell of a throw. Actually, he didn't see how it was humanly possible, unless Larsen played centerfield in college.

"That's one hell of a throw," said David. "You might want to rethink that plan."

"Did the sentry reach the big hangar yet?"

"He's almost there."

"I have a better idea," said Larsen. "Let me know if anyone else heads to the hangar."

"This is turning into a cluster fuck, Larsen," said David.

"I told you it was fifty-fifty," said Larsen.

David shook his head. It was looking more like twenty-eighty—not in their favor.

Chapter Forty-Eight

Larsen knocked on the pilot's window, getting Chang's attention. He signaled for Chang to kill the engine, and waited for him to shut down the aircraft. When the engine went silent and Chang opened the pilot's door, Larsen took a moment to adjust the scientist's helmet and night-vision goggles for a tight fit. Satisfied everything would stay in place for the escape, he patted Chang on the shoulder.

"I'll be back in a few minutes," said Larsen. "If something goes wrong out there, David and the others will hike to the edge of the cornfield in front of the hangar. Shut the door and hide out until they get there. You'll have to walk out of the quarantine zone."

"How will I know if something goes wrong?" said Chang.

"You'll know," said Larsen, walking backward. "If the fuel bladder goes up before I get back, don't wait for me. Taxi out of here and follow the plan."

"Wait!"

Larsen stopped, startled by Chang's tone. "What?"

"We have to remove the rear set of seats," said Chang. "Theoretically, I can only take off with another seven hundred pounds. Even if we stripped off most of our personal gear, my guess is that we're pushing a thousand."

"I'm not interested in the theoretical at the moment, Dr. Chang. Can you take off with a thousand pounds?"

"I don't know," said Chang.

"This would have been nice to know a little earlier," said Larsen. "You know, during the planning phase. Can you remove the seats by yourself? I'm on a bit of a timeline here."

"I've never done it before," said Chang.

"That's your only fucking mission right now. Understand?" said Larsen.

Chang nodded. "I'll do what I can."

Larsen didn't like the sound of that. He returned to the aircraft and opened the clamshell-type cargo door on the right side of the aircraft, pulling both doors wide open. He studied the bolting that held the seats in place, shaking his head.

"Figure it out, or we're leaving the rest of them behind," said Larsen.

Chang stared at him with disbelief.

"I'm not even close to kidding. You're too important."

"I won't fly us out of here if you leave them behind," said Chang.

"Then figure out how to fucking remove these seats," said Larsen. "I need to go."

Larsen dashed out of the hangar, hugging a lengthy row of hangar bay doors. When he reached the end, he peeked around the corner, scanning for any sentries that they might have missed from the cornfield. Finding the monochromatic green image clear of obvious threats, he jogged down the short end of the hangar and stopped again, surveying the area ahead of him.

The southern end of the long taxiway separating the western hangars from the main aviation complex would bring him to the three-story hangar. He'd have to cross roughly a football field of open ground to get there, briefly exposing himself to the small group of sentries standing between the fuel bladders and the tarmac, but the risk would be worth the gain.

Larsen took off diagonally across the taxiway, keeping his speed just below an all-out sprint. He needed a little something left in him when he reached the big hangar. Halfway across the taxiway, he heard a distinct change in rotor pitch coming from the tarmac. It was a deeper tone, giving him hope that it was one of the Black Hawks.

They really needed to blind the Kiowas before attempting their escape.

"Larsen, one of the Black Hawks is airborne. Heading right toward us," said David over the radio net.

"They won't see you," said Larsen. "What's happening with the Kiowas?"

"Nothing. Looks like they're disengaging fuel lines from another Black Hawk."

"Good. I'm almost at the big hangar. Is the sentry still inside?"

"I would have told you if he wasn't," said David.

Larsen didn't respond immediately, because he didn't see a side entrance on the northern side of the hangar, where he could remain unobserved from the tarmac. The entire western side was a two-story, closed hangar bay door. He reached the corner and kneeled, catching his breath.

"What door did the sentry go in?" said Larsen.

"Small glass door at the northeast corner of the hangar," said David.

"Got it. You're going to see me peeking around that corner in about twenty seconds," said Larsen. "I need you to watch the sentries and give me a green light when I'm clear."

"Copy that," said David.

Jogging as close as possible to the corrugated metal side of the hangar, Larsen came up on a twenty-foot-long, floor-to-ceiling bank of windows, which formed the corner of the building. He peeked inside, seeing an open lobby leading into the main hangar. Through a similar glass wall on the opposite facing side of the corner, he had a clear view of the sentry team guarding the fuel bladders beyond the tarmac. There was no way he was going in the front door. It didn't matter how good of a job David did—they couldn't miss him if they glanced in this direction.

"Change of plans," said Larsen. "I'm taking a more direct route. Let me know if anyone reacts."

He backed up a few feet from the first window panel and fired three suppressed bullets through the glass, shattering the door-sized piece in place. Using the stock of his rifle, he cleared enough of the panel to step inside the lobby.

"Give me a few seconds heads-up," said David.

"It's already done," he whispered.

"Then it looks like you're clear," replied David.

A quick glance around revealed the bathroom signs. Larsen drew the Taser from the holster next to his pistol and disengaged the safety switch, heading for the men's room. If the sentry popped out of the door right now, he was in trouble. A full kit of body armor didn't leave a lot of unprotected area for the Taser's probes to penetrate, and the Taser itself wasn't exactly what he'd call a precision device. He'd be better off firing his rifle center mass and praying that the ceramic armor plate did its job, allowing him to get close enough to fire the Taser at a limb.

The mental exercise turned out to be academic, since the door remained closed during his approach. He paused outside for a moment, rehearsing what he planned to do for each possible scenario in the bathroom. When the door squeaked on its hinges, the soldier immediately reacted.

"Hello?"

"Jesus. How long do you plan on sitting in here?" said Larsen, observing two feet under the single stall.

"I just called you, motherfucker! Got the shits from the jalapeno cheese spread you pawned off on me," said the soldier. "How long has that been sitting in your pack?"

The tiny bathroom smelled like Montezuma had already gotten his revenge. Larsen fought the urge to gag as he walked up on the stall.

"Breene? Is that you?"

Larsen kicked the stall door as hard as he could, knocking it open to reveal a young soldier in full combat gear—standing with his pants down. He aimed at one of the soldier's pale legs and triggered the Taser, dropping him to the tile deck in front of the toilet. A few minutes later, he had the guy hog-tied and gagged on the floor. A messy affair he would not soon forget. With the soldier's rifle in hand, he bolted out of the bathroom, gulping the hangar air.

A quick check of the sentry team's location relative to the fuel bladders reinvigorated his hope that the plan would work. His side of the plan. If Chang didn't figure out how to drop some weight from the plane, they were all screwed. With that cheery thought in mind, he rearranged his sling so the compact HK416 hung from his back, somewhat out of sight. He'd carry the soldier's M4 onto the tarmac, giving the soldiers out there one less thing to notice when he strolled toward the bladders.

"David, I'm coming out now."

Chapter Forty-Nine

David Olson watched in disbelief when Larsen opened the glass door and stepped onto the tarmac, standing there for a few seconds to look around—like he owned the damn place!

"Get your ass moving, Larsen," hissed David. "You don't look anything like any of those soldiers, except for the rifle."

"That bad?" said Larsen.

"That bad. Whatever you're going to do, you better do it and get out of there."

Larsen started walking toward the bladders, moving slowly and purposefully like a sentry.

"This was your plan?" said David.

"I can't throw that far," said Larsen.

"I could have told you that."

He couldn't believe this. Larsen thought he could impersonate one of the sentries and just stroll up to the bladders? Did he think they were blind? David decided they were getting the hell out of here. He'd grab the Harpers, too, unless they wanted to stick around for this madness. He started to move when his son nudged him.

"Are you seeing this?" said Joshua. "It's like he's invisible."

David put his eye behind the scope, finding Larsen's dark figure at the northern edge of the tarmac, walking straight for the fuel bladders. The four soldiers standing a few hundred feet away acted like he was—invisible. He'd barely finished the thought when one of the soldiers glanced in Larsen's direction, pausing long enough to note his presence before turning back to the group. Like nothing was wrong! Jesus. Even without night vision he could tell it wasn't the same soldier that went into the hangar.

"That's some serious magic," said David over the radio net. "I'd do what you need to do before it runs out."

"Yeah. I didn't think it would work either," said Larsen. "Think I should walk the rest of the way or use my centerfield arm?"

A light blue strip stretched across the eastern horizon, tinged with orange. In about fifteen minutes, the soldiers down there would ditch their night-vision gear.

"Use the arm," said David. "We don't have much time left."

"I set the timers for two minutes," said Larsen. "Once I throw these, I'm hauling ass out of here."

"What? You start running, and this invisible act is over."

"All part of the plan," said Larsen.

"I'm beginning to suspect that you're just making this up as you go along."

"You wouldn't be entirely wrong," said Larsen. "I need to focus here. See you in a few minutes."

"God speed, man," said David, turning to his son. "Keep a close eye on the four soldiers and Larsen. He's about to do his thing. Don't be surprised if Larsen starts hauling ass."

"In the open?"

"That's what he said," said David.

"What if they shoot him?" said Joshua.

"Then we have a decision to make. Do we stay, or do we go?" said David.

His son remained silent, and David saw why. Larsen cocked his arm, took several running steps in the direction of the bladders and threw the explosive device like he was trying to chase down a runner headed for home plate. He repeated the process, throwing another one toward a different part of the bladder field before turning and walking casually toward the nearest hangar.

"Any reaction?" said David.

"No. They weren't watching him."

"Start the timer on your watch for two minutes," said David.

"Yep," said his son, who put his binoculars down to mess with his watch.

David turned toward the Harpers, who were lying in the cornfield, next to the edge facing the runway.

"Two minutes until the fuel explodes," he yelled to them.

Jack Harper responded immediately. "Something's wrong down there!"

Joshua scrambled to get his binoculars back up while David sighted in on the tarmac. Two of the soldiers ran toward Larsen, who was in a full sprint now, while the other two soldiers were headed toward the fuel bladders.

"You attracted some attention," said David over the radio net.

"No shit," said Larsen, his words coming in garbled. "Part of the plan."

"Half the soldiers are headed toward the fuel," said David.

He saw Larsen slow down long enough to look toward the bladder farm before speeding up again. David didn't like his response.

"I need you to sort this out," said Larsen, breathing heavily over the radio. "I have to focus on Chang."

"There isn't going to be an escape if they find the explosives," said David.

"Then do something!" screamed Larsen. "Quit dissecting the problem and solve it! You're a cop and a Marine! Larsen out."

And just like that, David could no longer fool himself into thinking there would be any easy way out of this. He sighted in on the two soldiers jogging toward the fuel farm.

"Josh, what's happening with the helicopters and the refueling crew?"

"They're starting to pull the hoses," said his son.

"All of them, or just a few?"

"Hold on...hold on," said Josh.

"I need to know!"

"All of them," said Josh. "It's looking frantic down there."

He panned over to the soldiers following Larsen, who had already disappeared through the hangars. They barreled in the same direction at full speed, leading with their weapons. The entire airfield was on full alert at this point.

"Jack and Emma!" said David. "Get back from the edge of the cornfield. Fifty feet minimum! Be ready to run for the plane!"

While the Harpers responded, he turned to Joshua. "You too. We're gonna take some fire here. I don't see a way to avoid it."

"I'm staying," said Joshua.

"You're going," said David. "I don't have time to argue."

"You need me to spot for you," said Joshua.

"Move away from me, then," said David. "And leave the suppressed rifle. Hurry up!"

Larsen had left the other compact HK416 with them. Now David understood why. Larsen knew this would go to shit fast. When his son had settled into the new position, David grabbed the HK416 and searched through the ACOG scope for the soldiers near the fuel bladders. He found their dark forms a moment later. They were almost there.

"How much time has elapsed?" said David.

"Fifty-eight seconds!" yelled his son.

A lot could happen in a minute. Time to start shaping the little time they had left. He centered the ACOG's illuminated green reticle to the right of the soldiers and pressed the trigger. The rifle bit into his shoulder harder than he expected, probably due to the shortened barrel and lighter weight of the rifle. By the time he got the scope back on target, the two soldiers had stopped.

"What are you shooting at?" yelled Joshua.

He fired another bullet, this one a little closer.

"Are you firing at the soldiers?"

"I'm trying to get them away from the fuel!" he yelled, finding the soldiers again.

They were already headed toward the buildings a few hundred feet away. He fired two more shots immediately behind them, reinforcing their decision to seek cover. There was nothing they could do in the open, and they knew it.

"What's happening with the rest of the security team?" said David.

He figured they'd heard the bullets snap overhead and were frantically trying to determine the source of gunfire. They wouldn't have much luck. The sizable suppressor attached to the HK416 quieted the muzzle blast to a point where the actual supersonic crack of the bullet was louder. The soldiers on the tarmac would likely perceive that the bullet came from a different direction.

"They're looking all over," said Joshua.

"Move back a little bit. Slowly," said David. "Watch for anyone aiming in our direction."

With the soldiers running away from the fuel bladder and the rest of the security team confused, David switched rifles. His next rounds wouldn't be so discreet. Without a suppressor, the .308 cartridge fired by his M1-A1 would sound like a cannon and produce a muzzle flash easily visible from the tarmac. Hopefully, the soldiers would be too preoccupied by the fuel explosion behind them to take notice.

Chapter Fifty

Chang pulled the rear bench with every bit of strength he had, finally dislodging it. He'd found the quick release mechanism soon after Larsen left, but it was clearly a job designed for two people. Every time he released the catch holding one side of the bench in place, and let go of it to yank the seat clear, the latch sprang back into place, locking it down again. That had gone on far longer than he cared to admit.

In the end, he'd resorted to using some of the paracord in his backpack to pull the levers into the open position and tie them securely to the seatbelt loops above. With the levers open, he was able to pull the bench loose and wrestle it out of the aircraft. He'd just dropped it to the hangar's concrete floor when Larsen appeared in front of the open bay door.

"Hallelujah, Chang! I knew you could do it!" said Larsen, ducking inside the hangar. "Get her started. We have about twenty seconds until the fuel blows!"

Twenty seconds? It would take them at least that long to get out of the hangar! Larsen stayed next to the side of the bay door, pointing his rifle in the direction he'd come, giving Chang the distinct impression that something had gone wrong at the tarmac. He shoved the seat clear of the aircraft and climbed through the rear cabin to reach the pilot's seat. Two snaps drew his attention to Larsen, who took a few steps outside the hangar and kneeled, his rifle kicking into his shoulder twice, followed by two more cracks no louder than a mousetrap. Chang turned the ignition key to START, the engine catching immediately. He switched the key to BOTH and motioned for Larsen to get out of the way.

When Larsen was clear, he throttled up, bringing the Cessna halfway out of the hangar. As soon as the aircraft cockpit cleared the opening, Chang glanced to the right and saw two figures on the ground at the end of the hangar building. One of them appeared to be pulling the other toward the corner. Larsen ran into the hangar and pushed the bench seat with his foot, returning a moment later through the cargo compartment doors. He closed the front clamshell door, leaving the rear one open.

"That seat didn't feel very heavy!" he said.

"It was lighter than I thought," admitted Chang.

"Shit," said Larsen, shaking his head. "Just go! Get us moving toward the tarmac!"

Chang got them moving again, turning the aircraft onto the concrete hangar skirt. Before they reached the southern end of the hangar, the aircraft shook, followed by a blinding flash. He slowed the plane, afraid to make the turn toward the tarmac.

"What are you doing?" said Larsen.

"I don't think this is going to work!"

"Too late for cold feet, Chang! Get us to the taxiway," said Larsen, squeezing between the middle row of seats.

Chang gave the throttle a big push, swinging them through the turn. When they straightened on the southern skirt, bright orange flames reflected off the silhouettes of the few aircraft still on the ground. In the sky just above the refueling point, a few more yellow reflections rose to escape the inferno Larsen had unleashed.

"Hug the left side of the tarmac," said Larsen.

"That's closer to the fire!"

"I know it is, but all the soldiers are moving away from the fire. We don't want to run into the middle of them."

He scanned the brightly lit tarmac ahead, seeing dozens of soldiers either lying flat on the deck or scurrying to the right. A few of them fired their rifles in the direction of the cornfield hiding the rest of his group. Larsen talked excitedly into his headset.

"David, what's your status?" said Larsen. "Did you take out their MMS?"

Chang couldn't make much out of the conversation. He moved the aircraft forward as fast as he dared, easing it to the left side of the hangar skirt. Something struck the glass in front of him, putting a small hole in the windshield. Another hole appeared several inches above his head, snapping through the cabin. A quick shower of sparks flew off the propeller directly ahead of him, followed by several deep thumps against the airframe.

"They're shooting at us!" said Chang.

"Keep going!" said Larsen.

He glanced into the rear compartment for a moment, seeing Larsen kneeling on the deck, his rifle firing rapidly through the open clamshell door.

Chapter Fifty-One

David kept the M1-A1 scope's crosshair fixed on the leftmost Kiowa's mast-mounted sight as his son counted down the seconds. When his son yelled, "Three," he pressed the trigger, keeping the rifle tight into his shoulder. The second bullet was on its way a few moments after that. He heard the words *both shots on target* after firing the third bullet at the same aim point.

Shifting to the second Kiowa, he managed to find the sensor ball before the fuel bladders exploded. The heat hit him first, his face and hands instantly warming from the light released by the blast. The sound and blast wave struck simultaneously, pounding his eardrums and shaking the cornstalks around him. A second wave of heat produced by the exploded fuel hit next, leaving him wondering if Larsen hadn't miscalculated the size and magnitude of the explosion. Before David could react to this thought, the heat and blast passed, leaving a massive fireball rising into the sky behind the few remaining helicopters.

David fired three rapid shots at the second helicopter sensor and backed up a few feet into the cornstalks. Several bullets followed him, passing through the thick foliage above his head. He crawled to his right, keeping low as bullets snapped overhead, and came to a new firing position halfway between his old spot and the runway side of the cornfield. His son was deeper in the cornfield, already making his way to the Harpers. Bullets snapping inches above his head, he wiggled forward, catching a glimpse of the plane racing toward the tarmac. There was only one way out of here now, and his job was to make sure it got through intact.

He scanned the refueling point, seeing most of the soldiers lying flat on the concrete. The few firing in his direction had shifted their attention to the approaching plane. He sighted in on one of them, applying pressure to the trigger, when the soldier suddenly lurched backward. The next soldier David found spun in a circle and dropped to the ground before he even thought of pulling the trigger. Larsen was making quick work of the few soldiers threatening the aircraft. All the better. He didn't want to have anything to do with it.

The plane reached the tarmac just as the Kiowas lifted off, their refueling crews scrambling for cover and firing at the Cessna. Larsen's gunfire pressed them to the earth in front of the concrete, preventing them from shooting accurately at the passing plane. In the upper corner of David's scope, a backlit figure emerged, kneeling with a rifle. The soldier was in full combat gear, which meant he was a member of the security team. He adjusted his view, placing the crosshair in the center of the soldier's chest, willing him to lie down. It wasn't going to happen, so he removed most of the pressure on the trigger and waited.

At the first sign of a muzzle flash from the soldier's rifle, the M1-A1 bit into David's shoulder. He knew it was a clean shot as soon as the trigger broke. Center mass. All he could do at this point was hope the soldier's chest plate performed as advertised, and that the shot hadn't hit a soft spot adjacent to the armor. When he brought the sight picture back to the soldier, the man lay flat on his back, his arms wrapped around his chest. He'd shot an American soldier. David felt like throwing the rifle away and charging the tarmac unarmed—accepting swift retribution for his unforgiveable act. Instead, he thought about his greater responsibility to Joshua and searched for more targets. Mercifully, he found none, and the plane reached the long taxiway parallel to the runway in one piece.

Chapter Fifty-Two

Jack Harper lay frozen on the ground, shielding Emma from what he could only assume were bullets snapping above them through the corn plants. One crack after another—the intensity increasing as David Olson ran in their direction.

"Let's go! Down to the runway!" screamed David. "They made it!"

Jack lifted his body up far enough to see that it was true. In the early dawn twilight, he spotted the white plane turning off the tarmac—onto the taxiway. The hiss of a bullet inches from his head sent him back to the ground. As David had explained, the cornfield was on slightly higher ground, and if they lay flat, about twenty feet back from the northern edge, there was no way a bullet could hit them.

"Come on!" said David, grabbing his backpack and trying to pull him to his feet. "You can't stay here."

"We need to stay down," said Jack.

"You can't crawl to the plane," said David, kneeling next to him, the bullets somehow missing the police officer. "Jack, Emma, get the fuck up and get moving."

"I can't," said Jack.

He really couldn't. No matter how hard he tried, he just couldn't make his arms and legs work.

"Emma?" said David. "I need you to follow me."

"She can't," said Jack.

"The hell she can't," said David before jumping over them and pulling his wife to her feet. "Run! Now!"

Emma grabbed Jack's hand, bullets striking the leaves and stalks around her, and tugged at his arm. He suddenly found himself free of the paralyzing fear, running with her toward the taxiway. Glancing toward the approaching plane, he saw a screen of white smoke wash across the tarmac, obscuring the airfield complex. The volume of gunfire snapping above and between them nearly stopped, convincing Jack that they were going to make it. He ran as fast as he could with the backpack, his legs finally reaching their stride.

They reached David and his son at the edge of the taxiway as the plane pulled up, the gunfire increasing again. Larsen jumped out of the rear door, pulling open both hatches to expose front-facing passenger seats and a spacious rear cargo area.

"Harpers in the seats! David and son in the back!" said Larsen. "Drop your packs. We can't take off with the weight."

"What?" said Jack.

"No time to explain. Leave the packs behind. Everyone," said Larsen, pulling a small cylinder out of a pouch on his vest and throwing it behind the plane.

The cylinder exploded into a white cloud of smoke, which hung in place for a moment and started to drift left.

"Five seconds! Five fucking seconds and we're gone!" yelled Larsen.

Jack dumped his pack on the taxiway next to his wife's and helped her board the plane. The Olsons piled on board with their cache of weapons, and Larsen shut the rear doors before making his way to the copilot seat.

"Go! Go!" yelled Larsen, shutting his door.

The aircraft lurched forward, picking up speed as the cornfield raced by on their right. He felt the plane try to lift skyward twice, the plane vibrating with the fully throttled engine, but they never left the ground for more than a moment. Larsen pounded the cockpit dashboard, cursing wildly. Chang shook his head, yelling back at him. When the plane started to slow, Jack knew what was wrong. They were too heavy. David Olson appeared between them, grabbing Larsen's shoulder.

"What the hell is wrong?" said David.

"We're too heavy!" said Larsen. "Too fucking heavy."

"How far off are we?" said David.

"We're not far," said Chang. "She wanted to lift off. I mean, I can force it, but I have no idea what'll happen in the air."

Larsen threw up his hands. "Wait! Wait! So you can actually take off right now?"

"We're above the maximum takeoff weight," said Chang. "But it can be done. I just don't recommend—"

"Dr. Chang," said Larsen, suddenly calm, "get us off the ground, please. I don't care about the unknowns up there, but I know what's going to happen down here—if we don't get in the air really soon. Can you do that?"

Jack squeezed Emma's hand as the plane throttled forward again, picking up speed. This time, there was no bounce or soft takeoff attempts. The aircraft wrenched skyward, pressing him into his seat. Behind him, David and Joshua Olson slid across the cargo compartment, hitting the back with a thud. After several seconds of a steep climb, the plane leveled off, momentarily hanging there before banking slowly to the right. Chang was taking them north.

"Stay clear of the airfield," said Larsen. "And get as low as possible."

The aircraft descended at a reasonable rate, settling in about a hundred feet above the clearly visible treetops. The sun was about ten minutes from rising above the horizon.

"Can you get lower?" said Larsen. "I don't want to make it easy for their helicopters. You can fly without night vision now."

Chang flipped up the goggles.

"I'll give you another fifty feet," said Chang. "But that's it."

Jack looked at Emma, who barely managed to nod at him, her hand clamped over his as Chang took them closer to the trees. A two-lane, east-west road appeared directly ahead of them, quickly passing beneath the aircraft. They were out of the quarantine zone.

Chapter Fifty-Three

Chang frantically tried to focus on his instruments and scan the airspace ahead of the plane, still unable to see clearly enough to pick out approaching hazards mixed in with the trees. He didn't remember any in the area, but he never flew this low around here except on final approach to the airport, so he wouldn't have paid much attention. A cell phone tower he hadn't noticed before would put an end to their trip really quickly.

Larsen was busy scanning the skies above and around them for helicopters. He had been especially worried about the smaller helicopters because of their surveillance pods and forward-mounted guns. Chang didn't know much about military helicopters, but Larsen had assured him that they posed a serious threat. They could fly as fast as the Cessna, and the pilots could turn them on a dime. As if reading Chang's mind, Larsen turned in his seat.

"You got both Kiowas?" he yelled to David.

"Good hits on both!" said David. "At least three bullets per mast."

"I hope so," muttered Larsen, going back to work looking for threats.

Chang detected a significant change to the ground illumination several hundred yards ahead of them, momentarily thinking he had drifted toward the eastern horizon. He knew he hadn't, seeing the long line of bright blue sky in his peripheral vision and quickly confirming his northerly heading with a glance at his instruments.

Something big was coming up, lit up like a football field.

"What is that?" said Jack Harper.

Before anyone responded to Jack's question, the treetops came to an end, and they passed over a sprawling, brightly lit complex of tents and military vehicles. Chang instinctively pulled up on the yoke, wanting to put some space between the aircraft and this new facility. His instinct saved their lives. The left wing passed several feet over the top of an unlit radio tower mast. Larsen grabbed his shoulder as the top of the tower flew by, sharing a quick, knowing glance with him.

A few seconds later, their world went dark again, the ground and horizon ahead of them lit by rapidly approaching dawn.

"What the hell was that?" said David.

"Looked like a military base or something," said Jack.

"With guard towers?" said Larsen.

"I didn't see any guard towers," said Jack.

"I did," said Emma.

"So did I," added Chang. "I don't think that was a military base."

"Well, whatever it is, we don't have to worry about it," said David. "How fast does your plane fly?"

"Cruising speed of about one hundred and forty knots," said Chang.

"What is that in miles per hour?" said David.

"About one sixty," replied Chang.

"I think you should bring us a little lower," said Larsen, glancing nervously out of the windows.

"I'd rather not risk—"

A long burst of red tracers zipped in front of the plane, missing the nose by several feet. Larsen pushed the copilot yoke forward, sending them into a dive, which Chang fought against by pulling back on his yoke. The result was a momentary drop in altitude, which dodged the next burst of tracers. The bright red line of tracers passed directly above the cockpit. Pandemonium broke out in the cabin behind them—a combination of screams and cursing.

"Get us lower!" yelled Larsen.

"This is it!" said Chang. "Any lower, and we'll hit the trees."

"Then start some evasive maneuvering!"

He pulled the aircraft into a steep climb, rolling to the right as a torrent of red-hot steel passed beneath them, several of the bullets catching the bottom of the airframe. Blood splattered against the inside of the cockpit windshield and Emma screamed, but Chang was too focused on the maneuver to figure out who had been hit. Judging by Larsen's sudden expletive-laced tirade, Chang figured it had been him.

Chang rapidly gained several hundred feet of altitude, hoping to buy some time. Unlike an airplane, a helicopter couldn't drastically change the vertical angle of its airframe. By climbing quickly, the helicopter would be forced to rise to his altitude to fire again. The helicopter wasn't designed to dogfight, and Chang planned to take advantage of that fact. When he reached eight hundred feet, he rolled the aircraft left, searching for the helicopter.

He found the Kiowa doing exactly what he suspected: gaining altitude. The pilot would likely fly the helicopter a few hundred feet above the Cessna's altitude and circle back to re-attack. Chang straightened the aircraft on a due north heading and considered his options. He didn't know the range of the Kiowa's guns, but decided his best strategy would be to put as much distance between the two aircraft as possible and head in one direction, changing altitude frequently. He understood enough about helicopters to know that the Kiowa would have to trade more speed to climb than the Cessna. Both aircraft could drop altitude and maintain speed. If he did this enough times, the Kiowa would fall far enough behind to render the chase pointless. That was the theory anyway.

"David," yelled Chang over his shoulder.

"Yeah!"

"Keep an eye out of the back window," said Chang. "The second you see those tracers again, I need to know."

"Got it," said David. "Does that mean you're going to do something drastic?"

"Yes."

"We don't have seats back here," said David.

"I know. Sorry," said Chang, briefly turning his attention to Larsen, who had become uncharacteristically quiet.

The top of Larsen's right leg was covered with a yellow powder, a wide bandage pressed to the leg.

"How bad is it?"

"I thought you'd never ask," said Larsen grimly. "I'll be fine. Just need to wrap this up properly."

"Tracers! They're shooting." yelled David.

Chang immediately put the plane into a sharp dive, the red tracers passing at least a hundred feet above them. He could do this all day, or until they ran out of fuel, which would be hours after the Kiowa had to turn around. That was another advantage of the Cessna.

"Seems like a reasonable plan," said Larsen. "Until the second one—oh, shit."

"What?" said Chang, immediately seeing the problem.

Four helicopters approached from the north, their black shapes barely visible on the distant horizon.

"Anyone have binoculars handy?" said Larsen.

Jack passed a small pair forward, which Larsen pressed to his face.

"Turn us around," said Larsen, followed by another round of expletives.

"Back toward the Kiowa?"

"Take us high above it, then hug the ground heading due south," said Larsen. "One of the helicopters out there is an Apache."

"Shit," he heard from the back of the plane.

"What does that mean?" said Emma.

"It means we're pretty much fucked," said Larsen. "Unless we can maintain a good distance. They pack a very accurate thirty-millimeter gun mount. If they get in range, we are dead. No amount of maneuvering will do us any good. Chang?"

"Got it," said Chang, bringing them into a steep, rolling climb.

The Kiowa raced below them, starting a sharp turn before Chang lost sight of it through his cockpit door window. With the plane now headed south, he brought them as low as he dared to fly. When the sun broke over the horizon, he could nudge them a little closer.

"Keep an eye on the Kiowa, David," said Larsen. "We're not out of the woods yet."

"I'm on it," said David.

"We're headed toward the Eagle Creek Airport," said Chang. "I've landed there dozens of times. I could navigate us there by sight."

"The army will have it locked down like the other airport," said Larsen.

"Then what are we supposed to do?" said Chang.

"Try to slip out on a different heading," said Larsen.

"Under observation?" said Chang. "We're a little conspicuous."

"We need to land unobserved and try this again tonight," said Larsen. "How are we looking back there, David?"

"The Kiowa lost a lot of ground on that last maneuver. The other four are still coming," said David.

Chang racked his brain for an option that didn't involve a registered airfield. He could land on a reasonably short patch of ground, maybe seven or eight hundred feet long, but with six passengers and most of their fuel, he'd need at least twice that to safely get off the ground. Then there was the helicopter problem. There was no chance of landing unobserved at this point. Within minutes of landing, the plane would be destroyed. A thought popped into his head, but it was crazy. Really crazy.

"You have a plan," said Larsen. "You're grinning."

Chang shook his head slowly. "You're not going to like it."

"We're fresh out of options," said Larsen. "So let's hear it."

"I can land us on Interstate 70, just south of the downtown area," said Chang. "I've driven it a thousand times. My office is right there. It's long enough and wide enough. We can even hide beneath an overpass I take to get to work."

Chang momentarily thought about the data he'd hidden in the lab. That would come in handy, too.

"Jesus," said Larsen, taking a few seconds to think it over. "How far away is your office?"

"Less than a quarter mile," said Chang. "At the NevoTech

research labs."

"We both work for NevoTech," said Emma. "I'm at the financial building in the city. Jack is a sales rep."

"How long have you—" started Chang.

"We can do the small-world stuff later," said Larsen. "How secure is the lab?"

"Very secure," said Chang. "I can't imagine NevoTech would let anything happen to that facility. It's basically indestructible."

"I don't know," said Larsen.

"It's designed to withstand tornados and earthquakes. They have billions of dollars in research and development riding on the survival and security of that building."

"I'm more concerned about what might be waiting for us outside," said Larsen. "There were three more teams. One of them might have been sent to the lab, just in case."

Chang hadn't thought of that, or the other possibility. "I keep an apartment a few blocks away from NevoTech."

"Then we definitely have another team in the area."

"I don't see where else we can land?" said Chang. "This is almost perfect. I'll aim for the city, skirt around the western edge of the buildings, then cut hard left, dropping in for a landing. The interstate is right there. I know I can set us down."

"We're forgetting something," said David.

"What?" said Larsen.

"The city itself. That might be a long quarter mile, given what I've seen on patrol in the suburbs," said David.

"Our neighborhood was on the border of sheer madness when we left," said Jack.

"It had already gone mad," said Emma blankly.

"Do we still have company back there?" said Larsen, turning painfully in his seat to see out the back.

"The Kiowa is fading," said David. "I still see the other helicopters, but I can't tell if they're falling back or gaining."

"Do your best to make that assessment. Our lives will depend on it," said Larsen, passing the binoculars between the seats to Jack.

"Give those to David."

Larsen grimaced in pain with the movement.

"Are you sure you're all right?" said Chang.

"How long to the interstate?" said Larsen.

"Five minutes. We should be able to see the city center at this point," said Chang. "Right there."

He pointed at a small cluster of high-rise buildings in the distance. Without the first rays of morning sunlight reflecting brightly off the steel and concrete structures, they wouldn't have been able to see them this far out.

"I'll be fine," said Larsen. "Take us in, Dr. Chang. I don't see any other option."

Chang made a minor adjustment to their course, pointing them for the western side of the buildings. Without turning his head, Larsen spoke in a soft tone that was clearly not meant to be heard by the other passengers.

"Can you really land this thing on the interstate?"

He responded quietly. "There won't be much room for error, and if there's traffic—forget it."

"Early Saturday morning, in the middle of a citywide outbreak?" said Larsen. "My guess is the road will be empty."

Chang hoped so, although the sight of Indianapolis's usual light traffic on a Saturday morning would be a welcome sight, too. It would mean the city hadn't imploded, and there was still some hope for the people inside the quarantine zone.

Chapter Fifty-Four

David's stomach lurched, his back pressed tightly against one bulkhead and his feet pressed against the other. Joshua sat across from him, looking just as nauseous, his feet pressed against the bulkhead next to David. Pushing against opposite sides of the aircraft was the only way to keep them in place when Chang maneuvered the plane. They'd been tossed around like rag dolls during the first few minutes of their escape from the airfield, miraculously avoiding injury. He had no idea what was in store for them with this landing, but it didn't sound good.

The city's modest skyline suddenly appeared in the curved rear window above them, close enough that David could see office furniture inside the nearest building. The aircraft leveled, blue sky mercifully filling the glass. He prayed that was it. It wasn't. The plane dove wildly for a few seconds before easing into a calm, shallow descent—but the damage was done to his stomach.

He retched its meager contents over his shoulder against the back of the plane. Joshua somehow managed to hold it together as everything seemed to go still in the Cessna. For a moment, David thought they had lost power, but he could still hear the engine buzzing. He glanced between the rear seats and nearly gasped. They couldn't be more than a few feet above the interstate. He faced forward and closed his eyes for what seemed like forever.

The Cessna bounced lightly off the highway, grabbing the road on its return and slowing significantly. David opened his eyes and peered through the cockpit window, seeing what any commuter might see through their windshield.

A hearty cheer filled the cabin, everyone high-fiving and yelling for a few moments. David crawled forward, steadying himself on Jack's and Emma's seats. An overpass rapidly approached, and Chang slowed the aircraft, bringing them underneath like it was meant to be. The plane appeared to be completely covered by the overpass when it stopped, positioned between two on-ramps feeding the four-lane highway behind them.

"Let's go!" said Larsen. "We need to get out of here fast."

David opened the rear compartment's clamshell doors, giving Joshua a hand out. They grabbed the rifles while Jack and Emma got out of their seats and squeezed into the cargo area. He took a quick inventory of their weapons, handing the M1-A1 to Joshua.

Larsen ducked under the wing, looking morbid. From the right hip down to the knee, his camouflage pants were stained dark red. A bloodied bandage was crudely taped across the front of his thigh, evidence of some kind of yellow powder sprinkled under the compress.

"I want you to carry that," said Larsen. "You know how to use it better than anyone here. Give your son the other suppressed rifle. Jack, have you ever fired a rifle?"

"No," said Jack. "I fired the revolver for the first time last night."

"Dr. Chang, you get the other rifle," said Larsen. "It functions the same as the one I showed you last night."

Chang didn't protest, so David reluctantly gave him the AR-15. Chang immediately checked the safety. A good sign as far as he was concerned. Joshua looked a little too giddy to be holding the suppressed weapon, but he knew how to work an AR-15 weapons platform, so he'd be fine with the HK416A5. The distant thump of helicopters spurred them into action.

"Which way, Dr. Chang?" said Larsen.

Chang pointed up the embankment leading down from the overpass. "The road right above us is East Street. It leads right to the NevoTech campus. The lab is on the other side, but we can enter through one of the lower campus gates. The whole campus is enclosed and secure. I need to inspect the plane first. One of the wings doesn't look right."

"One of them was crooked to start, right?" said Larsen.

"We've been flying in a broken plane?" said David. "Not that I'm complaining."

"It wasn't crooked," said Chang. "Just needed a little adjustment to bring the two wings into better balance. I've been flying it like this for years."

"What's wrong with it now?" said David.

"Hold on."

Chang walked in front of the plane, staring at it, as they passed him.

"The right wing looks bent," said Chang. "Just barely, but you can see it. Maneuvering like that over max weight puts some weird stresses on the aircraft. We're lucky it didn't snap off."

Larsen stood next to Chang for a second. "Looks fine to me."

"It'll look fine until it isn't," said Chang. "That's kind of how aviation accidents work."

"We can take off, right?" said David.

"I don't see why—"

The helicopter sounds deepened, cutting off Chang's answer. They climbed the grass embankment and ran across an off-ramp to a thick stand of trees and bushes next to a run-down residential street. Larsen struggled the entire way, leaving David with the distinct impression that he needed medical attention immediately.

"Anyone see the helicopters?" said Larsen.

The group scanned the skies beyond the trees, each answering no in rapid succession. The rotor drumbeat didn't seem to get any closer as they listened. David walked to the far edge of the overgrown patch of land and took up a position close to the neighborhood. A woman dressed in denim shorts and a bloodstained bra sat at a picnic table behind the nearest building, staring at the back of the next building. A man sat across from her, clutching a half-crushed beer can, his bloodied head resting facedown on the table. He couldn't tell for sure, but it looked like the worn surface was covered by a thick sheen of blood.

A shirtless man in bloody jeans stumbled down the street next to the neighborhood, swaying like a drunk and drawing her attention. She stood up, grabbing something David couldn't see from the bench next to her. The stumbler caught sight of someone in the group and veered toward the line of bushes separating the street from their little oasis.

He tracked the man over the M1-A1's scope, the shot too close for the 10X-magnified optics. The disheveled man lurched through the thick bushes, falling to the browned grass in a heap. When he managed to push himself back up on two feet, a bloodstained kitchen knife appeared in his hand—previously concealed behind his leg. The man glared at him with pure malice, his eyes narrowing. David looked over his shoulder at Larsen, who took one look at the guy and raised his rifle. A single suppressed shot drilled through the man's forehead, dropping him below a bright red mist.

David swallowed hard, unsure what had just happened. Actually, he'd seen it before—and it had nearly killed him. The man had the same look as the woman on Maidenfield Road when she'd unloaded a pistol at David and his partner, then charged them for no reason. Inexplicable hatred and rage.

The woman in the backyard started toward the chain-link fence separating her from the street. David sighted in on the woman, who carried a semiautomatic pistol. Like the guy that stumbled through the bushes, she didn't look right. Glitchy movements, almost zombielike, characterized the way she climbed the fence, ignoring the gate a few feet away.

"Contact. Armed hostile approaching from north," said David. "I need some suppressed shots here."

"Fuck," muttered Larsen, hobbling over to David's position.

By the time he got there, the woman was in the street, heading directly for them. The woman started to raise the pistol, losing the top of her head a fraction of a second later.

"This is fucking crazy," said David.

"Swap weapons, Emma," said Larsen. "I suspect we'll be doing a lot of this on the way to the lab."

"I can't believe we're in the city," said David. "This is beyond fucked."

Larsen put a hand on his shoulder. "I wish I had better news for us, but this is our reality until nightfall. We just need to hold on until then. Not do anything stupid."

"Like go to Chang's apartment?" said David.

Larsen didn't respond directly. "Take a look across East Street."

David looked past a thick row of trees. A twelve-foot-tall black wrought-iron fence ran along the sidewalk on the far side of the street, extending as far as he could see.

"That's the NevoTech campus," said Larsen. "I think we'll be safe there."

"Unless another *team* finds us," said David. "Right?"

Larsen adjusted himself, wincing from the movement. "We need to get inside one of the secure buildings on the campus and wait for nightfall."

"I don't think you're going to last that long," said David.

"I've been worse off," said Larsen. "Let's get moving."

Chang ran toward them, holding up his cell phone. "Dr. Hale is in my apartment!"

"Keep it down, for shit's sake," said Larsen, pointing at the street. "They're everywhere. Who the fuck is Dr. Hale?"

The scientist went pale when he saw the body in the street.

"Dr. Hale is an emergency room doctor," said Chang, his eyes locked onto the corpses. "She brought me samples of the virus this morning. I left her with the codes to get into my apartment in case she ran into trouble. I can access the security system remotely. She's there."

"You could use a look from an ER doc," said David.

Larsen didn't fire back a smart-ass comment, like usual, so David guessed he agreed.

"We can't risk approaching your apartment," said Larsen. "How do you know it's her and not someone else?"

329

"I can see her sleeping on the couch," said Chang, shrugging his shoulders. "I know. It's a little creepy."

"The apartment will be under surveillance," said Larsen.

"She can head over to NevoTech," said Chang.

"That would work," said Larsen. "They'd send one person at most to trail her. We could have David let her in one of the gates. They don't know him."

It was David's turn to be pragmatic. "How are we going to take off with another passenger? I assume we aren't going to leave her behind."

Larsen laughed. "Well, look at you."

"I ditched my rose-colored glasses at the airfield," said David. "Thanks to you."

"The campus will be safer than you think," said Chang. "We might end up staying there until help arrives."

"I highly doubt we'll see any help," said Larsen.

A long burst of automatic gunfire cut through the new morning. He recognized the distinct sound immediately. So did Larsen, who gave him an uneasy look. M240 machine gun. Only the military would be equipped with a weapon like that. A second, shorter burst echoed off the buildings. The gun wasn't close, but it was close enough.

"We should get off the streets so no one confuses us with one of them," said Larsen, motioning toward the heap of bodies in the street.

"Then I guess we have a plan," said David. "Subject to immediate change. Let's go."

Chapter Fifty-Five

Chang followed Larsen closely as the group moved briskly down the wide sidewalk. They walked in a tight line, weapons facing the street on their right. The formidable fence separating them from NevoTech stood guard over their left flank. The normally bustling corporate campus stood eerily quiet, like a ghost town. He wished he could say the same about the neighborhood beyond the street.

One of the rifles behind him snapped twice, and Chang looked over his shoulder. A man dressed in a ripped and partially burned suit dropped to his knees in the middle of the street, trying to keep his body upright with a fireplace poker. Another shot from David's suppressed rifle knocked him flat. That had been the third shooting since they'd set off for the pedestrian gate farther down East Street.

"What happened?" whispered Larsen.

"Another aggressive type," said Chang. "Guy in a suit with a fireplace poker."

"We're not seeing many nonaggressive types," said Larsen.

"I was afraid of that," said Chang. "The virus was seriously modified. Almost reengineered. This could be way worse than I ever imagined."

"Worse?" said Larsen.

"If they somehow reduced the lethality, we could be looking at a city full of violently unpredictable lunatics."

"Great," said Larsen before abruptly shifting his rifle to the right.

STEVEN KONKOLY

"Contact. Ahead and across the street. Just past the Mexican restaurant. I saw some movement in the parking lot. Back me up, Chang. Everyone else, watch the buildings next to us."

Chang aimed his rifle in the direction of the red, one-story restaurant. Beyond the corner of the patio, he spotted why Larsen was alarmed.

"Looks like more than one person," said Chang.

"I count three," said Larsen. "They don't attack in mobs, right?"

Up until now, all of the attacks had been perpetrated by lone assailants, which made sense given the virus's neurological impact. The impulsive, violent behavior associated with temporal lobe deterioration was individualistic, directed at whatever and whoever caught the infected victim's attention.

At least that was what the limited scientific observation of diseases that target the temporal lobe had indicated. Limited being the operative term. Most cases occurred in single patients that never came in contact with other similarly affected patients. There was no telling what might happen if victims of low-level deterioration merged.

"I don't know," said Chang. "We've killed more temporal-lobe-deranged patients in the past five minutes than the entire international medical community sees in any given year. Anything is possible at this point."

"If I see a weapon, we're taking them down," said Larsen.

"I can't find any fault with that logic," said Chang.

He looked through his rifle's holographic sight for the first time, finding a bright red circle with a dot in the middle. The image looked fuzzy until he lined his eye up directly behind the sight. The circle and red dot appeared superimposed against the white patio spindles. Dark figures shifted beyond the wooden deck. A moment later they were gone.

"Three targets inbound," said Larsen, a single crack filling the air. "One down. The rest are yours, Chang."

"What?"

Chang lowered the rifle a few inches and looked past the barrel.

332

Two men sprinted in their direction, one carrying a machete, the other an aluminum baseball bat. He pulled the trigger without aiming, the rifle biting into his shoulder and having no effect on the attackers.

"Chang?" said Larsen.

He pulled the trigger three times, seeing one of them jerk sideways—but they kept coming.

"Are you using the sight?" said Larsen.

"No," said Chang, firing again to no effect.

"Center each target in the middle of the red circle and slowly press the trigger."

Chang raised the rifle level with his face, finding the red circle again. Both of the men appeared in the sight, and he shifted the rifle gently to bring one of them into the circle. He pulled the trigger twice, lowering the rifle to see what happened. One of the men had tumbled to the street, his steel machete clattering against the asphalt.

"Slowly press the trigger," said Larsen, firing a single shot that flattened the downed man as he tried to get up. "You were lucky to hit him at all."

"This is your job," hissed Chang.

"Not anymore," said Larsen. "If we're going to survive, we all need to be able to do this."

Chang wanted to argue, but the man holding the baseball bat was closing fast. He placed the dot in the middle of the attacker and eased the trigger back, surprised when the rifle dug into his shoulder.

"Perfect," said Larsen. "Center mass. Dropped him like a stone."

When Chang lowered the rifle, he found the man with the baseball bat motionless on the street.

"Don't make me do that again," said Chang.

"You passed the test. I'll take it from here," said Larsen, firing a single shot from his rifle.

A woman stumbled into the open next to the restaurant, grasping her stomach. A second bullet spun her to the parking lot pavement, a rifle skidding along the ground.

"It appears they are capable of attacking en masse," said Larsen.

"And covering their approach. Thankfully, she was a little slow on the draw."

The implication was both groundbreaking and devastating. The infected population was not only capable of cooperating in groups, but of higher level functioning. They needed to get safely inside the campus immediately.

"Can you move faster?" said Chang.

"Don't worry about me," replied Larsen.

"Then I suggest we pick up the pace."

"Music to my ears," said Larsen, immediately pulling ahead.

Chang turned his head. "We're picking up the pace."

They passed a side street before they reached the passenger gate, spotting a sizable mob a few buildings down. The mob started toward them immediately, screaming and yelling. Larsen's rifle barked several times, dropping the front row of the horde.

"David, take Chang and the group to the entrance. Joshua, stay with me. We need to buy the group some time."

"I want my son with me," said David.

"I need someone who can shoot," said Larsen. "I'll keep him safe. Get moving."

David hesitated next to Chang.

"No time to argue. Go!" said Larsen.

The police officer grabbed Chang's arm and pulled him toward the pedestrian entrance.

"Fast. Let's go!" he yelled.

Chang ran toward the turnstile gate with David and the Harpers while Larsen and Joshua fired bullet after bullet into the approaching pack. Rapid gunfire erupted from the mob, clanging off the iron fence around him.

"Get that door open, Chang!" yelled Larsen.

When they reached the turnstile, David raced toward the street, rapidly firing his rifle in the direction of the approaching horde. Chang dug through his pockets, suddenly realizing that he'd stuffed his ID in his backpack, which sat in a cornfield twenty-five miles away. Shit. He'd fucked up big time.

"I don't have my ID," said Chang.

"What?" said Jack.

"I left my ID in my backpack," said Chang.

"Are you fucking kidding me?" said Jack.

"What's the holdup?" said David.

Chang looked beyond the Harpers at Larsen and Joshua. The two of them fired nonstop at the approaching crowd, which had thinned considerably. Several bodies lay in the street, which didn't seem like enough to explain the sudden thinning.

"I can't get us through the door," said Chang. "My ID is back at the airport."

David didn't respond. Two men burst into the open behind the building directly across the street from the gate. David tracked them with his rifle for a moment before they ducked out of sight. He turned to Chang with a panicky look.

"Please tell me you didn't say you left your ID back at the airport," he said.

Chang's look must have said it all, because David immediately yelled to Larsen, "Chang can't get us in. What's plan B?"

Larsen patted Joshua on the shoulder and ran as fast as his leg would allow to the gate. When he arrived a few moments later, he cornered Chang. "Isn't there some kind of passcode?"

"You have to swipe your ID," said Chang.

The Olsons' rifles cracked repeatedly behind them.

"Something's brewing!" said David. "You better figure something out quick."

"Damn it, Chang," said Larsen, unsnapping the pouch that previously held his tablet. He removed a small package that was immediately recognizable as a plastic explosives device.

"If I blow this open, it stays open," said Larsen.

A bullet snapped overhead, striking the thick metal turn-bars, followed by another that glanced off Larsen's helmet—who barely acknowledged it.

"They're firing from the windows!" said David.

"That doesn't make any sense," said Chang.

A sharp pain creased the back of his right shoulder, causing him to stiffen.

"I think I'm hit," muttered Chang, surprised he hadn't screamed.

"You're fine," said Larsen, bullets ricocheting off the sidewalk next to him.

"Fuck it. This is getting out of control," said Larsen. "I'm blowing this thing open."

Emma Harper pushed Chang out of the way, holding a card attached to a lanyard. "Try my ID."

"Hurry up," said Larsen. "We're running out of time."

She pressed the card against the reader and the digital display turned green.

"Ha!" said Larsen. "Joshua! David! We got access. Compress your perimeter and suppress that gunfire until everyone is through."

Emma pushed through the turnstile and handed her card through the bars to Jack, who pressed it against the card reader. When the display turned red, Larsen exploded in a tirade of foul language. Chang knew what was wrong.

"She has to come back through," said Chang. "The system won't allow another entry using that card until she exits. We'll have to squeeze through two at a time!"

Emma pushed through the turnstile, returning to the group.

"I don't think there's room for two," she said.

Larsen examined the turnstile for a second. "One climbs the bars as high as possible and holds on. The other squats underneath and pushes," said Larsen. "Jack and Emma first. Leave your rifles."

Emma pressed her card against the reader, enabling the entry point, before grabbing the second highest bar of the turnstile and lifting her legs. Jack squatted below her and waddled forward, pushing the bars. A few awkward seconds later, they made it to the other side. Larsen slid their rifles through the horizontal bars next to the gate.

"Emma, repeat the process," said Larsen, flinching as a bullet struck the fence next to his head.

Emma came through again, this time taking Chang to the other side. He moved to the wrought-iron fence next to the gate, taking his rifle from Larsen. A bullet pinged off the metal in front of him, dropping him to the grass at the foot of the fence. He aimed his rifle through the thick horizontal bars, trying to find the source of gunfire. Something moved in one of the windows in the building across the street, attracting his attention. He pressed the trigger repeatedly, shattering the upper glass pane and splintering the wooden window frame.

"Nice shooting, Chang!" said Larsen, turning to the street. "You guys watching this?"

David backed up, pulling Joshua with him. "This is nuts. She's doing every trip?"

"She's the smallest," said Larsen.

A bullet struck Joshua's rifle, knocking it out of his hand. Before he could reach down to grab it, Larsen pulled him toward the turnstile.

"Leave it," said Larsen. "You're next."

Chang kept firing until his rifle didn't respond. He fumbled with one of the spare rifle magazines, unsure how to reload the rifle, while the police officer's son and Emma got through the gate.

"Chang, get everyone to the nearest building," said Larsen.

Chang turned and recognized his surroundings immediately. The Mexican restaurant, and Turkish restaurant next door to it, had been a once-a-week habit for years before he got serious about his weight. He'd rarely walked outside, preferring the climate-controlled campus buildings to the sweltering heat or raw cold. Chang set off for the nearest door, knowing it would put him in one of the wide-reaching access hallways that NevoTech employees used to range the campus.

"Follow me!" he yelled before taking off.

By the time he reached the door with Joshua, Larsen and David were halfway across the perfectly manicured grass, following the Harpers. Jack had gone back for his wife! Incredible. They were all incredible. When everyone arrived at the door, Emma pressed her card against the reader, admitting the group to the building. The heavy security door closed behind them, silencing the sporadic gunfire and yelling that had chased them inside. Chang was relieved to feel crisp, humidity-controlled air in the hallway. NevoTech's systems were still fully functional. He put his back against one of the walls and slid to the floor, happy to stay right here for now.

"Chang, you're hit," said David.

A bright red streak of blood stretched down the wall behind him. He'd momentarily forgotten the wound, which began to sting again.

"He'll be fine," said Larsen. "Nothing a little hemostatic powder can't fix—for now."

Larsen limped across the tile floor, bracing himself against the wall next to Chang and digging through one of the pouches on his vest. His leg was bleeding heavily again.

"Tell me about this ER doctor again," said Larsen, pressing a compress against the wound with a bloodstained hand. "This is going to require a little more than hemostatic powder and gauze."

"How soon?" said Chang.

"Not immediately," said Larsen, shifting uncomfortably on his feet. "After we get settled and figure out if this place is safe."

"My apartment is a quarter mile in that direction," said Chang, pointing toward the street they had just left.

"Through all of those crazies?" said David. "They seem capable of concentrating their efforts. We won't get fifty feet."

"We could use a different gate," said Chang. "My place is northwest of here. Not very far."

"What about the other teams out there?" said David.

"They won't be expecting us," said Larsen. "And I know exactly how they operate. We'll have to go soon, before they link what happened at Chang's house with the airport escape."

"And what exactly happened at Chang's house?" said David. "I don't believe we got a full report."

"Larsen disobeyed a direct order to murder me," said Chang. "One of his teammates had a problem with that, and—I can't even."

He couldn't continue. Larsen put a hand on his head, comforting him.

"Three of the four members of my team were killed within the blink of an eye," said Larsen. "I somehow came out of it unscathed. I don't plan on wasting that."

David nodded, looking too tired to pursue Larsen's story much further. "Any other secrets?"

"I think that about covers it," said Larsen.

"I'm sorry about your team," said David. "Nothing easy about losing teammates."

Larsen sank to one knee, leaning against the wall next to Chang. "It's always a fucking waste."

"I don't disagree," said David.

Chang pushed himself up to his feet.

"Then that's that," said Chang. "We've made a pretty damn good team so far. We stand a way better chance of surviving together. Is everyone with me?"

"Yeah," said Emma, her husband nodding his agreement.

"We're with you," said David, glancing at his son, who gave him a thumbs-up.

"Then it's settled. We're a team," said Chang. "First order of business is getting you some proper medical attention. The campus has an infirmary, but I think you need more than Band-Aids and ibuprofen."

"It'll be a risky operation," said Larsen. "The CHASE program is mostly comprised of clowns and poseurs, but they're heavily armed poseurs."

"Can the two of us pull it off?" said David.

"If there's a back door," said Larsen, turning to Chang. "Some kind of hidden approach."

"The parking garage attached to the apartment building would work," said Chang. "I'd be willing to go with you. It's a little tricky navigating from the garage to the building."

"Sounds like the beginnings of a plan," said Larsen. "For now, I say we do a little exploring. Make sure this place is as secure as Dr. Chang thinks."

"Gene. Please call me Gene. Everyone," he said, "I think you'll find this place to be very secure. Like a vault."

"Well, it feels quiet enough. Almost quiet enough to consider hunkering down and waiting this out," said Larsen.

"I'd rather be on a plane headed away from here," said David.

"I said *almost*. If that plane can fly come nightfall, we're out of here," said Larsen. "Gene, why don't you lead the way. Unless Ms. Harper knows the campus better."

"I don't work on campus. The financial buildings are a few blocks away," said Emma. "That's why I didn't offer my ID sooner."

"I'm starting to believe we've been put together for a reason," said Larsen.

"I was thinking the same thing," said Chang.

"I was actually kidding," said Larsen, grinning. "But I'll take what the fates throw me at this point. Even a ragtag team like this."

They all shared a light moment, briefly laughing at Larsen's wry comment. Chang was hopeful for this group and their situation. They just needed to survive the day and get the plane back in the air. He'd head south, as low as possible, until they were well clear of the quarantine zone, before turning toward the Indiana-Illinois border, where he'd find a quiet place to land to figure out his next step. The team's next step.

THE END

KILL BOX, Book 2 in *THE ZULU VIRUS CHRONICLES*, will be released in the fall of 2017. To be among the first to be notified of *KILL BOX*'s release, please visit **eepurl.com/D2D1j** to join my mailing list. Periodically, you'll receive exclusive news, content and discounts regarding my work.

UNTIL THEN, if you haven't read my very first novel, *THE JAKARTA PANDEMIC,* I think you'll enjoy circling back to this story. It's an intense thriller about a lethal pandemic outbreak—told from a street level perspective. Six years after its release, *THE JAKARTA PANDEMIC* remains my most popular and widely read novel.

81205459R00208

Made in the USA
Middletown, DE
21 July 2018